ALSO BY RINA KENT

LEGACY OF GODS
God of Malice
God of Pain
God of Wrath
God of Ruin
God of Fury
God of War

GOD
OF
WAR

RINA KENT

Bloom books

Copyright © 2024, 2025 by Rina Kent
Cover and internal design © 2025 by Sourcebooks
Cover design © Opulent Designs
Cover images © Rashevskyi Viacheslav/Shutterstock, Min C. Chiu/
Shutterstock, Vadim Vasenin/Depositphotos, PhotobyE/Shutterstock, tr3gi/
Depositphotos, 3dart/Depositphotos, avagyanlevon/Depositphotos
Internal art by Victoria Cavaleri @weirdowithluv

Sourcebooks, Bloom Books, and the colophon are
registered trademarks of Sourcebooks.

Published by Bloom Books, an imprint of Sourcebooks
P.O. Box 4410, Naperville, Illinois 60567-4410
(630) 961-3900
sourcebooks.com

Originally self-published in 2024 by Rina Kent.

Cataloging-in-Publication data is on file with the Library of Congress.

Printed and bound in the United States of America.
LSC 10 9 8 7 6 5 4 3 2 1

To the end of an era.

AUTHOR'S NOTE

Hello, reader friend,

God of War marks the end of the Legacy of Gods series and the Rinaverse until further notice. This has been the most bittersweet book I've ever written. I was excited throughout the entire process, but I couldn't help feeling a smidge of sadness at the thought of saying goodbye to these intense characters.

Eli and Ava consumed me, heart and soul, and I hope you experience the same when you read their journey.

God of War is a complete stand-alone. However, since this story takes part way after the timeline of the previous five books in the series, it might spoil some events.

If you haven't read my books before, you might not know this, but I write darker stories that can be upsetting and disturbing. My books and main characters aren't for everyone.

This book isn't as dark as my other books, but it contains sensitive subjects. I'll list them below for your safety, but if you don't have any triggers, feel free to skip the following paragraph, as it will provide spoilers for the plot.

God of War contains mental health issues, including

depression, anxiety, fugue states, and dissociative amnesia. There are on-page descriptions of a suicide attempt, deteriorated mental states, and violence. The main character struggles with alcoholism in the beginning and there are mentions of drug use. I trust you to know your triggers before you proceed.

For more things Rina Kent, visit rinakent.com

LEGACY OF GODS TREE

ROYAL ELITE UNIVERSITY

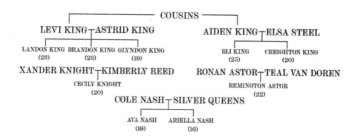

COUSINS

LEVI KING┬ASTRID KING

LANDON KING BRANDON KING GLYNDON KING
(23)   (23)   (19)

XANDER KNIGHT┬KIMBERLY REED

CECILY KNIGHT
(20)

AIDEN KING┬ELSA STEEL

ELI KING   CREIGHTON KING
(25)   (20)

RONAN ASTOR┬TEAL VAN DOREN

REMINGTON ASTOR
(22)

COLE NASH┬SILVER QUEENS

AVA NASH   ARIELLA NASH
(19)   (16)

THE KING'S U'S COLLEGE

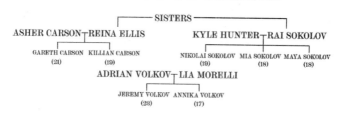

SISTERS

ASHER CARSON┬REINA ELLIS

GARETH CARSON KILLIAN CARSON
(21)   (19)

ADRIAN VOLKOV┬LIA MORELLI

JEREMY VOLKOV ANNIKA VOLKOV
(23)   (17)

KYLE HUNTER┬RAI SOKOLOV

NIKOLAI SOKOLOV MIA SOKOLOV MAYA SOKOLOV
(19)   (18)   (18)

PLAYLIST

Don't Fear the Reaper—Baltic House Orchestra
Breathe—Lø Spirit
Time—MISSIO
BLEAK—Michael Aldag
I Like Me Better—Lauv
Misery—Unlike Pluto
oUcHiE (medium)—Mitchel Dae
Nothing's New—Rio Romeo
Escapism.—RAYE & 070 Shake
Blind Spot—Saint Chaos
PARALYZED—Death and All His Friends
You Make Me Feel Like It's Halloween—Muse
Broken Smile—Lil Peep
Goddess—Xana
Half My Heart—grandson
Feel Something—Jaymes Young
Church—Chase Atlantic
Spell It Out—You Me at Six

You can find the complete playlist on Spotify.

CHAPTER 1

AVA

THE FOUL MIXTURE OF LIQUOR, THE LATEST drug on the market, and a sense of euphoria flows through me as I sway to the loud music.

Here, I'm okay.

As I blend into the middle of lost kindred spirits and empty shells, I don't feel alien.

No pressure. No lost potential.

No disturbing images.

Nothing.

Just the way I like it.

I lift the double shot of tequila to my mouth and slurp half of it. The bitter taste sits on my tongue, leaving a lingering aftertaste that coats my mouth. But it also brings a sense of excitement and reckless abandon. The burn rushes down my throat and settles uncomfortably alongside the inauspicious dose of tranquilizers I've flooded my stomach with.

My solution? Find more alcohol, drugs, and whatever I can get my grubby hands on.

Something. Anything to relieve the pressure of the latest images that have been crowding my head.

Blurry faces with blurry voices in blurry clubs.

The last thing I need is a reminder of my state of mind or the recent pickle I've gotten myself into.

So I choose to sweep it under the rug and pretend everything is fantastic.

Normal.

My friends chose this up-and-coming club in North London for the occasion. The grungy brick walls shine in a beautiful mixture of different shades of blue.

Violet laser beams glow on the crowd of people filling the massive downstairs hall. We have a VIP room upstairs, but it's always fun to get down and dirty.

The dirtier the better.

I've just lifted the half-full shot of tequila to my lips when a slim hand with milky-peach nails snatches the glass and puts it out of reach. I'm about to spout some profanity when my eyes meet her calm green ones. I'm instantly hit with a smidge of judgment and a copious amount of unconditional love.

"Cecy!" I shout over the music, my voice sounding surprisingly sober. "What are you doing here?"

She's wearing a beautiful pastel-orange spaghetti strap dress. Her silver hair is pulled up in a dainty ponytail, and her face glows more than ever.

I don't miss the fact she's comfortable wearing dresses now when she's always been a jeans-and-T-shirt kind of girl.

Or the fact she's put on a subtle hint of makeup. She wants to look beautiful. She loves herself more.

And to my shame, it's not because of anything I've done or even contributed to. It took me so long to figure out something was wrong. I could blame my condition, but that's no excuse. Not when she's been there for me our entire lives.

"You've had enough to drink, Ava."

"What are you talking about? I haven't even started." I reach for the glass, but she holds it behind her back.

"Don't even think about it." She grabs my elbow and starts pulling me from the middle of the crowd I've been happily nestled in. They all break out in a meltdown of questions.

"Ava, are you coming back?"

"You joining us for that Ibiza trip, Ava?"

"I have the latest gossip for you, Ava."

Ava, Ava, Ava...

I love the attention, the hungry gazes, the irresistible need to satisfy my every whim, every need, every demand.

I blow them kisses and wink at a few of the guys, whose names I can barely remember.

It's all part of my defense mechanism. My charm, my looks, my popularity.

I'm whatever they want me to be: A flirt. A social butterfly. A useless prodigy.

Anything. Everything.

As long as I confiscate their attention, I don't mind.

Attention keeps the emptiness at bay.

More importantly, the boisterous compliments and not-so-innocent touches ward off dark thoughts.

Even if only temporarily.

My best friend, Cecily, abandons the shot of tequila on a table and continues pushing her way through the crowd with me in tow.

I tug on her hand, pull her to a stop, and wrap my arms

around her neck, swaying to the loud club music. "Come on, let's dance!"

"This isn't my scene, Ava."

"Please, Cecy. For me?" I bat my lashes and twirl her around.

She sighs and moves slowly, in no way matching my energy. I wiggle my hips, and the shimmering pink of my dress catches the strobing lights. My skirt is so short, people behind me must catch a front-row view of my arse.

Some guys hoot, and I blow them kisses, throwing my head back with laughter, falling into the intoxication. The madness.

The nothingness.

Some guys surround us, and Cecily tenses, her hands coming protectively around my waist.

I used to take this subtle change lightly before, but not anymore. This time, I'm the one who pushes the swarming bees out of the way; I then drag my friend through a hall that leads to the toilets.

The dark walls are decorated with the grungy neon signs of London, the red lighting casting a warm glow on the otherwise-dim space.

The chaos filters behind us, the music lowers a notch, and Cecily releases a breath as she leans against the wall.

"Ready to go home?" she asks slowly, almost hopefully.

"You know the exact answer to that." I pinch her cheek. "You go. I know you don't like nightlife."

"There's no way in hell I'm leaving you here alone when you're drunk, Ava. This club is in the middle of nowhere and gives off sketchy vibes. No clue why you came all the way here."

"Something different from the usual Soho places. I'm all for adventures."

"Are you sure this isn't about your latest participation in the international cello competition?"

Phantom pain squeezes my chest, but I put on my best smile. "Nope. Maybe I wasn't made for classical music and should switch to DJing. It's much more fun anyway."

"Ava..." She's interrupted by a group of drunk girls giggling and swaying their way between us to the toilet queue.

Cecily takes my hand in hers. "Want to buy some junk food and rewatch *Bridget Jones's Diary*?"

"Don't you have a boyfriend you need to, I don't know, fly to New York with?"

So maybe I'm being salty, but I know I have no right to be. I always thought Cecily was my soul twin. My person. My sister. The one person who was always in my corner.

But that was before I realized how dependent I was on her. How inconveniencing I was to her. She took care of all my dumb drunk adventures. Kept me safe and sane, wiped my forehead after I got sick, then held me to sleep. She listened to my nonsense and let me invade her space with no complaints.

After she found the love of her life and he pointed out that I was taking all her goodwill and giving nothing in return, I hated him.

I thought it was logical to despise him. He's taking my bestie, and no one deserves my bestie. But no, the real reason I couldn't stand Jeremy was because he told me the truth I'd refused to see all along.

He was right. I've been too reliant on Cecily. Too

clingy. Too childish. A mess of epic proportions, if you will. But it's not Cecily's responsibility to keep me together.

Which is why I kept my mouth shut when she said she was moving with said boyfriend to the States, even if it's been killing me inside.

Just now was a slip. I blame the alcohol.

I trap my bottom lip beneath my teeth and bite down so harshly, I'm surprised no blood gushes out.

"So you're not okay with it after all?" She watches me carefully. "I knew it. I was surprised you didn't throw a tantrum."

"I'm just kidding," I lie through my teeth. "You go live your life, Cecy."

"I can stay a few more weeks."

"No. Don't stop your life because of me."

"You're not a burden." She clasps my shoulders. "I'm worried about you. Like, really, *really* worried. You've been drinking so much, it's almost an addiction at this point. You haven't been taking your meds regularly, and you keep spiraling into these destructive patterns more often than not."

"It's called having fun."

"Taking weird pills from strangers is not fun. It's suicidal."

"They're not strangers. They're friends."

"Not good ones." She sighs. "I'm not the only one who's worried, Ava. Your mum and dad are, too. Is it true that you haven't spoken to them since you left the competition hall?"

"I texted." My voice gets caught, and I swallow, then exhale deeply to release the tension.

"And you believe that's enough?"

"For now." I can't trust myself to speak to Papa and Mama and not break down. I've had three panic attacks in three days. I know I'm spiraling and a huge episode is growing in the distance, but no one needs to know about that. Least of all Cecy, who's finally found her well-deserved happiness. If she figures out what's wrong, she won't go to the States, and I can't be in her way anymore.

"I'll take the meds on time and cut down on drinking. I promise." I lean my head on her shoulder so she doesn't see the blatant lies in my eyes. "But only if you FaceTime me every day for at least three hours."

"Promise?"

"Promise." I push away reluctantly and jut my chin in the direction opposite to us. "Now go to your man and do your magic before he kills the guys who surrounded us on the dance floor."

Her eyes light up, and then her entire body angles toward a tall, broad guy with full sleeves of tattoos. A personality that's completely contrary to hers. And, wait for it, he's an *actual* Russian Mafia prince in New York.

Jeremy has been keeping his distance, but he's been following us around from the get-go. Like, everywhere. I'm sure the only reason he didn't glue himself to Cecily is because she asked him for some alone time with me.

Although he's standing across the room, his entire attention is on her. His dark eyes meet hers, and in that fraction of a second, I don't see a scary motherfucker with a reputation that sends people running. I see a man who loves my friend as furiously as she loves him. A man who'd level the world to the ground just to protect her.

"Want us to give you a lift?" she asks, ripping her gaze from him with obvious effort.

"I drove."

"But you're drunk."

"I only had half a shot, and you snatched it away before I could finish it. I'm perfectly sober."

"No, you're not."

"I'll call an Uber."

"That's not exactly safe."

"I'll ask Papa's chauffeur to pick me up. Is that safe enough?"

"I guess. I'd rather we take you home."

"I'll be fine."

"You sure?"

"Just go before Jeremy hates me some more for daring to occupy your time."

"Since when do you care what he thinks of you?"

"I don't. I care about you, and you love the twat, so I have to put up with him."

She gives me a quick hug. "Love you. Let's watch *Bridget Jones's Diary* tomorrow, deal?"

"Deal."

"Text me when you get home."

"Yes, Mum." I salute.

She gives a subtle shake of her head before she moves in Jeremy's direction. Cecily chances one last look at me, her brows drawing together, and I can see her contemplating either staying or forcing me to go home early like a granny.

I fake my best smile and send her kisses. Before she can change her mind, Jeremy appears in front of her like a mountain. His hand slips to her lower back with subtle possessiveness, and he drops a quick but passionate kiss on her mouth that makes her forget about me.

Only momentarily, though, because she keeps looking at me as he hauls her out of the club while warding off any unwanted attention.

She deserves all that and more. If there's anyone in the world who's owed happiness and a man who brightens up only when she's around, it's Cecily.

I'm slightly envious of what she has, but then again, to get something like that, someone needs to be as selfless and as purehearted as she is.

Innocent, maybe.

Less mentally sick.

More...normal.

So it's pointless for me to even hope for what she has—what all my friends have.

I snatch a glass from a passing man's hand, down it, and nearly cough.

Whiskey. Yikes.

Still, I have manners. So I kiss my finger and place it to his mouth as a form of thanks as I stroll back to the dance floor.

One more hour.

I'm not ready to face the emptiness that comes afterward.

If I'm drunk enough, I might forget a little.

Escape a little.

Live a little.

In no time, I'm surrounded by a group of people. Some are friends or classmates from the art school. Others are new faces.

The more, the merrier, if you ask me.

We're on holiday from uni, and it's our last year. Cecy already graduated, and it's no fun without her at Royal Elite University. If I weren't positively terrified about living in my parents' house again and letting them see me in raw, painful detail, I would've transferred to a London university.

Oh well.

Thankfully for me, I didn't come here to think.

I slide my fingers into my long blond hair, lifting the strands to reveal my bare back as I sway sensually to the music.

Warm hands drop to the exposed skin on my sides, and I playfully shove them away.

"You can look, but you can't touch, Ollie," I coo over the music.

Not sure if he heard, though I don't think he cares, to be honest, because he continues staring at my hint of cleavage, blatantly eye fucking my long legs, my bare shoulders, and anywhere his greedy eyes can reach.

Perfect dress, in my humble opinion.

The string tied around my neck keeps it in place, and the tiny microskirt barely covers my arse. Snakelike straps spring up from my stilettos and hug my legs in stunning glittery pink.

"You owe me for earlier, love," Oliver says as he dances with me to the beat, mirroring my every move, every bat of my lashes.

"Oh?" I play coy. "How much?"

"I'm expensive."

"Not more expensive than my trust fund, Ollie." I

stroke my fingers beneath his chin, tracing his skin with my chrome-pink nails as his nostrils flare. "Besides, we both know you're not thinking about money as a currency."

"Did I think right?"

"Possibly?"

Oliver is classically handsome—square face, light-hazel eyes, and sandy-blond hair. Pretty sure I dry humped him a couple of nights ago when he dropped me off.

He wasn't happy with how I left him unsatisfied, but he keeps coming back for more, so maybe if I'm in the mood, I'll go further.

Ollie groans as I move my hips. "You're killing me, Ava."

"I know." I laugh, the sound eaten by the loud music before it dies on a hitch.

A stare.

No. A glare.

Cold, calculating, and entirely destructive eyes hold me hostage.

Like a million times before.

And like all those times, my apprehension hasn't reduced one bit. If anything, my awareness has gotten a lot more daring. Suffocating.

It's impossible to figure out where he's watching me from if he doesn't make himself entirely visible. However, whether I see him or not, I'm extremely conscious of his presence.

Like a parasite. Or, more accurately, a high-tech security camera where I'm the sole focus.

Sweat trickles down my back, and my skin heats by several orders of magnitude.

Instinctively, my hand drops from Ollie's face, and my movements slow as I search the corners of the club. That's where he always lurks, like a shadow, the darkness's lord and master.

A fucking ghost.

I see him. And I wish I didn't.

Eli King stands by the bar, nonchalantly leaning back, one hand nestling a drink and the other tucked in the pocket of his pressed black trousers. He always wears something black. Like a Gothic duke in a faraway castle. A step above Dracula and Satan's favorite tutor. It fits with the sharp jawline, high cheekbones, and vile character.

His crisp white shirt highlights his broad shoulders and lean muscled frame. The cuffs are slightly rolled, revealing a Patek Philippe watch that's so expensive, it could buy everyone in this club. I know because I bought that watch. Got into shit with my dad about spending so much money as well. Seven years ago, I begged Nana to take me to Switzerland, we met a retired watch master, and I had to plead for weeks before he agreed to make that special edition.

Though Eli doesn't know that tidbit. I made Aunt Elsa give it to him and swear to never tell him it was from me. So he thinks it was a gift from his mum for his twentieth birthday, which is probably why he always wears it.

Despite the shadows, the chaos, the noise, and the endless people separating us, I see him clearly. Too clearly. As if the world is transparent and he's the only tangible being in its midst.

Eli King has been my damnation ever since I figured out what that word meant.

My nemesis.

The only man who's immune to my charms.

If anything, he disregards them with cold indifference. Like right now.

His eyes exude a bottomless darkness, and their stormy gray never rages nor revolts. Never deviates from the coldness I faced the day he shattered my heart to pieces and stomped all over it.

Turn around and remove your distasteful presence from my sight, and I'll pretend I didn't hear your embarrassing confessions.

His words still sting despite the years that have passed. Whoever said time heals everything has obviously never met Eli King.

He's worse than an infected wound that's refusing to heal and more brutal than a war without an end.

On the other hand, that terrible lapse in judgment on my part flipped my feelings for him upside down. I used to be blind, but now I just loathe him.

I want to annoy him.

Tug any feelings out of him just to disrupt his day and destroy his carefully put-together life.

He watches me and I stare back, unwavering, even if I'm burned by that icy gaze, if I'm pulled apart and shattered to pieces, I'll never back down in front of the prick.

Feeling particularly suicidal tonight, thanks to my spectacular failures and, possibly, the cocktail of substances, I grab Ollie's hands and place them on my bare sides again.

My skin doesn't catch fire. I don't break out in a sweat nor experience the shattering sensation of mysterious eroticism.

But it's good enough.

My arms wrap around Ollie's neck, and I dance slower than the rhythm, provocatively, swaying my hips, jutting my breasts. The music pulses through my body, the bass reverberating in my chest and making my heart race in a symphony of chaos and rebellion.

The feel of Eli's eyes is a toxic elixir, swirling and bubbling within me, a concoction that promises a temporary escape from reality and a false sense of bliss.

Ollie matches my movements, touching, caressing, and falling completely into it, but my attention is not on him. I never break eye contact with the dilemma leaning against the bar, his eyes still detached and completely unaffected by my show.

So I snake my fingers into my hair, pulling it up, biting my lower lip while I stare into his black soul.

"Fuck you," I mouth.

Then, and only then, does he react. The corner of his lip quirks up in the most amused, sadistic smile before he takes a generous sip from his drink.

Scotch. Malt. Straight.

I hate that I know all these details about him. I wish I could be hit with amnesia so I could just forget him, his favorite drink, his wardrobe choices, and his entire malicious personality.

Ollie gets closer until he's almost flush against me. His smell, oud and musk, nearly suffocates me, but I put up with it and trace my forefinger over his stubbled cheek, forcing my entire attention to stay on him.

Giving Eli the show he signed up for.

I have no idea why he doesn't leave me alone when he

clearly has no interest in me whatsoever, but I'll be damned if I don't play his game.

At least today.

Most of the time, I just avoid him like the plague. What? I'm not always drunk, and when it comes to Eli, my courage—or impulsive foolishness—largely depends on the level of alcohol and drugs pumping in my veins.

I lift my head, but my movements slow when I find his spot at the bar empty. A strange, crushing disappointment crinkles in my chest, and I hate it with everything in me.

Worse than I hate that man.

My phone vibrates in my bra, and I jolt, then disentangle myself from Ollie to check it out.

Ariella: Call me. It's an EMERGENCY!

My heart trips over itself as I storm off the dance floor, ignoring Ollie's and the others' objections as I fly up the stairs to the VIP room I rented tonight. I close the door behind me and pace the length of the tacky space with red faux-leather sofas and black walls.

My younger sister answers in a matter of seconds. "Ava!"

"What...?" I swallow. "What's wrong? Are Mama and Papa okay?"

"They're fine."

"Nana and Grandpa?"

"Living their best life on their latest cruise in the Mediterranean Sea."

"Okay...then what's the emergency?"

"Figured it was the best way to get you to call me."

I release a long, tortured breath and lean against the side of the sofa. "Ari, you little shit, you scared the hell out of me."

"Oh, please. No more than you scared the hell out of us during that competition earlier, then proceeded to ghost us."

"I didn't ghost you. Besides, it was…nothing."

"Only if 'nothing' means literally freezing midnote for, like, five minutes and then storming off the stage."

"I had…a block."

Of senses. Of existence.

I literally ceased to be me at that moment.

"And you couldn't, like, talk to us about it?"

"So you'd pity me?"

"So we'd support you, idiot. Mama and Papa are worried about you. I'm worried about you."

I bite the corner of my lip. Why the hell do I manage to be like this and concern every single person I love about my mental state?

"We'll talk tomorrow after I'm past the hangover. Can you tell Mama and Papa that I'm doing okay right now and keeping busy practicing for the next competition?"

"Sure. How much do I get paid for lying?"

"Bitch, please. You love lying."

"I love getting paid more." I can imagine her smiling like a little psycho. "How about you tell me Remi's schedule for the week and we call it even?"

"Ari…you're my baby sister and I love you, but you need to take a hint when a man isn't interested in you and move on."

"Didn't stop you when you were falling into a puddle at Eli's uninterested feet."

I touch my hair and clear my throat. "And I got over him and then some. In fact, I hate He-Who-Shall-Not-Be-Named."

"As you should, Sis."

"Maybe you can do the same?"

"Nah. Eli is unfeeling and has no trace of any human emotion in him. My Remi is different. He's lovable, a gentleman, and every woman's dream man. He just needs a little push to see the love of his life, aka me."

I smile despite myself. "You're not going to give up, are you?"

"Only after my ring is on his finger."

"Jesus. You're thinking of marriage at eighteen?"

"I've loved him since I was eleven. That's seven years too late, if you ask me."

"Oh Lord."

"Back to the topic at hand, are you going to get me that schedule, Ava?"

"Nope."

"Is this really worth losing my support when Mama and Papa grill you for actual answers? Think very carefully, Sis."

"Ugh, you're a little bitch."

"I take after my beautiful bitch of a sister. Mua ha ha."

I'm about to call her a few colorful names when I hear the door clicking open behind me. "Give me a sec, Ollie…"

My words trail off when I face the door and get instantly trapped in the depths of those eyes.

Cold. Indifferent. Stormy.

I swallow hard, not caring if my sister hears it. "I'll talk to you later."

"Only if you have that schedule for me. Byeeee."

She hangs up, and the sudden click nearly makes me jump in my skin. Though it has nothing to do with Ari and everything to do with the man whose height and broadness block the entire exit.

I straighten, forcing my shoulders back, but it's categorically impossible to make them relax.

"To what do I owe this displeasure?"

I'm proud of how bored my voice sounds. It took a lot of practice to sound as cold and indifferent as he is.

Eli shoves himself off the door, and even though he no longer blocks my exit, his presence overwhelms my senses in a fraction of a second.

Imposing. Intimidating. Suffocating.

I can't take my gaze off him because I know it will take only one misstep and it'll be game over for me.

One stupid move, and I'll strip away another chunk of my barely put-together soul.

"The real question is..." His smooth, deep voice touches my warm skin like a whip. "What have you done to owe me the displeasure, Ava?"

CHAPTER 2

AVA

A LONG TIME AGO, WHEN I WAS YOUNGER AND dumber, I used to look at this man like he was a god.

The only touchable god. One I could see up close and personal. One I could worship without fearing any system of reward and punishment.

I had the dedication of a religious fanatic and a lunatic fundamentalist until the grandiosity shattered right before my eyes.

The god was never a god after all. He's more akin to a devil: sinful, seductive, and destructive.

Now I understand why people who leave their religion have the most contempt for it. I completely get why they sabotage it, sully its name, and write hateful words about it in obscure online forums.

When you give an undeserving god your dedication and he ruins you through it, you're bound to loathe him so that you don't hate that stupid version of yourself who once worshipped him.

When I followed that god like a lovesick puppy and he looked at me once in a blue moon, I nearly gave myself a heart attack due to the excitement. I was lucky to have any form of recognition from a man who had girls falling at his feet, but I was the only one who got close.

Now I see it for what it is: indifference.

I meet Eli's frosty gaze with my nonchalant one. "Oh, I'm sorry. Did you just insinuate that I care about your opinion concerning anything I do?"

He steps closer silently, smoothly, almost creepily. I'm forced to tip my head back to stare at him.

I hate how tall he is, and I'm not short by any means.

It's just that Eli was made to look down his straight nose at most people, and he does it so well, with a pinch of arrogance and an unhealthy dose of utter disregard.

He has a way of making others feel like they're not worth a speck of dust beneath his shoe.

It's the handsome face, I realize. He was born with superior looks, thanks to his parents and due to no contribution on his part. A face that makes people stop and stare at the ridiculously sharp jaw, perfectly proportional high cheekbones, and stunningly full lips.

But Eli's most notable feature has always been those mysterious eyes.

People say eyes are the windows to the soul, but it's impossible to tell what he's thinking, no matter how long you stare at them. They run deep—so deep that I was pulled into them once upon a time. I fought and floundered and yearned to be the only one who understood them.

Good thing I'm out of that haze now and couldn't care less about whatever demonic plans he entertains.

He stops a few steps away, but it's enough to flood my senses with his scent, something subtle and masculine and definitely made specifically for him, because I've never smelled it anywhere else. "You clearly don't care about my opinion."

"Clearly." I cross my arms to stop my hands from giving away my mental state. If there's something I've learned about Eli, it's that he's a master manipulator and a predator who won't hesitate to use people's weaknesses against them. Ruin them through those potential loss-of-control moments. Absolutely decimate them until there's nothing left.

"But you do care enough to put on amateurish shows in front of me." The slight lilt in his deep voice catches me off guard.

"You might believe you're the sun and that the world revolves around you, and I'd hate to burst your bubble, but no, no show I do is for you."

"Even when you were looking at me the entire time you were acting like a stripper?"

I force a smile, refusing to fall for the provocation. "You know me. I love giving attention to admirers."

A curve touches the corner of his lips. "So I'm one of the admirers now?"

"Clearly. Or you wouldn't be following me around like a simp. Sorry, you're not my type."

"Is this the part where I get on my knees and beg?"

"I'm afraid that won't cut it."

"How about if I send flowers and a box of chocolates?"

"Unoriginal. Try harder."

"If I cry into my pillow?"

"Only if I get to witness it personally."

"So I have a shot. Fantastic."

I release an exasperated sigh, putting an end to the stupid back-and-forth. I hate his blatant amusement whenever he riles me up for sport. But what I despise more is how I still fall for it every time.

"What do you want, Eli?"

"From you? Nothing."

"And yet you're haunting me like a vengeful ghost."

"More like one of those mischievous ones that scare the ever-loving fuck out of you just for laughs."

"Ha ha. There, I laughed. We done?"

"You're supposed to be scared."

"Oh, hold on." I throw my hands up and shield my face, mimicking watching a horror film. "I'm so terrified. So scared. Get me out of this B movie scene. Is that enough for you tonight?"

"Your strap has fallen." He motions at my chest.

I slap a hand on it instinctively before I look down and see that the strap is perfectly in place.

A nick of annoyance mounts on the previous copious levels of annoyance, and I narrow my eyes at him.

"It didn't? My bad." He doesn't sound apologetic in the least. "But then again, you wouldn't have had to worry about it if you weren't dressed like a stripper."

"I'll call when I have any fucks to give about your opinion of me."

"You're funny."

"And pretty and popular. Your point?"

"Delusional, too. Apparently."

"Nah. I leave that to you." I hike a hand on my hip. "Now, if you'll excuse me, I have better people to spend my time with."

I walk past him, my head held high, ready to tuck this unfortunate encounter away with all the previous ones.

"I heard you made a fool out of yourself today. Again."

My heels click on the floor as I come to an abrupt halt

and turn around to face him. All of a sudden, I'm thirsty. For alcohol.

Or anything that's able to soothe the dull ache at the back of my throat.

Crossing my arms, I adopt my most mocking voice. "Whoa there, soldier. Slow down on the stalkerish tendencies, would you?"

"Don't even try to sass me, Ava. What was it this time? Your pills malfunction?"

"Screw you," I snarl.

"I'm not interested in contracting the nest of STIs from the losers you fraternize with."

"They're no worse than your fuck buddies."

"My fuck buddies are always tested, unlike the drug addicts you mingle with. And don't try to change the subject. Why did you flee this time? What did you see? Or not see?"

My lips part, and I stare at him like he's an alien. What does he know? *How* does he know?

It doesn't make sense.

Sure, since our families are close and his mum is my godmother, he's aware of my condition. But like everyone else, he must think it's depression, anxiety, and some mild case of psychosis. He could deduce the meds, and considering his stalkerish habits, he could figure out the alcohol and the occasional drugs.

But that's it.

There's no way in hell he's privy to what's eating me from the inside.

I lift my chin. "No idea what you're talking about."

He narrows his eyes. Gray. Stormy. Calculating.

I can see him concocting a plan to coax me to talk, but if that doesn't work, I'm sure he'll force it out of me. Even if I kick and scream.

Especially if I kick and scream.

"Speak, Ava. Don't make me resort to unpleasant methods we both know you're unable to handle."

A lick of heat sneaks its way beneath my dress, and the room's temperature takes a sudden hike. My throat dries, and it's exceptionally difficult to swallow.

"I didn't know you were this concerned about me." I flash him my sweetest smile. "I'm touched."

"Concerned? More like embarrassed."

"You'd have to care to be embarrassed by my actions, and we both know that emotion doesn't exist in your arsenal."

"It exists in my mother's. She called me to ask about your, and I quote, 'worrisome state of mind.'"

The thing I hate most about Eli is that his mother is Elsa King, aka my godmother and second mother figure after Mama.

Sometimes I can't believe a considerate, absolute green flag of a woman actually gave birth to this devil. I'm surprised he didn't eat her while he was in the womb like some parasite.

"I'll talk to Aunt Elsa myself. You stay out of it."

"Only if you stop being such a disgrace. You're becoming an embarrassment to your family. I'm certain your ex–prime minister grandfather will disapprove of your scandalous lifestyle if it's printed in gossip magazines."

I grit my teeth so hard, my jaw hurts. "Thanks for the touching concern. You might want to stop being so obsessed with my life. Desperation doesn't look good on you."

"Because it looks better on you?" His lips tilt in that infuriating way again, and it takes everything in me not to slap it away.

"If you're done..." I start to walk to the exit, but he steps in front of me, blocking the light, the door, and my oxygen.

Eli first and last touched me four years ago, when I was seventeen, and ended my birthday, turning it into the most shameful disaster.

Since then, he never does. Not even accidentally. But that doesn't stop his heat from engulfing me and his smell from invading my every sense.

He's too warm for a cold bastard.

"Go home, Ava."

"Since when do you get to tell me what to do?"

"Since you're clearly unable to think. Don't take anyone home. Don't drive. Take a black cab and leave."

"Aw, you're not going to offer to drive me yourself?"

He raises a perfect brow. "Would you take said offer?"

"No."

"So what's the point of making it?"

"Indulging me, perhaps?"

"You're far too indulged by others. I don't plan on making the list."

"You won't make any list, for that matter."

"Debatable." He steps closer, his body heat enveloping me like a threatening cloud as his rough voice deepens. "Now leave."

"The answer is no."

"Out of spite?"

"You're not my keeper."

"Let's go with that if it makes you sleep better at night."

"What is that supposed to mean?"

"Go home," he says again and then turns to leave. When he reaches the door, he throws me a dark look over his shoulder. "Alone."

I resist the urge to flip him the middle finger as I stand there fuming, my body warm and my heart thumping so loudly, I'm surprised it doesn't spill out onto the ugly carpet in the room.

My state is so extremely disoriented that I have to take some time to pull myself together again.

Ten minutes later, I find my way back to the dance floor. Screw Eli and his orders that definitely won't be met.

I let myself be absorbed by a swirling vortex of ecstasy, a concoction of substances, and emotions that transport me to a realm of hedonistic bliss. Among the lost souls and hollow shells, I find solace and acceptance, a sense of belonging that makes everything else fade into the background.

So I drink another shot, dance until I nearly drop, then agree to join Ollie and some others at an after-party.

Fuck Eli.

Fuck the cello.

Fuck my fucking head.

By the time we spill outside, it's somewhere after one in the morning.

I shouldn't be driving, but our friend Raj's house is, like, ten minutes away, and the roads are empty at this time, so I should be fine.

Besides, I hold my liquor pretty well, so I'm not even that drunk. Just drunk enough to see the world through pink goggles, like my favorite color.

I stumble into my car and tell the others to go ahead. Ollie offers to drive me, but I decline with a smile.

Before I pull out of the parking lot, I text Cecily that I'm home, like a world-class liar. But it's because she won't be able to sleep if she knows I'm still out.

What Cecy and my parents don't know is that I refuse the notion of spending any unnecessary time alone.

Jesus. I can't believe I'm graduating in a couple of weeks. What am I going to do without the buffer uni's offered me?

Make other cliques of friends outside? Join a thousand and one clubs?

I desperately need to stay out of my parents' orbit before they figure everything out.

With a sigh, I shove all those thoughts to the back of my mental closet as I refresh my makeup.

My phone vibrates, and I freeze when I see it's a text from Eli.

Tin Man: Are you going home?
Me: New phone. Who's this?
Tin Man: Your location better be on the way home.
Me: Guess where I am for a hundred quid.

I snap a selfie while doing a kissy face and send it over, then silence my phone and pull out of the car park. I nearly drive into a wall, but my car's camera saves me in time.

Oops.

I follow the GPS and voice command the car to play music. Bach's Cello Suite no. 2 in D minor fills the car, and I release an annoyed noise as I punch the radio button and listen to some pop music instead.

Classical music and I are officially divorcing.

That's what I said after my last failed attempt at winning yet another competition last year.

And yet I went back this year. Only to make a bigger fool of myself.

What did you see? Or not see?

Eli's words from earlier send a shiver down my spine.

He couldn't have known, right?

No one does—

I stare at my rearview mirror when I notice a car without headlights following me.

How long has that been there?

I look ahead but the road is clear.

Shit.

Okay.

I shake my head to come back into focus and speed up, just a tiny bit over the speed limit.

The car matches my speed, and my heart starts to gallop at a scary rhythm. I voice command my phone to call the police.

You can never be too careful in these situations. Even if I'm overthinking it.

I come to a junction and hit the brakes when a car flashes past. Jesus. A BMW. No surprises there.

The suspicious car comes to a halt behind me as someone picks up.

"Metropolitan Police Emergency Department. How might I help?"

"There's a weird car without headlights following me," I say as I hit the accelerator again, pushing the car forward with sudden speed. My body flings backward as the tires screech.

"I need you to remain calm, miss. May I have your name?"

"Ava...Ava Nash."

"Can I call you 'Ava'?"

"Yeah."

"Can you tell me where you are, Ava?"

"I don't know exactly. Near the M25. Hold on—" I steal a look at the GPS, and the next thing I hear is the loud, unbearable blaring of a truck's horn before its bright lights blind me.

I turn the steering wheel as hard as I can while hitting the brakes. My car swerves as I spin around and around, and then a sickening crash resounds in my ears.

The last thing I see are the eyes that follow me everywhere.

Dark. Cold. Destructive.

CHAPTER 3
AVA

A BITTER TASTE STICKS TO THE BACK OF MY DRY throat.

I cough but choke, the sound leaving my lungs in long, torturous heaves.

Darkness materializes around me with depressing finality, and I completely lose any sense of my physical body.

I don't know where I am.

My surroundings dive into pitch-blackness.

My head follows suit as tendrils of shadowy hands grab me.

A strangled sound gets trapped in my belly, and the tight noose of a panic attack wraps around my throat.

No…

No…

No.

I blink my eyes open, and slowly, almost like a slow-motion documentary, the grainy colors of reality engulf me.

The light condensation against the oxygen mask strapped to my face comes first, followed by bright white walls.

Darkness recedes in my peripheral vision with a snake-like motion, and with it, my awareness trickles back in.

A beeping machine.

The smell of hospitals and mint essential oil.

The gradual return of my physical body to reality.

My name is Ava Nash. Twenty-one years old. I love classical music and reading scandalous bodice-ripper novels. I watch cheesy rom-coms or true-crime documentaries—nothing in between. I'm kind of obsessed with the color pink, can eat candy floss for days, can't get enough of salted caramel popcorn, and can survive on smoothies as long as they have strawberries in them.

Like every time I get my episodes, I repeat the usual mantra I taught myself. It's my attempt to prove my existence to the shadowy version of myself. The version that seems to forget the entire world and succumbs to frightening numbness for extended periods of time.

I breathe steadily as the remnants of the fog clear, and I wiggle my toes. It's a habit I picked up to ensure I'm here. In the present.

My other self doesn't have the capacity to wiggle my toes. I watched some security footage from our house once. I look robotic when I'm in that state—too stiff, too emotionless.

Too lost.

The feel of my body returns in small increments, and that's when I sense that my right hand is warm.

Too warm.

I try to crane my head to the side, and the rustling of the pillow fills the quiet space.

"Ava?"

Deep, rough notes penetrate my foggy brain, and I find it hard to remember to breathe properly.

Eli's cradling my hand between both of his as he stares at me from the chair at my bedside.

I thought I'd already woken up.

Is this another episode—or, worse, a nightmare?

I swallow, but a ball constricts my throat. So I wiggle my toes again and, yup, still moving. This is real.

How…?

I stare at Eli's brutally handsome face as if it'll explode with answers for his bizarre existence in my vicinity.

For some reason, he looks older than when I saw him earlier. Slight stubble covers his harsh jawline, and his hair is longer, disheveled, and finger-raked. He appears to be a bit tired as well, his lips absent of some of their color, as if he's suffering from a cold.

Wait.

Can hair grow in the span of a few hours?

A day?

Two?

I narrow my eyes, trying to remember the last thing that happened. I was going to an after-party with Ollie, Raj, and the others, but then…I…

A car without headlights.

Calling 999.

Blinding lights.

A lorry.

A crash.

Stormy, harsh, soulless eyes.

The same eyes that are fixating on me right now.

"Ava? Can you hear me?"

The rough timbre of his voice nearly sends me into a more prominent panic attack. My heartbeat spikes, and the machines go crazy. Crazier than the fake note of concern in his voice.

He curses under his breath and pushes something above my head as he strokes my face.

"Breathe, Ava. Fuck, come on, beautiful. Breathe."

I actually stop panicking for a second because what...? What's going on?

He called me *beautiful*, and he's touching me. Matter of fact, he's been touching me since I woke up.

Eli never touches me.

The longer I stare at his eyes, the more my breathing slows. They're different. But how...? Why...?

"That's it. Good girl."

My heart trips over itself, and my breathing stutters. The machines beep louder, and my world tilts on its axis.

Did Eli just call me a good girl?

The Eli King?

Oh.

This must be a dream after all. Let's hope it doesn't turn into a nightmare where he jams a spear into my chest and laughs like a maniac as my blood splatters on his precious shoes.

I close my eyes and will myself to go back to reality. This is just so cruel, even by my strange-dreams standards.

"Ava...open those eyes. Look at me."

I peek at him and immediately regret it. His somber gray eyes are as angry as a hurricane and as tempting as the damn devil.

"You feeling all right?"

His words don't match his expression. He sounds concerned, but he looks bored. Cold. Indifferent.

Like the Eli I'm used to and the Tin Man we all know and hate.

This imposter needs to piss off or at least put more effort into sounding sardonic and unbearably sarcastic like the actual Eli. Two out of five on Trustpilot—could use more imitation skills.

I pull the mask from my face with an ease I didn't expect. Honestly, after that accident, with a truck, no less, I expected to die or at least end up with lifelong paralysis. In the best-case scenario, I'd get away with a few broken bones. I stare down at myself, at my hands, and move my toes again.

Nothing.

There's no way in hell I would've come out of that one unscathed.

Hold on. Was the accident a dream?

Though, if I were speculating, I'd bet money the current situation is the actual dream, not the other one.

Maybe I'm dead and this is a benevolent angel's effort to give me a dreamlike experience of what I couldn't have when alive.

Brilliant. Dead at twenty-one. What a loss of potential.

But maybe it's a good outcome, considering all the fuckery that's been happening in my life lately. And the burden I've posed to the people closest to me.

I start to sit up, then pause. Eli helps me and sets a pillow behind me so I'm comfy.

Maybe I'm disfigured and he's sympathizing? Though he doesn't do that.

If sympathy were to meet Eli in an alley, it'd stab itself in the eye, and he'd just step on it and be on his merry way.

I touch my face and feel the normal texture. No bandage. Hmm. I'm at a loss, to be honest.

"What are you doing here, Eli?" My voice sounds low, husky, a bit odd, as if I've been screaming for days.

Eli rises to his full height, looking majestic in a black shirt and gray trousers. His godlike presence and the tinge of intimidation that rushes through me whenever I'm around him pale in comparison to a different phenomenon.

His eyes.

They grow in size for the first time in my life. They're a lighter shade of gray, close to a cloudy summer's day.

"Say that again." He speaks slowly.

"What are you doing here, Eli?" Annoyance breaks through my voice, and I have to swallow past the discomfort.

Before he can answer, I catch the shadow of Papa and Mama walking through the door. They're both holding coffee cups and speaking in a hushed tone.

I think I hear *"again"* and *"it's not doable anymore."* My posture straightens to eavesdrop, but they both halt when they lift their heads and see me.

A rush of comfort mixed with a tinge of unease floods me. Yikes. I avoided them for as long as I could after the competition, but a strange car without headlights brought us to this less-than-glamorous scene.

"Hi, Mama, Papa..." I say with a guilty voice and trail off when they look positively shocked, as if I'm a ghost.

Something's off.

They both seem worn out, like they've aged five years since the last time I saw them. My father, Cole Nash, is the most collected man and the most loving father, and yet, right now, he looks to be on the edge of something. His beautiful green eyes, which have always reminded me of spring and sparkling exotic water, look half dead.

He's lost weight, too.

Mama is worse. Her usually shiny blond hair that she passed down to me is now dull and uncharacteristically gathered in a ponytail. Her skin is pasty white, and her face looks haggard.

Silver Queens Nash is a celebrity in this world. And it's not because Grandpapa is an ex–prime minister, my nan is an ex-politician, or my father is a business tycoon. It's because she chairs different charities and works extremely hard to make our world a better place.

She's how I learned empathy, sympathy, and to be abundantly aware of my privilege and how to use it to help others.

My parents are the reason behind my high standards for love, family, and communication.

They taught me and Ari our worth way before we were old enough to understand the term.

So it kills me to feel like I'm the reason behind their soulless eyes.

"Ava, honey…" Mum wraps her arms around me and squeezes me in a hug that nearly crushes me.

"She…" I can see Papa's calculating gaze straying to Eli. A look of mutual understanding passes between them before my father nods, and a fractured sigh falls from his lips.

What the hell is going on?

Papa has never liked Eli. And I mean *never*.

He's called him a little psycho since he was twelve and has often gotten into massive rows with Uncle Aiden—Eli's dad—over that.

He hated him even more when I had a stupid crush on him and warned me to avoid the nuisance, as if he were a spark of fire and I were a house pumped full of petrol.

It's safe to say that he's the only person who joins in enthusiastically whenever I talk shit about Eli. So the fact he's nodding in agreement with the same person he calls *a prison runaway* and *a privileged criminal* is bizarre, to say the least.

This is a dream after all.

Mama pulls away, but her touch doesn't feel surreal. I can feel her warmth and smell her favorite cherry perfume. It's her. My mother.

"Are you feeling okay, honey?" she asks, stroking my hair away from my face.

Papa sits beside her, and I stare at them, then at Eli, who's standing behind them like a wall, both hands in his pockets and a devious look in his eyes.

"Yeah," I answer. "Papa. What's going on? Where's Ari?"

"Ari went to get you a change of clothes." Papa strokes my hand. "Do you need anything else?"

"No..." I get distracted by Eli again, pause, swallow, then groan. "Seriously, why is he here? Wait. You can see him, too, right? Mama? Papa?"

Mama steals a glimpse behind her, and when she looks back at me with a furrow in her brow, my heart races so fast, I nearly throw up.

Is it my imagination again?

No.

Please no.

"Where else would Eli be?" Mama asks with a note of confusion.

"He better have stayed the entire night by your side."
That note of loathing Papa has for Eli rushes to the surface,
and I let out a breath.

Okay. It's a bit more normal now. Except where Papa
wants Eli to spend the night by my side.

And that he's here in the first place.

"Do you remember what happened, hon?" Mum
asks.

All of a sudden, a shroud of tension covers the room.
Three pairs of eyes dig into my skull in silent expectation.

Way to pressure a girl.

"Um, yeah. I called 999 before the accident because
someone was following me…" I trail off when I hear a
subtle *tsk* coming from Eli, then narrow my eyes at him.

"Someone was following you inside the house?" Papa
asks with a note of weird carefulness.

"Was someone else there when you fell down the
stairs?" Mama says.

"Stairs…? There were no stairs. It was a…"

My lips seal together when Eli shakes his head. I narrow
my eyes.

"It's fine if you're confused," Papa says. "You've been
under a lot of pressure lately, so let's leave it for now. We're
just glad you're okay."

I nod, but the confusion mounts to an unprecedented
level. I am so going to have a field day talking to Cecy
about this.

"Where's my phone?" I ask Mama. "I want to call
Cecy."

"She's on her way from the States."

I frown. "But she wasn't leaving until next week."

"She hasn't been here for about a month, Ava," Mama tells me, her voice soft but her face slightly paler.

What? There's no way. We were together a few hours ago.

My protests remain unsaid when a few doctors and nurses walk inside, looking like a prim-and-proper private crew that someone like Eli—or Papa—would insist on hiring.

"How are you feeling, Mrs. King?" the doctor asks, and I search my surroundings for Aunt Elsa—Eli's mum. Or maybe Aunt Astrid—Eli's aunt. Or Eli's grandmother. Those are the only Mrs. Kings I know.

I find none of them and redirect my gaze at the white-haired doctor, who's watching me with that fake sympathy.

"Mrs. King?" he repeats.

"Who is he talking to?" I whisper to no one in particular. "Is Aunt Elsa around?"

"He's talking to you, Ava," Eli says with a cruel tilt to his lips. "We got married two years ago, remember?"

CHAPTER 4
AVA

MY JAW NEARLY HITS THE FLOOR, AND MY mouth remains hanging open for longer than socially acceptable.

I stare at the countless faces surrounding me, searching for the joke. The *I got you*. The *you didn't see that coming, did you?*

Neither comes.

"Mrs. King?" the doctor asks again while adjusting his gold-framed glasses.

My heart squeezes and beats in intervals of uncomfortable pain.

Something must be wrong. There's no way I'm Mrs. King nor that I married Eli two years ago.

I was floundering in fucking depression two years ago. He mocked, ridiculed, and humiliated me two years before that.

He taught me the valuable lesson to never love again.

There's no way in hell I married him when I was nineteen nor that Papa would have allowed it.

I release a burst of nervous laughter before it chokes and dies down amid concerned gazes from my parents, sympathetic looks from the doctors, and a cold glance from the devil himself.

"Good one," I say with my usual cheerful energy. "Almost got me there. I don't know what I did to piss you off this time, considering you're always such a joy to be around, but I think you took it too far."

Eli's eyes narrow the slightest bit, and I think I catch a muscle clenching in his jaw.

"Mrs. King," says the impressively groomed doctor. "Can you start by telling us what year we're in?"

"Ava. It's Ava. Stop calling me 'Mrs....that'!" I snap.

"It's okay." Mama strokes my shoulder. "Try to relax, hon."

I realize my fingers are clenched in the bedsheets and my palms sting. I slowly release them and frown when I find my nails short and bare. I've always had a shade of pink on my nails and toenails since I was fifteen.

It's impossible that I've kept them bare.

Did the hospital remove my nail polish when I was admitted? That seems trivial and quite bizarre.

"I need this entire thing to stop." I sound more determined than I feel. "I'm not married to that prick, and I sure as hell am not Mrs. anything. I'm only twenty-one, for God's sake."

The sudden tension in the room slaps me across the face, and I freeze upon catching the note of horror in my parents' expression.

"Wh-what?" I sound terrified to my own ears. "What's wrong?"

Eli's gaze, which could rival Antarctica's frozen landscapes, falls on me. "You turned twenty-three a few months ago, and we've been married for over two years, Ava."

I realize I'm shaking my head and force myself to stop as I study my parents' gazes. "He's lying, right? Mama…? Papa…?"

Since I was young, I've known my father to be a massive figure in and outside our home. The man who could fill the horizon with his presence alone but who still treated my mum like a queen, and Ari and me like his princesses.

So to see him lower his head sparks a jolt of pain in me. Because I know, I just *know* I'm the only note of discomfort and shame in his and Mama's perfect family. The splash of black ink on his intricately woven life.

Ari is the normal, though mischievous, daughter. I'm the anomaly. The one they sometimes need to walk on eggshells around because I was born with a defective brain and a serious case of psychosis.

It was fine when I was living with them, when they could keep me under their watch and coax me to take the meds I hate more than my faulty brain.

But uni came along, and I think they gave up. Or maybe I forced them to by keeping my distance whenever they popped that unorthodox question: *Have you been taking your meds?*

I'd say yes instead of the truth. I'd been substituting those fuckers with my favorite cocktail of alcohol and drugs.

Now I can see that concern rising from the ashes as Mama shakes her head.

It's not a lie.

Even if Eli is devious enough to stage this masquerade and even hire an entire medical crew for it, my parents would never betray me.

My gaze falls on those eyes that have haunted me my entire life.

Stormy. Icy. Mysterious.

And reality slams into me worse than my disturbing nightmares.

I've lost complete recollection of my life for two whole years.

And somehow, someway, I managed to get myself in the worst trouble imaginable.

Married to Eli King.

This is just another nightmare I'll eventually wake up from, right?

———

So it's not a nightmare.

I lift my head from Cecily's shoulder and stare at her face. Her hair is shorter now, all pretty and wavy. She looks more mature; her eyes sparkle differently.

Happy.

I realize that's what she looks like: happy.

Though something's troubling her, and I can take a wild guess that it has to do with me.

After Cecy and Ari came along, I managed to kick Eli out under the pretext that I needed girl time.

My sister's style has also changed. She used to dress in these wannabe outfits that could rival the wardrobe of Satan's favorite underlings, but right now she's wearing a cute polka-dot dress and black Prada boots.

Her bowl-cut dark hair makes her look adorable, but like a gorgeous menace.

I can't believe she's, like, twenty now. Twenty.

The prospect that I didn't only lose two years of my life but also of hers and everyone I care about floods my veins with unease.

As I push away from Cecy, Ari shimmies out of her boots and sits cross-legged on the hospital bed, watching me like a rookie detective from those late-night mysteries. "You could use some skin care."

"Thanks for the concern, little shit."

"Anytime." She flips her hair, but I can see the hint of pain she attempts to hide. "I thought I'd never see you again."

She pauses and bites her lip when Cecily shakes her head.

I stare between them, feeling awfully like an outsider. An imposter in someone else's skin. "What's going on?"

Cecily releases a heavy sigh. "We thought something bad would happen to you after we heard about, you know."

"I don't know. What?"

"After you fell down the stairs," Cecily says.

"You really threw yourself down the stairs?" Ari asks in a vulnerable voice I'm not used to hearing from my rowdier-than-hell sister.

"What...? No? I don't know. I don't remember that. I don't remember anything after...after the party last—"

I cut myself off before I say *last night*, because that's not the case, confirmed by my doctor, who suspects I suffer from a form of dissociative selective amnesia.

There's no telling what the reason is nor how I'd be able to retrieve the missing memories except by being in a supportive environment.

Which is a lot of words to say he has no solution.

It doesn't make sense that my memories of that night at the club and everything before then are crystal clear, but somehow, I have no idea about my life over the past two freaking years.

I checked the calendar. It's been exactly two years and three months since that night.

"You really don't remember anything?" my sister asks.

"Not for the past two years or so."

"Well, I'm glad you didn't completely forget about us."

"Never."

Her lips tremble, and she looks away before I can see what her eyes are hiding.

"Cecy." I hold her hands. "It's not true, right? I need you to be the one who tells me it's not true. The last time we saw each other was in that shady club you hated while Jeremy had a hard-on for you and bloodlust for anyone who looked your way—you know, the usual for that guy. I promised to leave after we agreed to watch *Bridget Jones's Diary* before you went to the States. And you..." I stare at Ari. "You blackmailed me into getting info about Remi in exchange for having my back with Papa and Mama."

"That was over two years ago, Ava." The sympathy in Cecily's voice nearly obliterates me, and the rare empathy in Ariella's face doesn't help.

I start to release my friend's hand and pause when my fingers brush against a massive rock.

She's wearing a diamond ring so big, it'd be a drowning hazard if she wore it while swimming. I flip her hand back and forth, my mouth forming an O. "Cecy, you...you got *engaged*? When? How? Where?"

"A year ago." She gives me a sheepish smile. "On an island."

"Oh my God. I'm so excited for you! Tell me *everything*."

"Well, Jeremy called you for advice, and you said, 'However big you're thinking of going, go bigger, Jeremy. You better give Cecy a proposal worthy of her.' So he bought me an entire island as an engagement gift, whisked me there on our anniversary, and asked me to marry him."

I nod in approval. "Sounds about right. He could've gone bigger, if you ask me."

"Ava! You know I hate big."

"But you *deserve* big, Cecy." My voice lowers. "I can't believe I don't remember any of that."

"Hey…" She strokes my hair. "You'll be my maid of honor at the wedding. That's more important."

"Yes!" I pause, my body feeling foreign, as if my brain doesn't fit the reality I've found myself shoved into. "What else did I miss?"

"Well…" Cecy starts. "Kill and Glyn took the year off and are touring the world, backpacking, and completely disconnected from civilization. They've been on their trip for about three months now. They're engaged, too."

"Oh fuck. I missed that as well? Who else is engaged?"

"Anni and Creigh. Lan and Mia. Bran and Niko. They're getting married before Jeremy and me because Niko is in a hurry. Honestly, I wouldn't be surprised if they eloped any day now. Niko's definitely pro that option and keeps bringing it up daily, but Bran wants their families and friends there."

Her words hit me like an arrow. The fact that all this

happened during a time I have zero recollection of leaves me hollow.

Why?

Why did I forget a whole two years of my life?

How could I erase important moments for my friends?

Creighton is Eli's younger brother and the best of the King siblings, in my opinion. Landon and Brandon are his cousins. Bran is an angel and my favorite King man. Lan is an arsehole and a narcisSistic psycho, but he's still much better company than his older arsehole cousin.

Mainly because he helps me destroy the Tin Man's armor.

"Where does everyone live now? I assume they graduated uni and went on with their lives?"

"Yeah, well. Niko, Bran, Jeremy, and I live in New York. Lan and Mia are also there because Lan is getting an MBA, but they'll move back to London after they get married. Creigh and Anni are also moving back here, but they're now spending time with her and Jeremy's parents in New York. Uncle Aiden isn't a fan of Creigh not wanting to take his role at King Enterprises. All the weight is falling on Eli's shoulders."

"What about Lan?"

"He wants to continue sculpting for a few more years before he sacrifices his, and I quote, 'godly artistic talent for boring corporate work.' As you know, Bran never wanted anything to do with the business side of his family, so that only leaves Eli. He's also involved with the corporation from his mum's side of the family. Let's say it's not fun being Eli these days."

And yet he was here for the past two days after I woke

up. Even when my parents were around. Even now, I can feel his presence somewhere outside my room.

Why?

Is this another game?

If it is, the rules must've changed, because I don't recognize any of them.

We were supposed to annoy each other while remaining outside each other's lives. But now...what?

Married? Eli and me?

I still find it extremely hard to believe.

Ari clicks her tongue. "He's been a massive doucheface to my Remi, overworking him at Steel Corporation. He better watch his back, I'm telling you."

I narrow my eyes. "Don't tell me you're also engaged?"

"Unfortunately, no. Remi is still an idiot, but he's *my* idiot, so you're not allowed to call him names. I'm the only one who can do that. Anyway, he'll give me a ring sometime before he dies."

"You still like him?"

"Don't be daft, Ava. I don't like him. I *love* him. He loves me, too, by the way."

"Does *he* know that?"

"Deep in his heart, he does." She grins.

"How can you be sure? And no, delusion can't be the answer, Ari."

"I'm not delusional. *You're* delusional."

"Uh-huh." Jesus. At least something hasn't changed.

"Don't give me that." Annoyance bubbles to the surface through her voice. "You're the one who's delusional enough to think you're still single or something."

"Ari!" Cecily scolds.

"What? She got married against everyone's recommendations and made Papa angry. I've never seen him so mad."

"About that." I lean back against my pillow. "Something is wrong. You both know I'd never marry He-Who-Shall-Not-Be-Named willingly. I *hate* the bastard."

Ari lifts her chin. "Apparently not enough, because you said no one was allowed to interfere with your decision."

"*I* said that?"

"To Papa."

"No way."

"And Mama and Nan and Grandpapa and me."

"And me," Cecily says in a murmur.

"And Papa let me?"

"Not in the beginning," Ari says. "He was so pissed, I'm telling you. Like I'd never seen him before. He drove to the King household in the middle of the night and nearly drowned Eli in their pool. If Uncle Aiden hadn't been there, you'd be crying at Eli's grave as we speak. But even with that incident, and many others, including, but not limited to, Papa chasing him with a golf club and sending thugs to beat him up, you still didn't budge. Like, you weren't even feeling sorry or anything. You were...cold."

Cecily shakes her head at Ari again. "She wasn't cold. She was going through something."

"Stop defending her, Cecy. She nearly broke our family, okay?"

"Ari!" Cecily says.

"*What?*" I say at the same time.

Ari looks guilty. "It's nothing."

"Tell me. Now."

"Well, Mama and Papa were fighting because of the

stupid marriage. Papa said you'd only marry Eli over his dead body and that his decision was final. Mama tried to calm him at first, but when he got violent with Eli and refused to change his mind, she put her foot down and told him he doesn't get to dictate your life. Mama took you and left for the countryside for, like, two weeks until he calmed down. I hated that time."

She doesn't say it, but I can hear it in her unsaid words.

She hated me, too. For driving a wedge between our parents, whom we'd always seen as the epitome of a perfect couple.

I singlehandedly nearly drove them apart.

My worst fear materializes before my eyes in the form of a dark beast with hollow eyes and scaly, blurred features.

What have I done?

"And then what happened?"

"Ava, maybe you need to rest." Cecily pats my shoulder, forever the pacifist, but right now, I need Ari's brutal honesty.

And my sister gives it to me as she sighs. "He still didn't agree to the wedding. I don't think he does even now, to be honest. Especially after you asked that Eli be your legal guardian instead of him. Papa almost didn't walk you down the aisle, and Grandpapa offered to do it instead, but Papa changed his mind at the last minute. He was still mad, and you were crying while hugging him and apologizing. You said you didn't want to anger him, but you wanted to do this."

"It just doesn't make sense. I'd never go against Papa, especially not for that psycho Eli."

"And yet you already did." Ari pouts.

"Cecy." I face my friend. "What did I tell you? There must've been a reason behind that out-of-character decision."

"No one but you and Eli knows."

"But you're my bestie. I must've told you something. Anything?"

She shakes her head. "Honestly, I was a bit hurt you didn't want to confide in me, but you said it was for my sake. Whatever that means."

"Listen, what if I was possessed or something? I mean, I had an accident, and a ghost could've gotten inside me and lusted over Eli, which isn't that far-fetched since he attracts all sorts of attention. Now I'm back to normal, which is why I remember nothing of the past two years." I laugh, pleased with myself. "That makes total sense, don't you girls think?"

They don't join in, obviously not finding this scenario as hilarious as I do.

"Fine." I release a heavy sigh. "Can I see the wedding pictures?"

"Sure." Cecily scrolls on her phone for some time before she shows me an album titled *Ava's Wedding*.

The first picture is of me holding a bouquet of pink tulips and dahlias. Ten out of ten for the choice. Naturally, I approve, considering I already chose my wedding flowers when I was, like, twelve.

My dress is a sparkling champagne-pink strapless gown with glorious diamonds in the corset and a huge tulle and lace skirt that gives every Disney princess's dress a run for its money. Mine is more glamorous, with pink jewels carefully sewn into the fabric with explicit, masterful detail.

"Elie Saab," I whisper.

"You had a meltdown for it." Ari grins. "It was fun."

"As I should have." I nod in agreement with my past self. At least this part seems accurate and not entirely something a possessed version of me would do. I've wanted Elie to be my wedding dress designer since I was sixteen.

I eat up the details of the picture. My hair is gathered in an elegant twist, and my glam veil falls to the floor like a carpet. My hands are covered with dainty lace gloves with small sparkling jewels. The details. Oh, my heart. Dream dress.

A pink diamond necklace wraps around my neck, coupled with a matching ring.

"Pink diamonds…" I whisper.

"Eli's wedding gift." Cecily smiles. "He got you the entire set, which is one of a kind."

"Where's my ring?" I motion at my bare hand.

"Probably with Eli." Ari lifts a shoulder. "Maybe they removed it when you got admitted to the hospital."

Something isn't right. Not sure if it has to do with my bare hand or the fact the ring's absence feels…strange.

Bad strange.

Dangerous strange?

What kind of thought is that?

I scroll to pictures of me with the girls. Cecy, Ari, Glyn, and Anni looked hot as fuck. Especially Cecy with her shiny golden dress and soft features. But I'm biased.

There's a picture with me, the girls, Lan and Bran, who are clutching each other's shoulders, and Remi, who's laughing at Creigh while the latter remains poker-faced.

Can't believe I don't remember my bachelorette party and all the shenanigans I must've made them do.

A tremor rushes through me when I reach a picture of Eli and me. My gloved hand is snaked through his bent arm as we both stare at the camera.

He looks mouthwateringly sharp in a tailored black tuxedo. Perfect bow tie. Broad shoulders. Refined lines. Shaven face. Stubborn, set lips.

Stormy, cold, cold eyes.

My eyes meet mine in the picture. I look weird. Different. Almost like a version of me I don't recognize.

I realize with daunting clarity that I look cold, too. Detached. Indifferent.

And while I'm used to that from Eli, I've never been like that. Not even when I'm faced with his mocking, rude, and obnoxiously hurtful words. I might have pretended to be nonchalant around him, but that was only camouflage for what I truly felt.

Just because I acted like a badass doesn't mean I was immune to pain. He could and did hurt me, several times.

The way I stare at the camera is exactly what I wish my expression could be like whenever I face him.

I marry the guy and suddenly look terrifyingly like him. What type of sorcery is that?

I scroll to a picture where Eli and I are facing each other. He has one hand on my hip, the other lifting my chin. Our friends are surrounding us with their significant others. Killian hugs Glyn to his front, Jeremy holds Cecily at his side by the waist, Anni is climbing Creigh's massive body, Lan is Frenching the shit out of Mia, Nikolai hugs Bran from behind, his chin resting on Bran's shoulder, and

Ari holds her face in both palms and makes heart eyes at a Remi, who's shoving her away while grinning at the camera.

Amid all that chaos, the only thing I can focus on is the way I'm looking at Eli. Is that...fear in my eyes? Trepidation?

What fuckery happened for me to decide I needed to marry the devil himself to resolve it?

There must've been something.

"Cecy...Ari...that night I last remember, what happened after the accident? Was I injured? Did I hit my head?"

A furrow appears in both their foreheads.

"What accident?" Cecily asks slowly.

"The night you left the club with Jeremy. When I texted you that I was going home, I was actually driving to an after-party. I had a weirdo following me, so I called the police and then I think I was hit by a truck or pushed to the side of the road or something."

Cecily pauses, fidgets, opens her mouth, then stops.

"What now?" I whisper.

"There was no accident, Ava," she murmurs.

"Yeah," Ari says. "You came back home late that night. I saw you the next morning, and you were fine."

"No, I called the police, I—" My words get caught in my throat when a flash hits me out of nowhere.

Cruel long fingers squeeze my face as flashing anger engulfs me whole. "You'll keep your goddamn mouth shut, Ava, or so help me God, I'll sew it shut for you."

The door opens, and I jolt as I meet those eyes. The same eyes that threatened me. No, they *terrified* me. I can still feel the harsh grip of his fingers around my jaw and the tremor that passed through me at the time.

Eli is my husband, but something tells me this marriage is more of an imprisonment. A way for him to control me. Sew my mouth shut, as he promised.

But about what?

"The doctor agreed to your discharge." He steps inside in his tailored black trousers and crisp blue shirt, his cuffs immaculate, his hair pushed back, and his presence stifling. The only thing out of place is the slight stubble covering his cheeks as if he hasn't found the time to groom it.

"Get ready, would you?" he says. "I don't have all day."

"All day for what?" I ask with audible trepidation.

"To take you home, Mrs. King."

CHAPTER 5
ELI

MY LIFE IS BUILT AROUND WELL-TRACED LINES and impeccably connected patterns.

I'm a man of reason, strategy, and, most importantly, control—though the latter is often accompanied by the seductive taste of manic fixation.

Some might say I'm just...sociopathic. A perfect representation of plot holes and uncertain outcomes. A bit too black to be gray. Too gray to be black.

I'm nothing short of a conundrum for most people, which is exactly how I prefer it.

Dad taught me that people fear you when they can't figure you out. They respect you, fawn over the merest hint of your attention, and grovel under the weight of your authority.

Which is why I've made it my mission to remain as clear of the public eye as possible. The eldest heir to two of the world's largest empires is a mystery by all important accounts.

A handsome mystery.

A seductive-as-sin mystery.

Still a mystery, though.

They see my outer self and the persona I choose to

adopt in public, but no one can tell what I'm planning until it's too late.

Those details haven't deterred their attention, though. Far from it.

Heads turn wherever I go. Men envy my charm, charisma, and ability to get things done. There hasn't been anything I've wanted and haven't acquired in this world.

Not a single thing.

Women drop to their knees if I so much as look in their direction.

All except for the one who's glaring at me as if I pissed in her special-edition bag and stepped on the hem of her precious veil. On our wedding day.

No kidding. Ava gave me the stink eye when I accidentally stepped on her veil.

"Don't touch Elie with your sullied presence," she told me while pushing me away.

I grabbed her by the elbow, tightening my fingers incrementally. "Who the fuck is Elie?"

"The designer," she replied as if I was supposed to know that.

Now I'm treated with the same disregard after I've announced we're going home. Something we should've done yesterday if her dear papa hadn't inSisted that she needed to be kept under surveillance for one more night and convinced the doctor—whom *I* pay—with that ludicrous demand.

Father and daughter share the stubbornness of a blind mule and the logical thinking of a drunk politician.

Dull pain throbs in my abdomen despite the illegal amount of painkillers I've consumed. I slide my hand into my pocket and roll my wedding band twice as I stare back at this headache in the form of a woman.

"I'm not going anywhere with you," she announces, her chin up, her arms crossed, gearing up for a fight I don't have the goddamn time for.

"You're my wife and will go wherever I go, Mrs. King."

She swallows, her pale throat working up and down with the motion until I can almost see the saliva traveling down through her transparent skin. "Stop calling me that."

"Calling you what?" I step into the hospital room, crowding her and the sidekicks she chose for the day. "Mrs. King?"

"Stop it," she snaps.

"Get dressed, and I might consider it."

"Hey." Ariella, a nutcase with serious stalking tendencies and a prison sentence waiting to happen, stands up and puffs out her chest, which is comical at best because she doesn't even reach my shoulders. "Stop ordering people around like they're servants and you're their lord and savior."

I lift a brow. "Is this still about your sister?"

"It's about everything you do."

"And you're a legal counsel now?"

"Only when it comes to going against you. Anyway, Ava should stay with Mama and Papa for a while until she gets used to her new reality. In case you forgot, she's lost her memory and doesn't remember marrying you."

"But she remembers me." I let my gaze float to Ava, who regards me with the attention of a parasite.

Maybe a ghost.

Or am I the ghost?

After all, her last memory of me is of that night at the club, when she hated me.

She still has throughout our marriage, so that's not a major issue, per se.

Conveniently, or maybe inconveniently, depending on your angle, Ava erased all her memories from before our wedding to the latest incident that nearly decimated it.

The good news is that she hasn't and will not find out about how this happened.

The bad news is that she won't accept it easily and will fight tooth and nail to discover the truth.

"She still doesn't remember the marriage," Cecily supplies in an amicable tone that somehow manages to calm any situation.

Not this one, though.

Besides, Cecily is one of the reasons Ava is an absolute wreck of a human being. And while Cecily hasn't made her worse, she hasn't contributed to making her better. Cecily's constant attempts at placating and spoiling her like some blind mother hen have always irked me.

I should probably text Jeremy so he'll whisk her away from here as fast as possible. Save us both the pending headache.

"Do you want to go with your parents? Is that a wise thing to do?" I ask my wife, and she starts to nod, but then she stops.

I was listening to their entire conversation from outside. And yes, Ariella is a mere amateur compared to me and my superior stalking skills, but I digress.

I heard the nutcase telling Ava about the fuckup she caused in her family and could hear the guilt in Ava's voice, even if she didn't remember it. Besides, she was pretending to be asleep last night when Aunt Silver and Cole—not calling that man *Uncle* unless he calls me *son*; report me to the petty police—were arguing about her meds and the new psychiatrist.

An entirely pointless conversation, if you ask me, considering I'm her legal guardian and neither of them has a say in her treatment options anymore.

She doesn't have a say either.

As they talked, Ava turned away, but I saw the way she clenched the sheets and hid further into the pillow. And while she's an expert at hiding from the world, she can't escape me.

I'm neither a limp-dicked thick fucker burning for her attention nor a worshipper at her sparkly-pink glitter altar.

She's neither my benefactor nor my owner.

She is, however, my wife. My fucking property.

Rare calm cloaks her features as she stands. The hospital's plain gown swallows her with the ugliness of a potato sack, and yet she still manages to make it look effortlessly elegant.

The collar of the gown slips off her shoulder, hinting at the creamy skin that's begging to be marked, owned, fucking turned red.

I drag my gaze to her face, which is pasty white due to her nearly dying on me. Her shiny blond hair falls to her back in slick waves, and like always, she shakes it a bit before running her fingers through it, then pulls it up in a makeshift bun like whenever she's ready to tackle something.

It's always the little things: the jut of her chin, the gentle move of her hips, the goddamn way she ties her hair.

And yet those little things are enough to prove she's here. Right across from me.

Not at the bottom of the stairs.

Not in a pool of blood.

Not dead.

"I'll get ready," she says without emotion.

"You're going back with him?" Ariella whisper-yells. "But why? I can drive you home."

Before I can correct her and say that Ava's home is now my house—not that she would admit it out loud—she waves Ariella away. "There's no need."

I don't like the note in her voice. It's not a resignation to her fate. It's the intention to fight it until the very end.

The irony.

I reSist the urge to smile. Then again, I've never liked Ava for her meekness. I've had too many willing people in my life. It's refreshing to be presented with a fight for a change.

At every turn.

For every word.

Yes, I contemplate breaking her neck sometimes, but that neck is too pretty to be broken.

As if sensing my murderous gaze, she looks up and narrows her eyes.

For all intents and purposes, Ava is every man's wet dream. She possesses a model's face that somehow can also pass for an innocent girl next door. Rosebud lips in her favorite color—pink. Big intrusive blue eyes that rival the North Sea's depths and the sky's hollowness during an eclipse. A body made for fucking. And an attitude that will get her killed—and almost has countless times.

I'd like to take the opportunity to applaud my immaculate resolve to keep that pretty head in place all this time.

It takes massive control and self-discipline to remain calm in her provoking presence.

Though, to be fair, it's been a long time since she lost the spark, so seeing it back is a welcome change.

For now.

She hikes a hand on her hip. "Some privacy?"

"There's no privacy between a married couple."

"Yeah, well, that might be your version, but it's certainly not mine. Go away."

What was that about applauding my resolve? Oh yes, I can't actually kill my wife. That's a felony in almost all countries as far as I'm aware. "You have fifteen minutes."

"I can't even do my makeup in fifteen minutes!"

"Fifteen, Ava." I close the door before she throws something at me.

She doesn't need makeup, for Christ's sake.

But then again, she's always had this strange concept about herself.

A concept full of inferiorities and muddied thoughts—and until recently, extremely destructive actions.

I walk down the hall of the elegant private clinic that could rival a five-star hotel and bring out my phone.

"Sir," answers Henderson, my trusted special asSistant, as he likes to call himself, after the first ring.

"Have the car ready in ten."

"Already waiting outside."

"Have you taken care of everything in the house?"

"Yes, sir."

"If I find—or, worse, if Ava finds—anything she's

not supposed to see, I'll have your head on a spike before sunrise."

"Considering my absolute disregard for that ending, I can assure you that everything will be spotless."

"Talk me through it."

"Deleted surveillance footage. We installed a completely new security system. The clothes have been thrown away and replaced with exact replicas. The hazardous setting has been blockaded. All maids, gardeners, and personnel have been changed except for Sam and me."

"If you and Sam disappoint me, you know your fates, right?"

"The spike or the guillotine. We have the liberty to choose."

"I changed my mind. You don't have the luxury of picking your fate anymore."

"Noted," he says with the same emotionless tone.

I'm nothing short of an excellent judge of character, which is why Henderson fits the bill. I might have stolen him from my dad's personnel, and Dad might still hold a grudge over it. But it's not my fault people prefer my company over his. Though he'd tell you otherwise, like the delusional old man he is.

Besides, Henderson needs more stimuli than Dad's boring entrepreneurial efforts can offer, and I present him with multiple ways to indulge in his darker tendencies.

A few staged disappearances here, a deletion of records there, and he's living his best life.

I saved him from a dull existence. He's welcome.

"Sir?"

"Yes?"

"You need to rest. You've been exerting yourself the past couple of days, and that has a negative impact on your recovery."

"Let me worry about that. If my parents—or, worse, my grandfathers—hear a peep of this…"

"They won't."

The door opens behind me, and I hang up before I turn around, knowing full well it's not Ava.

She'll be late just to get on my last nerve. Pissing me off is her favorite sport and the center of her infuriating existence.

I'm faced with her firecracker sister, who's glaring up at me.

Rising to my full height, I raise a brow. "What can I do for you, stalker?"

"Funny coming from the master."

"Don't be jealous." I pat the top of her head, and she pushes my hand away.

"You still owe me an explanation, Eli."

"Concerning?"

"Don't fuck with me." She surveys our surroundings like a rookie detective on their first mission and leans in. "What the hell happened before she fell down the stairs?"

"I told you. It was an accident."

"We both know damn well that it wasn't," she hisses under her breath. "Why are you hiding the truth?"

"None of your business."

"Should I make it Papa's business?"

"Only if you wish to complicate things further. Keep your mouth shut, get on with your nasty habits, and leave this to me."

"You said the same thing the last time, but now she's ended up in the hospital. Again. How many more times can you hide this before everyone knows that she—"

I slam my hand over her mouth. "Shut the fuck up, Ariella. Don't speak of it again, or I swear to fuck, if you prove to be a liability, I'll keep you in the dark about any future plans."

She pushes my hand away, her chin trembling. "I'm worried, okay? I thought it was the last time I'd see her."

"It won't be. Not as long as I'm here."

"Well, you're doing a poor job at proving it by being controlling. You know she hates that."

"She doesn't remember. All the better."

"What if she does?"

"I'll take care of it."

A frown appears between her brows. "I don't know where you get the confidence to believe your words, but I sincerely applaud you."

"Thanks."

"She'll hate us both once she finds out everything."

"A position I'm willing to be in, though I'm starting to doubt if I can say the same about you."

"I'd do anything for her."

"Good. Start by keeping your mouth shut. Engage in your favorite hobby. Disappear if you have to."

"Give me what I asked for first." She juts her palm in my direction. "Remi's schedule."

"You lost the rights to that when you suggested she go to your parents' house." I sideline her and head to Ava's room.

"You petty wanker!" she screams behind me, and I can

imagine her fuming, face red, and mentally cursing me all the way to Sunday.

But I couldn't care less about Ariella and the dismal role she plays on my chessboard.

It's time to take my wife home.

And this time, I'll keep her there.

CHAPTER 6

AVA

AN HOUR LATER, I STEP OUTSIDE THE HOSPITAL, having survived falling down the stairs with a couple of bruises and no memories.

Oh, and I'm accompanied by a royally pissed-off Eli. Which can be described as his default setting.

He can blame himself for the tardiness, for all I care.

A girl can't get ready in fifteen minutes, and even if I could, I wouldn't miss the chance to bring the devil down a peg or two.

I might have made the horrible mistake of marrying him—sticking to my brain-damage theory, thank you very much—but he's not my keeper.

"The only reason I'm going with you is because I need answers," I inform him as I stop in front of a Mercedes, which I assume is his, considering the short guy with sandy-blond hair who's holding the door open.

Eli leans in behind me until his warm breaths send a hot flush against my ear. He's so close, his height towers over mine and his scent shoots straight to my head quicker than drugs.

"Whatever you say, Mrs. King," he whispers in a rough tone.

I stiffen, my skin crawling with deep-seated annoyance and dangerous awareness.

Brilliant. That stupid part hasn't changed despite the amnesia.

I slide into the back seat in a hopeless, slightly clunky attempt to escape his orbit. Eli places his hand on the roof inside the car to prevent me from hitting my head.

My mouth remains open in complete and utter surprise. Was he trying to be a protective gentleman just now or something equally ridiculous?

Someone call the imposter police and get this guy checked for authenticity.

On the outside, he looks quite the same, like a high-class replica, but something's changed about this man.

Yes, he's still the same crass Eli with enough unbothered audacity to give Satan a run for his money, but it's different now.

Only, I can't put my finger on it.

The blond guy, whom I think I saw with Uncle Aiden in the past, closes my door with a respectful nod. Eli rounds the car, unbuttons his jacket, and sits beside me.

All of a sudden, the space is dwarfed by his titanic presence, and I have to remind myself to breathe. Obviously, I'm shit out of luck, because I only manage to breathe him in with every inhale and fail to expel him with my exhales.

He smells like forbidden temptation and impending disaster.

Divine but so utterly wrong.

Sharing a space with him is entirely not in my best interest and could be considered a major test of my resolve, but I have to put up with it if I plan to uncover the truth behind whatever fuckery happened to me two years ago.

I refuse to believe I married him of my own accord but then, illogically, kept my closest people out of the loop.

There's no way in hell I wouldn't have told Cecy. Hell, I've always been so descriptive about everything, and she knows more about me than Mama or Ari. She's my person. My confidante.

If I didn't tell her why I inSisted on marrying this glamorous Tin Man, something's up.

And, apparently, Eli is the only person who knows the truth.

Getting him to divulge it, though, will be tricky. So my best shot is to familiarize myself with my new environment first.

I study the driver and the short man sitting in the passenger seat, then Eli, who's going through his phone.

My fingers clutch a pink kombucha that's sitting in my side of the cupholder, and I take a sip. The weird bubbly taste burns my throat, and I grimace.

But hey, it calms me down, and at least the can is a beautiful pink, so that's a win in my book.

I wonder how Eli knows I like this brand. But then again, it'd be weird if he knew nothing after two years of marriage.

And no, I'm still not used to the idea that I'm married. To Eli.

If I were to write my seventeen-year-old self about this and be like, *Guess what? I'm married to Eli*, she'd probably have a stroke. Naive, stupid bitch that she was.

"Where's my ring?" I ask absent-mindedly.

Still looking at his phone, Eli reaches into his jacket and retrieves a huge pink diamond ring that sparkles like a thousand lights.

It's the ring I saw in the countless pictures Cecily showed me. Turns out, I also have a folder with 3,523 pictures of the marriage. The title is *My Wedding feat. Tin Man.*

Which I buy, to be honest. I see myself naming it that. Other options would be *My Wedding and He-Who-Shall-Not-Be-Named as a Prop* or *I Got Married. He's Only Here for the Pictures.*

Eli holds the ring in midair, waiting for me to take it. Still not looking at me.

I jam the bottle of kombucha in the cup holder, my temper flaring as fast as the fizz that's spilling over. "If you are actually my husband, then look at me when you give me my fucking wedding ring."

He lifts his head, a flash of anger appearing in his stormy eyes. Under different circumstances, I'd probably run or cower.

Hell, under different circumstances, I'd never allow myself to be in a closed space with Eli. That's just asking for trouble.

Right now, however, I don't see a way out.

Instead of focusing on the confusion and the loss I feel without my memories, I direct that energy at him.

"Watch your mouth." He speaks in a deep, firm tone.

He has a way of moderating his words to intimidate his adversary. And while I'd be lying if I said I wasn't affected, I'm more pissed off than anything.

"Should've thought about that before you married me."

"A decision I question every day."

"As do I, for sure."

"For sure," he repeats with a hint of dark amusement. "Except for the small fact that you've been infatuated with me for years and then proceeded to beg me to marry you."

I can feel my cheeks warming and probably turning bright pink, and for the first time, I'm not a fan of my favorite color.

"Me? *Beg* you? You must be out of your mind."

"Out of my mind for tolerating your presence? Yes."

"I did *not* beg you to marry me."

"Does that mean you remember the proposal night?"

"Just because I don't remember it doesn't mean you can spout nonsense. Why on earth would I beg the person I hate the most to marry me? I'm neither desperate nor suicidal."

A hint of something unfathomable passes in his eyes as quick as lightning, and then they're back to their status quo—aka an unreadable gray cloud. "And yet you ended up marrying the person you hate the most. The irony."

"The horror."

"The reality, Mrs. King."

"*Stop* calling me that."

"But you are. We have the wedding certificate and the ceremony to prove it." He grabs my hand and slides the ring on my finger roughly, with no patience nor softness whatsoever.

But then again, there isn't a gentle bone in the devil's body.

I stare at the ring, and for some reason, it seems familiar. Comforting.

What kind of disturbed thought is that?

Choosing to steer clear of that territory, I cross my arms. "Well, there's something that can undo it. It's called a divorce, and I want one."

A burst of laughter rips from his cruel lips and fills the car with a dreadful undertone before it comes to a sharp halt. "There will be no divorce, Mrs. King."

"Well, I demand it."

"Demand declined."

"I have every right to decide the status of my marriage, and I want it to end. As soon as possible."

"Our marriage."

"What?"

"You said the status of *your* marriage, but it's *our* marriage, Mrs. King."

"Well, *our* marriage is obviously an anomaly, considering we can't stand each other. No idea what went on in my head when I agreed to this ridiculous wedding, but I'm no longer possessed and would like to do the right thing. Please and thank you."

"*Possessed…*" He repeats the word slowly as if he's letting it sit on his tongue to taste it, dissect it, probably slash it open like the countless hearts he's broken to pieces, often unknowingly and without regrets. "Do you believe you were possessed when you said 'I do'?"

"There's no other explanation for that daft decision."

"Interesting." He focuses back on his phone, completely and effectively erasing me.

This prick has a PhD in raising my blood pressure. If I were still hooked to those hospital machines, they'd be beeping all the way to the sky.

"I'm talking to you," I grind out.

"I'm not."

I snatch the phone from his hand and contemplate throwing it out the window. But that would make me look both dramatic and impulsive—two descriptions Eli loves shoving down my throat.

So I regulate my breathing and let the phone drop to my lap. "I said I want a divorce."

"And I said you won't be getting one."

"I'll take you to court."

"No, you won't."

"Wanna bet?"

"If you're in the mood to lose your money and time aside from your feeble logic, sure thing. I suggest you stop being impulsive for once in your life and think about this rationally."

"This *is* the most rational solution. There's no love lost between us, Eli. Why the hell did you even marry me?"

"As I said, you begged."

"Let's say I did, which is by no means true, by the way. You just said yes?"

"I've always had a soft spot for begging." His eyes shine with a gleam of lethal intensity, and I swallow, feeling suddenly parched.

"Be serious," I breathe out.

"I'm dead serious. Remove the idea of a divorce from your head. The sooner, the better." He reaches for his phone, but I hold it out of reach.

"I'm high-maintenance."

"Just the way I like it."

"I have extremely expensive tastes."

"Good thing I come from old money and I'm rich enough to outshine a few countries' GDP."

"I'll drive you crazy."

"Nothing new there."

"I don't like you."

"That's because you love me."

"In your damn dreams. I'm way out of your league."

"I can rope you back in if I choose to."

I'm fuming. My fingers tingle with the need to throw the phone at his stupidly gorgeous face and ruin it once and for all.

"Are we done?" he asks in a bored tone.

"No. I still don't understand why this marriage happened."

"Because it's beneficial for both of us. Now quit the pointless dramatics."

"In…what sense is it beneficial for both of us?"

He releases an exasperated sigh. "I needed a wife for my image, and you needed a husband to safely leave your parents' orbit and hide your self-destructive nature, reckless behavior, and alarming mental breakdowns. Does that answer your question?"

He jerks the phone from my slack fingers as I stare at him, speechless.

A hollow, bitter taste sinks to the bottom of my stomach, and nausea climbs up my throat.

I knew things didn't add up, but I hadn't thought I'd make a deal with the devil to put a stop to the ticking bomb in my head.

My marriage, just like my life, is one big embarrassing sham.

———

The rest of the drive is spent in tense silence. Eli never looks up from his stupid phone, and I look at everything but him.

The familiar yet strange London streets. The driver and the asSistant, who I realized belatedly probably heard everything, including my humiliating realization of what went down in my life.

Two years later, and it's still the same mess from my last year at uni.

According to Cecy and Ari, I married Eli the summer of my graduation and haven't done much since.

It was their way of insinuating that I'm still the fuckup I remember. I haven't participated in any competitions since the one I ran offstage from. Haven't gotten any contracts nor invitations to any orchestras nor even events. I simply withdrew from the music scene as quietly as a dwindling star.

And just like that, I set my talent on fire and drowned in copious amounts of alcohol as it turned into a huge rubbish can.

Brilliant.

Apparently, I still play sometimes, but what's the point if I'm my only audience?

I'm on autopilot when the car stops and my door is opened. I step onto the property's asphalt entrance, and my Jimmy Choo heels squeak when I come to an abrupt halt.

The grand Edwardian building in front of me looks imposing, with its signature brick structure and massive windows, surrounded by a vast garden and a greenhouse decorated with multiple pink indoor plants.

But that's not what makes me halt in my tracks. I swear

I saw this house in my dreams once. Down to the gorgeous pink greenhouse.

However, I've never been here before. I mean, I don't remember the past two years, so I was here before, but I forgot. Is that why it feels familiar?

"I assume the house gets your stamp of approval."

I flinch; Eli's rough voice sounds so close to me that my senses short-circuit. I clear my throat as I look up at him. "When did you buy this?"

"My family has always owned it. It was a wedding gift from Grandpa Jonathan to both of us."

"But I'd never been here before that?"

"No." He coaxes me forward with a hand on my back.

I reSist the shiver, but it's tragically pointless. I feel the pads of his fingers nearly burning holes in my soft-pink Ralph Lauren dress.

We stop at the entrance when we're greeted by well-groomed, impeccably presented staff I've never seen in my life.

A short lean woman with East Asian features and thick-framed glasses precedes them.

"Sam!" I exclaim.

Her usually standoffish face breaks into a rare small smile. "I'm glad you're well, Mrs.—"

She hasn't even finished the sentence when I attack her in a hug. Might have to do with the fact she's the only familiar face I've seen here or that something finally makes sense.

"There, there." She pats my back mechanically, her movements stiffer than Eli's nonexistent morals.

No wonder she's his nanny. Or ex-nanny or whatever.

"You're so standoffish." I push back and pull on her cheek. "Relax a little."

She steps away from my touch. "I left all the relaxing to you, Mrs. King."

"It's Ava. And was that sarcasm?" I tilt my head at the other staff. "Must be *so* much fun to be around her, am I right?"

None of them moves nor even acknowledges me.

"You let Sam handpick her clones, didn't you?" I give Eli the stink eye.

He's leaning against the wall, his arms and ankles crossed, looking more amused than a king watching his personal clown. "Anything for you, Mrs. King."

I grind my teeth to keep from falling into the trap he's goading me into and proving to these people I've never met that I'm a fuckup. "Well, this atmosphere sucks. Totally not a fan."

"You'll get used to it."

"Or we can change things up. Sam, I love you, but you need a chill pill and a proper introduction to smiling. How about a staff reshuffle like the prime minister does?"

"I'll have to decline," she says.

"But why? It's going to be so much fun if you let me help."

"I have my doubts."

"How can you be so cruel?" I pout.

"Henderson already briefed me about your situation, so I'll reintroduce myself." She completely ignores my earlier statement. "I'm the house manager and I cook Mr. King's meals. If you need anything, please don't hesitate to ask me."

"Henderson?" I ask.

She points at the blond guy who's standing by the car.

"Leonardo Henderson," he says in an eloquent tone. "I'm Mr. King's special asSistant."

"How special?" I ask.

"He's just an assistant," Eli says with a grumble.

"I prefer *special assistant*. Seems mysterious and cool." I grin at Leonardo, who smiles back.

"I'll take you to your room," Sam says.

"I will do it." Eli slides to my side. "You can get on with your tasks."

She nods, turns, then leaves, followed by her army of mini-mes.

"She totally scoured the entirety of the UK and Europe to find her own world-domination minions," I mutter. "We'll talk about that reshuffle later, Sam!"

She doesn't even acknowledge me.

What a thrill. Not only do I have to deal with Eli, but also with his loyal sidekick and the woman who loves and nurtures his monstrous nature.

While I love Sam, mostly because Aunt Elsa loves her, she's too standoffish and uptight for my liking.

I glare at Eli. "Is this a punishment?"

"Believe me, you'll feel it when I punish you, Mrs. King."

He waltzes to the stairs, leaving me in an alarming state of hyperventilation. I slap a hand on my chest, willing my heartbeat to slow down and stop being in utter shambles.

What the hell is up with that?

Was he flirting with me or threatening me?

At any rate, I shouldn't feel warm because of it.

I follow him, partly because I have no choice and partly because I need a distraction.

I catch a glimpse of the sitting area's decor and pause upon seeing pink paintings, sofas, and even a pink-and-white rug.

Did Eli and Sam let me decorate?

They had to have, since Eli's favorite color is the shade of his soul, black, and I'm pretty sure Sam is allergic to bright colors and would contract a serious case of nausea at seeing all the pink.

The sitting area upstairs also contains a grand champagne-pink sofa. A huge pink crystal chandelier hangs from the high platform ceiling, and the halls are filled with artistic pink paintings.

Ten out of ten for taste. It's mine, so of course it's perfect.

My head bumps into a wall, and only when I inhale the intoxicating scent and get assaulted by the warmth do I realize it's actually Eli's chest.

I was so preoccupied with my spotless taste that I momentarily forgot I wasn't alone. And the bastard definitely stopped abruptly and turned around on purpose.

I glare up at him. He smiles.

I glare harder. His grin widens.

"My, Mrs. King. We just got back and you're already throwing yourself into my arms? Control yourself, would you?"

I jerk away. "It was an *accident*."

"One of many."

"Stop it."

"Stop what?"

"Being a dick, for starters."

"And now we're talking about my dick. That desperate, huh?"

"Hell will freeze over before I let you touch me, Eli."

"You look adorable when spouting lies. Besides..." He lifts my chin with a curled index finger, spearing his cold eyes into my soul. "I already touched you. If I want to fuck you, you'll bend over and take it."

"Lie." My whisper is barely audible as my chin trembles.

"Want to bet?"

"You're messing with me because I lost my memory. I'd never sleep with you."

"There was no sleeping involved. I must say I wasn't impressed, but I can give you a chance for a redo."

"Fuck you."

I storm into what I assume is my room and slam the door in his face.

There's no energy left in me to even appreciate the glorious pink princess room that greets me. I slide down against the door and pull my knees to my chest as a tear stains my cheek.

I clearly remember making a promise to myself that I'd never cry because of Eli again.

Never, *ever* again.

And yet another tear follows, and another, and another.

Because I realize with crushing clarity that I'm mourning a part of me that I thought meant something.

Something I wanted to only give up for love, and yet I handed it over to the devil on a silver platter.

What the hell have I done?

CHAPTER 7
AVA

"DON'T TOUCH IT!"

I swat Sam's destructive hand away before she murders my beautiful dahlias more coldly than her favorite master would.

"Then you should do it properly." She gives me her usual blank expression that I'm sure means *murder* in at least one language, then sits on the vintage recliner in the greenhouse, nestling crochet yarn on her lap.

"I am doing it properly." I cut the stem and carefully bury it in the pot, then cover it with the soil we ordered.

"Those flowers will die within the week. Maybe you should leave it to the professionals."

"Stop being a buzzkill. Why are you here if you disapprove of everything I do?" I hike my gloved hand on my hip. Everything is pink—my gloves, wellies, and cute little off-the-shoulder Armani dress.

"I have nothing to do."

"Pishposh. You've been following me around for days, Sam."

She crochets with the precision of a surgeon, and considering how awfully mysterious she is, I wouldn't be surprised if she was one in a previous life.

All I know about Sam is that she's been with the King household longer than I've been alive, and although she has Asian features, she uses no Asian name, has no accent, and has never given any indication of her heritage. She certainly doesn't offer up the information. I've heard her give different answers to different people depending on the occasion. *Chinese, Japanese, Korean,* and *Filipino* all came into the conversation.

I nudge her foot with my cute boot. "I'm talking to you. Is Eli ordering you to babysit me or something?"

"Or something."

I narrow my eyes. "If that piece of shit thinks he's my warden, I will—"

I cut myself off because she glares up at me at the audacity of me bad-mouthing her lord and master. Besides, I'm so livid, I have no idea how to finish the sentence.

If I had any misconceptions about this marriage before, then they're long forgotten. Or, more accurately, confirmed.

The day after I got here, Eli took me to meet my new doctor, a serious woman named Dr. Blaine. Apparently, my doctor was changed, and something tells me it was all his doing. When I asked about my previous psychiatrist, Dr. Wright, Henderson said he's out of the country.

I didn't probe further, mainly because I was embarrassed. It's one thing for Eli to get a whiff of my mental state, but it's entirely different for him to supervise it.

Due to my psychoSis and constant mental breakdowns and fugue episodes, I'm legally required to have a guardian who'll be able to supervise and approve any major decisions, including, but not limited to, opening a bank account, having access to funds, and completing any administrative processes.

And while that has always bothered me, Papa never made me feel like he was my owner, and he gave me more freedom than most patients like me could dream of. In fact, he was accommodating and never stepped on my toes, partly because my parents aimed to give me as much of a normal life as possible.

But the truth is, I'm not normal.

And finding out that Eli, of all people, knows that in full detail *and* has complete control over approving my treatment programs left me in a foul mood.

Thankfully, I didn't have to face him, considering he completely ignored me for an entire week afterward. His driver took me to a previously approved session with my psychiatrist, to visit my parents—who keep inSisting I go back to live with them despite my refusals—to hang out with Cecily and to catch up with his parents.

Let's say I'd rather live with his mum and dad than with him.

Aunt Elsa spoiled me shitless, had the cook make all the desserts I love, and made me feel as if nothing has changed despite missing a two-year chunk from my life. Uncle Aiden told me in gloating detail how he won a one-million-dollar bet against Papa and how he's my and Eli's number one supporter for no other reason than to piss Papa off.

Honestly, I stay out of whatever bad blood my papa and my father-in-law have. I'm just glad Mama and my mother-in-law get along. In fact, the three of us and Ari had a spa day yesterday, and we spent it pampering ourselves and talking about everything and nothing.

I was relaxed and content for the first time since the

amnesia hit, but that was only until I came back home and was faced with Eli's closed office door and his incessant avoidance and religious disregard, as if I were the plague.

The only time he looks at me is to shake his head like I'm a liability he's stuck with.

Well, no one held a gun to his head and forced him to marry me. Besides, he's the one who needs me to polish his rogue image.

I might be a clusterfuck internally, but I'm the epitome of a social butterfly and the media's darling. So, of course, I'm an asset.

"Hey, Sam." I finger some tulip seeds after I lay them on a plate. I've been told not to even attempt to grow them as an amateur, but I've never liked being told what to do, and I'm always up for a challenge.

"Yes?"

"How long are you going to hide the alcohol from me?"

"No idea what you're talking about." Her eyes are zeroed in on her crochet, which gives me no clue about what she's trying to make. Maybe a witch's cloak for her Halloween costume—sorry, I mean everyday clothes.

"Don't think I haven't noticed there isn't a drop of alcohol in the house."

"Is that so?"

"Uh-huh."

"And that's a problem because?" She drags her eyes to mine, pinning me down like I'm a petulant child.

I narrow my eyes back. "I need to loosen up. You know, considering I'm living with an absent husband and all."

"I thought you were, and I quote, 'So happy I didn't see the devil's face this morning. Made my day. I should celebrate.'"

"Were you eavesdropping on me when I was in the wardrobe?"

"I was there to collect your clothes, and you made sure I heard your musings. Which I repeated back to him as you intended, miss."

My cheeks warm and I growl softly. If Eli doesn't drive me insane, his precious Sam definitely will.

"You know what? Forget it. Have a lovely time making your entry ticket into the witch coven." I remove my gloves and dump them in the box at my feet, then turn to leave the greenhouse.

Henderson mentioned this place was my idea, but I have no clue why. Yes, it's pink and I can practice my gardening skills, but as I shimmy out of my apron and wellies, I realize its purpose could've been to allow me to replace my only passion in life.

Music.

I feel like I haven't touched my cello in years.

"Where are you going?" Sam asks.

"Out. And stop acting like my warden!"

I put on my cute pumps with crystal jewels on the heels. Six inches. All ready to be shoved up the arse of anyone who tries to stop me.

My strides are determined as I go to the house, freshen up, change into a skintight silver dress, grab a purse that matches my shoes, and stroll to the huge car garage.

I tried to take it slow over the past week even though Cecy was still in town, and now I'm a bit heartbroken that she left yesterday because, boo-fucking-hoo, her stupid fiancé can't cope without her for a whole week.

What a baby.

Anyway, I told them to keep my fall down the stairs a secret from everyone else because I didn't want to worry them.

Now I regret it big time because my only genuine company is my little sister, who'll snitch to Papa if he so much as glowers at her. She's such a daddy's girl.

Oh, and Sam.

I smile at the image of her dancing in a club while wearing a witch cape.

Then I pause upon seeing the garage that's filled with a dozen cars you'll never see on the market. Sports, luxury, and...oh, my heart! A special-edition soft-pink Mercedes!

My feet take me to the beauty, and I snap a few pictures and then snap some selfies while hugging the distinguished lady.

"You also feel out of place here, Sis?" I pat the car. "Don't worry, I'll save you."

Maybe I can take this to my parents' house. Surely, Eli won't notice the loss of one car when he has so many of them. Besides, he's usually driven around, so I bet he never comes out here.

"I will drive you, Mrs. King."

I startle at the ghost of Henderson appearing out of nowhere. Considering all the times he materializes out of thin air, you would think I would've gotten used to the man's silent attitude and forgettable presence.

"Do you and Sam have trackers that give away my

location?" I peek at him. "Because this is starting to become creepy."

"Please follow me."

"I will drive myself."

"Mr. King wouldn't approve of that."

"Then you go to your Mr. King and ask him to tell me so himself instead of using middlemen. Not that I'd listen."

I stride to the key cabinet, grab the one for the Mercedes, then slide inside and take a few pictures of the beautiful off-white interior. Once I'm satisfied, I start the car and kick it into gear, but as I approach the garage door, it remains closed.

Gritting my teeth, I roll my window down and stare at Henderson. "Open it."

He's standing to the side in his smart casual suit, no tie, with both his hands clasped in front of him. "If you come out, I will drive you."

"I said I'll do it myself."

"I'm afraid you're not allowed to drive."

"Let me guess. Mr. King's orders?"

He nods once.

Trying and failing to keep my temper in check, I pull out my phone and dial the number titled *Tin Man*.

"Tell Henderson to open the damn garage door," I say as soon as he picks up.

"Hello to you, too, Mrs. King." The lazy amusement in his voice pisses me the hell off.

How dare he be nonchalant when my mind has been in shambles over the past week? Every time I put my head on the pillow, I think of him on the other side of the house, naked or half naked, doing fuck knows what.

Whenever I sleep, I dream of him talking about business on the phone and being an insufferable autocrat.

There's no such thing as *out of sight, out of mind* when it comes to him. If anything, it's the exact opposite. I find myself snooping in his office as if I'll find a secret letter or passage, like in those mystery films.

Alas, all I've found is work and a boring office library. The house library is fun, though. Probably because I filled it with my spicy books.

Inhaling deeply, I say, "Open the door, Eli."

"Let Henderson drive you."

"You mean let Henderson babysit me outside like Sam does inside."

"You figured that out?"

"Didn't take much effort."

"You're not that daft after all. I'm impressed."

"What will impress you more is my heel in your face, twat. I'm your wife, not your pet. Don't you dare try to control me, or you won't like the outcome."

"I'd love to see you try."

"Are you going to open the garage?"

"Not unless you let Henderson drive."

He hangs up without an attempt at a goodbye. I curse him a thousand times with a dozen colorful names.

This bastard will send me to an early grave if I don't control my emotions.

You know what? I'm in the mood to mess with him.

I step out of the car. "Hey, Henderson. Which one is Eli's favorite car?"

"The pink Mercedes."

"Be serious."

"I'm always serious."

I narrow my eyes. He probably sensed my plan and is trying to sabotage it. "Second favorite?"

He motions at a monster of a slick black Bugatti. Now, this one makes more sense.

With a smile, I search for the key in the display, then I slide into the driver's seat.

"Mrs. King, this is pointless, as the door won't open."

"Well, either it opens or..." I rev the engine, slightly shivering at the force of the vibration. Jeez. This thing could be used as a sex toy.

"Miss!"

I hit the accelerator as hard as I can. My whole body flattens against the seat. I really, *really* underestimated the power of this beast, because it sends me straight toward the garage door.

Yes, I mean to smash his car, but I don't want to die in the process. I slam the brakes, but thankfully, the garage door opens.

I still hit the bumper, but it's a win, considering I did damage his car.

The front gate also opens before I smash into it. Good. Henderson and his precious boss should know I mean business.

My breathing is more relaxed as I blast music and fly through the streets. Hello, speeding ticket.

But at least I'm alone for the first time since I woke up in the hospital. I can breathe properly without professional babysitters.

After I stop for a cup of coffee, I shoot some feeler texts

in the group chats I'm in. Instantly, people fawn over me since, apparently, I haven't been around for months.

Hi, stranger.
OMG, she's alive.
We haven't seen you in months, love!

What the hell? There's no way I'd withdraw from my social circle for months. It's that bastard Eli, isn't it? What the hell has he been playing at for these past two years?

I get invited to three gatherings, so I opt to meet my uni crew at a members-only club in Mayfair.

My phone rings, flashing *Tin Man*. I hit Ignore, and since I'm feeling petty, I use his card to buy everyone at the club a round of drinks. Make that three rounds of the finest liquor they have. Also, the gentlemen get expensive cigars because why not?

Caviar? Yes, please.

The waiter quotes me three hundred thousand quid. I tip him thirty thousand.

He tries to remain cool like all the professional peeps in exclusive clubs, but I can see the tears in his eyes. "Are you sure, miss?"

"My husband is very generous." I pat his hand as I place the black card in it.

"Ava!"

I turn around, beaming at the familiar face. Gemma, the one who called my name, runs toward me, her slick strawberry-blond hair shining under the lights. She interlaces her scrawny arm with mine and digs her pointy nails into my flesh. "You look stunning."

"So do you. Love the sparkles, Gem."

"Aw, thanks. I thought they'd be too much."

"Nothing is too much, Sis." I wave at our group of friends, who are sitting at the biggest table, sipping martinis I'm desperate for and wiping traces of coke from their noses.

My favorite mindless existence.

"Hi, guys. Miss me?" I pose as if I'm doing a shoot and accept hugs and kisses.

As I sit down, something feels off. Their smiles, welcomes, and...well, everything seems weird.

Granted, I ghosted them for months, and honestly, they're the blow friends. They're get-drunk-until-passing-out friends. They're not as genuine nor caring as Cecy and my childhood friends. Which is why I prefer this bunch now.

They don't really know me and don't stop me from being as reckless as a rock star in the nineties.

They also don't make me feel guilty for seeking out escapism. Gemma is probably the sanest of the bunch and never goes overboard, probably because her papa is an important member of the government's think tanks and she can't afford any scandals.

In reality, I can't either, but I'm desperate to feel something.

Anything.

As long as I keep believing I'm alive, I'm open to unorthodox options.

"So how's life?" I ask in my cheery tone as I reach for the bottle of alcohol.

Gemma grabs it at the last second and fills everyone's glass but mine.

"Hey, rude." I laugh it off and snatch Zee's glass, and she startles as if I murdered her baby. "Relax, I'll order us another one. The bill's on me."

Zee's dark-skinned fingers wrap around the glass and snatch it with more force than needed. Alcohol spills on my hand and the table.

"Jeez." I laugh, wiping my hand. "Since when did you become stingy?"

"You can't drink with us, Ava," she says with a note of...fear? No. Panic?

"Why the hell not? Of course I can. Anyone got a line?"

They all shake their heads.

"Okay, this is weird. Your noses are testifying against you, by the way."

"It's just..." Gemma starts, clinking her nails together.

We're all private/boarding school nepo babies. And while we have different ethnicities, we share the same posh white-collar, trust fund upbringings.

Shallow on the outside, broken on the inside. Or, in the case of some, absolutely hollow.

I'm some. Some is me.

"It's just that we heard you had an accident recently," Gemma says. Forever the mediator, the people pleaser with a big capital *P*.

"I'm fine." I go for her glass, but she smoothly keeps it out of reach.

"Gemma said you lost your memories," Raj, a politician in the making, points out.

"Just two years. Changes nothing."

"We don't run in the same circles anymore," Ahmed,

a tall man with olive skin and dark facial hair, who's been leaning back and smoking a hookah, says bluntly.

"Med!" Gemma scolds him.

"*What?*" He blows the hookah smoke through his nose. "None of us want to deal with her psycho husband."

"Eli threatened you?" My voice shakes with every word.

"Not exactly," Gemma says.

"He threatened our families, investment funds, and futures if we let you drink or use with us," Raj says.

"And he made sure to hold incriminating evidence against all of us, except for good-girl Gemma over there." Zee snaps her fingers in our friend's direction.

"I'm going to kill him," I mutter under my breath. "Is he the reason we haven't hung out for months?"

"Nope. That was all you," Raj says bitterly. "Apparently, you're too big for us now."

"I...said that?"

"In no uncertain terms."

"Come on. You know I care about you guys." I pause. "Wait. Where's Ollie?"

A daunting silence suffocates the table before Gemma smiles. "He's traveling around South America."

Ahmed mutters something under his breath that I can't hear with the chaos and chatter around us.

I blow out a breath. "Gem, do you remember that night when we were going to Raj's house after the club? Two years ago? Before graduation?"

"Oh, yeah." She smiles. "Zee and Sailor puked all over his Persian carpet, and he was livid."

"Did I make it?"

"No. I believe you went home."

"Did something else happen?"

She frowns. "Something like what?"

An accident.

But I don't say that again, because it seems it was all my imagination. The last thing I remember is a hallucination.

A rush of panic lunges through me. If I lost time then and also during the competition that day, what else did I lose?

According to what Gem confirmed, the club and the after-party happened, but what about the time in between? If no accident took place, then what did?

I steal a drink from a passing waiter's tray, then tell him to give whoever ordered this a bottle of their finest liquor on me.

Before the flute can touch my lips, a rough hand covers mine and subtly removes the glass from my fingers.

I can smell him before I see him, and when I look up, Eli stares down at me with carefully tucked rage. His eyes shine a dark gray under the dim light, and his black suit gives him an intimidating, sinister edge.

"You leave my sight for one minute and you're already wreaking havoc, Mrs. King."

I meet his glare with one of my own. "All thanks to your fortune, Mr. King."

"Ava just wanted a change of scenery," Gemma says in a honeyed tone. She's slipping her hair behind her ear and batting her eyelashes. Anyone from a continent away can see she's flirting.

With her friend's husband.

On paper only, but they don't know that.

Yes, Eli is an infuriating bastard who's not worth my attention, let alone this fire burning in my chest, but that's only because she's disrespecting me.

Gemma, the good girl with better morals than most religious leaders, doesn't find it amoral to flirt with my husband in front of my face.

Unless she knows it's all one big sham? Or he encouraged her? Did they have sex?

The fire burns hotter and wilder than the volcano that wiped out Pompeii.

I smile sweetly at her and then at Eli. "You don't have to speak for me, Gem. My husband and I are *excellent* communicators."

He grins back. "Precisely. Which is why she needs to be excused, as we have an engagement this evening."

"Do we, now? It must've slipped my mind, *darling*."

"Your forgetfulness is one of the many things I adore about you, *beautiful*."

Dick. "You go first, *babe*," I coo with a fake-as-hell tone. "I'll be right with you."

"We go together, *sweetheart*."

"Aw, can't breathe without me, *hon*?"

"I'm positively dying," he says and offers me his hand, and when I keep staring, his slightly rough voice drowns out all other noises. "I inSist."

I take it reluctantly, but when I stand, I swipe Gemma's drink and raise it to my lips.

"You don't want to do that." His concealed anger bursts at the seams.

"Or *what*?" I glare at him over the rim of the glass.

All of a sudden, it feels like we're the only people in the midst of a chaotic, faceless crowd.

"Or you'll pay the price. Put the drink down. Now."

The haughty order does it. He expects me to fall to my knees before His Majesty like Gemma has been itching to do since he walked through the door, but he obviously hasn't met my trouble-wired brain lately.

Keeping eye contact with the devil, I let a victorious smile lift my lips as I down the drink in one go.

Martini.

His eyes burn hotter than the liquor washing down my throat.

"Since you inSist." I let the glass drop to the floor with a shatter.

He doesn't like that. He doesn't like it one bit. For a fraction of a second, I wonder if riling him up is worth the frosty coldness in his eyes. The promise of something sinister and terrifying.

I yelp when the world tilts from beneath my feet.

Eli carries me in his arms, bridal style, and walks out the door, not giving a single fuck about everyone's attention zeroed in on us.

"Put me down," I hiss.

"Shut your goddamn mouth, Ava."

The anger in his tone makes me zip it.

I definitely, absolutely, and without a shadow of a doubt hit my head during the time I've been married to this man.

Or else I wouldn't be so terrifyingly excited at the promise of danger in his eyes.

CHAPTER 8

ELI

"LET ME GO, DAMN IT!"

I can't kill my wife.

I cannot lock her up either.

Those thoughts jam-pack my head like a chant. As much as I pride myself in being a fucking ice cube when faced with pressure, one woman is able to drill a hole in my frozen exterior, hollow out my black soul, and start a fucking riot.

"Eli!" she whispers-yells, then smiles at the cameras flashing in our direction.

Her dainty hands wrap around my neck, and even though she offers the world her blinding smiles, she pulls on the hairs at my nape, digging her nails into the skin with the intention to cause pain.

I grind my teeth, and she grins. "Oh, I'm sorry. Does that hurt, *hon*?"

"No more than how you'll pay for this stunt, *darling*."

Her eyes flare up in a bright, intoxicating, and absolutely ravenous blue. My favorite color until further notice. "Put me down. You're embarrassing me."

"Not more than your attempts to embarrass yourself, Mrs. King."

I contemplate dumping her in the passenger seat like a sack of potatoes but think better of it and deposit her caringly, like the gentleman I'm not.

But then again, the confusion in her eyes at the mixed signals is worth it.

So I slide into the driver's seat and lean over. Ava pushes back against the leather, the squeak filling the car and drowning out the outside world.

"What are you doing?" she whispers, her chest rising and falling in quick succession, her full breasts brushing my shirt with the teasing of a soft-core show.

My dick takes notice of her smaller size and how easy it'd be to conquer her.

Own her.

Once and for all.

But my brain recognizes that would be no different than shoving her back to the clusterfuck of a state she was in prior to the "incident."

If anything, I shouldn't be here, but she had to push my fucking buttons. She can't help it.

"What do you think I'm doing, Mrs. King?"

My face is so close to hers, I feel her shallow breathing against my mouth and watch the slight tremble in her chin and the parting of her pillowy lips.

I even catch the small scar near her hairline and the flecks of forest green in her wide eyes.

She slams both her small hands on my chest, and I suppress a goddamn growl.

Bloody fucking hell.

This woman exists in my vicinity, and I'm tempted to shred every ounce of control that flows in my veins.

"Don't touch me." Her low yet firm voice fills the car.

"Is that a threat?"

"A warning."

"And yet you're the one who has her hands on me. Can't reSist me, huh?"

"You wish, prick." Her words are merely a whisper as she pushes me away.

Or attempts to, anyway.

If I decide this is the place where I'll exist for the rest of my life, this is exactly where I will be, and there's nothing she can do to alter the decision.

That uncharacteristically reckless part of me that needs to be burned at the stake finds the idea tempting.

Dangerously so.

I pull the seat belt over her chest, fighting the urge to ogle how the dress hugs her curves. A fucking dress she paraded in front of a bunch of fuckers who have no business seeing her like this.

I wonder if Henderson is Superman enough to blow up the entire club and everyone in it, then somehow pin it on aliens.

I snap the seat belt into place and retreat into my seat, something sour clinging to the back of my throat.

A sigh of relief leaves Ava, but as I pull away from the club, she crosses her arms—and legs for good measure. "Why did you follow me?"

"You hit my car and nearly crashed it, spent a small fortune on people you don't even know, and were attempting to recreate your miserable alcoholic days. Need I say more?"

"Told you I'm high-maintenance. You said you like it."

"There's a difference between being high-maintenance and a spoiled brat who's an embarrassment."

I can see her eyes flashing in my peripheral vision, like two orbs of burning lava. "No one forced you to marry me. If you dislike my behavior, give me a divorce."

That's the second time she's demanded that in the span of a week, and I swear to fuck, if she says it again, I might lock her the hell up.

"So you can pick up the scraps of your useless, empty life, participate in blow parties, and fill your body with enough alcohol to give you liver failure?"

"What I do with my life is none of your concern."

"It is now. Get used to it."

"I'm warning you, Eli. You can't control me. The more you force me, the harder I'll rebel."

"The harder you rebel, the more insufferable I become."

"You're *always* insufferable."

Can't argue with that.

I steal a glance at her to find her digging holes in my face with eyes that were made to see only exotic things— namely me. "I'll take the dreadful, outrageous behavior up a notch, then. Whether you'll be able to endure it is another story."

"You can't do anything to me."

"Do you dare test that theory?"

I catch a glimpse of her lips pursing before she releases a long breath, clamps that beautiful mouth shut, and stares out the window.

Silence has always been a quality of mine, a strong preference, so to speak. It's a skill when used properly and an advantage to wield in dire times.

Ava's silence, however, has always been an irksome, absolutely maddening experience. It's like reaching an oaSis in the middle of the desert, only to find out it's a mirage.

"What do you want, Eli?" Her soft voice fills the car as she continues staring out the window.

"Some peace and quiet would be fantastic."

"From me. What do you want from me?"

"Behaving properly is a satisfactory start."

She swings her head in my direction and bats her long, curled, and fucking glittery lashes at me. "And how am I supposed to do that, exactly? Turn into your puppet? Worship at your feet?"

"Distancing yourself from the wrong crowd and refraining from throwing tantrums is enough."

"Aw. But those are my favorite pastimes. You know, since, and I quote, 'I'm lazy, shallow, and would rather splurge a fortune than use my airhead brain.'"

I let a smirk tilt my lips. "And who are you quoting exactly?'"

"You, prick. And here I thought I was the one with the memory loss."

"In sickness and in health, Mrs. King."

"I hate you."

"By all means."

"If I weren't struggling and didn't feel guilty about implicating my parents, I'd never stay with you."

"Lucky me."

"If I had a redo, I'd marry any man but you."

"Good thing you'll never get a redo." I pause and count to ten, a method I need to use so I don't accidentally bash her head in. Once I'm done, I look—or probably glare—at her.

She's fully facing me now, and if eyes could kill, I would've been murdered in cold blood, cut to pieces, and thrown into the Thames by now.

I stare back at the road because I can't trust myself not to get us into a freak accident. "What are you struggling with?"

"What?"

"You said if you weren't struggling, you wouldn't stay with me. So what are you struggling with?"

"Hello? Have you forgotten that I lost two years of my life?"

"And?"

"You're my psychiatrist now?"

"Try me."

"So you'll use it against me in the future? I'll have to pass."

"I've never done that."

"I beg to differ."

"Didn't you say you don't want me to control you? If we're going to find a solution around that and reach some middle ground, you'll need to communicate with me."

"Says the one who thinks glaring and staring are the hallmarks of communication."

"They can be. Now stop fighting for the sake of fighting, and tell me what's on your mind."

She stares at her nails, some shimmering pink with a fuck ton of sparkles. "Were you there that night?"

"Which night?"

"The last night I remember. When we met in that VIP room and you were such a delight."

"A delight as always, you mean."

"Naturally." She rolls her eyes in an epic theatrical show. "So you recall that night?"

"Yes, why?"

"I...clearly remember leaving the club, and well, I was driving to Raj's place, but there was a strange car without headlights following me. I called the Met Police, and I swear...I swear I had an accident."

I tap the wheel once. "But?"

"But Cecy, Ari, Mama, and even Gemma said there was no such thing. I went home as usual. There was no accident."

"What's the issue, then?"

"What's the issue? If that's not true, then there's something terribly wrong with me."

"Yes. It's called alcohol."

"Alcohol doesn't make you imagine a whole scenario."

"Drugs do. You took a hit or two of blow that night aside from your medication, didn't you?"

She opens her mouth, then clamps it shut, breathes shakily for a few beats. "Did you follow me out?"

"Why would I have?"

"You ordered me to go home. Besides, you tried everything under the sun to make my life miserable at the time."

"I did, huh?"

"You still do. You really didn't follow me?"

"And if I did?"

"Wh-what...?" she trails off and swallows. "What did you see me do?"

"You stopped by the side of the road, probably too drunk or high to realize where you were. I drove you home."

"You did?"

"It was either that or leave you to be kidnapped, assaulted, and murdered. Not specifically in that order. Before you get any ideas, I did it for Mum."

Her expression lights up like a myriad of fireworks. Fuck me. The innocence painted all over her face stabs me in the chest.

Good thing I have nothing there.

"You made sure I went home?"

I nod.

"Oh, thank God." The words are a low whisper. I don't think they were intended to be said out loud.

We arrive at the house, and I stop the car at the entrance. "Go in. Have a lovely evening."

She stops with her hand on the handle. "Why aren't you coming in?"

"I have other engagements."

"So you get to go out and have fun, but I don't?"

"Our ideas of fun are different. You go out to drink. I go out to earn money to afford your expensive tastes."

"In that case." She smiles sweetly, which I know is as fake as her social circles. "Have a horrible evening."

She nearly rattles the goddamn door off its hinges as she slams it shut and storms to the entrance with a ferocious yet entirely enticing sway of her hips.

I shake my head out of the reverie I'm in when I catch myself watching the door long after she goes inside.

Count to ten.

You can't fuck the attitude out of her. Yet.

Get it together.

I shoot Henderson and Sam a text, reminding them

of their pending execution if they let her out of their sight.

Sam replies with a thumbs-up emoji, and Henderson likes the text.

Bunch of unfeeling wankers.

My favorite type of people.

———

"Nice of you to grace us with your mythical presence."

I smile at my father as I grab a flute of champagne from a passerby. "No need for a standing ovation, Daddy dearest."

He's not amused by that. Not one bit.

But then again, my father is 100 percent bulletproof to my impeccable charms and finds my shenanigans extraordinarily tiring, insufficiently creative, and massively headache-inducing.

"Mind explaining why you left in the middle of a meeting?"

"An emergency." An emergency that caused damage to a one-of-a-kind car, a ridiculous liquor bill, and a migraine I had to down a few ibuprofens to drown. All because of an infuriating woman who has pink, glitter, and my pending demise up her sleeve.

I throw a fleeting glance at the men around us. Gentleman's club. Naturally, I was introduced here when I hit puberty and my father—and grandfather—decided I'd be the perfect successor for their empire.

I am.

Don't believe anything my cousin Landon tells you. He's not my competitor nor my counterpart.

He definitely is not the best King grandchild as he

claims. He'll have to work harder to be me when he grows up.

The men around us mingle in circles, wearing stuffy Ralph Lauren blazers, smoking cigars, and discussing the latest tax laws and ways to keep their money out of the king's treasury.

Old money reeks from the dark wallpaper like a stench I enjoy wallowing in.

My father steps into my space, looking sharp in a tailored dark brown suit Mum got for him. She spoils the man too much, if you ask me, but she loves him.

A useless emotion that's done no one any good—except for producing me, but my existence is a miracle for everyone.

"If you have no intention of taking your role seriously, kindly piss off to your mother's side of the family and leave the grown-ups to do business at King Enterprises." His calmly spoken words are neither a threat nor a jab. They're simply a statement.

One would think that since I'm a clone of him—same jet-black hair, build, frosty-gray eyes, and deep-seated disregard for other people's intelligence, or lack thereof—he'd spoil me more.

But then again, he's probably jealous because I'm better-looking than him. After all, I have some of Mum's genes, and he's beneath that woman's level. Just saying.

"You and I both know I've brought the most profit to the company since I became CFO, and my numbers are only exceeded by you and Uncle Levi. So how about you be proud of me and consider stepping down sometime soon with Uncle Levi so I can do things my way?"

"If your way is alienating possible partners by keeping

their children on a leash and threatening to expose, imprison, or have them killed, then I'll have to pass."

Well, well.

He knows.

After my grandfather stepped down as CEO and became the honorary chairman, my father took his place. My uncle is the COO, and honestly, I expect him to step down sooner than my father since he prefers his extended family's company and was never as ruthless a businessman as Dad and Grandpa.

I need them both gone so I can take over. Something neither of them will give me unless I fight for it.

And fight I will.

I pretend to take a sip of the champagne, measure my words—ironically, a trait he taught me—then smile. "If you have a choice between being loved and hated, it's better to be hated."

"Not if we need to expand the business. And this isn't the Roman Empire."

"I'll handle it."

He raises a sardonic dark brow. "Will you, now?"

"Trust me, Dad." I squeeze his shoulder.

"I don't trust your destructive methods."

"They won't be used unless absolutely necessary."

He shakes his head, a mysterious look taking refuge in his eyes. "If you don't focus and step up your game, Landon will come after your position."

"That prick hasn't taken a business class in his life and is more content sculpting statues and pretending the entire population is peasants who should start a cult to worship him. How could he ever be a threat to me?"

"He's studying for an MBA at Harvard. We both know he'll speed through it like lightning and roll back in here for your throne, even if it'll be purely out of spite and to prove himself to Levi and my father."

I grind my teeth. Just another complication to add to the list of fucked-up nonsense I have to deal with lately.

For the sake of my sanity, I blame a blue-eyed, pink-obsessed little minx who gives me a hard-on with a single glare.

"You're going about this entirely the wrong way," my father tells me matter-of-factly.

Though I respect the hell out of him, I seriously loathe that knowing look he directs at me as if he has me all figured out.

"Humor me," I say with no emotion. "Is this concerning business decisions?"

"It's more related to the reason you're losing concentration."

"No idea what you're insinuating."

"Marriage is not a joke, a bet, nor a way to inflate your mega-sized ego."

"Took that last one from the best." I wink at him.

He doesn't smile. "The moment you think you're in a competition with your wife, you've already lost, Son."

"We're not in a competition." Except for the fiery back-and-forth that somehow ends up happening whenever we're in the same room.

"What did I tell you before?" It's his turn to squeeze my shoulder. "Women need space. Doesn't matter if it's an illusion or if you can confiscate it whenever you wish. It's the gesture that matters."

"Ava would take that space, drown it with alcohol, fill her nose with white powder, then drive her car over a cliff while laughing like a maniac. She needs discipline, *not* space."

"Don't say I didn't warn you." He drops his hand. "Let's get this over with."

"What?" I nudge him. "Can't wait to go home to Mum?"

"Some of us actually miss our wives. I certainly prefer her company over this charade."

"Oh, the drama," I deadpan.

True to his word, Dad finishes the introductions, seals two business deals, and finishes two drinks in the span of an hour and a half.

Then he's out of the picture, leaving me to deal with the fallout.

I'm thankful for any opportunity that keeps me away from the house as long as possible.

It's become increasingly difficult to exist around the bane of my existence and not touch her.

Which could be considered an innovative form of torture, if you ask me.

By the time I reach the house, it's a bit after midnight.

I walk in and pause at the threshold, and that's not only because of Sam's and Henderson's alarmed expressions as they stand by the stairs.

Nor the absence of any other staff.

The sound of the cello coming from upstairs fills the space like a haunting doom.

"Why the fuck didn't you call me?" I snap at Henderson, my ears prickling at the damn sound.

"I did. You weren't picking up," he replies.

"How long?"

"An hour," Sam says.

"Has she been taking her meds regularly? You didn't skip a day?"

She shakes her head. "Every morning with her strawberry and banana smoothie, and she takes her nightly dose with her usual glass of milk."

"Fuck." I climb the stairs two at a time and stop in front of her door. Images from the last time I heard the cello slip into my head, and all of them end with a haunting smile, a scream, and a fuckload of blood.

One, two, three…

It's under control.

Four, five, six…

She doesn't remember.

Seven, eight, nine…

At ten, I open the door and stop at the entrance.

My wife is sitting on the bed, facing the window with her back to the door. She's wearing a baby-pink satin gown, the straps hanging off her pale shoulders, and her hair is tied in a messy bun.

The sad and absolutely lethal sound penetrates my ears like a doomsday song.

She's nearly wrapped all around the cello as she plays on and on, like a robot.

I walk toward her slowly, carefully. "Ava?"

No reply.

Not that I was expecting one.

I stop beside her, and a crushing weight lands on my chest and stabs my nonexistent fucking heart.

For a long horrendous beat, she keeps playing, her eyes lost, her expression muted.

Her face closed off.

She looks up at me with the same empty eyes, not blue. Ice.

It's the stranger again.

The demon that possesses Ava and leaves this hollow being in its wake.

A metamorphoSis of failed existence and shrinking presence.

It hasn't been long. She shouldn't be having an episode so soon.

And no, there's no way in hell I'd take Dr. Blaine's alternative option.

My fingers trace her face, gliding over her cheek and touching her lips. They tremble beneath my touch, and she breathes so heavily, I can taste her exhales on my tongue.

A frown appears between her brows, and then a curious blush follows.

The bow halts on the strings as her eyes widen. "What are you doing here? Get out, pervert!"

Bloody fucking hell.

A rush of life rips through me, and the noose slowly loosens from around my neck.

It's not the stranger. It's my fucking wife.

CHAPTER 9
AVA

AGE SEVENTEEN

TENSION RIPPLES THROUGH MY VEINS, AND MY heart thumps so loudly, I'm surprised no one hears the drums of dread besieging me.

I slip through the invitees, wearing my standard smile and acting on my best behavior. A "hello" here, a "how are you?" there.

Unfortunately, I register nothing of what they say. Not the chatter, the exchange of empty words, nor the fake-polite birthday congratulations.

I shuffle my huge tulle skirt that stops above my knees and check my sparkling glitter top to make sure every tiny crystal jewel is in place.

Everything needs to be perfect tonight.

Everything.

"Happy birthday!" two female voices scream at the same time.

I squeal as I turn around and hug Cecily and Glyn, who are respectively one year older and the same age as me.

"Aw, thanks!" I pull away to be greeted by their companions. Glyn's brothers, Lan and Bran—twins, who are four years our senior. They might share the same looks, but they couldn't be more different. Bran dresses like the posh, elegant boy he is: pressed khaki trousers, a polo shirt, and a sweater draped around his shoulders. His eyes are a warm blue, kind, and welcoming.

Lan, on the other hand, could rival a serial killer—one of those hot ones. He oozes dark princely charm, and he's dressed in jeans and a designer blazer that gives him an edge.

Bran hugs me as if I'm his precious little sister, and I wish I had a brother like him in my life. Cecy and I always say Glyn is so lucky to share DNA with him.

"Congrats," Lan says. "Can't tell if you're supposed to look like a princess or a wannabe-grunge junkie."

"You could've stopped at 'congrats,' Lan." Bran pinches his nose.

"Where's the fun in that, little bro?"

I reSist the urge to spar with him, mainly because I won't allow anything to sour my mood today. I'm so going to end the night with a shattering bang and I have no time to engage with wankers.

"Thanks for the compliment, Lan." I hug him and then step on his toe with my five-inch stilettos. He stifles a groan, and I release him with a grin.

So yes, I might not fight with words, but I'm still as vengeful as a ghost.

"Ava!" My sister comes running, wearing a glittery black top, shorts, and fishnet stockings. Her dark hair is held in a tight ponytail that enhances her cat-eye makeup. "Look who I found!"

She's dragging an uninterested Remi behind her. He's

tall, handsome, and reeks of aristocratic blood—part British, part French, as he likes to remind us. He's around Lan and Bran's age, already at uni, and thinks it's beneath him to hang out with secondary school kids.

The only reason we get together is because our parents belong to a tight-knit community in London. We share the same tax bracket and luxurious holidays in different guarded properties around Europe.

It's virtually impossible for us to avoid one another when our parents have been best friends since school, so we stick together. Ride or die of a sort.

"Let me go, peasant." Remi pushes Ari away and wipes his hand on his shirt as if he touched something foul.

Soon, however, he smiles upon seeing Creighton lounging behind Lan and Bran, then wraps an arm around his shoulder. I honestly didn't notice him until now. He's been silent, seeming bored to death as he munches on some shrimp.

"Creigh!" I squeal, attacking him in a quick hug, and disengage before he hugs me back with his shrimp hand and ruins my dress.

He's about Cecily's age, and more importantly, he's her cousin and Eli's younger brother.

But they don't share any physical traits. Where Eli mostly takes after his father, Creigh looks different. His skin is more tanned, his face shape is longer, and he's handsome in a medieval-prince kind of way.

Those who aren't close to the family aren't aware that Creigh is adopted. Probably because Aunt Elsa and Uncle Aiden don't treat him any differently than Eli. And because Eli is always pestering him for hugs, asking him to swim with him, and vying for his attention at every turn. But Creigh remains silent to a fault and barely speaks, even when poked.

Oh, to be Creigh in Eli's eyes.

But like a female version who's not sibling material.

"Here." Remi opens his arms. "I'll let you hug my lordship since it's your birthday. You can enjoy the honor while it lasts."

I roll my eyes and hug him. "More like *you* are honored."

"Don't be blasphemous. It's not a good start for your birthday."

"Strange birthday, if you ask me." Lan throws a look around, not bothering to hide his disdain for the entirety of the invitees. "What type of seventeen-year-old throws a party that includes parents? Trying to be a debutante in the sixteenth century or something? In that case, your clothes would be frowned upon and cause a scandal."

"I thought it'd be fun to have them here, and then we can leave. And my clothes are perfectly fine."

So maybe my skirt stops way above my knees and is a bit too short. But I have beautiful long legs, and I have to take every opportunity to show my assets. Especially today.

"Have Aunt Elsa and Uncle Aiden come around, Cray Cray?" I ask with a note of undisguised excitement.

"Just ask if Eli showed up and drop the act," Remi says with a dramatic shake of his head.

"I'm not asking about...him."

"But you're content to give him heart eyes whenever he's around?" Lan supplies needlessly.

"I do...not."

Glyn winces. "You actually do."

"Glyn!" I interlink my arm with my best friend's. "Cecy, tell them that's not true."

"Stop hiding facts when you're shit at it. You're totally going to confess to him like a lovesick idiot today," Remi says.

"Which is why you invited the parents. You knew he wouldn't come if his mum didn't drag him along," Lan says.

I stare at Cecy, my eyes nearly bulging out. "You...you told them?"

"I swear I didn't." She juts a finger in Remi's direction. "He eavesdropped when we were in the South of France and blasted it all over their little group chat."

My heart falls.

My skin crawls.

I think I'm going to throw up.

My voice sounds foreign when I speak. "The group chat with *Eli* in it?"

Bran offers me a sympathetic smile and nods once.

"Oh God." I nearly faint against Cecily.

"You went too far, Remi." She points at him again. "You had no business sharing that secret."

"Bitch, puh-lease. At this point, everyone from the royal family to the local delivery office knows about her little crush."

"Including Eli, if that doesn't imply it," Lan says with a wicked smile. "He just chooses to behave as if you're a wallflower whose existence he couldn't care less about."

"Lan!" Bran chastises. "There's no need to be mean."

"He didn't react in any shape or form to Remi's text," Creigh speaks for the first time.

"Or when Lan and Remi egged him on for days," Bran adds. "So maybe it's not as bad as you think."

I know Bran and Creigh are trying to make me feel better, but that's no consolation at all. Maybe the reason he didn't react is because he really doesn't care. Indifference is worse than disinterest.

"Are you both high?" Lan huffs. "That's the worst. It's no different than him pretending she's nothing more than a speck of dust on his shoe, like he's already been doing her entire life. You want my advice? Don't do whatever you're planning, Ava. You're the only one who'll end up with a broken heart."

"Leave her alone." Cecy hugs me and strokes the tremors in my shoulders. "This is not your place, and no one asked for your advice."

"I'm trying to save her the waterfall tears and an impending visit to her psychiatrist. But suit yourself. It's not my fault no one listens to me when I'm always right."

"Yeah, Ava." Remi keeps his attention on me as he swats Ari's hand off his bicep as if it's a mosquito. "He's twenty-three and gets more pussy than Casanova, but unlike that loser, he never actually works for it and doesn't pay any attention to the women attached to it. He never sleeps with the same woman more than twice and doesn't recall their names, even if he's hit upside the head with it. Do you honestly want to be one of them?"

"No. I'll be the exception."

"What exception? He barely knows you exist."

"That's…because I was underage. He didn't see me as a woman before."

"News flash, he still doesn't," Lan says. "You and Ari are the same in his eyes."

She's almost fourteen. I'm way older and definitely past the age of consent in the UK. I've had a crush on Eli since I was twelve and started to develop hormones. I visited Aunt Elsa all the time just to get a glimpse of him, even if he barely acknowledged me. Even if he didn't see me any differently than he did his cousin Glyn.

That was okay. I know the age difference didn't work in my favor, and an eighteen-year-old would've never looked at a twelve-year-old.

So I waited a whole five years to grow older and seem adult. I even stopped sleeping with stuffed animals to completely throw away the child phase.

"That's not true!" I say.

"How does Eli treat you, Ari?" Remi asks her.

She grins like a little psycho because he's finally looking at her for the first time. "He bought me a bucket of candy floss and told me to share it with my sister."

"My point, ladies and gents." Remi makes the motion of a mic drop.

"Adults eat candy floss," Cecily says.

"Stop putting ludicrous ideas in her head and inflating an ego that will burst to smithereens the moment she talks to Eli." Lan appears to be bored. "He's an emotionless prick who collects little girls' broken hearts in a jar and then sacrifices them to his demons. Don't be a heart in a jar, Ava."

———

My mood takes a sharp dive for the worse for the rest of the party. I say hi to Aunt Elsa and Uncle Aiden, then leave before I spot or run into Eli.

I know he's here. I can feel him in the air.

One thing about Eli is that he can make himself invisible if he chooses to. But usually, that doesn't work on me. I've always been aware of him and the unbearable hold he has on me.

I intended to confess to him with a letter that I carefully wrote a month ago and have since learned by heart. I hid it in my Chanel bag for safekeeping, but now that I've heard what the guys said—even Bran and Creigh, who said in no uncertain terms that it's not a good idea to confess—I feel like burning it.

With its dainty paper, metallic writing, and glitter hearts. All pink.

I'm being naive. I'm a little girl who's not allowed to exist in his godly vicinity.

Maybe if I wait a few more years, I'll have a better chance...

My thoughts trail off when I catch a glimpse of him standing by the pool with Mama's asSistant for one of the charities. Kylie is a leggy brunette with tanned olive skin, bright brown eyes, and a very mature figure and face.

Her hand is on his arm as he listens to her with his usual poker face.

Doesn't matter what type of expression he wears. Eli has and always will be a god with sharp features, a jaw that could cut my heart in half, and eyes that enchant anyone who stares at them.

He's wearing dark gray slacks, Italian loafers, and a crisp white shirt with the sleeves rolled to his elbows.

His hair is a buzz cut on the sides, and the middle is thrown back in a beautiful chaos I itch to run my fingers through.

Just once.

But he never lets me get close, let alone allows me the chance to touch him.

While I can't pinpoint when exactly I started to like him this strongly, I know that I always felt a sense of intimidation when we were growing up. Mostly because he played rough and didn't hesitate to pull on my hair or step on my princessy lace dresses or dirty my sparkly shoes.

It wasn't until I hit puberty that the dread turned into a heating of my cheeks whenever he was around.

My real infatuation with Eli started when I saw him play polo when I was around twelve. He looked absolutely majestic on the horse. Regal, handsome, and so attractive.

And then he saved me from a wayward ball, and I kind of fell head over heels. I yearned to get close so he'd grant me access to his true self and what hid behind his winterday eyes.

I wanted to be his exception.

But I was mostly invisible to him.

Even though I've been using my special relationship with Aunt Elsa to visit whenever possible, it's pointless since he moved to a boarding uni with Lan, Bran, and Remi.

He's allowing Kylie to touch him now, her coffin nails tracing a line on his forearm as she bats her lashes and probably speaks in that breathy tone that should be reserved for sexy times.

Maybe that's what they'll do later.

Don't think about it. Don't think about that.

I chase away the image of him embracing, kissing, and fucking her out of my head. Like I've done a thousand times before.

It's not our fault that we're six years apart nor that he hit puberty when I was arguing with Cecy about cartoons. In fact, it would've been entirely weird if he'd taken a liking to me when I was a kid.

It sucks that he thinks I'm still a child, but I don't blame him for sleeping around.

My only consolation is that he's never had a relationship and I haven't seen him with the same woman three times. As Remi mentioned, he doesn't sleep with the same girl more than twice.

What makes you think you wouldn't be another statistic in his endless women's adventures?

I used to think he'd just fall in love with me as easily as I fell in love with him, would see that I'm his best option, and would cherish me forever.

Obviously, that's the hopeless romantic in me.

Realistically, I know Eli is a cruel man who has no qualms about crushing people's pride and aspirations. But that's part of his charm.

Besides, he can be warm with a select few he considers his people—namely his parents, Creigh, and even Lan, Bran, and Glyn.

I just want to be added to the list.

Which is not a lot to ask.

I hide behind a pillar to watch him, creepily becoming aware of where Ari gets her stalkerish habits from.

Eli's still speaking to Kylie, or she's the one who's doing the talking while he listens with little interest, polite nodding, and the absolute opposite of the signs she's giving.

My eyes narrow on her hand on his forearm, the way

she leans closer to whisper something in his ear. She pulls away with sensual laughter. His lips tug in a small smile.

Why is he smiling at her?

A lick of jealousy burns my skin, and my feelings burst at the seams.

You know what?

There's no way in hell I'll be able to wait until I'm a few years older and he finally sees me as a grown-up. I have to take my shot.

As Papa says, you'll always fail if you never try.

Though he'd certainly break Eli's neck if he knew about my fixation on the mythically handsome gray-eyed prince.

Who's six years older than me.

But age is just a number. I've known I liked him since I was young. In the beginning, I thought it was because he was so cool and handsome and the face of every fairy-tale prince I read about.

As I grew older, I began to compare every boy, actor, and musician crush to him.

They all failed miserably to hold a candle to my Eli, by the way.

It's not a hopeless crush like Lan and Remi said, nor an unhealthy obsession as Cecy likes to remind me.

It's fate.

Otherwise, the universe wouldn't have placed him in my path.

Pushing my shoulders back, I walk toward him and Kylie, who, if I didn't know she was good at her job, I'd contemplate having fired from Mama's NGO.

I keep my eyes on him, and the closer I get, the more

dazzling he becomes. I can hardly breathe because of how beautiful he is—tall, dark, masculine—and he smells like mysterious cloudy nights.

He's very well-built: muscular but not bulky. A prince through and through.

"Hi, sorry to interrupt," I announce in my usual cheerful tone and touch Eli's bicep, trying not to feel up the taut muscles. "Aunt Elsa is asking for you."

It's subtle, but he slips from underneath my hold, steps back, and offers Kylie a smile. "It's been lovely talking to you."

"Hopefully we can do it again soon?"

"Hopefully."

She smiles at me, probably not seeing me as a threat, and I return it with a plastic one.

However, I have no capacity to focus on her because Eli's already walking away.

I jog, careful not to trip on my stilettos, and catch up with his long strides.

"She's not by the pool," I offer, knowing she's with Mama and my other friends' mums, probably sharing stories about their husbands.

His gaze strays to me, gray and mysterious, and it takes superhuman effort not to squirm.

Why is he able to effortlessly destabilize me? I seriously hope there'll be a day when I'm not this affected by his attention. It's both terrifyingly exciting and downright draining.

He raises an eyebrow. "Where is she, then?"

"Follow me."

He says nothing, but he walks a few steps behind me as

I lead him to the back garden. Some people are out here for a smoke and chatting. Many of them are my friends from school.

"She's just out there," I say in my happy-go-lucky tone, waving at some of my classmates.

"Happy birthday, Pink Princess!" Vance says and throws me a kiss.

I pretend to catch it and put it in my pocket. "Thanks, V!" I steal a glance at Eli, but he doesn't seem to have even heard the exchange.

My chest is pricked by a thorn of disappointment, but I ignore the sense of rejection. I still haven't hit him with my secret weapon.

The chaos dies down behind us as we keep walking until we reach the small greenhouse Mama helped me decorate with pink flowers and roses.

I've spent late nights dreaming about bringing him to my secret spot and days making Cecily's ears bleed with my plan for our future.

My and Eli's, I mean.

Three children, two dogs, and three cats.

He strides over as if he anticipated the location, stops by a bed of colorful flowers, and stares at me as he slides his hands in his pockets.

A blur of heat sneaks beneath my skin as I catch my reflection in his pitch-black eyes.

When he speaks, his rough voice sets my goose bumps on edge. "What's the purpose behind this?"

"You knew Aunt Elsa wasn't here."

"Partly because I saw her drinking with Aunt Kim on the way here."

I wince but hide it with a smile. "Aren't you going to wish me a happy birthday?"

"Happy birthday. Mum brought you whatever gift she thinks kids your age like."

"I'm not a kid. I'm seventeen."

"The *teen* there proves you wrong."

"Age of consent is sixteen."

"Thanks for the info. If that's why you brought me here..." He starts to sidestep me, but I stand in front of him and open my arms.

"I have something to say."

"Not interested in hearing it." His cold, dispassionate tone feels like a piece of glass wedging itself beneath my skin.

But I came this far. I can't back down now.

"Just give me ten minutes."

"No."

"Five minutes. Just five."

He looks at me for the first time, like *really* looks at me, instead of looking through me and categorizing me as invisible. His stare sears a hole through my heated skin, and my breaths shatter and my lungs burn.

"The answer is no, Ava. Save yourself the hassle and go back to celebrate with kids your own age."

I am *not* a kid.

Stop saying that I'm a kid.

Just stop it.

I lunge at him, ready to prove just how much I'm not a kid. His hard chest glues to mine as I grab his hair, run my fingers through it like I've always dreamed, and seal my lips to his.

My first kiss, which I always fantasized would be with him.

My first everything is his. Only his.

His lips taste of strong mint and a hint of alcohol. He tastes like my forever, the man who'll make me forget I'm mentally damaged.

A fiery explosion starts where we connect and spreads all over my body, dipping to my stomach, shaking my fingers, my lips—my entire being.

I can't breathe, and for a fraction of a second, I don't want to breathe.

At first, his lips don't move, and I keep brushing my mouth against his, licking and stroking. I have no idea what the hell I'm doing, but I let instinct guide me.

Despite the fact I watched videos and practiced on inanimate objects, nothing could've prepared me for the pure intensity that is this moment.

His lips finally move, and I can safely die here and now.

The caress of his lower lip is harsh, unforgiving, and leaves me heaving for air, but then it suddenly changes.

Pain bursts on my skin as he sinks his teeth into my lower lip and bites hard. A metallic taste explodes on my tongue as his hand slides up my nape, then fists my hair in a rough grip, and he tugs me back.

I'm panting as blood coats my tongue, my lip throbs, and my scalp burns. But the pressure only lasts for a second before he releases me and wipes my blood from his lips like a Gothic vampire.

"Why…?" I whisper.

"That's what happens when you touch what you shouldn't, Ava. You get hurt."

I shake my head, my chin trembling. "I just...I just wanted to prove I'm not a kid. I..." I take a step toward him and then another, wearing my heart on my sleeve despite the dull pain. "I like you, Eli. I always have."

"And I don't."

Three measly words nearly smash my entire world to smithereens. I struggle to remain standing, to look at him through my blurry vision as spikes grow in my naive heart. The heart that he blew life into—life that's currently being sucked out.

"Because I'm a kid? I'll be eighteen next year—"

"Because I couldn't care less about you or your glittery, entirely idealistic feelings. Turn around and remove your distasteful presence from my sight, and I'll pretend I didn't hear your embarrassing confessions."

When I do no such thing, too busy searching for the pieces of my splintered pride, he steps around me.

"This is my first and final warning. If you attempt anything this foolish again, I'll ruin you."

Then he's walking away, leaving me with a shattered dream, a broken heart, and a deep, crushing hatred for love.

And *him*.

CHAPTER 10

AVA

PRESENT

THE LONGER ELI STARES AT ME, THE TIGHTER the tension slithers around my neck and squeezes like a venomous snake.

I've been lethally poisoned by him before—it was both painful and irreversible. It took all my resolve to escape his orbit. I spent sleepless nights and precious tears on the bastard, and I had to adopt a complete change of mindset to escape him.

After the day he so cruelly stepped on my naive heart, I thought I wanted to die.

Stupid, really, when I think about it now.

But at that moment, everything morphed into black smoke, and I felt so miserable, I contemplated plotting my demise.

I'm so thankful Creigh found me in the greenhouse before I could entertain those dark thoughts. He let me cry on his shoulder for an hour without saying a word, and I'll never forget the comfort he provided me.

It's an absolute tragedy that I wasn't head over heels for him instead of his tyrant brother, but then again, one can't simply dictate the demands of their heart.

I threw the pink letter I wrote to him in the nearest rubbish can and, for good measure, kissed Vance to wash away Eli's bloody kiss.

Cecily stopped me before I did something stupider, like shagging the guy out of spite. My friend and I snuggled in my bed, and she listened to me blabber and cry and curse Eli while I drank myself to sleep.

Honestly, if it weren't for Creigh and Cecy, my life would've ended that night in the most embarrassing way imaginable.

To think I was naive enough to even consider that option grates on my nerves.

No, I'm not the healthiest person mentally, but I'm surrounded by people who love and appreciate me, and I have to focus on them instead.

So I spent the years that followed getting over him by converting all that admiration and affection to hot-blooded hate. It worked like a charm.

It's *still* working like a charm.

Except that he inserted his distasteful presence in my way after I got into his uni. For the record, I only did that to be with Cecy, Glyn, and the rest of my friends. It absolutely had nothing to do with He-Who-Shall-Not-Be-Named, as I preferred to call him.

Not one single bit.

Yet wherever I went, he was there either physically, like a dark lord lurking in the shadows, or virtually through others. He was like a damn parasite I couldn't get rid of.

That night before my imagined accident was one of many when he just dished out his orders and expected me to follow them like I was still the idiot Ava who ceased breathing whenever he looked in her direction.

He ruined all my relationships. Though it's a stretch to call them that since he scared the guys away before we even started dating properly.

James at school ditched me supposedly because I was high-maintenance. Later, I found out from Lan that Eli had threatened his application to Oxford and his dad's spot in the gentleman's club.

Harry said my tastes were too expensive for his liking, even though I never asked the loser for a penny. Eli apparently had worked his devious ways to nearly drive his family's business into bankruptcy.

My favorite, Marco, was shipped back to Italy on the first plane after he kissed me. He's banned from the UK as we speak.

That's not mentioning the abolition of any possible fling I attempted to start.

Apparently, I offended the mighty Eli King by confessing my naive feelings, so he set out to ruin my life.

The more I act out, the harder he represses me.

The stronger my reaction, the more brutal his consequences.

He told me not to go to clubs. I did. He got me blacklisted from half of them.

He told me to stop vying for attention and being easy. That one got me mad and destructive. I danced with any man I could find that night. The one I rubbed my arse all over? Yeah, no one knows where that guy is.

I just hope he was sent back to the States and not to somewhere more obscure.

My retaliations proved useless and only managed to provoke Eli's ugly side. All his sides are ugly, but there's a deadlier part of him that survives on psychotic viciousness.

That didn't stop me. Not when he glared at me as if I were a cockroach he couldn't wait to squash beneath his designer shoe. Or when my friends told me I was asking for trouble.

Even Cecily said it was like I wasn't doing it for my freedom anymore. I didn't even like any of the guys I flirted with. Didn't want to be in a relationship. And my little girl's dream of a big house, kids, and multiple pets had already been broken. So, according to her, I was only doing it because I did want the attention. Specifically, *his* attention.

I did *not*.

I just liked messing with him like he messed with me. Sometimes, when my head got too depressed, I thought it wasn't worth it and chose to avoid him.

Most of the time, however, I'd swing back with my own poison.

You can bet I secretly sabotaged any relationships or situationships he was in after I got to uni. Not personally. I'm not an amateur, thank you very much. I hired aspiring actresses and invented entire scenarios to make his possible girlfriends think he'd gotten a girl or two pregnant and was siring an army of fatherless children he'd cut from his life.

Annoyingly, some of the girls were so desperate to be with him, they didn't care about that moral dilemma. So I had to pull out the big guns and ask for Lan's help.

I should be ashamed about the leverage that psycho holds over me. If he chooses to, he could have me locked up for all sorts of petty crimes. But I have no regrets. I needed a psycho to battle a psycho.

Lan and I are a team against Eli. He participates because he loves instigating chaos more than breathing, while I'm dedicated to the cause because I can't lose to the prick anymore.

Eli doesn't get to mess with me and obtain an easy life in return. My parents taught me to hit back twice as hard and never back down.

So I'll die on this hill, please and thank you.

Or that's what I thought before.

Now that I have Eli's last name and I'm forced to share space with him, everything is crumbling.

I look up at him as my lungs empty of oxygen and fill with his scent. I'm unwillingly trapped in his frosty eyes, his tragically handsome face, and his sharp features.

And in moments like these, I have to squash any remnants of the old me with bloody hands and chipped nails.

Playing the cello isn't even a viable escape anymore. It took a lot of courage and effort to pick it up again, and surprisingly, it worked well, as if I'd never stopped playing. In no time, I got lost in the music and forgot my surroundings.

Until he barged into my space and touched my face like he owned me.

His fingers have left such a searing burn on my skin, I'm surprised I don't erupt in flames.

"Get out." My voice is barely a whisper.

Partly because I'm taken aback. I thought he didn't want to be in my vicinity, which is why he's been avoiding me like the plague. Partly because I don't understand the cryptic look in his eyes.

Morbid anger mixed with a strange sense of relief.

As fast as they appeared, those emotions retreat behind his fortified walls. My eyes widen as he sits on the edge of the bed. Beside me.

I try to ignore the lick of heat that touches my bare arm. "Didn't you hear what I said?"

"I did."

"Then why are you still here?"

"Never said I'd listen. Besides…" His lips lift in a sardonic smirk. "I heard you were moaning about my absence from your life, so I decided to grace you with my presence."

That snitch Sam.

"I'm honored," I say with enough bite to signal a third world war.

Eli grins. "I know. Try not to fall head over tits."

"I'll manage just fine, considering your presence bores me to tears. Now, I need to practice. Do you mind?"

"Not at all." He leans back on his palms, watching me with that dark gaze.

"Leave already. Shoo."

"Do I unsettle you?"

"You repulse me."

"I don't see how that would interfere with your ability to play."

You know what? Screw him.

I'm not going to allow him to ruin my newfound connection with the cello.

After grabbing the bow, I launch into a slow note

and then decide to play something angry so he'll get the memo.

The cello has always been my perfect outlet. Until I substituted it with unhealthy addictions—alcohol and drugs.

Maybe the fact I've been mostly sober for some time is the reason my cello is speaking to me again.

I play the sixth movement of Bach's Cello Suite no. 3 with every ounce of intensity in me. The entire time, I try my best to ignore Eli, but I'm dangerously aware of him.

His stare—or glare—nearly rips a hole in the back of my head. His warmth engulfs me, steals my breath, and charges the air with a destructive energy.

As I hit the last note, a slow clap comes from my side. My jaw nearly hits the ground as I stare back at my cruel, emotionless husband, who has not got one gentle bone in his ripped body.

I expect to find mockery, disregard, or his usual attempts to put me down, but all I find is a small smile and a bizarre glint in those dead eyes.

For a moment, I think he's an imposter.

Also, why am I dazzled?

The thing in my chest better stop beating so loudly, or I'll carve it out once and for all.

Eli opens his mouth, and I harden my pride for the hit, but then his deep voice fills the space. "Impressive. I have to say, the anger makes it more memorable."

"Is that sarcasm?"

"I didn't peg you as someone who can't handle compliments. You seem to ask for them on any occasion possible."

"I didn't peg you as someone who compliments people."

"Not people. You."

He stands before I can process his words. His fingers trace my cheek, leaving a trail of goose bumps in their wake before he grabs my chin. He looks down at me without his usual disregard and studies my face so intently, so lovingly, that if I were watching the scene from the outside, I'd mistake it for affection between a married couple.

His touch burns, but his intense stare leaves me frozen. It's like he's searching for something. What, I don't know.

Finally, he releases me. "Sleep tight, Mrs. King."

Eli walks out with firm, measured strides. The door clicks shut behind him, leaving me in a perpetual state of confusion and unbearable warmth.

What type of game are we playing now? Because no one informed me of the new rules.

He was supposed to regard me with contempt, so what the hell is up with this sudden change?

———

The following morning, I'm surprised to find Eli in the kitchen.

He's typically out of the house by the time I wake up at ten in the morning and comes back late in the evening, normally after I retreat to my room to fight my usual war with insomnia.

A battle I totally lost last night because I only went to sleep at, like, four in the morning.

I consider going back to my room and disappearing

until he screws off somewhere, but that would mean I'm avoiding him.

I'd rather die before giving him any ideas.

"Morning, Sam." I beam at the old lady as I grab my smoothie and completely ignore his sore presence.

Even though there's a whole dining room next door, he's sitting at the kitchen table, reading from a physical newspaper like an old-fashioned lord and sipping his coffee.

Crisp white shirt, dark blue pressed trousers, and my watch on his wrist.

Yup. Still as perfect as ever.

"Morning to you as well, Mrs. King," he says without looking up from his newspaper. "Nice of you to finally join us. I thought the stock market would close before you graced us with your appearance."

"Good thing I don't handle my own investment portfolio." I slide across from Sam as she also sips her tea and watches the exchange with no emotion. "I'm going to the greenhouse. Call me when the eyesore presence is gone, Sam."

Eli finally stares at me over the top of his newspaper. He pauses when he catches my champagne-pink velvet skirt. It stops a bit below my arse, stretching around my slender curves.

His gaze descends from my white muslin blouse, pausing at my breasts before it takes in my bare legs and cute bunny slippers. For a moment, I can feel his big veiny hands stroking a pattern on my naked flesh, searing and marking it for anyone to see.

Stop thinking about sex and Eli.

He slides his attention back to my face. "Sit down."

"Pass."

"Sit your arse down before I find you a less pleasant chair."

"Still pass. Bon appétit." I blow him a fake kiss and make a beeline for the door.

Before I can move out of his orbit, two strong hands lift me by the waist, and I shriek as Eli shoves me down on a hard surface.

His lap.

What the—

The smoothie sloshes in the cup before it settles like the weight in my stomach.

His taut bicep encloses me. He's all hard—his chest, his thighs, and holy...shit. Is that his erection pressing against my arse?

"What do you think you're doing?" I sound more horrified than a nun.

"Finding you the less pleasant chair I promised."

"Let me go."

"Should've thought about that before you defied me. You need to learn how to pick your battles, Mrs. King." His voice is so close, I can taste his words and feel the rumble of his chest as my legs part, revealing my thighs.

A microskirt was definitely not the best choice.

It rides up my legs, dangerously close to exposing my underwear. I fight the urge to tug it down because that would make me look meek in front of the devil.

"I'll sit on the chair."

"Missed your chance." He flips open his newspaper, and even though it's right in front of me, the words are a blur.

I chance a look at Sam, pathetically asking her to help me, but the damn woman is busy folding napkins at the counter with her back to us.

Refusing to seem affected, I slurp my smoothie and squirm. Jeez. It's physically impossible to ignore his erection.

"Did you gain on any stock investments today?" I ask, examining my nails.

"Certainly."

"That explains the celebration happening beneath me."

He raises a perfect brow, a smile tugging on his lips. "How so?"

"Making yourself rich and the world population poorer is the only thing that turns you on. Is there a paraphilia for money fetishization?"

"I ought to ask you since you're an expert at splurging. Also"—he folds the newspaper and snakes his arm around my stomach, pulling me back against him until his cock settles at the crack of my arse, where the hem of my skirt meets my naked thighs—"money isn't what's sitting on my lap."

Warmth spreads through me like a burst of fireworks as the straw falls from my lips. Swallowing the contents of my mouth is exceptionally hard as I stare into his dazzling eyes.

A spark of lust stares back at me, strangles my throat with invisible fingers, and licks its way beneath my skin.

No.

"I must say, I'm heartbreakingly disappointed." I pat his cheek, thankful that I sound coherent enough. "It's okay. There's no shame in mediocrity."

A soft snort comes from the other side of the room,

and I could swear Sam is laughing, but I can't turn and see, because I'm winning this round.

I'm met with Eli's poker face. "Is that so?"

"Uh-huh. Had better." I fake a yawn.

"Doubtful."

"Aw. Hurt?"

"Apathetic."

"*Doubtful.*" I smirk, but it dies out when he tightens his grip on my waist and slides me up and down his erection.

Oh God.

His cock engorges, thickening and lengthening until it settles right between my thighs.

I reSist the urge to clench my legs or pull the damn skirt down.

"You seem quite impressed now." His dark words land on the shell of my ear in a low whisper.

"Hardly."

"You're drooling, Mrs. King."

"More like fuming."

"Enough to attempt dry humping my cock?" His words lower, eliciting sharp tingles on my nape.

"I'm trying to get comfortable under the miserable circumstances."

He slides his other hand up my back, erupting a volcano beneath the muslin shirt, and I bite my lower lip when his fingers skim my nape.

Eli fists my hair by my ponytail and jerks my head back so that it's leaning against his chest and he's staring down at me. His lips nearly touch mine with every word. "Comfortable enough, Mrs. King?"

I cease breathing, partly because if I open my mouth,

I'll brush my lips against his. The part that's daring me to go for it, see who can win this battle, should be chucked over a cliff.

Movement comes from behind as if it's reaching us from a basement before a familiar voice announces, "Isn't it too early for this show?"

I snap out of my alien state and straighten when Eli reluctantly releases my hair, looking positively annoyed.

My eyes land on Creigh first, but then a smaller girl who's wearing a purple jumpsuit and matching headband and earrings slides from behind him, covering her eyes.

"Anni!"

"Ava!"

I shove Eli away to attack her in a bear hug. Even though I only met Anni at uni, we clicked right away. She's the purple to my pink and the only one of my friends who's obsessed with looking like a princess. All the time.

Once we break apart, I stroke her long brown hair and the locks she curled. "Love the new haircut!"

"Love your skirt!"

We hug again. "Missed you, Anni."

"Missed you, too, future Sis-in-law."

Right.

We're that now.

I reluctantly let her go and wrap my arms around Creigh. "Hi, you."

He barely returns the hug before he's pulled back and Eli envelops him in an embrace. "What a very pleasant surprise, little bro."

Creigh pushes him away. He looks different now. He's happier, I guess, thanks to the fireball of sunshine that is Anni. He's been a changed man since she came into his life.

She altered him for the better, despite all the odds that were stacked against them.

Ari says Anni is her role model because she got the guy who had absolutely no interest in her in the beginning and even considered her annoying. She takes notes from her.

Not from me.

Since I'm obviously a failure.

"You knew we were coming," Creigh tells his brother.

"In the afternoon. Does it look like teatime to you?"

"Every time is teatime."

"You need to work on your disastrous timing."

A rare smirk lifts Creigh's lips. "I have my dear old brother to blame."

Eli looks like he's contemplating punching Creigh, but then he wraps an arm around his shoulders and shakes him roughly. "Did I say how much I *missed* you?"

"Not in the past..." Creigh checks his watch. "Ten hours."

"I'll only say it again next month, due to your poor timing."

"Don't think you'll survive that long." Creigh smiles at me. "Anni wanted to spend time with you. Want to join us?"

"Absolutely!"

"*Not,*" Eli finishes.

I glare at him. "I'm going out with them."

"Not in that skirt."

"It's perfectly acceptable."

"For the bedroom. In case you didn't notice, there are kids in the streets."

"Pretty sure that's not what you're worried about," Creigh mutters under his breath.

Eli pokes him in the side. "You're uncharacteristically chatty today, little bro."

He pokes him back. "Only for you, Brother dearest."

Eli's cold eyes send icy spikes in my direction. "Either you change, or you don't go out."

I want to defy him just for the hell of it, but I could really use some friends and a change of routine. Real friends, not fake-ass ones who are easily threatened by the resident prick.

Not gracing him with a response, I shove past him toward the stairs.

He is so going to regret this.

I have the perfect plan for a long-overdue payback.

CHAPTER 11

AVA

ANNI AND I SPEND THE ENTIRE MORNING shopping on Bond Street, gushing over all the exclusive beauties we get our hands on and boosting each other's confidence through the roof.

Creigh is bored out of his mind the entire time, and he lets us know that with his constant sighs of disapproval and "are you done yet?" His attitude changes only when Anni walks out of the fitting room wearing a purple spaghetti strap dress that hugs her petite curves.

He definitely isn't bored then, and judging by the heated, dark look in his eyes, I'm surprised he doesn't undress her then and there.

Talk about fiery chemistry.

The type I'll never have.

I ignore the images from this morning and even last night because that's the wrong type of person to have that chemistry with. Once upon a time, my fantasy was being whisked away by a dark knight, but now I want to have a normal Prince Charming, thank you very much.

Besides, I'm pretty sure I stopped breathing a few times when Eli touched me, so it's more of a hazard than anything enjoyable. Which is why I'm content being my friends' third wheel today. I'm willing to try anything to escape Eli's orbit and my own head.

After we fill the car with shopping bags, Creigh drags us to a sushi place owned by a famous chef in South Ken.

The restaurant is situated downstairs, and we're given their best table, across from the colorful Japanese mural art. The bright pink of the sakura flowers slithering around a black dragon makes me swoon.

I take a selfie of the three of us, then make Creigh take a dozen pictures of Anni and me as we pose and air-kiss. He gets bored after five minutes and forces us to sit back down and order.

Pretty sure Uncle Aiden owns part of this place and delegates its management to a different company. Creigh only had to give his name to get in, while people normally have to book months in advance to secure a spot.

And while the King name can open any door, Creigh doesn't use it much. His brother, however, throws it around whenever possible to force people to their knees in front of him.

But then again, that devil has an obnoxiously terrific sense of making money. Might have to do with his unfeeling nature.

"So." I take a sip of my yuzu water and smile at Creigh and Anni, who are sitting across from me. "How long are you guys staying in London?"

"Maybe a week." Anni gathers some of her sashimi with her chopsticks and places them on the plate in front of Creigh, who, in turn, shares some of his sushi with her.

"Stop being so sweet. I'm swooning, you guys."

She grins and blushes, then attempts to fill her mouth with food.

Creigh raises a brow. "Get used to it."

"So now you can speak?"

"Only when my Annika is involved."

"Creigh," she squeals, then quickly kisses his mouth.

Apparently, that's not enough for him, because he traps her lower lip between his, and she barely manages to push him away.

"Get a room." I pout. "Some of us live a life that's as dry as the desert, you know."

"With Eli around?" Anni asks after she swallows a bite of food.

"Especially with He-Who-Shall-Not-Be-Named around." I scowl at my rolls.

Anni laughs. "You're back to calling him that? I thought you stopped after..."

She trails off, and I think I see Creigh's arm moving under the table.

"After what?" I ask.

She grins, but it's a bit forced. "After you married him."

"It's worse now." I stuff my mouth with my straw to stop from blurting out everything. Pretty sure no one knows about my arrangement with Eli, and I'm not ready to face their questions, as valid as they may be.

Also, something tells me there's a big chunk missing from the story he fed me. It'll be a cold day in hell before I take his word for anything. Though I haven't given up on finding the truth, I know I have to do this carefully.

My husband is a scheming, manipulative sociopath.

If he feels I'm snooping where I shouldn't, he might shut down any available routes to find out the truth.

So I have to do this carefully.

"But aren't you glad you can stalk"—Anni clears her throat—"I mean *follow* his movements in person instead of creating fake profiles and stuff?"

I nearly choke on my water. "Anni!"

"Creigh knows," she says apologetically.

"Everyone knows," he supplies.

"Including your brother?"

"*Everyone*," he enunciates.

"That prick Landon is horrible at covering tracks. Two out of five—would not use again," I mutter under my breath.

"You're the one who sucks at concealing your plans, if we're being honest," Creigh says. "You're rubbish at hiding your emotions around him."

"He makes me angry."

"Uh-huh."

"He does, and you're channeling his energy right now, which I don't appreciate. Talk some sense into him, Anni."

"He's not wrong."

"I can't believe this." I gasp. "Friendship is dead these days."

"Don't be like that." Anni takes my hands in hers. "We're just worried about you."

Great.

Every single one of my friends thinks I'm a clusterfuck they probably wouldn't trust to watch a goldfish.

"I'm fine." I pat her hand and pull away. "Now tell me

stories about the time I forgot. Did I make his life hell more than he made mine?"

"By miles," Creighton says, his voice uncharacteristically darkening.

Anni pinches his bicep. "He meant you got back at him."

"Good. What type of things did I do?"

"You know. This and that."

"Like?"

She spends longer than usual chewing on her sashimi and even takes one sip of her purple-colored mocktail, then another.

"You're familiar with your shenanigans," Creigh says instead. "You don't need us to remind you of them."

"So I drove away all his girlfriends and started a small fire in his designer-shoe room?"

"Something like that," Anni says. "Though you guys are exclusive, so there were no girlfriends. Only admirers."

A warm, fuzzy feeling mixed with triumph shoots through me. "And I kicked them to the curb?"

She nods.

"I crashed his car the other day and spent a small fortune on strangers."

This time she laughs. "I wouldn't expect anything less from you."

"It's his favorite car, too. Once he gets it repaired, I'm contemplating scratching the hell out of it, and when the paint is done, I'll chuck it over a cliff and film it in slo-mo."

"Badass." She clinks her glass with mine.

"More like foolish," Creigh supplies like the worst sidekick. "If you believe these childish attempts will sway

Eli for the better, then you've learned nothing from the past."

"Let her blow off some steam, Creigh." She strokes his shoulder. "She doesn't remember the past two years."

"That doesn't give you the green light to act like a spoiled brat, Ava."

I swallow, his words hurting me more than they should.

"Creigh!" Anni scolds.

"You're channeling too much of his energy today, Cray Cray. If I'd wanted to be chewed out, I would've stayed with him."

"I'm just saying you're lost, and that's understandable." His voice softens—as much softening as Creigh is capable of. "But you're going about solving this situation the wrong way. Over the past few years, whenever you've caused trouble, he's made it his mission to retaliate tenfold. Don't you think it's time to try a different tactic, especially since you tied the knot?"

I purse my lips before I say I don't know any other way. It doesn't help that the past few interactions have left me with a mountain of confusion and a morbid yearning.

For what, I don't know.

"Knots can be untied," I mutter instead.

Creigh watches me for a beat before he shakes his head. "I highly doubt that."

"You said you wanted to marry him," Anni says.

"People change their minds all the time. If I want to be out of this game, I can simply retreat."

"If you believe this is a mere game to Eli, then you're sorely mistaken," Creigh says between bites.

"He's always playing games, not fairly, might I add. Why can't I do the same?"

"You certainly can, but we both know you're unable to handle the consequences."

I stab my sushi as I glare at him, and the worst part is that I have no comeback because he's right.

My battles with Eli have no goal nor aim. It's as if I'm floating in the air, hoping to find a port somewhere.

"So, Ava. In the group chat, you said you're practicing the cello." Anni changes the subject not so subtly. "Are you thinking about participating in any competitions?"

"Nope. I'm just having fun on my own." If I put pressure on myself again, I'll lose my newfound connection with the cello.

And with reality.

That's probably why I've been religiously taking my meds and didn't order a drink even when I had the chance to.

I'm here, and I want to be here for as long as possible.

Dr. Blaine said my amnesia is not related to my mental condition, but I highly doubt that.

"I'm glad you're enjoying yourself." Anni beams, then goes back to fawning over Creigh and sharing her food.

Third wheeling sucks.

Thankfully, they soon realize I'm still here—or more like Anni does. Creigh seems to shut out the entire world when she's around. We talk about life, her ballet shows, and Creigh's MBA at Princeton, which he's only pursuing so he can be with her in the States.

It's weird hearing how all my friends' lives have moved forward and I'm stuck in two years ago.

No, it's much worse.

I'm stuck several years back, in a muddy swamp of lethal emotions, numb awareness, and sudden breakdowns.

The thought that one of those episodes will sneak up on me and engulf me in a silent white cloud haunts me day and night. In part, that's why I don't want to sleep.

The other part is that I've starved my body of sleep so much, it now refuses to knock itself out.

"Ava?"

I lift my head and pause when I'm met with a familiar face. He's taller now, more muscular, but he's still the same guy. Shiny blond hair, sparkling blue eyes, chiseled nose— the epitome of a European prince.

"V?" I ask.

"I'm honored you remember me," Vance says with a blinding smile.

"Of course I'd remember, you silly oaf, come here." I stand and hug him, and then I point at my company. "This is Creighton and Annika, my friends. Vance is a school darling."

"Your favorite darling, Pink Princess?"

"You know you are."

Creighton stands and shakes his head not so gently. "Nice to meet you, Vance. I'm Ava's brother-in-law."

Prick.

Is he getting paid by Eli today or something?

"I'm aware. No one in this country missed the infamous marriage that could only be rivaled by a royal wedding." Vance's cordial tone doesn't change, letting Creigh's peacock behavior fly past him.

In an ideal world, I'd be married to someone like Vance right now. Beautiful, respectful, and would worship me like a queen.

Instead, I'm stuck with a psycho.

"Wrong." Creigh releases him. "We're much wealthier than the royal family."

"Creigh!" Anni tugs on his sleeve.

"So I've heard." Vance keeps the perfect polite smile. "Might I join you?"

"Certainly." I usher him to the seat beside me before Creigh indulges in his rare dickish behavior.

I'm thankful Vance doesn't seem to let it affect him as he orders some food, and I get more yuzu water.

We catch up on the past few years we haven't been in touch. He went to study at Harvard after school and then went to Australia to help manage a branch of his family's business. He's now back in London at the headquarters of their company that manages this restaurant and a few other places in Chelsea and Belgravia.

The entire time he speaks, Anni and I try to be amicable, but Creigh seems to be possessed by his brother's demonic soul.

It's actually challenging for Vance to say a word without Creigh either mocking him or being passive-aggressive for no apparent reason.

"You've been doing so well." I smile.

"Not as well as you, obviously." He points at my hand. "That ring is a blindness hazard."

"And yet you can still see. Looks like I need to up my game." Eli's deep, dark voice rushes beneath my skin like a shot of adrenaline.

My pulse spikes, and a shiver crawls down my spine as I look to my side.

There he is.

The bastard.

There's masculine beauty, and then there's Eli in a black suit, powder-blue shirt, slicked hair, and a jaw so chiseled, it has the capacity to cut people in half.

I'm people. People is me.

It's tragically unfair that the devil looks mouthwateringly tempting. No wonder people sell their souls.

I'm dangerously close to offering mine up for pennies.

His big palm lands on my nape beneath my hair, and he strokes the skin there like a doting husband before he leans over and brushes his lips over my cheek.

My breath stutters, and a fiery warmth explodes where his mouth touches my skin.

As he rises to his full height, I feel the redness spreading on my face.

"You have company, beautiful."

Even though I recognize he's putting on a public persona, a shiver crawls into my belly whenever he calls me by that nickname.

"Vance Elliot." My friend stands and offers his hand to Eli above my head.

If I thought Creighton was unnecessarily rough, I'm scared my husband will break the poor man's bones with how firmly he squeezes.

"Eli King," he says in a cool tone that doesn't betray the darkness in his eyes. "I see you've been keeping my wife company."

"We met by coincidence."

"I'm sure. She has a lot of coincidences in her life."

"V is an old friend." Whom he's met countless times, including the night he broke my heart. But to expect Eli to remember people is beyond absurd.

"I hope I'm not intruding," Vance says with his usual gentlemanly smile.

"You perfectly are," Eli says without missing a beat.

"In that case, I'll take my leave." Vance buttons his jacket and smiles again at me. "Let's meet up sometime, Ava. Don't be a stranger."

He leaves, and immediately, the waiter clears his plates. Before he disappears, I stand.

Eli tightens his grip on my nape and whispers in my ear: "Sit the fuck down."

"No," I murmur back. Then, armed with the knowledge that we're in public, I elbow him and run after Vance.

I catch up to him by the steps leading upstairs and touch his arm. He turns around with his usual welcoming expression. "Everything okay?"

"I'm sorry about Eli. He can be..."

"Territorial?"

"I was going to say a prick." I smile. "Please don't be offended, V."

"It'd take more than that to offend me. Especially when it comes to you."

"That makes me so happy."

"Which can't be said about your husband, I suppose."

I swallow. "I am happy."

"You don't even smile anymore."

"I'm smiling."

"It's not as cheerful as before."

"There's that thing called growing up. It sucks."

He pats my hand. "I'm always here if you need a shoulder to cry on, Pink Princess."

"Rude. Ladies don't cry."

"My offer still stands." He chances a look behind me. "Should I leave before your husband shoots me with his eyes?"

"You know what?" I wrap my arms around his neck. "Play a game with me?"

"Always."

Maybe this is my chance to watch Eli lose control for once in his life.

Just once.

Because of me.

I angle my head as if I'm about to kiss him. I don't even get on my tiptoes properly before harsh fingers dig into my waist and I'm hauled back with a force that leaves me breathless.

My back slams against Eli's harsh chest, and I swear I can hear the animalistic breaths rumbling behind me, but when he speaks, it's annoyingly, disappointingly calm. "Forgot something, Mr. Elliot?"

"Not really."

"Think again, because next time you forget your manners and put your hands on my wife, I will make sure your soul leaves your miserable body."

"I meant no disrespect."

"On the contrary."

Vance pauses, squinting, but then he nods at me before he silently takes the stairs, leaving me in the company of a dangerously boiling Eli.

I steal a glance at my husband. His nostrils flare, his eyes narrow, and his face closes off with a speed that prickles my skin.

I know I was playing a little game to ruffle his feathers and provoke him, but I'm beginning to regret it big time.

My intuition is proven right when he brushes his lips to my ear and whispers darkly, "You're so fucked, Mrs. King."

CHAPTER 12

AVA

WITH A STROKE OF LUCK—THE LUCK BEING A passing waitress who looks like she'd get on her knees and beg Eli for forgiveness for walking by at that moment—I manage to escape to our table unscathed.

Mostly.

That is, if I don't count my heavy heart and my shaky feet, which barely carry me.

"No world war happened?" Creigh tips his glass to his mouth once I sit down. "I'm surprised."

"My Tchaikovsky." Anni grimaces after using her favorite composer as God's substitute. "I love you, Ava, but you tend to be quite...impulsive."

"*Suicidal* is the actual word you're looking for," Creigh says with his usual poker face.

"Stop adding fuel to the fire." I huff.

"You're doing that on your own just fine."

"Well, your brother needs to learn that he doesn't *own* me."

"Repeat that." Eli's rough voice lowers with a threatening edge as he sits beside me, his presence consuming all available air.

"Repeat what?" I fake a smile, then sip on my water.

"The part where I don't own you."

"You don't." My voice isn't as confident as usual, probably due to the tension that, unfortunately, didn't leave with Vance.

"I see." The simmering anger in those two words seeps beneath my skin like a shot of poison.

"For the record," Creigh starts with a smug tone, "I introduced myself as her brother-in-law and gave that tool a hard time on your behalf."

Eli clinks his glass of water with his brother's. I'd snort under different circumstances, but right now it feels as if I'm being suffocated by Eli's invisible hands.

Instead of ordering food like a normal human being, he is content with messing with my mind as I narrowly avoid choking on every bite of sashimi.

Anni tries to lighten the mood, but she ends up conversing only with Creigh. I couldn't speak even if I wanted to, and my dear husband seems to have chosen the silent treatment.

Fifteen minutes later, I'm fuming.

Both at the unbearable silence and the fact I'm letting it affect me.

Who cares about Eli's opinion of me? He doesn't like me, never did and never will, as he so blatantly put it. Our marriage is merely a business transaction that plays in both our favors.

I cannot and will not read anything into his caveman behavior, for its sole purpose is to drive away any prospect of my happiness.

He's still the same infuriating Tin Man with not an ounce of emotion inside his metal exterior.

I excuse myself to the ladies' room just to escape the ridiculously charged atmosphere. If someone lights a match, the entire place will catch fire.

Once I'm in the loo, surrounded by bamboo-decorated doors, sakura flowers hanging from the ceiling, and gold-colored sinks, I dump my bag on the marble counter and stare at my reflection in the mirror.

For a moment, it feels as if I'm back to two years ago—or more like a week or so, since that's the last thing I remember.

Drunk, high, aimless, and utterly hopeless.

The last two are still there, but in a way, I'm thankful for the disappearance of my less glamorous habits. I don't even crave alcohol much, and even when I do, Eli loves to make a whole theatrical drama out of it.

There's not a drop of alcohol in the house. I know because I snooped around, and guess what? The wine cellar that comes with our type of house? It's full of buckets of candy floss instead of alcohol bottles.

Not that I'm complaining.

I wonder how the hell I got clean.

And I know I got clean, because the last couple of months I can remember—from two years ago—I suffered from a massive headache if I didn't consume alcohol every three hours. I mixed it with my coffee and smoothies and consumed approximately a barrel a night.

The blow was easier since I wasn't an addict and only indulged whenever I was offered. Alcohol was a different story.

To go from consuming a ton to nothing must've been hard. Cecy and Ari said Eli had signed me up for this program, but they were vague.

Problem is, it's impossible to imagine myself willingly getting locked up for anything.

Not with how creeped out I am about mental institutions and being labeled a madwoman.

How did Eli manage to get me from a raging alcoholic to this state? It must've not been too easy—

A static-like flash lights up my head, and I grab the sink for balance as the bathroom spins.

An image appears before my eyes like an old grainy film in the mirror.

I lie in the dimly lit bedroom, the pink silk duvet gleaming under the soft glow of a bedside lamp. My sheer white nightgown clings to my trembling body as I pull on my wrists, which are bound to the bedposts, my legs flailing and tangling in the swirling sheets. The bed is a chaotic sea of twisted fabric and rumpled pillows.

While the silk feels smooth and cool against my heated skin, the tight rope bites into my flesh. My legs kick wildly, my muscles straining and aching in protest.

A faint scent of rose petals and frantic adrenaline lingers in the air, mixing with the musty smell of sweat and fear. Beads of perspiration cover my skin, and my hair sticks to the sides of my neck. The thumps of my heart are so loud, I hear them in my ears. However, my entire attention is on the man hovering over me, his eyes hard.

Frosty.

Stormy.

His legs are on either side of my waist, and then his fingers dig into my cheeks so roughly, I feel my jaw about to snap.

I clamp my trembling, dry lips shut and shake my head.

"Open your fucking mouth, Ava."

I shake my head again and try to wiggle free, but he forces my mouth open and shoves something between my clenched teeth.

I bite.

He plunges deeper until his fingers are nearly down my throat.

I gag, and I swallow in fear that I'll throw up all over myself.

Eli rises to his full height by the side of the bed, blood dripping from his fingers and slithering to the rug.

Drip.

Drip.

Drip.

My glazed eyes follow the crimson droplets as my defeated body slumps. For a second, my skin dissipates into a cloud of nothingness and I'm floating inside myself.

As if I'm an imposter. A parasitic entity that shouldn't exist here.

But I am here, and I'm staring up at my warden. The man who shattered my life to pieces, prevented me from gathering them up, and is continuing the mass slaughter.

"Let me go." My voice is low and weak.

"No," he breathes out with unconcealed darkness.

"Please…"

"No."

"Will you ever get enough?"

His hand wraps around my throat, and he leans over until his voice vibrates against my ear. "Never."

The door swings open, and I'm thrust back to the

present, my eyes huge as they clash with the same frosty coldness I met in the dream. Or perhaps a memory.

It felt too raw and gritty to be a figment of my imagination.

Eli's stare darkens like he wants to throttle me.

And he'd probably succeed.

"What do you want?" The question leaves my lips in a weak whisper.

The images—memories—that invaded my head still rattle me to my bones. I don't see the Eli I've known my entire life.

He's neither the man who broke my heart nor the man I played cat and mouse games with at uni.

Right now, I see a man who tied me up and forced me to swallow whatever poison he jammed down my throat.

The man who looked down at me as if I were a mission he needed to complete.

Maybe that's the reason I lost my memory.

Maybe Eli was already successful in destroying my life and the story ended. Or this is the sequel, where the wife is found dead in her bathtub.

He clicks the door shut behind him, the sound echoing around us like a curse. I hold the edge of the marble in a tight grip, tracking his movements through the mirror.

Eli has always been intimidating, but it's tenfold worse now as he rolls his sleeves to his elbows, exposing muscular forearms.

No idea why he discarded his jacket and is performing this ritual. But for some reason, the image unsettles me.

Warmth floods the base of my stomach, but I turn around, stand tall, and square my shoulders.

"What do *I* want?" He repeats my question, still meticulously rolling a sleeve. Everything about Eli is precise, cold, and decisively calculated.

He's too controlled, too damn emotionless, and yet he exudes a terribly destabilizing sexual energy. Without even trying.

"I should be the one to ask you that, don't you think?" He steps forward.

I instinctively step back, and my arse slams against the marble counter. The cold shock makes goose bumps erupt on my overheated skin despite my clothes serving as a barrier.

Eli stops a few inches away from me, tall, muscular, and imposing. My air vanishes, and I inhale through my tingling nose and trembling lips.

He has no business being so disturbing, but for the first time, he looks as terrifying as the monster from Nan's stories.

"Care to explain the meaning behind your little stunt just now?"

"What stunt?"

"Wrapping your arms around another man's neck in my presence."

"V is my friend." I'm beyond grateful my voice doesn't crack under the pressure.

"Vance. His name is Vance."

"Last I checked, you don't dictate what I call my friends. As I mentioned earlier, you don't own me, Eli."

As soon as the last sentence is out of my mouth, I realize the colossal mistake I've made.

His fingers slide up my throat, leaving a war of tingles on my skin before he wraps them around my neck.

It's not strong enough to choke me, but he exercises the right pressure to forbid me from moving even if I choose to.

My skin throbs beneath the pads of his fingers, and I hold my breath, not daring to breathe openly.

"I've been more than accommodating. I allowed your pointless rebellions and spoiled-princess behavior. I have turned a blind eye to your attempts to provoke me with every inhale you take and piss me off with every exhale. I have looked the other way when you plotted to infuriate me with every word out of your mouth. But you seem to mistake my tolerance for a green light to indulge in your old repulsive, attention-seeking patterns. It is *not*. And I advise you not to mistake my patience for foolishness. The show from earlier is the last time you let another man touch what's fucking mine. Are we clear?"

His grip tightens with each word, still not suffocating, but it's engulfing enough to drive every sentence with a punch.

My thoughts are possibly the toxic ingredients of a suicide attempt, especially considering how pissed off he appears. It doesn't matter how calm and collected he sounds. I feel the lash of his disapproval and his barely concealed rage simmering beneath the surface.

But how dare he threaten me?

After everything he did—and continues to do—to me?

And because I'm in the mood for a war, I go with confrontation.

"I'm not yours. Also..." I get on my tiptoes and stare at his frosty eyes. "V didn't touch me. I was the one who was hot and bothered and couldn't keep my hands off him."

One second passes of us staring into each other's eyes.

Two...

Three...

Four...

On the fifth, Eli grabs my waist roughly and flips me around in a blur of movement. My stomach pushes against the edge of the counter as he shoves me down.

I'm disoriented as my head rests on the marble, his hand wrapped around my nape like a noose, keeping me immobile.

"Eli, what are you—"

My words get caught on a startled sound of fear and anticipation when he uses his other hand to bunch my miniskirt to my waist, exposing my arse and the white lace panties I had to change into this morning after he caused me to dampen the previous ones.

I smell my own arousal and a whiff of Eli's cologne as it mixes with my flowery perfume. My senses overflow with him, and my body feels like a pawn in his hands, completely under his control. My exposed thighs tingle with anticipation, adding to the pool of electrifying energy between us.

His palm strokes my arse cheek gently, almost lovingly, and I suppress whatever alien sound is pushing itself into my throat.

I'm not supposed to be attracted to this bastard, but I can't help it when he touches me. I blame it on the sexual frustration he awakens every time he's near me.

Or the way he provoked that carnal part of me this morning before we were interrupted.

The urge to tell him to stop is on the tip of my tongue, but I can't say the words. Not when his fingers skim my skin in a slow, torturous rhythm. Sharp tingles start in my tummy and spread to my aching pussy.

"You seem to need a reality check on who the fuck you belong to, Mrs. King. This"—he pinches my arse cheek until I whimper, then slaps it, hard—"is mine." Still gripping my arse with one hand, he releases my nape and reaches beneath my blouse, crumpling it and freeing it from the skirt, and then moves to my breast under the bra and squeezes my nipple in a painful erotic pull. "These tits are also mine. But above all." He slides his grip from my arse, cups my pussy through my panties, and strokes his finger on my swollen clit. "This cunt is fucking mine. The next time you offer it to someone else, I want you to remember that."

His fingers trace the curve of my breast, his thumb grazing over my sensitive nipple as he bunches my underwear against my clit, rubbing, sliding the fabric up, down, and up again with practiced precision. A flush erupts on my skin, and my lips part in a gasp before I bite the lower one.

I can't stand the man, but he touches me, and I'm so close to begging.

He releases my nipple sooner than I'd prefer, and then his hand disappears from beneath my shirt. He fists his fingers through my hair and tugs my head up. The scent of my arousal fills the air as his hot breath dances over my skin.

"I want you to remember this view, Mrs. King." He thrusts the middle and ring fingers of his other hand inside my mouth. "Suck. Show me how much you want me."

Or more like my lips remain open for him to use as he sees fit. My mouth waters with anticipation, a soft moan escaping me as he lathers his fingers against my tongue and forces me to lick him. His intense touch ignites sparks of pleasure, and I arch against him, needing something. Anything.

I don't recognize the reflection in the mirror.

Not my crimson-colored face, my saliva coating his fingers, my hooded, lust-filled eyes, nor the way my hands tremble as I grab the edge of the counter for dear life.

A deep part of me recognizes I should stop this. That I'll regret it when it ends.

But right and wrong blur in a magnitude of indifference.

No, not indifference. Reckless impulsiveness.

I always knew my tendency to go with the flow would get me in trouble. I just never thought it'd lead to this.

Eli stands behind me, looming, like a god of war right in the middle of battle. His fingers tangle in my hair, gripping tightly as his dark, commanding eyes bore into mine.

His touch is both sensual and violent, a paradox that leaves me breathless. His intense gaze holds more weight than any words, nearly pushing me to the brink of madness. My sanity hangs by a thread as I'm trapped in the clutches of this enigmatic man.

He swipes his fingers out of my mouth, parts my underwear, and thrusts both of them inside me. I slide forward from the force of it and stare down at the golden sink, catching my erotic face.

I know he said we've had sex before, but I've never felt as full as I am right now. The delicious, slightly painful sensation sparks my insides with novel excitement.

I'm so wet, my thighs are sticky with evidence of my pleasure. The in-and-out of his fingers is loud and erotic, echoing in my ears like a spell.

"Your tight cunt knows who it belongs to." His muscular chest covers my back as he angles my head with his grip on my hair and whispers hotly in my ear: "*Me.*"

A throaty moan leaves me when he rubs a sensitive spot inside me. My vision dances, and I lower my head, unable to face the alien version staring back at me.

Eli tightens his hold and tilts my head back. "You will look at your face when you come on my fucking fingers. The ring you wear isn't a decorative item, Mrs. King. You're my wife. My property. Fucking mine. It's time you properly start acting the part."

"Not yours..." I whimper the words, even as I lose the battle with my flimsy control. I rock back and forth on his fingers, flat-out chasing my pleasure and reveling in every lick of pain and control he holds over me.

"The fuck you just say?" He speaks so close to my mouth, he nearly kisses me with every word.

The impulse to seal my lips to his is as overwhelming as the pressure pooling in my belly. But the reminder of bleeding lips and a broken heart makes me say, "I'm not yours, *husband.*"

And then I fall.

My body trembles with the force of the orgasm that rakes through me. It starts at my pussy, rips through my stomach, and expands to my heavy-lidded eyes.

My legs shake so badly that I'd drop to the ground if it weren't for Eli's fierce grip on me. He's still thrusting his fingers in me as I ride my orgasm. His touch is firm, and his face no different from that of a tyrant warlord about to order the massacre of a few villages.

My insides liquefy, and I find myself lured into that gaze and the dangerous promise in it.

This man can hurt me, in more ways than one.

Yet as he strokes my clit with his thumb and adds a third finger, I'm there, ready for the second free fall and all.

"Not mine you say?" His eerily calm tone should alarm me, but I'm too horny to care, too close to another explosive release.

I'd do anything for a bit more pressure.

"Mmm," I whine.

While I hate the man with every fiber of my being, he's hotter than sin and infuriatingly knows the right buttons to push.

Which he does, again and again, hitting that spot inside me while stroking my clit.

White stars form behind my lids, and the rush of adrenaline nearly engulfs me. "Yes, yes, yes...right there..."

I'm downright begging now, but I couldn't care less.

If I'm suffering the misfortune of being married to Eli, the least he can do is satisfy my basic needs.

"Here?" he asks with an amused tone, but he's not fooling anyone. I can feel his engorged cock against my arse, and I wiggle some more, rubbing against him and sliding my covered breasts over the edge of the sink for friction.

"Yes, oh God. More." I moan as a wave stronger than the first grabs hold of me. My core tingles in preparation for the orgasm.

Before it can hit, however, Eli slips his fingers out and rips my underwear off my starving pussy.

"Wh-what?" I try to turn in his direction, but his grip on my hair keeps me in place.

He shoves the scraps of my knickers in my mouth with his fingers, stuffing me full. "Lick them clean, Mrs. King. I want you to swallow every last drop."

My tongue laps around his fingers, which is a bit awkward with my underwear in the mix. I don't know how nor why I do it. Maybe it's hope that after I do, he'll finish what he started.

My cheeks warm the more I taste myself. On Eli's fingers.

God. This is fucked up.

But I do it more enthusiastically, lapping my tongue around his fingers and deep throating them as I stare at his eyes. Then I slow my pace and bat my lashes at him.

A muscle clenches in his jaw as he slips out his fingers. "Don't flirt."

I spit out the underwear and slide my arse up and down his erection. "Finish what you started."

"You lost that opportunity when you challenged me. Only good girls get rewarded." He shoves the underwear in my mouth again, releases me, and retrieves his phone.

I'm disoriented as he snaps a picture of me propped against a bathroom sink, my skirt bunched to my waist, my arse in the air, and my underwear filling my mouth.

"Fascinating," he whispers before he turns around and disappears.

Leaving me unsatisfied, infuriated, and feeling dreadful about how this little episode changes everything.

CHAPTER 13
ELI

Landon: I've learned something distinctively interesting.

Remington: And? You're going to have us beg before you spell it out?

Landon: That's a good start. On your knees, peasant.

Remington: This bitch seems to forget that my lordship outranks him in every sense of that word. You're the one who needs to bow down before my noble presence.

Landon: I'd rather be stranded in the Sahara and survive on eating sand.

Creighton: @Landon King, is this by any chance concerning my "beloved" brother?

Eli: Why is the beloved in quotes?

Remington: *GIF of a kid rolling their eyes* Because he doesn't mean it. OBVIOUSLY. My spawn Creigh loves me more than you. Trust.

Eli: Keep floundering in your delusions while the rest of us are busy doing grown-up things.

Remington: Such as?

Eli: Building actual empires.

Remington: And making the world a worse place.

Eli: Not worse than the possible spawns you've littered all over Europe.

Remington: Hey. I believe in protection, thank you very much. I have a line of earls to protect. You, however, are only interested in foolish power.

Brandon: Aren't you being too hard on yourself, @E.King? I know how passionate you are about King Enterprises and Steel Corporation, but I don't believe it's worth the stress.

Landon: @Bran.K That's where you and our dear cousin differ, baby bro. Eli is content with swallowing half the world for breakfast and plotting to devour the other half for supper. It's not greed. It's his intolerably incessant need to fill that black hole inside him with some semblance of power. Kind of camouflages the perished soul he left in his mother's womb.

Eli: My. Did the psycho become a doctor? Stunning progress, Lan. *GIF of slow clapping*

Remington: He's not entirely wrong, you know. Stop pressuring the rest of us to be your version of control freaks.

Eli: Because laziness is more becoming of you?

Brandon: Remi's mum and both his/your grandparents are still part of the corporation. Perhaps you should take it easy on him.

Remington: My man. Thank you! Finally, someone said it.

Eli: Our grandparents are only there in name at this point. All the weight falls on your mum and me.

Either you help out properly or remove your unpleasant presence from my vicinity.

Landon: Someone didn't get his cock sucked this morning.

Creighton: Worse. His wife nearly kissed her secondary school sweetheart in front of him two days ago. He's been an utter joy since.

Eli: He is not her secondary school sweetheart.

Creighton: Denial doesn't negate facts. Bro was stressed.

E.King removed C.King from the chat.
Lord.Remi added C.King to the chat.

Remington: My, my. No wonder he has his head so far up his arse, he can hardly breathe. So Ava's playing with fire again?

Creighton: Safe to say, she's dousing herself with petrol at this point.

Eli: Since when are you this talkative, @C.King? Shouldn't you be sodding off with your girl and saving us from your unwanted presence?

Remington: Details, @C.King?

Brandon: Did it turn ugly?

Creighton: Pretty sure shagging happened in the bathroom while they stranded us in the restaurant.

Eli: No such thing.

Creighton: Please. You stayed in there for twenty minutes and she came back with so many murder plots in her eyes, you could've seen them from across the pond.

Landon: *GIF of evil laughter* My favorite firecracker Barbie.

Eli: My wife will be your least favorite anything once I'm finished with you.

Landon: Shaking in my boots as we speak. Brb, let me call my mummy for emotional support. Also, word on the street is that you dragged her kicking and screaming to the altar, so you can drop the act and stop calling her your wife whenever you get the chance.

Brandon: Stop provoking him, Lan.

Landon: Only after I die. Though I've thought of ways to haunt all of you from the grave *slow smirk emoji*

Remington: I don't understand why someone as gracious as Mia would ever be with a heathen like you.

Landon: Stay jealous of my perfect relationship.

Creighton: What's the interesting tidbit you learned, @Lan.King?

Landon: Oh, nothing much. Only that something drastic could've happened to Barbie prior to her latest unfortunate "accident."

Remington: The plot thickens.

Creighton: You mean it wasn't an accident?

Landon: We can only call it an accident if Eli wasn't involved. Seeing that he was clearly present at the scene of the crime, I have my doubts.

Brandon: He's just messing with you, right, @E.King?

Creighton: Eli?

E.King has left the chat.

I have come to the grim conclusion that my wife has the destructive energy of a world war and the emotional IQ of a plastic flower.

And while I pride myself on being a man in control concerning all the happenings in my life—emotions and future plans included—I have inevitably hit a jarring obstacle in the form of a pink chiffon skirt and a cream crop top.

"What are you wearing?" I grit my teeth as I stroll into my kitchen and glare at the material hugging her perky round nipples and stopping right above her exposed belly button.

"Burberry." Ava doesn't even lift her head, choosing to pretend to be fascinated with Sam's crochet work.

My ex-nanny gathers her unrecognizable work and trudges out of the kitchen to avoid our usual bickering.

"Go change. You're not walking around with unfinished clothes among the staff."

"Hmm. Let me think about it." She taps a perfectly manicured finger to her lips. "I'll go with no."

I grab the edge of her chair to keep from throttling the fuck out of her. My hand flexes, and I count to ten.

A tactic that failed miserably a few days ago after she almost kissed that wannabe boy. If she'd actually placed her lips anywhere near his vicinity, he would've been decapitated on the spot, Middle Ages style.

Though the question of his disappearance is a matter of when, not if. I have already extended my shadowy hands to his parents' corporation and will axe him the moment he moves.

Ava stares back at me with a honeyed smile that's faker than her rubbish acting. My gaze flicks to her lips—full, glossy, and tempting. The image of them wrapping around my fingers, sucking my soul through them, flashes in my head.

They'll look divine choking on my cock.

No.

No more fantasizing about my wife's lips and cunt. However, that's proving to be challenging after I had a messy, enticing taste.

The only thing I've thought about since is how to shove her back against the nearest surface and reacquaint her body with mine. How to fuck every other man out of her.

And once those damning images formed in my head, it's been impossible to purge them.

Despite fully recognizing that this could be a dangerous trigger.

"What did I say about picking your battles?" I speak so calmly, even I start to believe I'm completely unperturbed by this chaotic human being.

"One day. Not today. Now, if you'll excuse me, I'll ask Sam to join me in the greenhouse. This place is rather suffocating due to a certain person."

"You're not going anywhere until you change, Ava."

"Want to bet?"

"Want to test me?" I slide my hand from the chair to her bare shoulder.

Her dewy skin is electric to the touch, or maybe it's because I want her, so much that it's starting to mess with my equilibrium. Not to mention I've been suffering all manner of blue balls since the day she rode and came apart on my fingers.

I close my hand around her nape underneath her hair and look down at her as she sucks in a stuttering breath.

My head lowers, and I nibble on her earlobe until she shudders. Once she angles her head to the side, baring her delicate throat and pulse point, it's physical torture not to feast on it.

And her.

Because there's no way in fuck I'll be able to keep myself in check once I start. It's challenging enough to watch her walking around in skimpy clothes and tiny pajamas that I swear were made to taunt me.

"Do I need to remind you of what will happen when you misbehave, Mrs. King?"

She clutches her smoothie cup tighter, digging her nails into it so harshly, I'm surprised it doesn't break.

"Or are you doing this on purpose so I'll use you again?"

This time, she elbows me in the side. Hard. "Don't flatter yourself. I have no interest in a redo of your subpar performance."

"Your cunt, which shattered all over my fingers, would argue otherwise. In fact, if I reach beneath your skirt, I'll find you dripping for me, wife."

"You wish." Her words are low, barely audible.

"Do you dare to bet?"

"Unless I can bet to keep you a few continents away from me, I'm not interested."

The clearing of a throat prevents me from putting

my wife in her place—or attempting to, however temporarily.

Sam has returned, and she juts her head in the direction of Henderson, who's at the entrance of the dining room.

I rise to my full height and button my jacket, but I don't release Ava. She doesn't seem to loathe the contact either, or perhaps she forgot about my hand surrounding her nape.

"We have the post, sir."

"And that's important enough to interrupt me?" I don't hide the venom in my tone.

Ava elbows me again. "Stop being a dick." And then she directs her sunshiny smile to my asSistant. "Thank you, Leo."

"My pleasure, Mrs. King."

"His name is Henderson," I say.

"That's his last name, and this isn't the twentieth century," she shoots back. "Besides, Leo is a cute nickname."

He smiles a little, but it promptly disappears when I level him with a glare.

Perhaps it's about time to act on my murder threats and bury the sorry sod where the sun doesn't shine.

As if sensing my thoughts, Henderson places the letters on the table before me and retreats, probably to polish his casket.

Ava skims through them, placing mine and the house bills to the side, then flies through her subscription fashion and music magazines and mail from the dozens of orchestras of which she's a top patron.

The woman donates to orchestras as if they're charities. Apparently, some of them are struggling, and they wouldn't be able to continue doing cheap shows for the general public without hefty donations from families like ours.

She pauses on a familiar envelope, then opens it carefully. Her eyes skim over the lines, and with every word she reads, they sparkle, turning glittery blue by the time she finishes.

Her lips fall open with a gasp. "Oh, my word."

"Good news?" Sam asks when I remain quiet.

Partly because I read the letter over her shoulder.

"The best. I've been asked to play at an event organized by one of the arts foundation NGOs."

"And you'll do it? I thought charities were beneath your musical talent," I say.

She whips her head in my direction as if she just realized I've been there all along. The blasphemy of forgetting my existence. No one but this headache of a woman is able to do that.

Not only that, but she has the audacity to glare. "I never said that."

"I thought it was a given with how snobbish you were about competitions."

"You thought wrong. I'm lucky to be part of a cause. Besides, I only did the competitions to prove something."

"Which is?"

"My ability to perform... Forget it. I don't know why I'm talking to you about this." She shrugs me away as she stands up, but her mood doesn't seem dampened in the least. "I need to go practice and shop for a new dress! This is so exciting."

She walks away with that gentle sway in her hips, then turns around. "Can I use the pink Mercedes? If you say no, I'll use it anyway."

"Since when do you ask for permission to use our cars?"

"*Your* cars."

"*Our.*"

"There is no 'our.'"

"I beg to differ."

She narrows her eyes, but, apparently, she has no intention of ruining her mood, because she shakes her head. "Thanks."

"My, and here I thought you were incapable of gratefulness."

"Don't make me regret it."

I press my lips together to stop myself from laughing, but a smile must escape, because Ava stares at me as if I'm a curious world wonder.

One that solely exists wherever she is.

It's a ridiculously meticulous obsession at this point, and the worst part is that I have no intention of altering anything.

"The driver will wait in the car," I say. "I also called you some company for shopping but can also join you while you practice or whatever you fancy."

She blinks twice, and I see the innocence that provoked this entirely foreign part of me.

The part that's made it my mission to steal her, cage her, and allow her no way out.

"Who's the company? Not Mama and Papa, I hope?"

"Considering your father still goes into phases where he loves to chase me away with a knife, I'll say no to that."

She tips her head back and laughs, the joyful sound echoing around us like her favorite Bach music.

I'm enchanted, enthralled, absolutely rooted in place with nothing better to do than watch her smile at me genuinely for the first time in...six years.

Up until now, I've been the subject of either her glares or fake smiles. Never the reason behind her laughs and cheerful personality.

"Is your father's illogical hatred toward me so funny?"

"Well, he doesn't trust your character, which I find nothing wrong with. I'm glad that at least one thing hasn't changed."

"Many things haven't."

"I suppose." She shrugs. "So who's the mysterious company you called for me?"

Henderson reappears, accompanied by a tall ginger girl, all legs and no curves, unlike my beautiful wife.

But then again, no other woman is comparable.

"I hope I'm not interrupting." Bonneville pats down her knee-length dress that's fit for Wimbledon or horse racing events.

Ava's smile falters only for a bit before she hugs her. "Gem, what a lovely surprise. What are you doing here?"

"I was invited by Eli for some brunch."

"You were, huh?" Ava stares between us with a mysterious glance I can't decipher, but she's been a fucking vault these past two years, so I'm lucky she's even talking again.

"I gathered Ms. Bonneville would keep you company," I say.

"Please, call me 'Gem' or 'Gemma,'" she says with a toothy grin, and did Ava just roll her eyes?

"I'll leave you to it." I grab Ava by the waist and drop a kiss to her cheek, dangerously close to her parted lips. "Behave."

"Only if you do," she throws back with a venomous tone before she turns and walks to the stairs—or more like stomps.

A disgusting skeletal hand lands on my arm as Bonneville offers me a polite smile. "Don't worry. I'll keep an eye on her."

"I don't remember giving you such a task, Ms. Bonneville. Just be a good sport and entertain my wife to the best of your ability."

"Yes...I mean, I understand."

She's a sheep, but she's the only useful person in Ava's unorthodox former friend group, and she doesn't hesitate to offer any form of information I ask for. She's the reason I was able to effectively ruin all of my wife's ex-love interests.

I'm well aware Bonneville is doing this because she's hoping I'll fuck her, but unfortunately for her and all other women, I'm only interested in my wife's cunt. Doesn't mean I won't use her, though.

"Gem. You coming?" Ava stops in the middle of the stairs, and even though she called to her friend, her eyes throw daggers at me.

I suppose that smiling episode was a one-off.

Bonneville flashes me a grin before she reluctantly releases me and heads to my wife. She casts one last look at me, and Ava's glare turns so wild, I'm surprised no lasers come out.

"What's wrong with her now?" I ask no one in particular after they disappear up the stairs.

"I must say, for someone so smart, you can be quite obtuse," Sam says.

She was supposed to have stayed inside crocheting away, but she's now standing by the door and shaking her head.

"Indeed," Henderson agrees with a grim look.

I stare between them. "What's this about?"

Sam sighs, turns around, and leaves.

"With all due respect, one simply does not invite a snake to their house and expect it not to bite them, sir."

"Is this about Bonneville? She's as harmless as a fly."

His poker face remains in place, but I can sense the judgment licking my skin like acid. "At any rate, we're ready to go."

We walk together to the entrance, and I roll my wedding ring. "Have you found out what Landon knows?"

"Not quite, but he does know something."

"Which is?"

"I'm not positive yet, but I suspect he's been kept in the loop about some happenings in this house."

"Your and Sam's necks are under the guillotine, so you wouldn't be suicidal. Previous staff?"

"I'm afraid it's more complicated than that."

"Ariella?"

"I'd rather not throw around accusations without proof."

I unbutton my jacket. "Leave Landon to me. I'll take care of his silence."

No one will know the extent I had to go to for Ava to be this way right now. Even if it's not permanent and is bound to be shredded to pieces, I'm happy to prolong this phase as long as possible before she forgets me.

Again.

Maybe this time, it'll be for good.

CHAPTER 14

AVA

"I SHOULD PROBABLY BOW OUT NOW BEFORE it's too late."

I pace the length of the boxy changing room for the hundredth time, the round hem of my French tulle dress dragging on the floor behind me.

Ari fingers old framed photos of the artists who've passed through this venue throughout two centuries. Artists whose vicinity I have no business existing in when I'm such a failure. "You've done this before. You can do it again, Ava."

"If by 'done this before' you mean I made an epic fool out of myself, then sure, I've totally done that before."

She trudges toward me in her killer black leather skirt and white top, then grabs my shoulders. "You're different from two years ago. You might feel like only a few weeks have passed since that last competition, but it's been years. People forget."

"Well, I don't."

"This is your chance to. Maybe try to remember those competitions you won as a teen?"

"Those seem like a lifetime ago."

"Maybe. But you looked like a goddess, Sis. You still

do whenever you touch the cello. I've never seen you shine so brightly as when you play."

A shaky breath escapes me as I nod. "Okay. I'll try."

"Yes!"

"Mama and Papa don't know about this, right?"

"Nope. You said you didn't want the pressure."

"Yeah. At least if I screw up, you'll be the only one to witness it."

"You won't screw up anything. Trust me."

"Thanks, little Ari. I'm glad you're here."

"Wouldn't miss it for the world. And FYI, I'm not little anymore. I will soon get married to Remi and pop out beautiful children before you and Eli get around to it."

"Be my guest." I plaster on an automatic smile that hurts.

The last thing I need in my current jumbled state is to be reminded of my dear husband, who's not only been away from the house for an entire week, but also shoved Gemma my way as if we're tight buddies.

I told her the date of the event was tomorrow in an attempt to create some distance. She's not a welcome guest today. Besides, I haven't missed the heart eyes she automatically shows whenever she brings up Eli, and Sam also caught her snooping near his bedroom.

The nerve.

Even *I* have never snooped in his bedroom, but then again, there's no love lost between me and the husband I'm stuck with.

Gemma, however, would be delighted to warm his bed and act as his mistress if given the chance.

Maybe I should present her with the option so I can

regain my freedom and stop obsessively thinking about the man's presence—or the lack thereof.

The only hint of him I've seen has been in the form of either Leo or Sam. The latter accompanied me today and is sitting at one of the tables up front so she can report my failure in HD detail to her boss.

Eli's actions have no business affecting my mood anymore, but the fact he hasn't checked on me, offered me his company, nor asked how practice has been going is fouling my mood more than it's supposed to.

And no, his limitless black card and Sam's emotionless face are no substitute for his interest.

Ari releases me and stares at me expectantly. "Is he really not coming to watch you?"

"Why would he? He never has before, and there's no reason he'd start now."

"But you want him to?"

"Absolutely not. He-Who-Shall-Not-Be-Named's presence would only sour the atmosphere."

She flops onto the worn-out faux-leather sofa. "You're still a horrible liar."

"Am not."

"Are too. You've been checking your phone and staring at the door since we got here."

"It's about Sam. She's not a joy to be around, but she's a marvelous listener and basically a close friend at this point. I wouldn't survive in that house without her."

"Uh-huh. More like Sam's boss."

I throw a pillow at her, but she catches it and giggles away like a know-it-all. While I love my sister, I'd like to strangle her right now.

At the same time, I'm grateful to have her by my side when everything seems to be falling apart.

Cello is the only thing that makes sense, and while I did consider abandoning it in the past, I'd never have been able to do it. That would be no different than discarding a part of my soul—the sane part that's not brimming with bizarre hallucinations and decisively sickening coping mechanisms.

"You know..." Ari stands, ready to take her place in the venue, possibly beside Sam so she can annoy the hell out of her.

For the first time, I feel sorry for the woman.

"Hmm?" I check my nails, even though I made sure they're not too long to get stuck in anything.

"I could call Eli and chew him out for being a horrible husband and not supporting his wife in her special endeavors."

I look up. "And make me look desperate?"

"So you *are* desperate." Her grin could match the Joker's.

I stand, grab her by the shoulders, and push her out. "Go away."

She slams her feet together like a soldier and salutes. "Will fight in your corner, Sis."

I can't reSist laughing as I close the door and sag against it.

A knock startles me, and I pull the knob, ready to give Ari a piece of my mind. Instead, I find a small woman smiling at me. "It's time, miss."

I return the smile even as a dozen knots form in my belly. "I'll be right there."

With a heavy heart, I walk to the vanity and check my

makeup, then touch up my hair. A vibration makes my phone dance on the table before it lights up.

I pause, my heart dropping to my stomach when I find a text from none other than my husband.

Tin Man: Breathe. You've been playing the cello since you were five years old. With nearly two decades of experience, you ought to conquer the instrument, not the other way around.

Ava: Someone hold me. Is the mighty Mr. King offering words of encouragement right now?

Tin Man: I'm offering facts. And I'm the only one who can hold you. There will be no someone who'll offer the service.

Ava: You're awful.

Tin Man: So you've been telling me. Back to the topic, imagine no one is there. It's just you and your cello.

Ava: I'll try.

Tin Man: Show them what you're made of, Mrs. King.

Ava: *GIF of three men saluting while drowning in a boat*

I slide my phone onto the vanity and leave with a smile on my face. For some reason, the knots ease little by little, and even though they don't disappear, I can breathe properly.

Thankfully, this is neither a competition nor a recital. With a sharp inhale, I walk to the podium, which is decorated with white and red roses and approach the white leather chair against which my cello lies.

The hustle and bustle of the attendees remains alive. They don't all go silent because I'm the main attraction—and possible ridicule—of the night. Everyone is mingling about the tall tables, sipping drinks and chatting.

Still, the sheer number of people present sends a tinge of nervousness through me.

I bow anyway and smile at Ari and Sam, who are standing by one of the front tables. My sister offers me two thumbs-up, and Sam smiles at me, which I know took effort because it looks as creepy as a serial killer's.

Every swallow is exceptionally dry as I slide onto the chair and grab the neck of the cello with clammy fingers. I fine-tune the pegs, although I've done it a thousand times already.

My hand stiffens and I pause, knowing full well that if I start playing, I'll break a string. The need to run away beats beneath my skin like a one-eyed monster.

Maybe I should spare myself the humiliation again—

I lift my head to check the crowd and pause, hugging the cello tighter when I see the two men standing beside Sam and Ari. Leo and, surprisingly, Eli.

He looks sharp in his black suit and studded cuffs, with that unreadable handsome face that should be studied by neuroscientists—and artists.

Despite his usual indifferent expression, his presence charges me with hollowing relief.

He raises a glass of champagne in my direction, and I offer a tight smile. Not because I don't want to smile, but because my muscles aren't entirely cooperating.

I close my eyes for a brief second and breathe deeply. Then, when I open them, I hit the first energetic note of

Kodály's Sonata for Solo Cello. I could've gone with something more modern that doesn't require much focus on technique, but I've been a classical cello junkie for relatively all my life.

If I don't challenge myself, who will?

I focus on my breathing as the passion of the allegro fills the space. The second note follows. Then the third…

Soon, I let the cello play itself, the melancholic music spreading through me like a healing balm.

For a moment, all the noise and people disappear. It's just me and my cello. Like it's always been my entire life.

But in the middle of the darkness, a maddening enigma of a man with frosty gray eyes stands—tall, unmoving, intimidating.

And, for some reason, his presence sends a chill of apprehension through me.

I'm not playing for any of these people, judges, nor critics.

For the first time, I'm playing for me.

However, I want him to see me at my brightest. I want him to look and regret everything he's done to me.

I want him to realize that he's lost me. And while he's exponentially allergic to feelings, I hope it stings a little.

Or a lot.

Or enough to allow me to stitch my infested wounds.

I hit the final note of the sonata's first and only part I'm playing tonight with an ardent breath.

Scattered applause fills the hall before it transforms into louder and louder noise. I slowly peel my eyes open to people applauding and shouting, "Bravo," led by Ari.

Only, now, Eli isn't with her.

My inner monologue from seconds ago plummets to the floor as a stronger emotion hits me: rejection.

I stand on unsteady feet and bow a few times, mainly to hide the trembling of my lips.

As I straighten to leave the stage, my heel stutters on the floor, and my lips part.

Eli walks toward me, carrying a massive bouquet of beautifully arranged pink flowers.

I blink twice, trying to shove myself back to reality, but all I see is my husband eating the distance with his long legs and then offering me the flowers.

"You've done well." His cool, rough voice carries in the air like a lullaby.

"Who are you, and what have you done to my cruel, unfeeling husband?"

A small smile touches his lips. "Enjoy this version while you can."

"You mean before your evil twin enters the chat?"

"Something like that." He places the flowers in my hands, and I'm acutely aware of the camera flashes. "I never doubted you."

"That makes one of us." I can feel my cheeks flushing a shade of pink darker than the flowers, despite my every attempt to remain unaffected. "I'm ready to go home and have some soup, then make Sam's ears bleed by talking nonstop."

"Nonsense. We should celebrate."

My lips fall open for the second time in a minute before I recover. "I won no competition. This doesn't call for a celebration."

"You're comfortable with the cello for the first time in a long time. I believe that's reason enough."

"Will Ari join us?"

"No. I'm pitching her back to your parents' house as we speak."

Sure enough, Leo is trying to drag a mildly pissed Ari, who keeps chattering away.

No kidding. My sister and I can talk for entire nights. Neither of us has the physical ability to end a conversation and simply shut up.

I smile. "Pretty sure she's sullying Leo's prim-and-proper ears with more profanity than he can endure."

"*Henderson* could use some real-world education." He places a hand on the small of my back and guides me down the stairs, his touch sending a shock wave through my clothes and heating my skin. "I'll see you at the car in fifteen?"

I stroke one of the flowers as I stare up at him. "If I didn't know better, I'd think you were asking me on a date."

He stares down at me with those cryptic eyes that somehow feel too familiar now. Too raw. Years ago, Eli was an idea, a deity, and a nonsensical idolization.

For the first time, he feels real. Close enough to touch and smell and breathe in.

"Do you *want* a date, Mrs. King?"

"Maybe I do."

"Then maybe I'm making your wish come true."

He releases me by the entrance to the hallway, and the lack of his touch is destabilizing. I open my mouth to say something but close it when I realize I'm speechless.

As soon as I'm inside the changing room, I grab my phone to take pictures of the flowers.

I pause when I see another two texts from Eli from around the time I walked onstage.

Tin Man: You look stunning.
Tin Man: My wife is many infuriating things, but she's undeniably beautiful.

I hold on to the chair as heat slithers through me and wraps its greedy fingers around my neck like a noose.

What is he doing?

What's this complete change from a certified bastard to...a flirt? An *actual* husband?

This doesn't play in favor of my latest revenge plan.

Maybe he's also plotting something himself? Like breaking me into pieces once and for all?

If that's the case, I'll drag him with me to the depths of hell even if it's the last thing I do.

My phone vibrates again, and I hold my breath but release it when I see my sister's name.

Ari: I can't believe that bully actually kicked me out before I got to congratulate you in person! Sending your performance video to Mama and Papa as we speak. You were the bomb, Sissy! So proud of you!
Ava: Thanks, Ari. I'm lucky to have you.
Ari: It's the other way around, silly. Also, should I come back in there and teach my brother-in-law a lesson or two? But, like, bring Lan for backup?
Ava: Drop the act. I know you like Eli and that the two of you talk all the time behind my back.
Ari: How...do you know that?

I pause. Right. How do I know? Before the accident, Ari was always an annoying little shit that neither Eli nor anyone aside from Bran, Cecy, and Glyn gave the time of day. I would've never accused her of liking Eli when she conspired with Lan to start a small fire in his car after he rejected me when she was barely fourteen.

Truth is, I'd have to recall something in the past couple of years to make that allegation.

My sister comes to the same conclusion.

Ari: You remember something?

Ava: No, not really. I'm not sure why I thought that. I have no actual memories to back it up.

Ari: That's fine. I'm glad you're getting there little by little.

Ava: Me, too.

Ari: I love you, Ava. You know that, right?

Ava: Love you, too, Ari.

Ari: Would still kick Eli for you. Want me to come back?

Ava: That's okay. I think it's time I properly face my marriage.

I don't tell her that while I'm finally accepting this wretched marriage, I'm doing it for very wrong reasons.

Once I'm done with Eli King, he'll regret ever marrying me.

CHAPTER 15

AVA

THE LAST THING I'D ACCUSE MY HUSBAND OF IS being romantic.

He'd need to have feelings to ever be endure such a task, and the world knows he's Machiavellian at heart and a devil in his soul.

So imagine my bemused surprise when he takes me to a refined rooftop French restaurant with a stunning night view over London.

Luxurious velvet chairs in a deep wine-red hue encircle round tables adorned with delicate lace and shimmering silk tablecloths. Glamorous dimmed lights cast a romantic glow over the elegantly decorated platforms. Soft music fills the air, creating an atmosphere of affluent sophistication.

Heads turn when we enter the restaurant, following an eager-to-please waitress. The blond is definitely not deterred by Eli's hand at the small of my back and bats her fake lashes at him.

I wouldn't be surprised if she slipped her number beneath his napkin or in his coat.

It takes everything in me not to roll my eyes. It's been years, but he's still annoyingly popular with girls. In fact, his irreSistibility is possibly way worse if one whole wife and the ring on his finger don't seem to discourage the flirtatious behavior.

I might be married to him, but I don't have any sense of ownership over him.

Not that I would want that.

I'm probably more peeved about the disrespect.

Eli orders nonalcoholic champagne with our food. Once the waitress is gone, I sip on my water. "Can't you be less obvious?"

He takes meticulous care in unfolding and placing his napkin on his lap. "About?"

"Your attempts to keep me off alcohol. You can drink, you know."

"And present you with temptation? I'll have to decline."

Your existence is the worst temptation, so I don't see the problem.

I press my lips together, furious at myself for even entertaining that thought.

Clearing my throat, I nibble on a piece of bread with butter. "Can I ask you something?"

"Since when do you need permission to ask me anything?"

"True." I shrug. "How did I get off my...alcohol issues?"

"Alcohol addiction, you mean."

"It wasn't *that* serious."

"It was serious enough that you were drunk more often than you were sober."

"Yeah, well. Not all of us have the mental capacity of a sociopath. I don't need you to judge me. I only want to know how I got off it. Did I undergo rehab?"

"Do you believe yourself to be the type of person who'd willingly admit herself to rehab?"

My knife and bread suspend in midair as I purse my lips. He's mocking me. I can see it in that tinge of amusement mixed with fierce interest in his eyes.

But if I get into a row with him, there's no way I'll be able to execute my plan.

So I take a sip of water to douse the burning need to claw out his throat. "If it wasn't rehab, then what was it?"

"A less conventional method."

"Like tying me to a bed and forcing me to take medication?"

His eyes narrow, and I think I catch a muscle clenching in his jaw, but the change is so fleeting that I barely notice it before he reverts to his normal facade. "Is this another one of your dreams?"

"Daydream."

"A dream all the same."

"It felt real."

"You also said slicing your own throat and watching yourself die in the mirror felt real."

My hands tremble, and I have to drop the bread and knife on the plate, its *clink* loud in the relative silence. "How...the hell do you know that? No one does."

"I do."

"How?"

"You told me."

"I don't believe it. There's no way in hell I'd confide in you."

"We've been married for over two years, Mrs. King. I know more about you than you might think."

"I'd never *ever* share something so intimate with you."

"You'd be surprised." His jaw tightens again, and he sips on the revolting fake champagne, savoring it as if it's centuries-old French wine.

I can't bring myself to grab my utensils again for fear that I'll make a mess.

No one is supposed to have access to that part of me. Even my psychiatrist gets a diluted version of my harrowing hallucinations. Partly because being admitted to a psych ward scares the bejesus out of me.

All of a sudden, I'm hit with a memory of when it all started.

When I was about thirteen years old, I accidentally eavesdropped on my parents in our Cotswolds summer house. I was supposed to be taking a nap with Cecy and Ari, but I couldn't sleep because of my sister's obnoxious snoring.

I was on my way to get something to drink when I heard my parents discussing my recent nightmare. I should've left and pretended to be oblivious like usual, but my feet remained frozen, and I couldn't leave my position by the door.

"She's been having them more often lately. I think we need to get her help, Cole," Mama says, nursing a cup of tea and standing across from Papa at the kitchen island.

Papa has a wretched expression on his face, as if he's in physical pain. I've never seen him like this before, not even when Ari fell and broke her arm after climbing a tree a couple of months ago.

"I was hoping it was nothing," he says, looking through the tall French windows at the pond outside. "I was hoping

we'd be rid of this pain by now, but that was all a pipe dream. I shouldn't have procreated."

"Cole." Mama abandons her cup of tea and wraps her arms around his waist from behind, resting her chin on his shoulder. "Please don't say that. Ava and Ari are the best things that have happened in my life after you. I refuse to think of our present without them."

"But can't you see?" His hand balls into a fist, his knuckles turning white. "It's because of my vile genes that Ava suffers. She's scared of sleeping, Silver. I know because she keeps reading or watching lighthearted shows way past her bedtime just to escape what awaits her when she closes her eyes."

My fingers tremble on the doorframe. I thought I was doing a marvelous job of hiding my frightening sleeping patterns, but it seems that I can never fool Papa after all.

"That doesn't mean anything, Cole." Mama kisses his cheek. "Many teenagers experience an atypical surge of hormones during puberty. It might just be a phase."

"What if it isn't? What if, a few years down the road, she turns into...into that woman?"

"Then we'll deal with it accordingly. Your mother had no support, and part of the reason she did what she did was due to the lack of care from anyone surrounding her. Ava will always *have us, right?"*

"Absolutely." My dad turns around and wraps Mama in a tight embrace.

At that moment, two distinct thoughts hit me.

One, I knew nothing of my paternal grandmother except that she'd died in an accident.

Two, I was a burden to my parents.

Even though Ari is the wild one who likes to do everything unconventionally, I'm the one who worries my parents more. The one who makes Papa feel guilty and forces Mama to try to put up a courageous front.

And the worst part is that I have no clue how to stop it.

"Ava?"

I look up at Eli through my blurry vision, my heart galloping so loudly, a buzz ricochets in my ear.

"Why are you crying?" His voice is a strange mixture of softness and anger. A stark contrast that pulls me apart.

He, of all people, can't know how messed up I truly am. I couldn't stand his mockery or, worse, his disdain.

It's tragic enough that he broke my heart. It'd be disastrous if he destroyed my spirit—or whatever's left of it.

I blink away the moisture and look up as I wipe the tear with the edge of my napkin. "Something got into my eyes," I say with an automatic plastered smile.

"Don't." The rough warning in his voice sparks a chill through me.

"Don't what?"

"Don't pretend in front of me. Don't put up a facade as if everything is fine."

"Isn't that what's expected from a couple like us? A pretense, a front, and an illusion that everything is glamorously perfect?"

He cuts his steak into minuscule pieces and places them in meticulous parallel lines. I'm pretty sure Eli has a mild version of OCD. He doesn't touch anything used by other people, including his parents.

Leo and his driver always wear gloves whenever they're in his vicinity—though Leo probably shares the disregard for touching anything. And I just realized that Eli barely eats anything whenever he's at a restaurant.

Even now, he's been content drinking and cutting meat, but he hasn't eaten a single bite.

Hell, I don't remember the last time I saw him eat anything. I know he has to, but he probably won't touch any food unless it's cooked by his precious ex-nanny, Sam, although I've never witnessed that myself. At least, not since I woke up in the hospital with spotty memories.

He used to eat fine at his parents' house, if I remember correctly. But I don't recall him consuming anything but drinks elsewhere.

"It doesn't have to be," he finally says, his attention still on the medium-well steak he's not eating.

"Doesn't have to be what?"

He lifts his head, pinning me with that dark gray look. "It doesn't have to be fake, a facade or a front."

I laugh. I can't help it. "So you mean to tell me you're willing to give me love, children, and your boundless protection?"

"You already have my unbound protection. I can give you children if that's what you want. But love isn't something I'm capable of. I presume you wouldn't want that from me either."

"You presume right." My voice rolls out steadily, despite the ball that forms at the base of my throat as constrictive emotion floods my stomach.

I thought my heart had already mended, but a few words from the bastard are enough to tear the messy stitches surrounding the useless organ.

The retort—*In fact, I want nothing from you, including*

children and protection—is on the tip of my tongue, but I douse it with the disgusting nonalcoholic champagne.

If I want to initiate this revenge properly, I can't keep antagonizing him or pushing him away.

He needs to believe that I'm falling in love with him despite all his warnings. I have to make him attached to me, crazy about me, and then divorce him and move on with my life.

Preferably not in a psych ward.

Though marrying this prick in the first place was surely a giant step in that direction.

He swirls the champagne in his glass. "So you agree to dissolve the fake status?"

"I'll have to think about it, though your behavior is far from convincing."

"Oh? I thought my behavior was the reason you fell head over heels for me."

"*Fell* is past tense. I'm not foolish anymore."

"I stand corrected."

"As you should." I square my shoulders. "Also, if you want me to agree to anything, you better start by giving me what I want."

"Such as?"

"Companionship."

"You have Sam, Bonneville, Ariella, and Cecily, whom you FaceTime every couple of hours."

"I'm not married to them, am I?"

"I'm a busy man with a tight schedule."

"There's no such thing a as busy man. Only an unavailable one. If you wanted to make time for me, you would."

"Make time to do what, exactly?"

"Court me properly, for starters."

He releases a bark of laughter that stabs an icy spear through my chest. "Why would I need to court you when we're already married?"

"Because while I don't remember, I'm sure you didn't court me the first time around. You must've forced your way in as usual."

His face remains impassive, and my doubts come true. I've never believed the marriage-of-convenience part anyway. Now I'm sure it was under duress somehow.

The problem is, I'm not sure why on earth Eli would force my hand to be with him. He doesn't even like me.

Right?

Eli's facial expression remains as frozen as Antarctica as he says, "I still don't see why I'd do a nonsensical thing such as courting when you have my name attached to yours."

"Because I said so, *Mr. King*. Take it or leave it." I clink my glass to his with a triumphant smile.

"And if I leave it? Will that change the fact you're my wife by all conventional and societal laws?"

"No. But it'll forbid you access to what you truly want."

He raises a brow. "And what is that, pray tell?"

I slide my shoe up his leg beneath the table and caress his dick. A rush of blood saturates my ears as his erection thickens beneath my touch.

"You know," I say in a sultry voice.

"Get on your knees and suck my cock, and I might agree."

"Agree first." I press my shoe against his erection. "And I'll get on my knees and suck your cock."

He suppresses a sound, whether a curse or a grunt, I'm not sure, but it's enough to prompt me to drop my foot. No idea what I was doing in the first place, but I was obviously playing with fire in the devil's lair, and I need to protect myself from a fire hazard.

As soon as my foot disappears from his vicinity, any sense of being affected vanishes, and I'm greeted with the cold Roman statue I've known all my life.

So much for trying seduction.

"As tempting as that offer is…" He lifts a piece of meat to his mouth, then drops it back to the plate and squashes it with his knife. "I'll have to pass."

I lift a shoulder even as a thorny stem pricks my heart. "Your loss. Many other candidates are willing to take me up on my advances."

I realize I've screwed up the moment Eli drops his utensils on the plate—calmly, I might add—and dabs his mouth with the napkin even though he ate nothing. He has the effortless talent of making every single action look sexually charged and dangerously attractive.

"It's not terribly smart to ignore my warnings, you know."

"Not sure what you're talking about."

"You know exactly what I'm talking about. Suggesting or, worse, threatening me with an affair is the most foolish thing you can do. I draw the line at other men touching my property. Are we clear, Mrs. King?"

"I'm *not* your property."

"You are whatever the fuck I say you are. Let's not go down that road, for I'd hate to make you cry. Again."

"And here I thought you loved seeing me cry."

"Think of me as you will, but your tears don't bring me any form of joy whatsoever."

"Could've fooled me." I wipe my mouth and toss the napkin down as I stand and then round the table. "If you refuse to satisfy me, I'll find a man who does."

I'd planned to walk away with my head high, but the moment I'm beside him, Eli jerks up, grabs my arm and tugs me against his chest.

My body explodes in a volcano of violent emotions when my breasts glue to his hard muscles. A lick of heat penetrates my skin as his scent seeps into my bones.

He stares down at me with frosty coldness eclipsed by furious fire. The longer he looks at my face, the more astonished I am that I don't melt into a puddle on the floor.

The feel of his touch and his attention is too much, and yet a part of me, a foolish, suicidal one, yearns for more.

For something other than the rejection I've been swallowing like a bitter pill since I was seventeen.

For his loss of control.

For the Eli no one else knows.

And I figured the best way to do that is to threaten him with another man. It seems to be what makes him tick. Aside from OCD tendencies.

Yes, I'd never act on those threats—cheating, ew—but that doesn't mean I wouldn't use the possibility to my benefit.

Keep him on his toes and all that.

"Do not ever bring up another man in my presence if you know what's good for you."

"Marrying you proved that I do not, in fact, know what's good for me."

"Ava…"

"Yes, *darling*?"

I'm inexplicably thankful for our strict gun laws, because if Eli had one, he'd shoot me between the eyes.

"May I help with anything? Dessert, perhaps?" The waitress comes back with a plastic smile and heart eyes directed toward my prick of a husband.

I wonder if she would still jump his bones if she knew he's not capable of love and collects broken hearts in a jar like Lan once warned me.

Pretty sure mine is the most smashed of them all.

Who am I kidding? She totally would. People like her and Gemma probably don't care about the Tin Man as long as he fucks their brains out and provides them with power and prestige.

Since I'm well equipped with the last two, I have no interest in anything he offers me.

"No, thank you," I say, shrugging free. "I'm leaving."

"How about you, sir?" The waitress gets so close, she's just short of rubbing herself all over him.

Professionalism has left the building.

I should walk away and leave him to his own devices, but then again, my mama didn't carry me for nine months so I could be trifled with.

Plastering on a smile that matches her plastic one, I slide my arm into Eli's. "Didn't you hear the part where I said we're leaving?"

"I thought you were…"

"We're married, so of course we'll leave together, or did you deliberately miss our rings in your attempts to gold-dig? He'd eat you for breakfast and still be in the mood for more, so you should be grateful I'm keeping him off the market. You're welcome..." I pretend to read her name tag, *Hannah*, and pronounce it "Anna."

Then I say, "I'll be waiting outside, *babe*." I flash Eli my sweet smile, pat his arm, and then walk out with my head held high, ignoring Eli's all-knowing smirk.

As soon as I'm outside, I'm hit with a chill. Damn. I should've brought a jacket.

I forgot my phone and purse inside, so I can't tell Leo to bring the car around. Brilliant.

Hugging myself, I rub my arms and pace the empty side street.

The area is illuminated by dimly lit lampposts, casting a shimmering hue on the wet pavement. The constant showers in the UK have left their mark, and passing cars create small waves on the road. A gust of wind blows through, and I shudder from the sudden drop in temperature.

"Ava Nash?"

I stop and turn around, slightly perplexed since no one has called me that since I woke up in the hospital.

I'm basically Mrs. King now.

"Yes?"

I observe the old woman's haggard appearance. Deep lines etch their way around her tired eyes and thin lips, telling tales of a long life. Wispy strands of gray hair peek out from underneath a hat that has faded from its original cheerful yellow to a dull, muddy green. The fabric is worn and frayed, giving away years of use. Despite her rough appearance, there is a sense of resilience emanating from her weathered features.

And for some reason, she looks...familiar? Like a grainy picture I've stumbled upon in an old magazine.

But where do I recognize her from?

"Do I know you?" I repeat when she remains silent.

The woman keeps studying me with hollowed eyes, not blinking. I search my surroundings, noting the absence of cars. A chill that's not from the cold forms goose bumps on my bare arms.

"I'm sorry, I don't have cash," I say with a smile. "I can buy you a meal if you can wait—"

"I don't need your money."

I physically jerk at how uncharacteristically deep her voice is. Probably a longtime smoker.

"Then I'm at a loss as to how I can help you." I pause. "How do you know my name?"

"You'll pay for what you've done, you sewer rat. Don't think you'll ever get away with it when I haven't."

"Pardon?"

The sound of a door wrenches my attention from the strange woman. I look back to find Eli carrying my purse and phone, and even though I'm still mad at him, a crushing wave of relief washes over me at his presence.

"Eli, this lady seems to be mistaking me for someone else—" I point at thin air.

The woman who was standing in front of me has vanished.

"No..." I whisper, my heart hammering.

A plush woolen jacket falls onto my bare shoulders, cocooning me in a wave of warmth and his alluring scent.

But that doesn't distract me from the fact I conjured up an entire woman just now.

And not just any woman.

The familiarity hits me like an arrow between my bones.

After my parents' conversation about my maternal grandmother, I searched all our family albums, but there was no trace of any pictures of her with Papa. So I scoured the internet. That did bring results because she was a famous horror-thriller novelist, and Papa donates all her royalties to various children's charities.

The old lady from just now seemed familiar because that's exactly how my grandmother would look if she'd aged.

The same hollow eyes. The same frozen expression.

But I know she's dead. She's been dead for over thirty years.

So why the hell would I conjure up her image?

"What's wrong?" Eli asks, wrapping an arm around my shoulders as if he feels I'll collapse.

"You...did you see a homeless woman just now?"

His brows dip together, and my heart plummets.

"She was wearing a puffy jacket, a torn skirt, and a hat that looked green but was originally yellow and..." My voice is turning panicked with every word, and my breathing becomes so shallow, I'm panting.

"Hey," Eli does something I never thought he would and rubs my arm in soothing circles. "It's okay."

"No no no no no no no, it's not okay!" I scream as panic floods my bloodstream. "Oh God, no, no, please, please, please."

"Ava...Ava..." Eli stands in front of me, his firm hands clutching my shoulders and his face blurred. "Breathe, come on, I need you to breathe. Mimic me."

He sucks in a deep inhale, and I follow with my shattered one.

"She...she was real, right? Right? Right?"

"Exhale, come on."

"Right." I release a long breath. "She must've been real. This is real."

"It's all real, beautiful."

"You?" I touch his face as I blink away the blurriness. "Are you real, or is this whole thing a hallucination?"

"I'm always real."

Slowly, my breathing goes back to normal, but I'm so drained, so ashamed, so unable to face him after my epic meltdown.

Closing my eyes, I sag into his welcoming embrace, knowing, for some reason, that he will prevent me from falling.

The world disappears from beneath my feet as he carries me to the car.

He said he's always real, but a depressing thought keeps banging on the walls of my sanity.

What if everything is still a figment of my unruly imagination?

CHAPTER 16
ELI

"TO WHAT DO I OWE THIS TOUCHING HEART-TO-heart displeasure?"

I narrow my eyes on my cousin through the huge monitor in my home office and stare at his nonexistent soul.

A step below mine—or maybe above.

Proving who's superior is a competition neither of us would forfeit, but it's a known fact that Landon breathes chaos and would sacrifice his firstborn to watch the world go up in flames.

Appearance-wise, we're similar and share the King genes. Especially the straight nose and frosty eyes that unconsciously prompt people to shake in their boots.

The similarities end there.

His brown hair, courtesy of his mother, and blue eyes, the only thing he got from his father, distinguish him from my better genes.

He's also tragically less refined than me, considering his casual gray T-shirt and finger-raked hair. One more reason why the parasite won't fit King Enterprises' image, especially if I have any say in it.

Rain patters outside, barely reaching my ears through

the double-glazed windows as I stretch my legs beneath my desk and cross them at the ankles. "Your recent plans to start trouble. Maybe I need to sit you down and break the unfortunate news that Hannibal Lecter isn't real."

"Don't insult my intelligence by comparing me to a loser who has no capabilities in controlling his basic impulses. Additionally, I wouldn't have started any trouble if I hadn't been presented with tempting receipts."

"I see your vacationing with vulgar Americans has taught you bad habits."

"Not vacationing; keeping my beautiful fiancée happy while annoying her brother and looking out for my brother's interests."

"Sounds tedious."

"Wouldn't have it any other way." He grins. "You should see Nikolai's face when I steal Bran's attention and purposefully cockblock him. That could be the stuff of an interesting psychological thriller. But enough about my stunning adventures, dear Cousin. Did you hear the news?"

"About your pending assassination by your fiancée's Mafia family? Already booked the coffin. Will put some drops in my eyes and pretend to shed a tear as they lower you into the ground."

"The Russians love me—like everyone who has the honor to encounter my godly presence. Don't you worry about that. What you should be concerned about, however, is the news I learned recently. Something about Ava's former psychiatrist somehow, by a stroke of luck, disappearing."

"Oh?" I remain in the same position, my face muscles unmoving.

"What unfortunate news." Lan shakes his head with

a pretense of sympathy. "He was bright, professional, and particularly close with Barbie. I wonder if she learned about the tragic turn of events."

"Ava. My wife's name is Ava."

"Thanks for the info. Anyway, is Barbie still awake for a quick catch-up call from her favorite King?"

"Seeing as she shares a house with her favorite King, the one she married, I don't see where you come into the equation."

He barks out mocking laughter and even slaps his knee for good measure. "You're effortlessly funny, dear Cousin. Sometimes, I wonder whether or not you truly believe your words."

"If you're done." I reach for the mouse, but he holds up a hand and leans in.

Behind him, a gust of wind hits a couple of willow trees, their wild leaves scraping the huge window.

He was apparently gifted the mansion he's currently residing in by his fiancée's Russian grandfather after he proved to be undoubtedly worthy of Mia Sokolov. It's a fact he never stops shoving down everyone's throats, especially Grandpa Jonathan's, so he can score more points as the potential favorite heir.

The joke's on him. I'm Grandma's favorite, and since Grandpa worships at her feet, no one else has a chance. Except for maybe my cousin Glyn, who's always been Grandpa's spoiled princess.

"I'm not playing, Eli. I can barely contain myself from sharing Barbie's grief, so unless you're not bothered by that outcome, I'd suggest you try to placate me. We'll start with a *please*."

"Please drop dead so I can go ahead with my funeral plans."

"Aw. Didn't know you were eager to shed tears for me. But let's postpone that for at least sixty more years." He tilts his head to the side. "You're really unperturbed about your wife learning the truth, possibly digging deeper, and shattering the illusion you've been miraculously maintaining?"

"No. Because if you tell her that, you'll have no ammo to piss me off with."

"Now. Don't be so pessimistic. There's that tidbit where her fall down the stairs and subsequent memory loss wasn't an accident, no matter how much effort you put into making it appear otherwise. I don't believe Barbie would appreciate the lies and deceit."

"Stay out of it, Lan." I lean forward and steeple my fingers at my chin. "You do not want to cross me, not when it comes to this."

His eyes shine with a challenge. "Or *what*?"

"Or I'll make it my mission to interfere in your relationship."

"That's where you're mistaken. I didn't build mine on incorrigible lies, unlike a certain someone."

"Lies can always be invented. I am not above shoving you back into the void you floundered in until very recently. You touch what's mine, whether by actions or words, and Mia will disappear faster than the doctor."

His lips lift in a snarl. "Is that a threat?"

"Only if you act foolishly. I'm presenting you with a warning because you're family, Lan. A generosity you're well aware I don't offer to others who get in my way."

I finish the call before he can say anything else. The screen turns black, then flicks back to the dozens of surveillance cameras I have all over my house.

The rain grows louder in the otherwise-peaceful silence.

No, not peaceful. Perhaps *ominous* is the word I'm looking for despite not believing in its effect.

The clock on my desk clicks to five minutes past one in the morning, but the last activity I'd like to engage in is sleep. Not after Ava nearly slipped back into that unrecognizable version of herself.

If anything, I need to keep an eye out the entire night.

She fell asleep against my chest on the ride home from the restaurant, but she wouldn't stop shivering or murmuring no.

That soft, haunted word still rings in my ears. The feel of her lifeless body left a massive hole in my thought process.

I'm not one to deviate from my patterns and the way I like things done, but as I carried Ava to her bed, I wanted to stay and ensure her chest kept rising and falling and that she did not, in fact, fall down that slippery slope of complete and utter loss of control.

It seems ironic that I, a man built on the very definition of organized control, have been plagued with a sickening fixation on chaos.

I've long since given up believing that my wife is merely a phase I'll eventually bypass and am slowly trying to accept that this hollowness is, whether I like it or not, a default setting.

My fingers pause on the mouse when I find Ava's silk bed crumpled and empty.

A strike of lightning flashes against the window as I scroll to her bathroom. Yes, I have a surveillance camera in my wife's bathroom. Sue me.

When I find it empty as well, my fingers clench around the mouse as I fly through the locations she could've gone to.

The kitchen—for her usual late-night popcorn and candy floss bucket. And if she's in the mood, strawberry ice cream could be added to the mix.

The cinema theater in the basement, where she consumes all those while watching romantic comedies from the early 2000s.

A guest room she turned into her music lair, as she calls it, and stuffed with five cellos—one of them pink—a violin, and a piano. All instruments she plays like a pro.

The library, where she fluctuates between reading books about classical music artists and porn-filled romance novels. She has a pink corner with a fluffy reading recliner, where she tabs, highlights, *and* writes notes in the damn books. A habit that infuriates me immensely and makes me cross-eyed with rage.

The greenhouse, where she can be found attempting amateur flower arranging and crossbreeding—and failing miserably. The poor gardener will have a stroke the next time she kills his precious plants.

She's in none of those places.

Fuck.

I go room by room, for the first time despising the size of the property. However, she's nowhere in the house.

Considering her closeness with Sam, she may have gone to the guesthouse to look for her. But I don't think she'd do that this late at night.

Despite her tantrums, obnoxious spending of my money on charities I didn't know existed, and her usually entitled behavior, my wife has proven to be much closer to those who aren't near our social standing.

She's learned every staff member's name and often invites them to watch her cringey films with her, even with Sam's attempts to create distance between Ava and them. She also always scolds me if I attempt to ask people to do their job.

It's about the tone. Yes, they work for you, but this is not the age of aristocracy anymore, and you're neither their lord nor their keeper, so stop being a dick and speak to them like they're human beings.

She fails to remember that I find 90 percent of the human population is either dull or has a neurodevelopment that stopped at the age of ten.

Still screening the cameras, I pull out my phone, ready to speed-dial Sam and Henderson. Who cares if it's past one in the morning when Ava is missing?

My fingers pause when I spot her standing in the middle of the back garden. Still wearing her evening dress.

While the rain pours down on her.

I curse under my breath, then storm out of the office and grab an umbrella on my way outside.

A cold gust of wind tightens my face, and the heavy rain, now unconcealed by the house, roars in my ears like crashing waves.

It takes me some time to reach the back after narrowly escaping slipping on the cobbled path zigzagged by patches of grass.

My feet come to a staggering halt when I finally see

her standing in the middle of the rain. The wet dress sticks to her body like a second skin, outlining the slope of her breasts and the curve of her arse.

She's staring up at the sky, and the lamppost behind her casts a soft halo on her face as rivulets of rain stream down her temples, cheeks, and neck before clinging to the dress and dripping to the ground.

My steps are careful as I approach her and hold the umbrella over our heads, battling the stubborn gust of wind that's scrambling to whisk it away.

"Ava, is everything okay?" I ask the rhetorical question because I can see nothing is okay.

I'm not even speaking to her right now. Instead, I'm talking to a ghost of her. Someone who checked out long ago despite my desperate attempts to revive her.

She steps away from me and out from under the umbrella to continue staring at the cloudy, starless sky. So I slide beside her and hold the umbrella far back so as not to block her view but still protect her from the downpour.

"Let's get you inside, beautiful." My arm wraps around her waist as I apply slight pressure to push her forward. For a moment, she follows my lead, but then she comes to an abrupt halt.

Her head tilts back in a mechanical movement, and she faces me, but she's not really seeing me. Her eyes are pale, unfocused.

She's not herself.

My wife is nothing more than a stranger right now.

Not even a shadow of herself like in some instances.

If her parents, or even Ariella, find out about this,

they'll take her away to where they think she should receive treatment.

I've been there, done that, and would not repeat it even if a gun was held to my head.

Besides, I'm her legal guardian, not them, so they can't do fuck unless they're ready to sabotage and sully her lucid moments.

"You think I'm beautiful?" Her voice is low, a bit haunted, lethargic, and nothing like Ava's snarky, energetic one.

But I nod anyway.

"Say it again." She sucks in a sharp breath and slides a cold hand on my chest, her movements awkward and stiff. "Tell me you find me beautiful."

"I find you so extremely beautiful, it hurts to look at you sometimes."

"More beautiful than your ex-girlfriends?"

"I've never had a girlfriend, and even if I had, they wouldn't hold a candle to you."

The wind howls, nearly blowing the umbrella away as the rain falls harder, soaking my arm that remains unsheltered to offer Ava the entirety of the space.

She slides a wet hand to my face, caressing and poking my cheek as if I'm a doll. "Are you real?"

"One hundred percent."

"What if you stop being real?"

"I won't."

She strokes my lips. "I think you're beautiful, too."

And then, in a massive upturn, she grabs both my cheeks, stands on her tiptoes, and seals her lips to mine.

I'm momentarily taken aback, considering she's never

touched me intimately when in this state. She barely tolerates my touch and would honestly prefer Sam or even Henderson over me.

Sam is usually the one who bathes her, provides her with her comfort candy floss bucket, and stays by her side until she finally tires out.

In fact, my presence seems to upset her and trigger these episodes, which is why I limit my time with her and don't touch her unless absolutely necessary.

But then she's been fine for weeks, despite that miscalculation when I couldn't reSist finger fucking her. She's been talking, walking, reading, practicing cello, and annoying the hell out of me with every word out of her mouth.

So I made the mistake of thinking this was a fresh start. Which is why I made the further fucking error of continuing to touch her, dating her, and presenting her with a chance to pick up her passion again.

Ava's teeth sink into my lower lip, and a metallic taste explodes on my tongue as she whispers against my mouth. "Do you want to know a secret?"

"What secret?"

"I'm going to hurt you." She speaks even lower before she gets down from her toes, her eyes lost and her posture hunched, lacking the elegance of her usual self.

"Why are you going to hurt me?" I ask.

"Shhh." She places a finger on my lips. "It's a secret. Don't tell anyone, okay?"

I nod, and she drops her hand, looking as stiff as a board as she trembles in her soaked dress.

"Do you still think I'm beautiful?"

"Yes."

"Even though I'll ruin you?"

"Possibly."

"Liar." She laughs, then wraps her arms around me. "Hey, Mr. King?"

"Yes?"

"Fuck me."

"Not now."

"When, then? I want to get laid."

She rubs her stomach against my cock, and I hate how my dick jerks to attention at her merest touch.

"You know you want me." She peppers kisses on my jaw, my throat, and my lips and even licks the blood she drew. Then she whispers in my ear, "You can tie me up and do whatever you please."

It takes an obscene amount of control not to succumb to her provocations and take her on the grass like a caveman. But that would be no different than taking advantage of her when it's obvious that sober Ava isn't at all open to that option.

My bruised lip throbs beneath her pillow-soft mouth, her gentle kisses, her innocent humping of my thickening cock, which is about to burst.

I wrap a tense hand around her shoulder and shove her away. "You have no idea what you're asking for."

"I do. I'm not a kid anymore."

With a curse, I grab her by the wrist and drag her behind me to the house, not caring about the water trail we leave behind.

Logically, I should call Sam, then disappear and hope she'll wake up better tomorrow without my triggering presence.

However, logic seems to have fled me tonight, because I take her to her bathroom and stop to watch her as she stands in the middle of the white-and-pink space with a huge Jacuzzi tub and golden taps.

I throw a towel on her head and rub it a few times. "Stay here."

Then I walk back to her bedroom and grab the first thing I put my hands on—a white silk nightgown. When I return, I find her in the same position, staring at the floor with the towel still on her head.

With a sigh, I stand behind her and pull down the zipper of her dress, revealing porcelain-white skin covered with a sheen of water.

I help her shimmy out of the dress, trying my hardest not to stroke her hard nipples, touch her pussy, nor slap her arse for good measure.

Jesus Christ.

Wanting to do the right thing with this woman is harder in practice.

I try to push her toward the shower, but she refuses to budge. She also seems to have checked out. Which isn't always a bad sign, because at least this way, she's less destructive.

My hands are steady as I dry her to the best of my ability without lingering too much on her breasts or pussy. Then, to eliminate the temptation, I slip on her white gown.

No. It's not better.

Her wet blond locks frame her face angelically, and the silk material clings to her skin with soft elegance.

I pick her up and carry her in my arms, then place her in the bed and pull the duvet over her body.

She lies on her back, staring at the ceiling as if I'm invisible.

My lips brush over her forehead. "Good night, beautiful."

I'm about to pull away, but she clutches my cheeks and shoves my mouth against hers. The cut stings, but I couldn't care less, because when she releases me, a soft smile brightens her face.

"Good night."

And then her eyes flutter closed.

As I watch her peaceful expression, I almost forget that I'm married to what's societally known as a madwoman.

Worse, she doesn't even know it.

And I'll make sure it remains this way.

CHAPTER 17
AVA

THE MORNING COMES WITH A SURPRISINGLY refreshing start. I haven't slept so soundly in...well, ever, now that I think about it.

Except for in my very distant, barely memorable childhood, I've often had a crippling problem with sleep.

Eventually, it scared me to the point where I always made sure I slept on my own and never with others.

The only person I trusted not to sell out my chaotic mental state and tragic future was Cecily.

When we were at uni, she often checked on me before bed, stood there until she was satisfied I'd taken my medication, and even prepared me a glass of milk or some herbal tea.

Part of the reason why I fell with less grace than broken china in my final years of uni was because I was hit with the reality that she had her own life. Expecting her to stay with me forever when I knew for a fact she yearned for a family of her own was both selfish and shameful.

My own thoughts—jealousy of Jeremy and the inability to accept my new situation—were what drove me over the edge.

Alcohol, drugs, and any form of escapism. I lost my

grip on reality more often than not and stressed hard about the very possibility that Papa would figure everything out and shove me into a mental institution.

Despite having forgotten two years, I find my current life seems the most stable I've had in a long time.

The most confusing, too.

On one hand, I'm extremely grateful and content with my balanced routine, but on the other, I feel dreadful about the fact my tyrant husband has had something to do with it.

My steps are careful as I cast a glance to the opposite side of the hall, where Eli's room is.

I hesitate at the top of the stairs and run a hand over my floral muslin dress that hugs my waist and stops right above my knees.

It's pretty modest compared to the crop top and micro-skirt I contemplated wearing.

Might have something to do with my inability to muster the will to antagonize my husband. Not this morning.

It's embarrassing enough that he witnessed my epic panic attack and even let me sleep against him on the way home. And I know he allowed it, because if there's one thing I know about Eli King, it's his lack of capacity to practice any form of sentimentality, so it's strange that he made such an exception.

I'm well aware that I shouldn't read too much into it and that he probably did it because he doesn't appreciate being humiliated in public, but that doesn't negate my gratitude.

My gaze drifts to the empty hallway, but I decide against the stupid idea of knocking on his door and head to the kitchen instead.

I'm not grateful enough to make him think I'm desperate.

"Morning, Sam." I stroll inside with a grin.

The middle-aged woman looks up from towel drying a pot, her gaze scanning me for a beat too long. "Did you sleep well?"

"Pretty well, thanks." I stifle a yawn as I climb onto a barstool and grab my pink-jeweled smoothie cup in one hand and a piece of avocado toast in the other. "Though I did have a bizarre dream."

Sam glimpses at me over her shoulder. "How bizarre?"

I check our surroundings, then whisper, "Is he here?"

"Who's he?"

"Who else? Your precious boss."

"It's past eleven in the morning, miss. He left for work hours ago."

"Um, okay." I ignore the sinking feeling in my stomach and drown it with a long pull of smoothie and a bite of my toasted sourdough.

"What was the bizarre dream?" Sam appears in front of me with the posture of a Roman gladiator, which is comical at best when she's still towel drying another pot.

"It's stupid, really. I dreamed of Eli taking me to bed. I think he dried my hair. Not sure why it was wet, though. And...um...he kissed my forehead and wished me good night." I let out a soft laugh. "What are the odds, huh?"

"More likely than you think."

"Yeah, right." I drop the half-eaten toast on the plate and play with my straw. "I probably had that weird dream because of how he helped me last night."

Sam's movements slow as she stares at me. "What else was in the dream?"

"That's all I remember." I squint. "And only in fragments. It's strange because I don't have dreams." *Only nightmares that make me wake up in a cold sweat and cause me to refuse to ever fall asleep again.*

Sam says nothing. Like my cold husband, she's a woman of few words.

I swirl my nails on the sparkling jewels. "Were you the one who changed my clothes last night?"

"Who else would it have been?"

Right.

"By the way." I opt for a different subject. "You didn't congratulate me for yesterday."

"Congratulations," she says with a poker face.

"That sounds performative, as if you were dragged into saying it."

"If you say so."

I scowl but choose to let it go as I jump down from my stool. "Hey, Sam?"

"Yes?" She's turned away to place the pots in the cupboards.

"What are you making for lunch?"

"Basil soup, shepherd's pie, and broccoli salad."

"And dessert?"

"Salted caramel flan."

"Make it strawberry and I'll help."

"Why would you?"

"Well...I'm bored."

"Considering you're able to watch films and read books for hours on end, I find that hard to believe."

"Fiiine. I want to learn how to cook."

"Why?"

"Just stop asking questions and teach me."

"So you can burn dishes faster than you murder the poor flowers?"

"Oh, please. I'm trying to make something fun from those flowers."

"Afraid Mr. Pratt does not agree with that view."

"He's just being dramatic. He'll survive." I interlink my arm with hers. "So will you? Please?"

"As long as you promise not to poison Mr. King."

My lips part.

"You *will* poison him?"

"Nooo, what are you talking about?" I laugh. "You're so funny."

"I'm anything but funny."

"True." I sigh with a mock pout.

She flips a sliding drawer open, places the pot inside among an incredibly organized set of similar pots, then pushes it closed.

OCD runs in this household, I swear. They should be thankful I'm adding more liveliness to their existence for free.

"So? So?" I place my hands together in a prayer. "Pretty please?"

"Fine. But only if you promise not to mess with his food. He's iffy about it as it is and would possibly fast for eternity if something were to happen."

"Aye, Captain." I salute, and I swear she suppresses a smile.

I wonder if I can convert Sam to the bright side and

steal her away from her tyrant boss. Being exposed to that gloomy energy, stone-faced orders, and dark soul on a daily baSis will suck the life out of her.

We just need a little bit of fun in this house. Though, *apparently*, my random watch parties with the staff and dancing sprees with Ari are already too much fun for my grump of a husband.

He'll come around. The entire house will.

Sam says we'll change the menu to cook something I love, so if I screw it up, I'll be the only one who has to eat it.

Rude.

We opt for lentil soup. Simple enough, I guess.

I lay out the ingredients as she instructs and start by adding more water than required to a pot.

"You said he's iffy about food," I start in a nonchalant voice. "Why is that?"

"He eats just fine."

"But not at restaurants, and now that I think about it, I've never seen him consume anything but drinks at parties, public gatherings, weddings, funerals, et cetera."

"He rarely attends weddings. Just funerals."

I roll my eyes. "Yeah, yeah. He's a great enemy of fun. We are all well aware."

"Maybe not entirely." She glares at my hand. "Stir faster, or you'll burn the pot."

I up my pace. "What's the reason behind his food snobbishness?"

"Why don't you ask him yourself?"

"As if he'd tell me."

"You'd be surprised. He's drastically different from the Eli you knew six years ago."

I swallow. Of course, Sam knows about my embarrassing confession and the heartbreaking rejection.

Bet he laughed about my misery when he told her the story.

"I very much doubt that," I mutter.

"Then you'd be very much wrong." She sorts through the tower-high spice shelf and retrieves a few jars. "And, deep down, you know that."

"Well, I admit he's a bit different." Old Eli would never offer me encouragement, bring me flowers, take me on a date, nor, God forbid, carry me, but I can't help thinking this change is due to an ulterior motive.

"A bit?" Sam flashes me an incredulous look.

"Yeah, a bit. He still ignores my existence most of the time."

"If you want his company, ask for it."

"I did, and he laughed at me."

"Did you ask nicely?"

"If by 'nicely,' you mean I offered an ultimatum, then sure, I said it with a blindingly *nice* smile."

"Why am I not surprised?"

"He's the one who keeps inSisting that we're a married couple, but, apparently, he only extracted controlling behavior from the institution. No idea who he takes after, considering his dad treats his mum like a queen. You sure he wasn't switched at birth?"

"What I am sure about is that this push-and-pull game needs to have less pulling before it turns tiresome."

"What...do you mean?"

She fixes me with a look, but she offers no other words except for instructions to cook.

I end up burning the soup, only slightly, and am put on Sam's shit list for endangering her special pot.

What I enjoy the most, however, is making a chocolate-strawberry cake, and it turns out pretty decent, though not as spongy as it should be.

Half a day and a gigantic mess in the kitchen later, Sam is so done with my antics. She chases me out after I break a crystal glass. In my defense, it looked ugly.

Anyway, after I take a shower, I change into a similar dress with a more daring neckline, then slip on my soft-pink slippers with fluffy pom-poms.

By the time I'm downstairs again, it's around six.

I spy on outside from the reception area, but no car comes.

So I go up to the music room, practice my Bach for over two hours, then go down again.

This time, I'm more annoyed than disappointed.

"You should have some dinner," Sam says, pointing at the dishes on the table, among which lie my soup and two slices of my cake.

"I have no appetite."

I fling the cupboard open, snatch my bucket of candy floss, and slip to the library to read about fictional romance and distant worlds.

Thinking better of it, I grab Eli's stupid political, historical, and finance books and stack them on the plush Persian carpet in a few chaotic rows. I can imagine the twitch in his eyes if he sees them in such a disorganized manner.

Perfect.

I lie on my stomach and proceed to eat my candy floss as I flip the pages of a giant book about the Hundred Years' War.

I'm not even reading. Nor interested.

The entire point is to mess up the books.

I take a picture of my sticky fingers, the bucket of candy floss, and the mountain of his books, then send it to him.

Me: Interesting stuff.

I can't hide my smile when his reply comes immediately.

Tin Man: Did you mark the pages with candy floss, Ava?

Me: And here I thought your deduction talents were getting rusty.

Tin Man: Move away from the library and take that evil bucket with you.

Me: But I don't want to. Btw, can you explain this?

I circle a line in the book in red without even reading it, underline and highlight a few others, then dog-ear the page for good measure. Satisfied with my handiwork, I snap a picture and then send it over.

He doesn't reply for one long minute. I believe I gave him a heart attack.

Fun.

I should've played on his organized-freak tendencies before. No wonder he placed a whole room separator between my side of the library and his. In hindsight, he should've built a wall.

Me: Hellooo. You still there?

Tin Man: Perfectly am, but you won't be once I'm finished with you.

Me: Oh, please. I'm just asking for help innocently.

Tin Man: There's nothing innocent about you. What's the reason behind this tantrum?

Me: I'm just reading ever so quietly.

Tin Man: Chaotically is more like it.

Me: You're right, there's no quietness involved. I have screaming metal on. Our neighbors would've reported me to the police if not for the soundproofing system. Sam has evacuated most of the staff from the premises, so it's only me and your books. No one will save them from my rigorous highlighting system. What a shame.

I send more marked pictures, but this time, he doesn't reply.

He's no fun.

Just when I think I've figured out a way to mess with him, he effortlessly shuts me down.

My level of frustration mounts to dangerous heights, so I grab a bodice ripper from my prized collection, then lie back down on my stomach in the middle of his pretentious books.

They could use an introduction to better and less snobbish literature if you ask me.

Lifting my legs in the air, I cross them at the ankles and get lost in the world of a rakish duke with questionable morals as I consume more candy floss than should be allowed.

This is unfair. Why are men better in fiction?

Petition to transform the entire male population into men written by women. Please and thank you.

"What in the ever-loving fuck are you doing?"

I hate the tinge of excitement that rushes through me at his deep, refined, and suspiciously calm voice.

This shit is really good if it managed to keep me from noticing his arrival.

"What does it look like I'm doing? I'm reading," I say without acknowledging his presence.

"And you couldn't do that in more decent clothes?"

I glance at him over my shoulder and kind of regret it because, apparently, I've forgotten just how illegally dazzling my husband is.

Clad in a navy-blue suit with a hand in his pocket, he looks straight off a fashion runway despite having been at the office all day.

I let my gaze roam over him shamelessly. Slick jet-black hair, frosty eyes, stone-cold face, and pursed lips…

I pause. There's a cut on his lower lip that's big enough to stand out.

"What are you wearing?" he asks.

I sigh. "Max Mara. Seriously, since when are you so interested in my dresses' designers?"

"Since they're not decent."

"They're decent enough."

"Enough to show the crack of your arse."

I glance over my shoulder, and, yup, the edge of my lace underwear is visible all right.

My cheeks heat, but I shrug. "Didn't realize we're entertaining the king. I'm on my own, relax."

"And if a staff member walked in?"

"Then they'd have something fun to remember me by."

I twirl the fluffy strands of candy floss around my fingers before bringing them to my mouth and sensually sucking on them. The sugar explodes on my tongue, but it's not just the sweetness that sends a rush of endorphins through me.

His eyes darken to a molten gray as they zero in on my hand.

I'm aware this is a dangerous strategy when I also want him, but I have to disarm him somehow. And if seduction is the only way, then I'll gladly play the game.

When I trace my tongue around my middle and index fingers suggestively, his nostrils flare and his jaw tenses. I take it further, deep throating my fingers and sucking and licking them with fervor, mimicking what I did to his fingers just the other day.

Although he remains still, I can feel his desire simmering beneath the smooth facade like a fire waiting to ignite. As he casually touches his watch, I think I sense his restraint slipping away, but then he remains still.

It's frustrating how he doesn't show anything on the surface.

Like a damn psycho.

Feeling like I won't get what I want, I slide my fingers out with a pop. "If you're done brooding, I have a very important scene to get back to—"

One moment I'm lying there, and the next, strong hands are wrapped around my ankles. I yelp as I'm flipped over, my legs parted, and Eli slams both his hands on either side of my head.

He looms over me, his body dangerously close to mine,

and I struggle to catch my breath. The air around us crackles with a charged intensity, every nerve in my body on edge. His scent fills my senses, overwhelming me with its intoxicating familiarity and drawing me in further. It's as if we're two magnets, irreSistibly pulled together by an invisible force.

"In that case, dear wife, it's better *we* give them something fun to remember us by."

And then his lips crash onto mine.

CHAPTER 18

AVA

A BURST OF WHITE STARS EXPLODES BEHIND MY eyelids as demanding, harsh lips claim mine in an abandon of fiery passion.

For a moment, my spinning head is so disoriented that I believe I'm in a strange dream.

But would I feel his heavy weight on top of me if I were? Would my stomach cramp at the sensation of his abs flexing and growing taut with every nip at my lips?

My mouth opens of its own accord—I blame the shocking turn of events—and he plunges his tongue between my teeth. It's a mess of biting, twisting, and sucking my soul through my lips.

He's kissing me.

After years of rejecting and humiliating me through a kiss, Eli King is the one who's kissing me right now.

And it's not a mere kiss. It's a possessive claim that's brimming with simmering darkness.

It strikes me with a stunning realization that Eli has the ability to perform every action with eclectic intimidation. And while he's controlled in everything, down to how many breaths he releases per minute, there's a raw quality about his kiss. The brush of his lips and the tug of his teeth are beautifully unrefined and abundantly unhinged.

He nibbles on my bottom lip and sinks his teeth into the soft cushion. I tense, expecting the bite, the blood, the humiliation, but he sucks on the assaulted skin and conquers my tongue again.

The sloppy sound of our clashing echoes in the air like an aphrodisiac.

I try to think why I should stop this, and while I fail miserably, my shaky hands lift to his chest in a half-arsed attempt to put an end to this or at least slow him down.

He's too intense. Too hard-core. I think he'll suck me dry and leave me hollow.

Still feasting on my mouth, Eli gathers both my wrists in one hand and slams them above my head. Over the cold pages of a book.

His other hand wraps around my throat in a vise grip until I feel my swallows against his palm.

A shock wave of desire rushes through my starved limbs and pools between my thighs. I rub them together in search of much-needed friction, half-amazed, half-horrified at how little it took to work me into a frenzy.

All of a sudden, Eli wrenches his mouth away from mine. Every fiber of my being mourns the loss, and I dart my tongue to lick my lips. I taste metal as I catch a glimpse of his reopened cut lip.

My pants echo in the air, and my skin prickles and throbs as if I've undergone a ruthless workout. Eli, on the other hand, breathes deeply and heavily, still looming over me with apprehensive power.

I want to sink my claws into that control and mess it all up.

Mess him all up.

It's only fair after he irrevocably ruined me.

"Is that all?" I try to sound nonchalant, which is partly a failure due to my trembling, slightly husky voice. "I'm kind of disappointed."

"Shut the fuck up, Ava." His rough voice echoes around us as he watches me with an edge of dangerous intent.

Apparently, I threw all my survival instincts out the window, because I wiggle underneath him and whisper, "Or what? You'll *make* me?"

A deep growl rips from his throat and sends a chill of dread and want through me. "Don't test me when I'm barely stopping myself."

"Stopping yourself from what?" I slide up and down again, this time opening my legs farther and rubbing my inner thigh against his erection.

His face tightens, the mask cracking around the edges and revealing a hint of the man I want to reach. "You don't want to know."

"Oh, I definitely do. There's nothing I want to know more than what goes on in that head of yours. Go ahead, humor me."

"What will I get in return?"

I smile sweetly. "My cooperation?"

His darkened gaze falls to my swollen lips, and any attempts at sarcasm fall flat. I grow hotter and stickier at his vicious undivided attention, squirming despite myself.

Damn him and his disruptive eyes.

They could win a war without any battles or troops.

He's going to kiss me again. I can feel it and taste it in the cloud of desire humming around us.

My eyes flutter closed in preparation for the beautifully fierce claim, but Eli releases and pushes off me in one seamless movement.

The protest that's about to fall out of me morphs into a yelp as he slides a hand around my waist and flips me onto my stomach as if I'm a doll.

I slap my hands on the floor for balance, my hair forming curtains on either side of my face.

"You want to know what I'm stopping myself from?" Eli's heavy body covers my back.

I quiver beneath his warm and ridiculously muscular frame. He's definitely packing for someone who looks lean, and even though I struggle to breathe, I don't dare protest.

I hear the rustling of clothes as he brushes my hair behind my ear, the feel of his big hand eliciting sharp tingles from my heated flesh.

His lips close around my earlobe before he sinks his teeth into the soft skin. I clamp my mouth shut to trap a whimper, but it escapes as a muffled moan.

"You had no business playing with my fire, Mrs. King, for you will *not* survive what I want to do to you."

A stroke of fabric touches my hands as he grips them and shoves them in front of me on the carpet. Though he threateningly covers me whole, he's holding his weight off, or he would've crushed me by now. A death I, astonishingly, wouldn't find revolting in the slightest.

I watch with bemused fascination as he wraps his tie around my wrists, securing them in a knot I couldn't undo even if I wanted to.

A deep thrill bursts inside me in magenta colors at the idea of being tied up by Eli. Never in my wildest dreams did I imagine this scene. My skin burns with excitement so fervent, stickiness coats my thighs and dryness takes refuge at the back of my throat.

"And what do you want to do to me?" I hear myself murmur in a voice I don't recognize. I didn't even know I could sound so crazy with desire, so turned on by a man I was sure I'd written out of my heart and soul.

But maybe I overlooked my body in that process.

"I want to mark you, Mrs. King." He fists my hair and lifts me so my back is flush against his chest as his dark, lust-filled words roll into my ears. "I want to hurt you, bruise you, and own you so thoroughly, you'll be ruined for all other men. I want to feel your pain, see my welts on your porcelain skin. I want to choke your throat, bite your lips and nipples, and leave my presence across your whole body before I pound into your tight cunt so ruthlessly, you'll beg me to stop."

My temperature hikes up dangerously, and I'm surprised I don't go off like a box of fireworks. I'm so embarrassingly wet and burning with need, I'm afraid if I move and accidentally rub my pussy on the floor, I'll come right here and now.

A part of me knows I should be alarmed by his words, but I was never normal anyway.

My breaths leave me in shallow pants that bounce off the carpet and condense on my upper lip.

"So beg me to stop," he orders in deep, calm words. "This is your only chance to say the fucking words that will push me away for good."

"Don't…"

"Don't what?"

"Don't stop." I'm ashamed of how needy my words sound, but that feeling only lasts until his voice fills my ears again.

"You have no idea what the fuck you've signed up for, beautiful." The nickname is spoken as a snarl as he drops me back on the floor and positions himself behind me. "On your knees, arse in the air."

Awkwardly, and surprisingly, might I add, I comply, my elbows sinking into the carpet as I lift my hips slightly.

I can feel his hawklike gaze following my every movement with fierce intent, but before I contemplate looking at him, he shoves my dress up to my waist.

A sudden gust of cool air prickles across my skin as he forcefully shoves his hand beneath the fabric of my clothes. I gasp as he tears the material, exposing my bare breast to his grasp. His rough fingers wrap around it and twist my engorged nipple, sending waves of pleasure through me. I bite down on my lower lip in an attempt to stifle a whimper. But the sensation is too intense, too raw, and I can't help but let out a soft moan as he continues to explore my body with his skilled touch. Every nerve ending is on fire, every inch of skin tingling with desire as he takes control over me.

"You were walking around with no bra, wife?"

"The dress would be ruined by one."

"My male staff's careers would be ruined due to the lack of one." He pinches and twists again, sending jolts of pleasure to my core, then moves to the other one. "If you're in the mood to get them fired, all you have to do is ask."

"Don't be a dick…oh God."

"Don't be a flirt. I don't appreciate others looking at what's fucking mine." His shadow feels so massive right now, so grand in its ruthless intensity.

He shoves my underwear to my knees while still torturing my breasts and runs his finger along my dripping-wet slit.

My knees nearly fail me, and my elbows give up on me. My head falls on my bodice ripper novel, and my nostrils fill with the sweet scent of printed pages as Eli strokes my wetness with lazy fingers.

"So messy, Mrs. King. So fucking messy."

"It's your fault." I pant when he twists my nipple and then removes his hand.

"Promise you'll conduct yourself properly around the staff. You'll act like my wife."

"No…promise… Oh fuck." My words die out when he slaps my pussy. Throbbing pain mixes with pleasure, and I think I come a little.

"We'll try again. Say 'I promise to act and dress decently.'"

"N-no."

His hand comes down on my arse cheek this time, and I jerk, even as a foreign rush injects itself through my veins. "Again."

"No…"

His palm meets my pussy with a slap so hard, I reel, my cheeks about to implode from warmth, and yet my arousal looms so high, I feel an orgasm building with vicious intensity.

"Wrong answer. We can do this all night, Ava."

"It's still a no."

Three consecutive slaps come on my arse, and I cry out, my lips quivering and my pussy so wet, arousal drips between my thighs.

"You seem to be enjoying your punishment. Interesting." He parts my thighs, and I catch a glimpse of him kneeling behind me.

I moan when he grabs my arse cheeks, digging his fingers into the bruised skin.

And then he dives in, his tongue ravaging my swollen cunt. My nose sinks between the book's pages, tears, snot, and drool destroying the paperback thoroughly as Eli ruins me. The scent of my arousal mingles with the musty smell of books, creating a heady and intoxicating aroma that fills the air.

His tongue is rough yet gentle, devouring my pussy with a skillful touch. The texture of the book pages scratches against my nose, adding to the overwhelming sensation. He sucks on my clit until the pressure becomes unbearably hot. White stars dance behind my eyelids as I whimper in short, choppy breaths.

"Eli... Oh fuck, please..."

He wrenches his lips from my clit. "Say that again."

"Please..."

"My name. Say my name as you come on my face."

He thrusts his tongue in my opening, and I shamelessly ride his face, rocking back and forth. "Eli...I'm coming, I'm coming."

The orgasm hits me with a strength I haven't experienced before. It's as intense as that time in the bathroom, but it's...so much *more*.

The throbbing pain in my arse mixes with the pleasure he wrenches out of me, turning it cathartic, alien even.

It's a moment of pure, pulsating abandon, like a fire burning through every inch of my body, igniting my senses and melting my inhibitions.

I don't think I'll ever come down from the high, and for a while, I seem to lose all sense of my surroundings. When I'm coherent again, I'm slumped forward, the pages of the book are stuck to my cheek, and my ruined dress falls in tattered shreds around me.

Eli flips me around again like a doll and kneels over me with the aura of a deity.

I can see my juices glistening on his cut lip, and that somehow injects me with a strange sense of emptiness.

Who's the reason behind that cut?

Was he kissing some other woman behind my back?

"Ava?" he asks with his usual calmness, though two lines form on his forehead. "Can you hear me?"

I reach my bound hands to his face. "Who gave you the cut?"

Whatever concern gripped him flies away in a shroud of mist as he grabs my hands before I touch him, and although he undoes the knot, the rejection nearly obliterates me.

Gently but dispassionately, he massages the red prints his tie left on my skin, then lets my hands drop like lifeless snakes.

"It's nothing to concern you with."

He stands, casts one last cryptic look at me, and then walks out of the room, leaving me throbbing and feeling rejected with a searing sense of pain.

———

Eli left the house the night he shattered my world to pieces and went on a business trip to the States for a whole week.

After his swift exit from the library, the house, and my immediate vicinity, the only form of care I received was through Sam.

She found me in my bedroom with my nightgown bunched up as I stared at his angry flushed-pink handprints on my arse. So she produced some soothing gel, pills, and her usual poker face.

For the first time, I was happy for her emotionless existence because I couldn't bear the shame that was probably written all over my face.

She also probably ate a piece of the cake as a form of compassion for all the hours I spent stupidly making him the dinner he never ate. I spilled the soup down the drain and dumped the cake in the bin as if I were burying the humiliation that tugged on every corner of my soul.

The whole week, I indulged in overspending, pumping charities with Eli's money to cleanse his satanic soul, and practicing my cello harder than when I used to prepare for a competition.

After my last performance, I was called again to play for a nonprofit event that I think I aced. This time, there were no flowers, but there was a text.

Tin Man: Heard you're playing tonight.
Me: To what do I owe this honor? Do you finally realize that I exist?
Tin Man: Good luck.
Me: You're the one who'll need luck when I get my hands on you.

Tin Man: What will you do? When you get your hands on me, I mean.

Me: Oh, nothing much. Claw your eyes out, for starters.

Tin Man: Not a strong incentive to invite me to put myself in your vicinity.

Me: That's because you're a coward, dear husband. You can't handle me, so you run away as far as you can. Why don't you divorce me and spare us both the hassle?

Tin Man: The D-word is not going to happen, so you might as well remove it from your vocabulary. And it's not that I can't handle you. It's the other way around.

Me: You were the one who left, not the other way around.

Me: ?

Me: ??????

Tin Man: Better not agitate you before a performance.

Me: I hate you.

Tin Man: *thumbs-up emoji*

Me: If you don't come back by tomorrow, I'm moving out.

I did do well with that performance, mainly because I was fired up and so pissed off, I took the allegro up a notch. I was brave enough to invite both my parents and parents-in-law. A decision rather foolish in hindsight, considering Papa can't stand Uncle Aiden.

I'm glad I booked a private room at a members-only

Asian restaurant, so at least the rest of the guests won't call the police on us.

While I sit between Mama and Aunt Elsa—both women elegant in stunning cocktail dresses and chic hairstyles, Papa and Uncle Aiden, who are facing us, are more concerned with glaring at each other instead of consuming their food.

Papa is wearing an impeccable tuxedo with a white tie. His lean and muscular frame still fills the jacket and the room with a charismatic aura. Uncle Aiden, on the other hand, is clad in a tailored suit and a cocky smirk that I swear he passed down to his less likable son.

While Uncle Aiden has a ruthless reputation in the world, he's always been a doting uncle when it comes to me. Probably because Aunt Elsa takes her godmother role very seriously, just like Aunt Kim, Cecy's mum, takes hers when it comes to the headache, Ari.

Seeing the atmosphere tonight, I could've used my sister's presence. But apparently, she had a *very important secret mission*, which is probably following Remi around like a puppy. Or more like the Grim Reaper if we're being honest.

But then again, I'm the one with a social-butterfly reputation. Surely, I can handle this.

With a smile, I refill both their glasses of wine. "So, how are things lately, Papa?"

"They were fantastic until I saw this eyesore. Why is he here again, princess?"

"Because I'm her father-in-law," Uncle Aiden answers with a mocking edge. "And you're just livid that little Ava married into the King household. She even has our last name now. Must be sad to be you."

"A reality that can be rectified."

"But it won't."

"We'll see about that."

"Cole…" Mama says with the exasperation of someone who's dealt with this a thousand times. "It's Ava's night."

"Yes, Aiden," Aunt Elsa supplies. "You promised to play nice."

"I'm anything but nice, sweetheart. And this prick deserves everything but nice."

"I'm going to knock your teeth out," my father threatens.

"Papa, please," I plead. "Can't we enjoy dinner as a family?"

"Since when is Aiden your family?"

"Let me see…since she has *our* last name?"

Papa glares at him, and he smirks.

"Admit it and cut your losses, Cole."

"Ignore them." Aunt Elsa pats my hand and places a dumpling on my plate. "I'm so proud of you, honey. You looked so bright on the stage."

"Yes. You looked like a shining star, baby. I'm so happy you decided to follow your passion again." Mama strokes my shoulder.

I smile. "Aw, thanks."

"I'm sorry Eli couldn't make it," Aunt Elsa says in a sympathetic note.

My smile falters, but I refuse to let him ruin this for me, so I shrug. "You know him. Money and investment are more important to him than anything else. I don't mind."

"Well, I do. I'll have a talk with his father, who's been overworking him lately."

"Pretty sure he's overworking himself."

"If you need me to talk some sense into him, I'm only a phone call away."

I contemplate her offer. Aunt Elsa is the perfect weapon to use against her son, since he respects and cares for his mum a great deal.

"I'll take you up on that offer if needed," I say with a sly smile.

We dig into our food as Mum and Aunt Elsa work their diplomacies with their husbands who seem hell-bent on leaving the restaurant with black eyes and bruised ribs.

After a while, I excuse myself to the bathroom, and Mama says she'll come with me.

Brilliant.

I stay as long as possible in the stall, hoping she'll leave, but, sure enough, when I emerge, she's standing by the backlit mirrors, redoing her lipstick.

Hiding my disappointment, I wash my hands and retrieve my powder puff.

"You have anything to tell me, Ava?" She slides the lipstick back into her bag and stares at me.

I keep looking at the mirror, touching up the powder more slowly than necessary. "Um, no, why would I?"

"Am I imagining it, or have you been avoiding me?"

"Definitely imagining it." I plaster a smile on my face. She frowns.

Mama opens her mouth, then closes it. Ever since I was diagnosed as a teenager, she often has these moments of hesitation where she needs to measure her words before she says them. "How's the new medication treating you?"

"New?" I pause. "Oh, you mean compared to what

I remember from two years ago? It's fine. I take one at night."

"Only one?"

"Isn't that what the doctor changed it to? Sam told me that's the new prescription."

"Right." Another pause, another rolling of words in her mind. I wish she'd stop treating me like delicate china. This is part of the reason why I couldn't live with my parents anymore.

I love them, but they're too careful, too scared about touching me the wrong way or saying something that will trigger me into a fit of psychoSis.

That's partly why I enjoyed Eli's touch and, begrudgingly, his company. He's never treated me like I'm weak.

He's a bastard, yes, but he's always talked to me as if I were normal, even though he's fully in the loop about my issues.

"Is it affecting you negatively?" Mama asks. "If we need to have another consultation…"

"I'm fine. I live normally, arrange plants, read books, binge-watch films, and even meet friends—and not at clubs anymore. I play my cello comfortably, without pressure, and I enjoy every second of it. I've had no serious side effects, and I certainly don't want another consultation with a psychiatrist that makes me feel like I'm insane. I wish you'd stop suggesting that every time there's a problem, which there isn't at the moment."

"Oh, honey." Mama pulls me into a hug, and I realize my eyes are wet as she pats my back. "I'm sorry. So sorry. I just worry about you."

"I know." All too well. More than necessary. *This*

is why, even if I move out, I won't go back to her and Papa.

The desperation and hopelessness in their eyes would undo me.

While they've never purposely made me feel bad, I can't help thinking I'm the failure in their lives. If they only had Ari, they wouldn't be worried like this all the time.

When we pull apart, Mama fixes my hair. "I just want you to go out with me for brunch or coffee sometime. Nothing serious. I only want to catch up with my beautiful daughter."

"Yeah, sure. I can do that." I sniff and dab beneath my eyes.

She stands behind me as I fix my makeup again. "Is Eli treating you well?"

I meet her eyes in the mirror as I apply my lipstick. "Not well enough, but he will."

"That's my girl. Let me know if you need tips."

"Why do you have tips?"

"Because I used them on your papa."

"No way. He treats you like a goddess."

"Let's say that hasn't always been the case."

"You had to catch him?"

"Not entirely, but I kept him in his place when I had to."

"I love you more now."

She laughs, kisses my cheek, and tells me she'll wait outside.

As the door closes with a silent thud, I jerk and knock my bag and all its contents onto the tile floor.

With a curse, I squat and pick up my lipstick. My perfume bottle has opened, releasing a soothing floral scent in the air. As I grab it, static passes through my head, and a blurry image hits me.

The sweet, heady scent of blooming flowers fills my nostrils, mingling with the musky aroma of sweat and desire. Rough, calloused hands grip my naked waist, pulling me closer to a hard and powerful chest. Our bodies press together, skin on skin, igniting a primal heat between us. My nipples harden against the firm muscles beneath them, sending shivers of pleasure through me.

My arms reach up to encircle the neck of a man whose face is shrouded in darkness, but his presence is commanding and alluring.

And then I hear my voice echoing in the stillness: "We shouldn't do this. My husband would kill me if he found out."

CHAPTER 19
ELI

"IF YOU INVITED US TO WATCH YOUR DULL, brooding face, I suggest we do better things with our time."

I look up from my glass of water and glare at the headache Lan, who flashes me a wide grin.

"There he is. I thought we'd lost you for a minute there, Cousin, which wouldn't have been tragic since I can simply carry on your legacy."

"Lan, stop provoking people for fun." Bran elbows his brother.

They might be identical twins, but Lan could be spotted from outer space as a nuisance in the form of a ticking bomb. Bran's expression is softer and lacks all the maliciousness his brother managed to absorb in its entirety when they were in the womb.

Since I'm in the States, where most of my family members decided to lounge for a while, I thought I'd meet up with them.

I'm regretting the decision immensely.

We're in a recently opened bar with gaudy black-and-red wallpaper that clashes against the dimly lit atmosphere. Vintage posters and old-fashioned beer signs hang all around, giving off a nostalgic yet edgy vibe. Our group huddles in a booth toward the back of the establishment, seeking refuge from the deafening music blaring through the speakers and the never-ending buzz of conversation.

"You should've seen him during this entire week," my brother says from beside me, alerting us to his usually silent presence. "He's been in a worse mood than a presidential candidate losing the election."

"And you chose to shove this energy on us, Cray Cray?" Lan feigns a pout. "I'm disappointed."

"It's only fair you guys suffer along."

"Thanks for the support, little bro." I glare at him. "Greatly appreciated."

He merely shrugs and focuses back on his phone, probably texting with his fiancée. Bastard is so pussy whipped, he can't survive without her for a couple of hours.

The same is true for Lan, who only separated from his girl because she had some sort of spa retreat with her sister.

Bran was talking with his boyfriend on the phone during what was supposed to be a bathroom break while smiling and shaking his head. Sorry, he was talking with his *fiancé*, as that crazy heathen Nikolai loves to remind everyone. Honest to God, I can't see why the most well-mannered and possibly the most normal King grandchild is with a man who's the definition of a disaster.

They suspiciously work together, though, as stamped and approved by Uncle Levi.

The only reason Nikolai isn't here watching Bran like a creep and smiling to himself right now is because he couldn't get out of a meeting with Jeremy and their Mafia wagon.

"You should've brought Ava," Cecily says from my other side, still cross with me about the fact I came alone.

"What makes you think she would've wanted to

come?" I conceal the fact that the whole point behind this trip was to remove myself from her proximity.

"Of course she would've," she argues. "Even just for a get-together."

"Now, Cecy." Lan swirls his drink. "Can't you see that Eli's brooding episode is entirely because he's suffering from a distance?"

"You'll suffer from a distance between your food and toothless jaw," I say calmly.

"My, a threat. I thought you didn't deliver those, and if you do, only *sparingly*?" He smirks.

"Lan, come on," Bran says. "You're being unreasonable."

"Not to mention a twat," I add.

"I'm just stating the obvious. Not my fault everyone prefers to bury their heads in the sand and carry on with their merry lives."

"So you're a wake-up call?" Cecily asks with a roll of her eyes.

"A wake-up call, a hazard alarm, a breath of fresh air in the midst of stifling hypocrisy. Take your pick. At any rate, I'm indispensable."

"In hell and only possibly," I mutter.

"Don't worry, dear Cousin. I'll fight you fair and square for Satan's throne when we're there."

I stand. "I'm out."

Creigh follows, but I pat his shoulder.

"Seeing as I was bothering Your Highness, you'll be happy to know that I'm flying back home."

He nods.

"Pretend to be affected, wanker."

He clears his throat and adopts a fake-ass sorrowful expression. "I'll miss you, but I won't miss your awfully moody presence. Hug Mum and Dad on my behalf."

My brother envelops me in an embrace, and I return it, knowing full well he's as allergic to mushy shit as I am. Or probably more.

When my parents brought him to our house and introduced him as my new brother, I despised the idea of sharing space, personal possessions, and parental dedication with someone else.

But then he followed me around everywhere, albeit silently, and participated in every sort of mayhem I dished his way. Though he did accidentally snitch to our parents about our endeavors.

In a way, Creigh wormed his way into my life slowly but effectively—something he shares with my wife.

The only difference is that he's always—mostly—on my side, and I can say without a shadow of a doubt that I was lucky to have gained a brother. We might not share a drop of blood, but he's one of the few people I'd sacrifice anything for to keep safe.

"You're leaving?" Bran asks.

I nod. "It was good seeing you. As for your twin brother, it was a taxing hassle."

"The pleasure was *all* mine." Lan clasps my shoulder with a wide grin, then leans closer to whisper, "I'm coming back soon to raze your efforts to the ground, dear Cousin. Please prepare the red carpet."

"I'll prepare your funeral."

With that, I walk out of the bar and head to where Henderson is waiting with the car.

I'm only a few steps out when I hear a female voice call, "Eli."

I stop near the mahogany double doors and turn around to find Cecily hurrying in my direction, her silver hair flying in the wind.

When she reaches me, I continue staring at her without saying a word. She's the one who's stealing my precious time, so she better have a good reason.

She rubs her nose, a habit of discomfort, before she finally blurts, "Is everything okay with Ava?"

"I thought you FaceTime her all day?"

"Not *all* day."

"Every couple of hours for a few hours?"

"Why do you have to be so mean?"

"I'm not mean. I'm busy. If that's all…"

"Wait." She clears her throat. "Is there anything wrong concerning…you know."

"You can name it, Cecily. Her condition has a diagno-Sis, and it's called *psychosis*. Shying away from putting a name on it or treating it like it's taboo won't do anyone any good, least of all her. And she is fine, considering she picked up the cello of her own accord and is enjoying the spotlight again."

"I know. She sends me updates and footage of her performances."

"There you have it. I hope you told her you're proud of her courage."

"I don't need you to tell me that. I've been there for her our entire lives, and that will stay the same, even if we live continents apart." She pauses and watches me peculiarly. "You've changed."

"All human beings do."

"I'm still not sure whether it's for the better or the worse."

"I'll leave you to ponder that."

"Hold on." She steps in my way before I can move. "I'm thinking about going back to the UK for a couple of months until I'm sure she's okay."

"I strongly advise against that, and by 'strongly advise,' I mean don't do it."

"Why not?"

"Because you treat her with kid gloves. You baby her and cater to her every demand. You spoil her worse than her parents, and that is the exact opposite of what she needs."

"Well, I'm sorry I care for her mental well-being."

"Not with methods that help."

"And yours do?" she whisper-yells as she searches our empty surroundings. "Like that falling-down-the-stairs *accident*?"

"It *was* an accident."

"Yeah, right. No need to put on an act, Eli. Both of us know she becomes unpredictable during her episodes, which is why you should've gone with the more intense therapy option."

"And kill her spirit? Murder her creativity? Stifle her entire being?"

"Only temporarily. She would get better."

"The last time we did something *temporarily*, she almost vanished."

"We just need to keep an eye on her. Your vain false hope will make things worse. Her current medication only dulls her symptoms and doesn't target the root of the problem."

"You treating her like a delicate flower is what made things worse and caused her to spiral down that addiction path."

"But—"

"Enough," I grind out. "I'm her legal guardian and will not tolerate any interference in my decisions. Not even from you."

I walk away, but I hear her whisper, "She'll hurt you, you know."

"Good thing I'm the Tin Man," I say over my shoulder and catch a glimpse of Cecily's sad downward smile.

She probably recalls that time during Remi's birthday party a couple of years ago when Ava got drunk, which wasn't novel at that point in her life.

Once she had enough liquid courage, she stumbled toward me and jutted a finger in my chest. "I hate you, Tin Man."

Then she nearly fell and would've drowned in the pool if Cecily hadn't dragged her away.

I wish I were still at that point where I mildly noticed her and only found her slightly annoying.

Right now, however, I have a horrible feeling that if she cries again, I'll be prepared to do anything to stop the tears.

On my way to the car, Henderson appears by the driver's seat, his brows pinched together. He has a rather distinct disregard for the U.S. in general, and New York in particular, so he hasn't been especially thrilled about this business trip.

"There's no need to sulk like a snobbish Victorian, Henderson. We're leaving in a couple of hours."

"It's not that," he starts in a strange, careful tone. "Sam and I didn't wish to bother you until we'd done our due diligence and checked the facts."

"What facts?"

He hesitates for a beat. Henderson never hesitates. "Mrs. King is missing."

"She's *what*?" While my voice is calm, the roar of emotions rattle around me with the discrepancy of violence.

"After the recital, she sent Sam home and said she was having dinner with your and her parents, then spending the night at her parents' house. Sam saw them go to the restaurant together. The CCTV footage shows that she left the restaurant with them and got into her father's car. Sam checked with the butler of Mr. and Mrs. Nash, but he reported that Mrs. King did not, in fact, arrive home with her parents."

"Then where the fuck is she?"

"We're not sure. Sam thinks she told her parents to give her a lift somewhere, and since they did, that means they thought she was safe. Sam didn't want to alert them until we consulted with you."

My fist clenches and unclenches. She couldn't have already moved out like she threatened. Not without luggage, and definitely not without any of her precious cellos and her flamboyant pink car.

Or did she?

Cecily's words from earlier about how unpredictable Ava gets during her episodes strike me in the marrow of my bones.

She couldn't have gotten worse.

I stayed away so she wouldn't get worse. It was torture

to peel myself from her inviting body and that satisfied look in her eyes after I wrenched that orgasm out of her.

But the momentary blankness proved that I was wrong to touch her. *Again.*

That my inability to control my impulsive feral needs whenever I see her will prove to be the end of everything I've built during these years.

Sometimes, she'll walk around in barely there seductive clothes, and I'll hear the tick of my control slipping away. She'll smile in her signature sunny, bubbly way, and I'll reSist the urge to shield my eyes from the brightness.

Truth is, I couldn't have controlled myself for long, not when I've yearned to own her, shove her down and tie her up, eat her pussy, and then pound into her. Not when I've fantasized about watching her cunt stretch to accommodate me as she releases those panting moans.

Truth is, I've craved her so much that it hurts to look at her at times.

If someone had told me I'd come to want Ava in this absurdly carnal manner, I would've chucked them into the river like stale goods.

But here we are, years after she softly and courageously confessed her feelings to a cruel monster, knowing I'd hurt her, and now I think about nothing but that infuriating woman.

"How about the tracker on her phone?" I ask.

"It's turned off."

The need to plow a hole the size of my fist into the car pulses beneath my skin, but I keep a cool head. It's the only way to find her.

"Contact the Nash family driver, wake him up if need

be, and ask where they dropped her off. Get access to all surveillance cameras in the area." I slide into the car and tell the chauffeur, "Airport. Now. If the jet isn't ready, we'll take the first commercial flight."

Henderson slides into the passenger seat, phone to his ear, and talks to his connections with the Met Police.

This is why I shouldn't have removed the security detail. But, tapping my finger on the back of my phone, I recall what happened the last time I had someone tail her.

She was triggered and nearly threw herself off a building.

That shit will never happen again.

I'll personally find my wife.

———

After a thorough scanning of the area where Ava was dropped off and hours of restless flying on my part, we locate her.

My wife decided to attend a house party with her despicable waste-of-space friends at Bonneville's flat in Chelsea's suburbs.

It's seven in the morning, but I ring the doorbell impatiently, my mood having darkened to its worst after more than twenty-four hours without sleep.

When no answer comes in the first two seconds, I ring again. And again.

On the fourth ring, groans can be heard from inside. *Male* groans. Pieces of absolute rubbish who'll be chucked through a window if they happen to be breathing the same air as my wife.

The door finally opens, revealing a sleepy Bonneville,

who's still wearing her shimmering silver party dress, her hair messier than her life.

Her puffy eyes widen upon seeing me. "Eli...? Ava said you were in the States."

"Key word being *were*." I push past her, forsaking any manners as I march into her upper-floor flat that she only managed to afford due to trust funds.

A plush rug spills beneath my feet as I step into the room. The walls are adorned with wallpaper in dark classical tones, adding an air of sophistication to the space. Crystal chandeliers hang from the ceiling, casting a warm glow and highlighting the luxurious furnishings. It's a grand display of opulence and excess, a testament to wealth and indulgence. But there's a chaotic mix of modern and vintage decor, as if the owner couldn't decide on a specific style and simply bought everything she could afford.

Like Ava, Bonneville is a spender, not an earner. However, unlike Ava, who's a classical music genius with technical prowess that made her teachers weep, Bonneville has no talent aside from dressing up as if every day is a party.

My feet halt at the edge of the spacious living room, where at least a dozen people are sleeping in unflattering positions. One guy is hugging a plant. A girl is sleeping in a U shape over the arm of a sofa.

I don't give any of the hedonistic empty shells a second thought, because the reason I even walked into this mess isn't here.

"Where is she?" I whip my head toward Bonneville, who's trying to stroke her hair into submission.

"Uh...she was here. I don't know where she went. You see, we might have gotten a bit crazy last night—"

"Did you let her drink?"

"No, I didn't, but…"

"But you threw a party where alcohol was more available than your morals."

"She crashed the party. She said she wanted to catch up. I swear I didn't do it on purpose."

I stride past her and into one of the bedrooms, walking in on unflattering bodies in naked slumber, but since none of them is my target, I walk to the next.

It's not until I reach Bonneville's upper-floor pool that overlooks the city that I pause.

And it's entirely due to a soft string of laughter. *Very* familiar laughter. And it's not directed at me.

I shove through the entrance with the devil on my shoulder.

Sure enough, Ava's sitting on the edge of the pool, her dress hiked up dangerously close to her upper thighs so that she can dip her sparkly pink toes in the water.

My blood roars in my veins upon seeing a half naked man floating in the pool and grinning at her with boyish charm.

"So what is it you wanted to ask me? You can do so after you join me. Come on," he says with a note of flirtation that I'm well aware the likes of him can't help.

Ava is nothing less than a goddess whose altar every man with a functioning dick yearns to burn incense at. She's a beautiful rose with mesmerizing energy that intoxicates the flies circling her, but like all roses, her stem is crowded with thorns.

It's me. I'm the thorns.

"I don't have my bathing suit." She's still smiling at the motherfucker.

If I hold his head underwater, how long will it take for the waste of space to spit his last breaths? Or perhaps I can smash his skull on the edge of the pool?

Choices. Choices.

He opens his mouth, which will be ripped at the corners Joker style. "You can improvise."

"I'll improvise your early death if you're not careful, Mr. Elliot." I stride into the scene and stand by my wife.

Ava looks up at me, and a sudden tension overtakes her. Her once-relaxed expression is now frozen in shock, and her mouth hangs open, devoid of even a hint of a smile or playful energy.

I hate that she regards me with obscene hatred. That my mere presence is enough to sour her mood. I thought she was getting comfortable around me lately, but perhaps I was sorely mistaken.

"What are you doing here?" she whispers.

"Weren't you the one who begged me to come home, *darling*?"

I expect the usual retort of *I did not beg you* or *you wish* or, better yet, for her to play along with the married-couple antics we engage in when in public. However, she lowers her head and chooses to stare at the water.

"We're leaving." I grab her arm and yank her to her feet in the midst of her splashing. She follows the motion, and the dress finally drops.

"Do you want to go, Ava?" asks the idiot who's begging to be waterboarded.

I step forward. "Do you want to breathe for one more minute?"

My wife places a firm hand on my chest. "Thanks, V, but I'm fine. Have a nice day."

"You, too," he says with a note of disappointment.

Before I can contemplate his fate once and for all, Ava slides her arm into mine and basically drags me out of the area.

"V was only keeping me company because I couldn't sleep. No need to be a dick."

I narrow my eyes on the top of her head. She couldn't sleep because she didn't take her meds, and the one person she chose to entertain her was Vance Elliot.

Not me. *Vance.*

"You know," I say in an eerily calm tone, "the more you take a liking to him, the faster he'll disappear."

She swallows and stares up at me with fear mixed with mysterious apprehension.

This is new.

Ava has never been scared of me. Not really. She wouldn't have battled me every step of the way if she were.

She resents me, yes, but she doesn't fear me.

Her emotions for me went through a long phase of idolization that morphed into chronic hatred and remained there. In the hatred.

"And me?" she asks in a low whisper.

"You?"

"What will happen to me? Will you make me disappear as well if you catch me with another man?"

I stop at the bottom of the stairs and lift her chin with two fingers as I speak with chilling calm. "Will I catch you with another man, Mrs. King?"

She shakes her head twice.

"Then the question is redundant."

"And what if it happens…hypothetically?"

"Hypothetically, I'll claim you on his corpse so you recall who the fuck you belong to."

Her lips part, but before she can say anything, Bonneville reappears, all freshened up and with a fake smile plastered on her face.

"You found her. Great! Do you want to join me for breakfast?"

"No." I grab my wife's hand and drag her out of the house.

She follows, but it's abnormal. My wife feels too pliant, a bit lethargic, and lacks the usual spark that shines brighter than the northern lights.

The deterioration of her state that I was afraid of didn't happen, but something else did.

What, I don't know.

Henderson releases a small breath upon seeing us.

Ava shields her eyes from the rare English sun before she gets in.

As soon as we're in the back seat, I turn toward her as she stares at the streets, too absent-minded. "Was the party worth missing your medication and worrying Sam shitless?"

"I took my meds and Sam is allergic to concern."

"When you speak to me, you look at me."

She reluctantly turns around and crosses her arms, her defiant streak barely visible beneath the sheen of mysterious meekness.

Something's off. Logically, she'd be giving me attitude for disappearing on her for a week by now.

But she's not.

In fact, she looks a bit guilty.

"What happened?" I ask with practiced calm.

A delicate swallow works her soft throat. "Nothing. I just wanted to catch up with friends."

"Those people are *not* your friends. I know it, your brain knows it, and even your heart would know it too if you opened it wide enough."

"Last time I opened it, you cracked it to pieces."

I grind my molars. "If this is your attempt at changing the subject, I'd like to inform you that it's an epic failure."

"It's my attempt to remind myself that I shouldn't be feeling this way. You have no morals, so why should I?"

"Feeling this way about what?"

"Forget it." She throws a hand in the air. "I'm surprised you showed up, after all. Were you scared I would move out?"

There she is.

I raise a brow. "Would you have?"

"No." She stares out the window again. "But I would've moved all your stuff to the garden and left it to soak in the rain."

CHAPTER 20
AVA

MY ATTEMPTS TO AVOID ELI FALL APART THREE
days later when I shove the door to his home office open.

I stand there in the entrance, keeping my distance.

During my hiding episodes whenever Eli is in the house,
I realized that the main reason for my tormented thoughts
and foolish moral code was because I believed the lie that
is our marriage.

When, in reality, this is a charade that was agreed upon
merely for convenience reasons.

We're not in a relationship, and therefore, I shouldn't
feel guilty about my supposed cheating episode that I barely
recall.

I went around asking the possible suspects at Gemma's
party, but I came up with nothing. Of course, the devil
himself interrupted me before I could pop the routine
question to V.

Gemma said she had no idea, so I wondered out loud
if it could have been Ollie, because I clearly remember his
interest from my last year at uni. Gemma mentioned that
was impossible since he left for some tropical island a long
time ago.

Which struck me as weird, because he gets red as a

tomato in the sun, and I never thought of him as the type who would indefinitely cut himself off from our gang in the UK.

But anyway, after my husband interrupted my conversation with V, I could've texted him. The real reason I haven't is because a part of me doesn't want to find out.

That part also believes that despite our lack of feelings for each other, our marriage is based on commitment. My husband is many things, but I've never witnessed him giving any other woman his attention. Even when they do everything possible to vie for it.

And that's part of the reason for my crushing guilt.

Upon my intrusion, Eli looks up from the screen in front of him, and I'm struck by how sinfully beautiful the man is.

Control oozes from his set lips and neutral expression down to the rolled cuffs of his shirt stretching around his veiny muscular forearms.

Something is distinctively out of order, though—his eyes.

They take me in from top to bottom in a blur of heat and a whisper of danger. He observes my pink silk camisole, matching shorts, and fluffy slippers with undivided interest.

The man is a national security hazard trapped in taut muscles and lurking behind a gentleman's facade.

Sometimes, I feel like I'm the only one who sees him unfiltered like this. Other times, I recall that I hold no importance in his life and quietly put myself back in my place.

His gaze slides back up to my face. I grow hot under his attention, but I refuse to appear bothered, so I stare back, unblinking.

"Does this mark the termination of you throwing a tantrum?" he asks with veiled amusement.

"Throwing a tantrum?"

"Wasn't that the case? You were clearly upset about my impromptu trip to the States and naturally couldn't move on without throwing your own punches."

He thinks I'm avoiding him because of that? Well, I suppose anything is better than him finding out the actual reason.

During this time, I've been obsessing and trying to find myself loopholes. I remember Anni mentioning we were exclusive. So I asked Cecily if that no-other-people agreement was really in place.

My bestie just laughed. "Are you kidding? He didn't allow other people around you for years. You think he would've started after he married you? I've never seen him with any other woman, if that's what you're worried about."

Only, that was *not* what worried me.

Though it was a nice confirmation, despite my telling Cecily, "As if."

To which she shook her head and smiled. I'm telling you, she will be so proud of me when I bring this prick down in an epic revenge comeback.

Though I don't feel like I'm fit for that after what I've done.

I cross my arms as if that will hide the hardening of my nipples and choose to ignore his comments. "Sam mentioned you wanted me to get ready for a charity event?"

"Correct."

"And what makes you believe I'd want to attend?"

"The very simple fact that you're my wife."

"And that magically transforms me into a doll you parade around at events?"

"It transforms you into my plus-one. Quit the dramatics." He goes back to typing away at his laptop, dismissing me entirely.

No, he didn't.

Plastering on a fake smile, I enter his expansive office that reflects its owner's enigmatic personality. The walls are a deep shade of forest green and worn dark brown. The leather sofa is large and dull and could use some color and fluffy plushies. The sleek black glass table reflects the light from the window and shares the color of his soul.

I saunter to the bookshelves across from his desk, retrieve a boring book about corporate management, then throw it on the floor.

A few more follow and suffer the same tragic fate before I feel done with my endeavor.

Then I push the coffee table so that it's not symmetrical and shove the perfectly placed throw pillows onto the rug.

"What are you doing?" The edge in his voice would scare me if I weren't burning in a furnace of pettiness.

"Being dramatic, so when you ask me to quit the dramatics, it'll be due to something concrete." I lift a fountain pen cube and then hold it up.

"Don't."

I smile sweetly as I let it fall to the ground. It shatters, and black ink splatters on the rug, pillows, shelves, and me.

Everywhere.

"Oops," I say genuinely. I didn't think it was full of ink.

There go my legs and my fluffy dog slippers. How long does it take to clean ink from the skin?

I fully expect Eli to lunge at me and bite my neck off leopard style. This would be a good time to apologize and say I only meant to tease his OCD tendencies and not yank them out in a barbaric fashion.

"Come here. Now." He taps the desk twice, his eyes tapering, his voice so eerily calm, it sends a chill through my veins.

"Wh-why?" I curse myself for the stutter.

"Don't make me stand up and come get you."

My legs move of their own accord, a languid feeling settling at the bottom of my stomach.

I stop at the far side of the desk, leaning my back against it for balance more than anything.

His scent seeps into my bones and intoxicates me worse than any alcohol. To avoid looking at him, I pretend to be bored as I study my nails. "So, um, maybe you shouldn't have kept a full inkpot in your office if you have OCD?"

"Shut up, Ava."

"I'm just offering a useful suggestion."

"I said." He stands up threateningly and presses his hands on either side of me on the desk surface, then slowly lowers himself so that his face is level with mine. I cease breathing when his lips skim my ear. "Shut that fucking mouth before I fill it with something that's guaranteed to keep it occupied."

My held breath comes out in a strangled pant. His lips burn my skin, but it's no worse than the volcano of his words, because why the hell do I feel thirsty all of a sudden?

"You're easier on the eyes when you behave, Mrs.

King." He still speaks in my ear, as if injecting sweet poison into my veins. "So, how about you be a good girl, change into a decent dress, and meet me downstairs?"

His warm lips leave my ear, but he doesn't budge. His nearness and intimidating presence sear into me like a cigarette against paper. It's hopeless to deny my desire for his touch when every inch of my body aches for it.

I'm wet just due to the vibrations of his deep, rough voice.

It's ridiculous at this point.

"Or what?" I hear myself whisper as I steal a glance at him, then regret it immediately.

His gaze darkens to a sinful gray as he gathers both my wrists in one hand, holds them hostage at my back, and drops his other hand to my waist.

"Or..." His large palm slides up, squeezing my breast through the flimsy camisole, and my nipples harden under his touch as he lets his hand trail down, grabs my arse, and shoves me against him. "I'll punish you, Mrs. King."

A shaky whimper leaves me as his unmistakable hardness settles against the bottom of my stomach. "How will you do that?" I murmur.

"Don't play with fire."

"Maybe I'm craving the burn."

"Fuck, Ava." He releases me and steps back slowly, almost as if he doesn't want to. "Go get ready before I do something I can't undo."

The sizzling print of his skin on mine still burns, heat coils damp and warm between my legs, but I refuse to surrender to the whip of rejection.

Again.

What a fool.

I came here intent on giving him a piece of my mind and retreating, but I ended up like a mouse between the cat's claws.

And I would've let him go further if he'd so much as kissed me.

Obviously, my pride packed up and left the building at some point.

I cross my arms over my chest. His eyes zoom in on my cleavage, and I will myself to breathe properly.

"If you want me to come with you, I have conditions."

His brows rise as he focuses back on my face. "Conditions. Plural?"

"Two, actually."

"And what makes you think you can dish out conditions?"

"A small fact called 'being your wife,'" I throw his words back at him with a sweet smile.

"I don't see the correlation."

"You have to treat me like a queen, duh, and that means making me happy. Complying with my conditions makes me happy. As the saying goes, happy wife, happy life."

He narrows his eyes, and I can tell he's done with my shit and is losing patience faster than his receding morals. "Carry on. Let's hear the conditions."

"One, if you want me to go to a cocktail party or event or whatever, you have to give me ample time to prepare and ask me first."

"You have an hour to prepare, and I already had Sam ask you."

"She didn't ask me—she carried out your *order*. So it's time for you to rectify that."

"And how am I to do that?"

"Simple. Ask me."

I know Eli is used to having his orders met. He single-handedly made our friend group, Cecy included, scared of his wrath because he told them that if I strayed off the crystal—also spelled *boring*—path he'd drawn for me, they'd regret it.

The only rebel is Lan, and Eli always makes him pay for it, whether by revealing his questionable actions to his parents, smashing a few of his precious statues (did it three times; one of them was prior to an important competition), or simply broadcasting his weaknesses to Mia after they became an item.

Eli is cold, merciless, and, above all, perSistent. If he delivers a threat, he'll act on it.

And he doesn't, under any circumstances, take orders nor compromise on things that don't benefit him. If you see him compromising, it's because he already has the upper hand and methodically planned out the situation to play in his favor.

So I fully expect the rearing of his monster horns and harden myself to stand my ground. This is the hill I choose to die on, thank you very much.

"Will you be my plus-one for the charity event, Mrs. King?"

My lips part. "You...asked."

"Isn't that what you wanted?" He sounds fully exasperated and on the verge of pulling away.

"Yeah, um. I will honor you with my presence."

"I couldn't be more *thrilled*," he says with a complete poker face. "What's the second condition?"

This one is tricky, but here goes nothing. I push my shoulders back. "You'll spend time with me."

"I am currently spending time with you."

"I don't mean like this."

"Then?"

"Like I asked you that night."

"I am *not* going to court you, Ava."

"Then don't. It's not the Middle Ages anyway. But you must spend time with me."

"Doing what exactly?"

"I don't know. Talking?"

"Is that another word for fighting?"

"Reading books?"

"We don't read the same books. Besides, do you expect me to sit there and watch you vandalize precious paperbacks?"

"I'm highlighting passages that stand out to me. No vandalizing happens. But you're right, we'll need to call the ambulance for your issues if you witness that for an extended period of time. Besides, no offense, but your taste in books sucks. How about we watch films?"

"I don't watch films."

"Who doesn't watch films?"

"And who does for half a day every day?"

I shrug. "I'll think of something, but you must promise to dedicate time, and I don't mean after hours when you're done being Machiavelli. I mean a proper afternoon."

So that was me shooting for the moon, but, hey, doesn't hurt to try. The guilt of cheating on him might not stop eating me from the inside, especially since I have no idea who the man was, but the only way to move past it is to dedicate myself to the here and now.

I should be as faithful as he is. Even if we're fake.

And then I'll break his heart. Well, maybe spirit, since he doesn't have a heart.

Eli watches me for a beat, and I try my hardest not to crack under the pressure and compromise.

To my utter astonishment, he nods.

"Really?" I ask in bewilderment. "You won't change your mind?"

"Do you want me to change my mind?"

"Nooo!" I jump him, wrapping my arms around his neck. My feet lift off the ground because he's too damn tall.

He plants a hand on my waist, swaying back a step at my sudden attack.

It isn't until his scent saturates my nostrils that I realize I'm hugging Eli.

Shit.

I fall back to the floor as naturally as humanly possible before I bolt to the door.

"I'll see you in an hour!" I say with unabashed excitement, and I catch the most peculiar view in my peripheral vision.

Eli's smiling, but it's hauntingly...sad.

———

So when my husband mentioned putting on a decent dress, he didn't specify the color, cut, nor tightness level.

I gracefully descend the stairs, my feet lightly tapping against each step as I make my way down in a flowing maxi dress. The deep-red chiffon fabric drapes off my shoulders, exposing just a hint of my cleavage when I'm standing up, but it will reveal half my breasts if I bend.

He doesn't know that, though.

As I move, the high slit of the dress shows off my slender leg, accentuated by the stunning golden studded shoes that adorn my feet. My matching clutch dangles from my fingers while my long red-and-gold earrings sway with every step, complementing the intricate design of my necklace.

I swept my hair into an elegant twist, leaving a few wispy strands to frame my face. A bold shade of red paints my lips, completing the glamorous look I've carefully put together.

While I felt beautiful when I looked in the mirror, none of that compares to the flashes of warmth that sizzle through me as Eli freezes upon seeing me.

He looks sharp and maddeningly masculine in a tailored tuxedo, black bow tie, and studded cuff links that match my—and, apparently, his—favorite watch.

The trimmed sides of his hair are precisely groomed, while the longer top is styled to perfection, highlighting his rough and raw features.

His jaw clenches as he watches me while absent-mindedly rolling his wedding band around his finger.

Wild energy radiates from him, drawing me closer despite my better judgment. Tension grows stronger between us as his piercing gaze roams over my face, lingering on my breasts and legs with a hunger that sends my senses alight. It's as if his hands are shoving the dress off of me, caressing me roughly, manhandling me, *taking* me.

For a moment, I forget how to walk properly, and I remind myself to do it one step at a time.

When I reach the bottom of the stairs, I keep my distance, afraid I'll catch fire if I get too close.

"No need to scowl." I try to lighten the mood with my joyful energy. "I was only twenty minutes late. That's, like, a record."

"You'll change immediately."

"But why?" I stare down at myself. "I'm perfectly decent."

"You're perfectly *tempting*."

I swallow past the dryness in my throat. "I'm not changing. It took me a long time to get ready and feel beautiful. You won't take that away."

"Ava…"

"Either I go like this, or I don't go at all."

"Don't go at all."

I release an exasperated sound. "Nope. I'm going. I didn't get ready for nothing."

Before he can lock me in my ivory tower, I breeze past him to the door, where Leo is waiting.

He opens the car door, dutifully not looking at me, probably because his boss would fire him faster than he could blink.

"At least remove the lipstick," Eli says as soon as he slips into the back seat beside me.

I pout. "But it's part of the outfit."

"Remove it, Ava."

"Nuh-uh." I blow him a kiss in an attempt to lighten the mood. "Relax, *darling*, it's only lipstick—"

The words aren't completely out of my mouth when his hand wraps around my throat, killing any protest.

His face is so close, I can taste the mint on his breath.

"Don't fuck with me, Ava. I do not appreciate sharing my things with others, am I clear?"

A tremor of fear and something unashamedly sexual course through me. He really will give me hell if he finds out about the cheating, won't he?

I attempt to pull back, but he grabs a fistful of my hair until his lips brush mine with every word. "Am I fucking clear?"

I nod, merely so he'll release me.

"Use your voice."

"Yeah, fine." My lips stroke his with the words, and a rush of heat pools between my thighs.

The car moves, and Eli does release me, then lounges back in his seat like a monarch. I give him the stink eye as I retrieve my mirror and start to salvage my hair.

"It took me half an hour to do this," I grumble.

"And only seconds to ruin," he shoots back with that dreadful sadism. This man is a hard nut to crack. I honestly have no clue what makes him tick aside from OCD tendencies.

He's as opaque as a muddy pond ravaged by a downpour.

I stare at my reflection in the mirror and gasp. "Eli!"

"Yes?"

"You left finger marks on my neck."

"Good." He stares at his handiwork. "That way everyone will know who the fuck you belong to."

Frustration bubbles in my veins, and I express it by kicking his feet and spending the entirety of the ride powdering the hell out of my neck and somewhat managing to fix my hair.

When we reach the venue, I'm hit with the beautiful smell of sage that the organizers picked for the event. A charity for protecting endangered trees and the planet.

The grand hall seems to stretch on for miles, large enough to hold multiple events at once. However, on this particular evening, it's filled to the brim with influential and self-important individuals, all dressed in elegant tuxedos and sparkling cocktail dresses. Among them, a handful of celebrities sign autographs on cards and even body parts.

In the background, a quartet plays a sophisticated arrangement of pop songs in classical compositions, filling the air with enchanting melodies. Waiters glide through the crowd in their smart uniforms, expertly balancing trays of drinks while guests indulge in the opulent buffet spread out before them.

The atmosphere is one of luxury and extravagance, a true feast for all the senses that seems to bore my husband to death.

I walk in with my arm draped through his and a blinding smile on my face. I say hi to all my acquaintances and even people I don't recognize when they greet me.

Eli's face remains stone-cold like the grinch he is. Honestly, he should be thankful I'm offering my social skills to balance his lack of diplomacy.

As we're stopped by some of his acquaintances, he disentangles his arm from mine and drops it to my waist, his palm covering my hip and sensually stroking the dress.

Although a whole piece of clothing separates his skin from mine, it's no different than if he were wedging his tongue inside me.

I blink away the erotic image of him doing just that

the last time he touched me and focus on the conversation. He's speaking to a business partner, a tall Black man with salt-and-pepper hair who's probably in his late forties. He looks both elegant and easygoing, his broad smile instantly inviting.

"Matthew, meet my wife," Eli says. "Ava King."

"How do you do?" Mathew grabs my hand, but before he can bow and kiss it like a gentleman, Eli swiftly pulls it away.

"I told you to meet her, not to touch her," he says with calm collectedness.

Before I can reprimand him, Matthew bursts out laughing and then raises his glass. "I better go find my wife before this one here starts a riot. It was nice to meet you, Mrs. King, and I wish you the best of luck. You'll need it."

"Nice to meet you, too." I smile and wave.

As he walks away, Eli faces me as he grabs a glass of water from a passing waiter. "Stop smiling so much."

"Stop being a dick. I'm trying to be nice since you're obviously not."

"I'm not, huh?"

"Hello? Have you seen your face in the mirror lately? It could be effectively used to scare children so they'll behave."

His lips tip up in an amused smile, but before I can bask in that, Leo walks in silently and whispers something in his boss's ear.

When he retreats, Eli looks at me. "I need to check on some business associates. Will you be fine on your own for a while?"

"Sure."

"Behave, Mrs. King." He leans in and brushes his lips to my cheek.

As he walks away, I can feel my face getting as red as my outfit.

Talk about teasing.

I mingle with some acquaintances and manage to refuse every alcohol offer. It's easier to settle with water and some mocktails now.

As I'm standing with a group of musicians, insanely jealous of their accomplishments and thinking of a way to escape the line of questioning about competitions, a familiar face strides toward me.

I excuse myself and walk to Vance. "Oh, hey, what a lovely surprise to see you here, V."

"I should be saying that. You look absolutely ravishing, Ava."

"Don't let my husband hear you say that." I laugh.

"Then he should appreciate what he has, don't you think?" The suggestive tone in his words doesn't escape me.

Oh God.

Is it him?

I fooled around with V in school, mostly out of spite, and he's a true charmer, nice, understanding, and really gentle.

He's the exact opposite of my husband, and although I've never thought of myself as the type who cheats, I can see why Vance would fit the profile of a man I'd choose for an affair.

"Hey, V." I step closer so no one overhears. "As you know, I forgot some events the past couple of years."

"Yes, you mentioned that the other time."

"Did something happen that I should be aware of?"

"I'm surprised it took you so long to ask." His blue eyes brighten up. "I knew you wouldn't forget everything."

I think I'm going to be sick.

His head slides close to mine, but before he can say anything, he's shoved away and then punched so hard, he hits the buffet table and plunges into the extravagant food. Blood explodes from his nose as a shock of red instantly covers his face.

Did...Eli just break V's nose?

A collective gasp from the attendees echoes in the air as my husband stares at his handiwork with ferocious eyes. "I warned you, but you didn't listen."

Gemma grabs Eli's arm. "It's okay..."

He pushes her away before I can think about her presence beside him, grabs my arm, and drags me behind him.

"Eli, wait..." I literally jog in freaking heels to keep up with his wide strides.

"I'm done waiting." He shoves me into a supply room, jams the door closed, and presses my back against the wall.

"Don't you think you went overboard—"

My words are cut off when his angry words roll off me. "Is he the fucker you cheated on me with?"

CHAPTER 21

AVA

MY LIPS PART AS I STARE UP INTO ELI'S EYES.

Cold.

Harsh.

Filled with rage.

I've never seen him like this before. He's calm and collected to a fault. It's alien to see him lose his cool, let alone drift into the lawless territory of anger.

His grip tightens on my arms, fingers digging into my flesh. It hurts, but I show no reaction and release no sound. I'm enchanted and completely taken in by his ruthless aura and...

Gray.

His eyes are so gray and enraged, it's a miracle they don't flash into darkness and suck me into their depths.

"Answer the question." His calm words are deceptive, too clipped, too wild.

"Wh-what...?" I swallow past the dryness making my tongue stick to the back of my throat. "What do you mean?"

"You know exactly what I mean. Did you fall into Vance Elliot's arms while wearing my fucking ring, Ava?"

"I don't remember marrying you, let alone anything

that happened after, so how could I know?" I sound too defensive to my own ears, and I hate it. I hate how guilt chips at my emotions and how utterly horrible I feel when faced with his anger.

"You told Bonneville you had a flashback in which you saw yourself kissing another man and asked her who it might be."

My limbs shake as my lips part in complete bewilderment. Gemma is supposed to be the nice friend who's never confrontational nor a trouble stirrer, but I should've known better. Her true colors have been showing ever since she set her greedy eyes on Eli.

In the beginning, I thought it was a harmless crush, even if it annoyed me. I told myself she thinks he's hot like a million other girls do and stopped my mind from conjuring a plot to get rid of her like I did with his previous conquests at uni.

I'm paying for my kindness. I should've known a spoiled princess like her gets everything she wants. Her target is now my husband, and if it means she has to slander me and break my trust to get him, that's exactly what she'll do.

And just like that, my worst nightmare about Eli finding out has come true.

I clear my throat. "It...was nothing."

"Don't you dare lie to me."

"It was a flashback, but you said the other flashback I had, about being tied up and being forced to consume pills, proved to be wrong."

A muscle clenches in his jaw.

A violent blare goes off in my head.

"You lied," I say instead of asking it as a question, because I'm sure he did.

He made me believe my memories were false.

"Why?" My voice carries in the silence like a ticking bomb. "Why did you lie to me?"

"Because you weren't ready to find out that tying you up for hours on end and forcing you to undergo rehab was the only method to stop your alcoholism."

I flinch, my head thudding against the door as if he slapped me. No. It wouldn't have hurt this bad if he'd actually slapped me.

And it's not only due to my forced rehab nor that he, of all people, was the one who performed it.

No.

It's the confirmation that I did, in fact, cheat on him.

All this time, part of me has felt guilty, but the other part has held on to the hope that it was a false memory like the one where I was tied up in bed.

But now that I know it's true, my bad morals crush me. In reality, I shouldn't be feeling this bad when I'm planning revenge for my broken heart, but I do.

My form of revenge should never include something as despicable as cheating.

It hurts me more than it does him. If I stooped that low, surely that would give him the green light to cheat as well.

There's no way in hell I'll be able to survive that.

"How many?" he asks in a voice tighter than my insides.

"How many what?"

"How many times did you offer what's mine to another man?"

I shake my head.

"Answer the fucking question, Ava."

"I don't know! I don't remember." My voice burns with my strangling tears.

"But you do remember fucking someone else." His eerily controlled voice sends a shiver through me as he releases my arm and wraps a hand around my throat. "What did you give him access to, hmm?" He shoves my dress down, and it rips as my breasts pop out, my skin flushed. I quiver when he twists my hard nipple. "Did you let him touch my fucking tits?"

Letting my dress hang in tatters at my waist, he wedges a hand between my legs and cups my pussy. His eyes flash when he's met with my naked skin. "Did you wear nothing beneath the dress in preparation for your rendezvous with your lover, Mrs. King?"

I want to say it was mainly to tease him, but apparently, my tongue is twisted in knots. Once again, my only reaction is a shake of my head.

"That doesn't deny that you let him touch my property. *My* cunt."

"I—I really don't know." My whisper translates the smashing weight of my guilt and utter loss, but to my shame, it also communicates my absurd arousal, which he can touch with his fingers.

"But you do know. You love blowing men kisses, having them eat from your fingers like fucking dogs. You love the attention and making those fools come back for more."

"That was before we got married."

"Was it, though? You still love the attention, the spotlight, the role of a goddess to men, but here's the thing." He releases me, flips me around, and shoves me against the door. His fingers press against my nape as warm lips meet my ear. "I'm the only man who'll offer you attention, and my cock is the only cock you'll take between your legs."

Then he's on me, his hand shoving my dress up to my waist, his heavy frame gluing to my back as he parts my legs.

I can hear the rustle of clothes before I feel the prodding of something large and unmistakable at my pussy.

A trembling breath escapes me as I grab the uneven edges of the door. The cool surface hardens my nipples and stimulates my warm skin.

He slides the crown of his cock up and down my slick slit, eliciting sharp, horrifying pleasure from the depths of my soul. "I'm going to fuck you, hard, until you're officially owned and dripping with my cum, Mrs. King."

Any protest I have ends in a strangled whimper when he slides inside me.

My body tenses, my insides clench, and he meets unmistakable reSistance.

Eli's movements halt.

I cease breathing.

The world stops rotating.

His hand wraps around my throat, angling my head back so his lips are inches from mine.

"Tell me you're just tense, and this isn't what I think it is."

"You...you said we had sex." I pant.

"I never said that."

Oh God.

Oh God.

This is actually the first time I've had sex. Against a door.

In a supply room.

While he's angry.

Pain explodes inside me in tones of bright orange as the reSistance finally breaks against his cock. Without him even having to do anything.

As usual, he destroys things with his mere existence.

Eli starts to pull out, but I sink my nails into his arm, digging them violently into his jacket. "Don't you dare fucking stop. You took my virginity, so you better make this worth it."

"Fuck." He plunges in again, panting in my ear like an animal.

I cry out, the pain spreading from my pussy to my stomach, then straight to my heart.

Everything hurts, whether my body or my soul, but I bite my lower lip, adamant to take it.

"Fuck," he murmurs again as he finds a rhythm, deep but slow and sinfully consuming.

My head bangs against the door as the pain slowly morphs into pleasure. My tongue wets my lower lip over the aching marks my teeth left. I'm shaking all over, my legs unstable and my head trapped in a messy fog. In a sense, Eli's hand around my throat is the only thing keeping me upright.

And sane.

So I bite his forefinger that's resting near my mouth and sink my teeth into it as I rock against him.

"Fuck." He goes stronger, his rhythm increasing in both depth and intensity as he breathes harshly. His thumb finds my clit, and he rubs and teases me in circles as he fucks me into oblivion.

I'm so wet, the in-and-out of his cock echoes in the room like a dark symphony of lust. It's obscene that I'm even getting so into this considering the circumstances, but I am, so much so that I grow more aroused with each measured thrust.

Eli pulls out almost completely, then drives in again, hitting a sensitive spot inside me.

A violent sensation thrashes through me. White stars dance behind my eyes as I let it wash over me in a consuming wave. I bite his finger harder as muffled moans slip out of me.

The orgasm is the strongest I've ever had, but also the most painful.

"Christ. Fuck!" He grabs a handful of my waist as he goes deep and fast, his teeth sinking into the side of my neck, sucking the flesh. "Mine," he growls against my neck as he comes inside me in one ruthless go and warmth fills me.

And then his lips replace his finger as he kisses me senseless. It's a mess of teeth, tongues, and primal frustration that spreads from inside me to where we're connected.

Being kissed by Eli is a beautiful torment. It's addictive. It's toxic. It's sweetly poisonous.

He pulls out of me, and I feel sticky wetness sliding down my thighs.

I'm still reeling from the throbbing orgasm as he nips my lips one final time before he pulls back.

He holds my arm as I turn around, probably sensing I'm unable to stand on my own.

My dress is still bunched up to my waist, and I follow his darkened eyes as they take in the sight of his cum mixed with my blood. The pink fluid slides down my thighs and pools in my precious shoes.

"Guess this means I didn't cheat on you," I whisper, my voice hoarse, my body aching everywhere.

Down to my stupid heart.

He steps toward me.

I hold up a hand. "Stay the hell away from me."

I straighten my dress and clean up as much as possible, my lips set in a dignified line as I reSist the urge to bawl my eyes out.

There's no way in hell I'll let him see me break down. Not now.

Once I'm done, I turn around to leave.

A jacket is draped around my shoulders, and Eli pulls the pins from my hair, setting it free. His scent saturates my nostrils, and I loathe that I take any form of solace from it. Or the fact he smells a bit like me.

Though something tells me his darkness will stifle my flowery scent soon enough.

He's destructive like that.

"I told you—" My words end in a yelp when he picks me up and carries me bridal style in his arms.

"To stay away. I heard. As it seems, I refuse to let you walk out in front of the entire world looking freshly fucked and allow small-dicked simpletons to picture how you look in the throes of passion. So unless you're in the mood to watch me go on a murder spree, stay fucking still."

I look away as my chin trembles and a bitter tear slides down my cheek.

———

The ride back to the house passes in a blur. My thoughts are a jumbled mess of violent emotions and hungry desire. A sick need for more and a wish to never do this again. I'm so tired, I want to fall asleep and possibly not wake up.

Not face the reality of whatever happened tonight.

So I do just that. I lean my head against the window and close my eyes. My hyperawareness of Eli's presence doesn't stop me from going under.

In my sleepy haze, I feel large hands pulling me away from the window. Something soft wipes the insides of my sticky thighs and gently strokes my sore pussy.

I let out a whimper. Eli curses under his breath.

Or I think he does.

When I come back to the world of the living, I feel him carrying me in his arms. I'm still wearing his jacket and morbidly invaded by his scent.

I can't escape it nor him.

It's like I'm stuck in a loop.

Instead of opening my eyes, I keep them shut. The last thing I want is a confrontation with him. I feel so raw. So fragile. So emotional.

If I speak, he'll dish out his favorite description of me—dramatic—and shelve me as mentally unstable.

And that's not what I want him to think of me.

Even if I actually am. Even if he's well aware of my situation. The panic attack he witnessed a few weeks ago should be the only thing he knows of my true self.

So I remain relaxed, my eyes closed and my hands tucked in my lap as he walks to what I assume is the entrance hall.

"Is everything okay?" Sam's voice filters through.

He comes to a halt, and I feel his eyes studying my face so intently, I resist the urge to squirm. "Not quite."

"Is she…?" Sam clears her throat. "Want me to help put her to bed?"

"I'll do it." He starts walking again, and I contemplate opening my eyes and asking for Sam.

As much as I liked comparing their emotionless behavior, she's by far much better company than he is. At least she listens to me talk nonstop, doesn't judge me, and even helps out with my different endeavors and half-baked hobbies.

But the chance to wake up and call for her slips between my fingers like sand as Eli takes the stairs with impressive speed.

He places me on my bed and disappears.

Oh. That wasn't so bad. Though one would think he'd at least cover me.

What a prick.

I start to open my eyes, but I hear noise coming from the bathroom. I go back to playing asleep, managing to relax as his footsteps echo in the room. Soon after, he sits me up and the mattress dips under his weight as he removes the jacket. Goose bumps erupt on my skin, and heat pulses through me. However, I remain still as he pulls down the zipper excruciatingly slowly and trails his fingers over my back in a sensual caress. Then he slides the dress away attentively, as if he's preventing the fabric from hurting my skin.

As I sit stark naked in front of him, I feel his gaze taking in my every slope and curve as he grabs my hip and wraps a hand around my throat.

Tension burns in the air hotter than a furnace, and I

can't banish the images of him fucking me against the door from my head.

I wish I'd hated it. I really, really wish I regretted it, but the truth is, it was everything I wanted and more.

I just dislike the circumstances.

Eli carries me in his arms for the third time tonight and walks me to what I assume is the bathroom. Warm water envelops my skin as he carefully sinks my entire body in it and leans my head against the bathtub's pillow.

The temperature is a much-needed balm for my aching core, and I reSist wiggling my toes. There's a rustle of clothes before the water swirls with movement.

I don't realize he's joining me until I feel him position my body between his legs, and then he leans me back against his taut muscles and rests my head on his shoulder.

Holy hell.

Is Eli taking a bath with me right now?

My skin heats, and I'm thankful for the water that acts as a camouflage to my chaotic state.

This is such a cruel predicament. How am I supposed to play pretend when his majestic body molds to mine? Hell, I can feel his semi nudging against my arse.

The first time he's gotten naked in my presence, and I don't get to see it. Fantastic.

Only, Eli didn't just join me in the bath. I smell my favorite honey-and-roses shower gel, and then, to my utter surprise, Eli washes me. He starts with my arms and my breasts, then goes down below. I relax as much as possible, despite the circumstances, and he lifts each of my legs up to clean the insides.

Most of the time, his arm is draped around my waist to keep me balanced.

It's almost impossible to not let out any sounds, so whenever I don't feel his eyes on my face, I bite my lower lip.

Being bathed by my emotionally stunted husband wasn't on my bingo card this year.

Excuse me while I freak out a little.

He takes his time cleaning every bit of my skin, exhibiting an amount of patience I know for a fact he's not capable of.

Wait.

Is this another cruel dream of mine?

My stomach sinks at the very possible realization, but instead of surrendering to the gloom, I choose to live in the moment.

Even if it is a dream.

After what seems like forever, Eli wipes my face with a lukewarm towel, removing every ounce of dolling up I attempted.

This time, I contemplate stopping him. Yes, he saw me without makeup when I woke up in the hospital, but that's the only time he has and, if I have a say, ever will.

I just don't feel as confident without a layer of high-end products. Especially not in front of him.

The pampering session ends too soon as he lifts me in his arms, wraps a towel around me, and carries me out. Again, he takes his time drying me gently and with ease, as if he's used to this.

Used to this?

What a bizarre thought.

He sits me on the bed again. Only, this time, it's against the headboard instead of himself. With featherlight touches, he slides a soft nightgown over my head and tucks me in, pulling the silk duvet to my chin.

I can feel his eyes on my face, and before I can hide underneath the covers, he wraps his fingers around my throat and strokes my pulse point as he brushes his lips against my forehead.

My mouth parts, and I'm surprised I don't explode like a box of dynamite.

Who is this person? He's not the Eli I know.

This is definitely not the Eli who accused me of cheating on him and claimed me like an animal less than an hour ago.

However, when he says, "Sleep well, Mrs. King," I do just that, the bitterness from earlier slowly withering away. I surrender to the darkness, even if it means I'll have to wake up from this gut-wrenchingly sweet dream.

CHAPTER 22

AVA

IT'S NOT A SURPRISE WHEN I WAKE UP TO FIND myself alone in the vast cold bed.

For a moment, I believe everything was a cruel dream. However, the soreness between my legs negates that thought.

I did, in fact, lose my virginity to the man I vowed to hate for the rest of my days.

And I loved it.

Kill me now.

Seeing as it's eight in the morning, I change into the first dress I get my hands on, put on some makeup, and run down the stairs.

That's the worst idea ever. My sore pussy aches, and my legs shake with every little movement. So I walk slowly, grabbing the handrail for balance like a toddler who's learning how to walk.

My heart shrinks behind my rib cage when I find only Sam in the kitchen, going about her cleaning rituals.

She doesn't hide her surprise upon seeing me. "Morning. I didn't think you'd be up this early. I'll prepare your smoothie in a minute."

"It's fine, I'll do it myself." I open the fridge and grab a banana and a bowl of strawberries.

"I insist." She smoothly pulls them from my hand.

"I can handle a smoothie. I won't break your precious blender."

"Doubtful." She doesn't even sound sarcastic.

With a sigh, I slide onto one of the stools across from her, cradling my chin on my palm. "Hey, Sam?"

"Yes?" She's turned away, washing the strawberries and then putting them in the blender.

"Were you the one who bathed me and changed my clothes last night?"

"Who else would it have been?" she says absent-mindedly.

My lips part.

She's lying to my face.

Makes me think about the times she might have concealed the truth from me. Why would she? Why would Eli? He also lied about the rehab.

Additionally, Ari and Mama lied about that and said I decided to get clean and Eli helped. He didn't help. He *forced* me to get clean, and while I'm thankful for the lack of alcoholism in my life, that doesn't negate how it came to be.

Unless they don't know? I wouldn't be surprised if he hid the facts from them so they wouldn't interfere with his madness.

Cecy is the only one who said she was just happy I got over it, without providing details.

Why is everyone lying to me?

Frustration bubbles in my veins with the lethality of a ticking bomb.

I'd expect that from my family, from Cecy even,

because they all love to be overprotective, but not from Eli. I thought he was the only one who didn't pity me.

The thought of him being with me, marrying me, just because he decided to be a philanthropist all of a sudden makes me sick.

I'll lock myself in the psychiatric ward if he so much as feels sorry for me.

I won't be able to handle it.

Not from him.

Not after everything that's transpired between us.

I can't handle feeling small in front of him, of all people.

"Are you sure Eli didn't help?" I ask Sam with a calm I don't feel.

The sound of the blender echoes in the air before she stops it and pours the smoothie in my cup, taking her time as if she didn't hear me.

Finally, she slides the cup in front of me and wipes her hands with a napkin. "What makes you believe that?"

"My memories, maybe."

Unless...they were my imagination. The thought of that sends a tremor through me, and I take a huge gulp of the smoothie to stop myself from hyperventilating.

Are my hallucinations getting more real now? I swear I could feel his hands all over me, his lips on my forehead, his gentle care.

"Please tell me they're real memories," I say in a small panicked voice. "Please, Sam."

"They are," she says simply. "He carried you and refused my help to get you to bed."

"Oh, thank God." I breathe heavily until my rhythm

goes back to normal, then narrow my eyes on her. "In that case, why did you lie?"

"I figured it'd make things simpler."

"Well, it doesn't. I want the truth, even if it hurts." Which, in this case, it doesn't.

She offers me a small smile, then turns around to disassemble the blender while I wallow in the truth that everything from last night was real.

No idea which I liked better. The sex or everything that followed.

"Did Eli leave early?" I ask.

"Yes." As always, Sam doesn't elaborate and never will, even with a gun to her head.

"Can you give more detail?"

"Like?"

"Why did he leave early?"

"You'll have to ask Henderson. I manage the household, not his schedule."

"Speaking of the household, why don't I see half the staff? The men, in particular?"

"They were sacked. The replacements will be women."

My mouth hangs open. "Don't tell me Eli did that?"

"Who else has that type of authority here?"

The fucking tyrant. He really kept his word about the male staff.

"By the way." Sam reaches into her apron and retrieves a small box. "He left this for you."

I clutch it with a questioning look until I see the label.

The morning-after pill.

The ticking bomb reaches the explosion point, and the burst shocks me to my bones.

That's it.

I'm going to unleash all hell on the bastard.

———

That afternoon, I change into the raciest, most revealing black miniskirt I own, which barely covers my arse, and pair it with a deep-V-neck pink top that reveals a generous portion of my breasts. Just to be extra, I finish the outfit with knee-high pink boots.

Then I head to King Enterprises, armed with pettiness, rage, and my husband's least favorite genre—drama.

I walk into the company's grand reception hall, smiling and waving at anyone who looks at me. Once I'm by the reception area, I demand family access. The guy ogles my chest for a solid ten seconds.

His colleague, a Black woman with short hair and adorable earrings, who looks young enough to have freshly graduated from uni, stares at him uncomfortably.

I knock the counter. "I'm over here, Mister..." I read his tag: "Tyler."

"Certainly, Mrs. King." He looks at the girl, who smiles at me shyly. "Do your job properly, Hailey! Call the security team and ask for an access tag."

"I'm sorry, sir." She falls over herself with apologies and grabs the phone with a shaky hand.

I narrow my eyes on him. "You do it, Tyler."

"Mrs. King, Hailey is a junior receptionist..."

"Did I ask you to talk back? Pick up that phone, and do your job." I stare at him, unblinking.

"Certainly." He cowers and takes the phone from her still-trembling hands.

Pricks like him only bark at those lower than them. It makes them feel grandiose about their miserable lives.

As he speaks on the phone, I lean over to Hailey and smile. "Love your earrings. They're so pretty."

She blushes and smiles tentatively. "Thanks. They're actually my late gran's."

"Your gran had fantastic taste."

"She did. She was a fashionista."

"Badass."

"I love your boots," she says in a low voice, surveying her surroundings. "You look like Barbie."

"Aw, that's so sweet. Thanks, Hailey."

Her smile widens, but it soon disappears when Tyler speaks. "I'm afraid Mr. Eli King and his asSistant joined Mr. Aiden King and Mrs. Teal Astor for a site inspection today."

"I didn't ask you to inquire about his whereabouts. I only need the access. Or do I have to repeat that slower so you'll understand?"

He purses his lips, but he nods again. "Certainly."

Soon after, a big buff security guy smiles at me and gives me a tag that he says gives me access to the management floors. Sweet.

I start to walk, then stop and smile at the girl. "You look after yourself, Hailey. It was nice meeting you."

"You, too, Mrs. King."

"Call me 'Ava.' We're about the same age, girl."

I offer Tyler a disappointed shake of my head and saunter to the lift. Naturally, I go to snoop in Eli's office. Leo's asSistants—he has two—don't even attempt to stop me.

If anything, the middle-aged woman and the young guy stare at me with unmasked fascination, as if I'm an exotic animal.

I smile, compliment the guy's tie and the woman's beautiful lipstick shade and ask her for the brand's name. After I make a mental note to add it to my extravagant shopping cart, I walk inside.

My husband's office is as cold as his soul. Neutral beige colors, a skyline view of London, and rows of horrific books about management, finance, and things he can bullshit his way through better than Machiavelli.

I walk to his desk and stop when I find a framed picture from our wedding. Lifting it, I sit in his chair and stare.

He's kissing me at the altar, a possessive arm wrapped around my waist and his lips almost eating my face.

My eyes are closed, and I look happy. *I think*.

For some reason, I don't like that I don't remember that kiss. It seems vital.

A question nags in the back of my mind. Why does he have it on his desk? He has no pictures of our wedding in his home office.

Not ones that I've seen, at least.

After what seems like half an hour of useless pondering, I slide it back to its previous position.

Hmm. What can I do to inject some life into this mechanical space?

I mess up the pens on his desk, mix the papers together, and wish I'd brought my candy floss to dirty his sofa.

I leave his office, a new idea popping into my head. There's nothing my husband hates more than other men. He made that clear way before he married me.

To this day, I have no idea why he became my watch-dog after I started attending uni. He made it impossible for me to go home with any guy. However, I did the same for him with girls, so it seemed like a little game we played.

Pathetically, driving away each other's romantic interests was the only thing we shared at the time.

Who knew there'd be a day when we'd have a legitimate claim on each other?

Anyway, Remi is a perfect candidate to ruffle Eli's feathers. As I leave, I tell Henderson's asSistants, "When Mr. King comes back, can you tell him I'm catching up with Remi at Steel Corp?"

They nod. I thank them and then head to the other unnecessarily huge corporation my husband holds a role in.

This time, it's easier to get in since the receptionist isn't as insufferable as Tyler. Instead of going to Eli's office there, though, I go to Remi's.

His secretary, a tall redhead, stands and tries to stop me. "Mr. Astor is...rather preoccupied, miss."

"Don't worry, he'll love this." I place a forefinger to my mouth. "I ordered his favorite sushi. When it arrives, please bring it in."

I open the door to Remi's office and stand in a dramatic pose. "Surprise, Rems!"

My jaw nearly hits the floor when I find Remi kissing a girl against the wall. And it's not just any girl.

It's my headache of a sister. Ari.

Upon hearing me, he immediately wrenches himself away from her, but the little shit wraps her arms around his neck. "Go away, Ava."

"Ariella Jasmine Nash!" I stride toward them with big-sister rage radiating from me in waves.

"What's up, Ava Dahlia King?" she asks with visible annoyance.

"You think this is funny?"

"Nope. I thought we were calling each other by our middle names."

Remi has the decency to appear a bit ruffled and even gives me an apologetic look. "It's not what it looks like."

"It's *exactly* what it looks like." Ari slides her arm around him and leans her head against his bicep. "We're getting married in maybe six months."

"No, we're not." He gently pushes her away.

"He'll come around." She continues smiling at him like an idiot, then gives me an exasperated glance. "He'd come around sooner if you hadn't interrupted. Thanks for nothing, Sis."

"So it's *my* fault?"

"Duh."

"I can't believe this." I catch her by the ear. "Shouldn't you be at uni?"

"I have two hours free."

"And you chose to spend them here?"

"I do that every day. Let me go."

She manages to release herself while I'm distracted with glaring at Remi.

"Don't look at me. I never encouraged her."

"Your tongue down my throat certainly did," my sister says with glee.

"Ari!" I shout.

"Ariella," Remi scolds at the same time.

"Don't care. I'm going now. Try not to miss me too much. I'll text later." She attacks Remi in a hug before he can dodge it, then she kisses my cheek once and whispers, "Don't pussy block me again. That's totally against the girl honor code."

Then she saunters outside, humming a happy tune and probably planning to broadcast what just happened to the entire world.

"What the hell did I get myself into?" Remi plops on the sofa after she disappears.

"One word." I join him. "Trouble."

He stares at the now-closed door. Remi is classically handsome. High straight nose, slightly curly brown hair, whiskey-colored eyes, and sharp, unforgettable features. A European prince through and through. He literally has aristocratic French and English blood, as he likes to remind us.

A heavy sigh rushes out of him. "Is there a chance she'll give up?"

"Not when you encouraged her. Besides, seeing as she's had a major crush on you since she was thirteen, I don't believe giving up is on the menu."

"Sort of like you, huh?" he jokes.

"Yeah, well, if you break her heart, you'll have me to answer to."

He smiles with no apparent humor, then seems to sober up. "What brings you here?"

"Your company?"

He finally notices my outfit, and his brows shoot up to his hairline. "Does that include my funeral? Because if Eli sees you dressed like this beside me, he'll have my head."

"Don't be a wuss. Why are you scared of him?"

"I'm not scared of him. I just value my life."

I roll my eyes. "Honestly, all of you seem to be my friends until he tells you to back off."

"Hey! I refuse to take part in any fight. Especially a nonsensical one like this."

"Nonsensical?"

"Come on, Ava. Everyone knows you love him."

"I do *not*."

"You surely look at him like you do."

"You mean as if I *hate* him?"

"There's a fine line between love and hate, and you've been teetering on it for a long time."

"You're talking nonsense."

"And you're still in denial. But anyway, bugger off before he comes back. He's graced us with his tiresome presence today and is hell-bent on turning everyone into insufferable workaholics like himself. I don't need to give him incentive to up the wanker behavior a notch."

"You're just jealous because he has a better position than you even though you only have to work for one company."

"If you want us to believe you don't love him, you might want to tone down the protectiveness."

I raise my hand to pinch him when the door nearly flies off its hinges.

My husband stands there, his glare seeping into me so deeply, I struggle to breathe.

He looks at me with renewed intensity.

Nefarious intent.

My own god of war.

CHAPTER 23
ELI

I'VE ALWAYS BEEN A CREATURE OF CONTROL.

Emotions, mild or strong, are a nonnegotiable sign of weakness.

I never lose my cool nor let feelings cloud my judgment or, worse, interfere with my decisions.

Sangfroid is the way of life Dad and Grandpa implemented in me from a young age.

They said the moment I allow any form of emotion to take over, it's too late.

In my twenty-nine years of life, I've been the epitome of detachment and the personification of pretend indulgence. I've never liked anything too much nor too little. Never succumbed to impulsiveness nor addictions. Never wanted anything and didn't get it.

Never lost my cool.

I've never started a fight nor punched someone—except for that fucker Vance. If a person crosses me, they get eliminated swiftly and silently.

Dirtying my hands is out of the question.

Being obsessed to the point of madness should be entirely blasphemous.

Yet the woman who's looking at me with a spark of a

challenge is single-handedly smashing all my principles into a fucking abyss.

A hot edge of bright red rage seeps from my chest to the tip of my thumb that's rolling my wedding band.

This unsettling feeling hasn't ebbed since Henderson whispered in my ear that Ava didn't only show up at King Enterprises, but she also got bored and decided to visit Remi at Steel Corporation for some *fun*.

I stood up and walked out of an important post-inspection meeting with overseas government officials and couldn't hear whatever excuses my father offered on my behalf.

Henderson and his asSistants failed to mention that my hindrance of a wife did all this while dressed in what looks like unfinished clothing.

Sexy-as-fuck erotic clothes that show half her tits and will expose her arse and cunt if she stands in the bloody wind.

Remi rises, buttons his jacket, and raises both hands in the air. "For insurance and criminal record reasons, I didn't invite her over."

"Seriously?" Ava slides her sparkling blue eyes to him. "You just become a traitor upon seeing him?"

"The right description is *pacifist*, peasant. My lordship is at the height of my impressive youth and would rather not end up floating in the Thames's unsanitary water."

"Then maybe you shouldn't have endangered said youth, Rems." It's a fucking miracle I sound calm as I stroll in, shoving a hand in my pocket.

"Mate." He wraps an arm around my shoulder. "Surely, you know I'd never look at Ava that way. Matter of fact, she walked in on me on the verge of shagging her sister and saved me and the universe in time."

"Oh my God! You just said it was a mistake and it wasn't what it looked like."

"That was before a pissed-off Eli showed up at my door hell-bent on murder. I must set the record straight. If I were to look at any of the Nash sisters, it would never be you." He observes his surroundings as if searching for a hidden camera. "But I ask that you don't repeat those words to Ariella, or she'll camp outside my house with an engagement ring."

"Is that so?" I say while glaring at my wife's generous décolletage and crossed long bare legs.

As if the whole debacle isn't enough, she's wearing pink fucking boots.

She purses her lips and glares back, although red covers her cheeks. God. This woman doesn't back down from a fight, even while knowing full well I'd crush her to smithereens.

But she never breaks, not really.

A few cracks might appear in her armor, but she's fully equipped to bounce back up and glue her fractured parts together one piece at a time.

"Absolutely," Remi says, choosing to actively ignore the brewing war happening in his office. "Actually, I asked her to leave right before you came in."

"And I refused." She examines her fingernails, feigning nonchalance she obviously doesn't feel. "In fact, you're interrupting. Do you mind?"

"I do." I release myself from Remi's grip and stand in front of her. She has to crane her head to peer up at me. "We're leaving. Now."

"You don't tell me what to do."

She's such a fucking brat sometimes; I want to punish her for it.

Turn her skin red.

My sick desire for her rages inside me, demanding that I throw her down and tie her up before I proceed to choke, pound, fuck, and own every inch of her rebellion.

The image of my cum mixed with her blood shouldn't have turned me on, but it did, and I'm not even sorry.

She's mine.

Only mine.

Body and fucking soul.

And the harder she fights that, the more drastic my measures to own her become.

I punched someone publicly for her last night, generated a few headlines that Henderson suppressed and my father shook his head at me for.

However, the need to do it again hasn't left me. That and the fucking seething lust that flows in my veins instead of blood.

Maybe I need to see a doctor for my issues. Surely, it's entirely unacceptable that I want her so much, a rush of heat engulfs me day in and day out like a vengeful curse.

Tension radiates between us as she holds my glare. Something she's been doing more often lately. So I say, "Either you get up and stand in front of me, or I throw you over my shoulder."

She narrows her eyes. "You wouldn't."

"Try me."

"You'll offer every single one of the employees a front-row view of my arse, so *you* try me. By all means, *babe*."

I shrug my jacket off with methodical movements. Her eyes widen when I grab her hand and shove it into the sleeve.

She attempts to fight, but it's no use as I slide her other arm in, then unfasten her belt and use it to tighten the jacket around her waist.

"What are you doing, Eli?!"

"Removing access to the view." I lean in and whisper in her ear, "*My* view."

Then, as promised, I throw her over my shoulder. The jacket almost reaches her knees, but I still wrap an arm over the material at her upper thigh so no accidents happen.

Ava yelps and I feel her reaching both hands out. "Rems! Help me."

I level him with a glare.

He rubs his ear. "I'm afraid I have temporary loss of hearing. Oh my, better check with my GP. Shit's serious."

"Remi!" Ava shouts, but I can hear the suppressed laughter in her voice. "Are you blind, too?"

"No, I ain't seen nothing. I ain't seen nothing. Matter of fact, I'm blind in my left eye and forty-three percent blind in my right eye. I don't see much of nothing. Matter of fact, I can't even see you, sir."

"Are you quoting a meme? You damn traitor!" She tries to hold on to the doorframe, but I easily pull her free.

"Byeeee!" Remi calls as his asSistant cranes her head, gawking at the scene. "Have fun, kids! Remember, play safe!"

"Remiiii!" Ava shouts, pleading her case one final time.

When I round the corner and press the lift's button, she lets her head fall to my back but only after she bangs on it with her fist a few times.

"Put me down. I can walk on my own," she hisses.

"You should've accepted that option when I first gave it to you."

"Eli! Everyone is looking."

"And? Don't you love attention?"

"Not like this. Oh God." She groans and buries her face in my back. Her hands grab my shirt, and she sinks her nails into my sides like a kitten.

I ignore the inquisitive gazes and suppressed giggles from the female staff as I walk my wife, caveman style, to my office. Henderson trails off in the midst of talking to his asSistants while they nearly fall over from shock.

"Send me the report for the afternoon meeting and any decisions made in my absence, Henderson."

He takes a few more seconds than needed to recover before he nods. "Already done, sir."

I nod back and then stroll inside my office. The space is a bit smaller than the one at King Enterprises, but it's an identical copy in everything else.

Same decor, the same sofa, the same coffee table, and the exact same books.

After I kick the door closed, I throw my wife on the sofa.

She bounces right back up, her face red and her nostrils flaring.

I ignore her and go to settle behind my desk. "Give me thirty minutes to salvage the mess you caused before I take you home."

"How...?" She storms in my direction and stops in front of my desk, and although I'm not looking at her, I can sense the flames erupting from her with the rage of an active volcano. "How *dare* you humiliate me in front of everyone?"

"I wouldn't call it humiliation, considering you're my wife, but even if it were, it's not my fault that you picked the wrong choice."

"You...you...you caveman!"

"That insult was extremely anticlimactic after all the stuttering. Surely, you could've come up with something better." I skim over the notes Henderson sent. "Now be quiet so I can focus."

"I only came here to return this." She slams a pill on the desk and glares at me. "Next time, don't delegate your dirty work to Sam, and have the balls to look me in the eye when you give it to me."

I grab the pill and then place it in her hand again, all the while staring her in the fucking face.

"There. Are we done?"

Her chin trembles. "You bastard...you...damn Tin Man! You don't get to tell me what to do with my body. Whether I take Plan B or contraceptives is only up to me. Do you think you have a say in it?"

"No, which is why I gave you the fucking choice, Ava. You think I don't want to pump you full of my cum, put a dozen children in you, and tie you to me for life? Because I very much do. But we both know you are *not* ready for that, so I gave you the option. I didn't force you to take the pill—I only put it on the table in case you want it."

"Do you want me to take it?" Her voice has lost some of its fire, but it's still as antagonizing as her entire existence.

"I will offer no say in the matter."

"But I want to hear your thoughts."

"You won't." Because I do want to fucking tie her to me and offer her no way out.

I hadn't thought much about it before, but after last night, blind possessiveness has been rushing in my ears and constricting my chest.

There's no way in fuck I'll let another man touch her after I put *my* mark on her. She still has a faint hickey on her neck despite the obnoxious amount of makeup she used to hide it. and I'll make sure that never disappears.

So she's always stamped with evidence of *my* ownership.

A kid—or a few—would make her mine for good. Though there are two pesky inconveniences. One, I genuinely dislike kids. They're messy and illogical—my least favorite characteristics. Two, I'd be forced to share their mother with them.

I'm ready to overlook both. Barely. My dad loathes kids more than I do, but he loves me and Creigh, so I choose to believe I will at least tolerate my own kids. I might even like them if they look anything like their mum.

But even I, and my optimistic plans, know that making Ava pregnant in her current state isn't only reckless—it could be catastrophic.

She's not stable, *yet*, and a child might wreck all my progress and spill it down the drain.

Last night, I knew she was pretending to be asleep the entire time, which is why I shook my head at Sam so she wouldn't accidentally reveal anything. After I put Ava to bed and she fell asleep, she woke up half an hour later and walked all over the house before I carried her back to bed and stayed with her until she went under again.

Then I showered, changed, and went to work.

I'm operating on no sleep, and I choose to believe that's the reason why I'm particularly irritable today.

Fine, it's because she paraded herself around with virtually no clothes on.

"So you really wouldn't mind either way?" she asks with a note of expectation.

"I thought I shouldn't since, and I quote, I have no right to tell you what to do with your body."

"But what about your aspirations? Your goals? Do you even *want* kids?"

"I don't see why that should concern you."

"The fact you're my husband, maybe? If I plan on having children, I need to know you'll be there for them since you're hardly there for me."

"Well, there's your answer."

It's a blow below the belt, and she flinches as if I punched her in the gut. But that's better than painting the sky pink and giving her any form of hope.

Not in her state.

Even though I know how much she adores kids and dreams of having her own. She always stops and plays with children and dogs in the street, and she volunteers at a charity to offer free cello lessons to children from humble backgrounds.

But that doesn't negate the fact she's not ready for them.

"You know," she murmurs. "I really hate you."

"So you keep telling me."

Staring me down with eyes less sparkling than earlier, she swallows the pill dry and heads to the sofa, then throws her weight on it. I watch her movements, searching for any sign of numbness, but she retrieves her phone and proceeds to text. She's probably yelling at Ariella about whatever fuckery she witnessed earlier.

Truth be told, my sister-in-law can and will drag Remi down the aisle kicking and screaming sooner or later. I better help her so I can get rid of that nuisance sooner.

Though it's virtually impossible to concentrate when my wife is sitting there like a snack waiting to be devoured, I try to get some work done.

I send Henderson my decision notes on the meeting—or whatever I attended of it. His answer is immediate. My father removed me from the project since I lack respect for it. He'll get Aunt Teal, Remi's mother, on board with his decision.

Motherfucker.

I roll my wedding band back and forth until I nearly snap my finger off.

This is a massive project to get governmental aid for international development, and *I* made it happen. I was the one who worked behind the scenes so King Enterprises and Steel Corporation won the bidding. It's my fucking work, and my father *cannot* take me off the project.

Well, he can since he's the CEO. Worse, Aunt Teal will probably agree with him since she has zero tolerance for nonsense—it must've been a hassle bringing up a child who's the definition of the word.

"If you're done glaring at your screen and making people's lives more miserable, can we go?" Ava stands and yawns. "I'm bored, and if this mood goes on, I'll start rearranging your stuff for revenge."

I glare up at the reason that I'm in this predicament.

Your reaction to her is the reason you're in this predicament.

My wife must sense my mood change, because her eyes widen a little, and she grows breathless. "What?"

"You're a fucking headache."

"Hold on." She rummages through her purse, then slaps an ibuprofen capsule on the desk with a sweet smile. "This should help."

"Is that supposed to be funny?"

"No. It's supposed to help with headaches. Oh, look at that. It's the day we give each other pills. We should make an anniversary out of it."

"As I previously mentioned, I didn't force you."

"As I previously mentioned, screw you. Oh right, I didn't mention that before, so here it is again: screw you."

I shouldn't touch her again so soon. I really, *really* shouldn't, but I don't seem to care as I stand and round my desk.

Ava pretends to hold her ground, but when I reach a hand up her back and grab her hair in a fist, she sinks her teeth into her bottom lip. A muffled sound rips out of her nonetheless.

"That mouth of yours is begging to be punished so thoroughly, you'll only sing my praises afterward."

"Highly doubtful." Her voice is throaty, so thoroughly aroused that I bet her cunt is weeping for me.

"If you don't shut the fuck up, I'll break, stretch, and split your tiny cunt in half."

"Promises, promises."

"Jesus fucking Christ." I wrap my hand around her throat, my fingers skimming the hickey I gave her. "Why are you like this?"

"Why are you?" That spark returns to her eyes with a

vengeance until I can see my reflection in them. "Why did you lie to me, Eli?"

"About?"

"Us having sex."

"I never said that we did."

"But you implied it. You mentioned something about seeing and not being impressed."

"I meant seeing you naked."

"You were lying about that, too."

"I did see you naked, Ava."

"Not that. The part about not being impressed. You obviously were."

I reSist the chuckle that rises to my throat. This woman will be the death of me. "You lied, too."

She frowns. "Me?"

"You made me believe you lost your virginity to some stranger in the back of a car during a party."

"I was telling Cecy that story."

"When you knew full well I was in the hallway."

"It's not my fault you believed I would ever lose my virginity to a nameless nobody in the back of a car."

"I see that now. I also see that your grandiose sex life was nothing but an illusion."

"Nope. I did a lot of things with guys, just not proper sex."

"A lot of *things*?" My fingers tighten around her throat. "Like what?"

"Like things girls did with you, Eli. Blow jobs, dry humping. That sort of thing."

"Keep talking."

"So you'll kill me?" She strains. "Let me go. You're choking me, and it's not the fun version."

I release her with reluctance and step back because she's right. I might accidentally snap her neck if I keep thinking about other dicks near her. "What else did you do with the guys?"

"Why does it matter? You had your sex life. I had mine. That's over now."

I touch my watch, roll my ring, narrow my eyes. "Is it, though?"

"What do you mean?"

"You said you remember cheating on me."

"I was a fucking virgin last night, prick!"

"Apparently, you don't need penetration to cheat, as per your earlier admission."

Her face falls as she comes to the same realization. "I...I wouldn't do that. I despise cheating."

"Not enough to refrain."

"Don't do this to me, Eli. I already feel guilty. Maybe it was a hallucination. I'm sure you know I have those... uh...sometimes. I mean...it's not that I'm crazy or anything, but like...you're my guardian, so you have an idea that I'm..."

She trails off, not wanting to disclose too much. If only she knew the things I carry because of her.

Things she'll never, *ever* find out about.

"Who was the man?" I ask, my voice closed off. Maybe it was the previous psychiatrist. He was the only one who could have had that sort of access to her.

While I hit Vance, and I'm arranging to have him leave UK soil, he's not a viable option. He only recently came back.

However, I'm well aware he wants to rekindle their

teenage fling, which is why he'll be removed from her vicinity effective immediately. For criminal charges—allowing the dealing of drugs in the bars and restaurants managed by his family. They're fake charges, but the threat of it is enough to force his father's hand.

My name is enough to make a nonexistent offense a tragic reality.

"I don't remember his face." Her eyes brighten with an unnatural shine as she holds on to the desk with both hands.

"Then what did you see in the memory?"

"Just that he was, um, half naked, and I wrapped my arms around his neck and said my husband wouldn't like this."

She watches me closely, her face pale as if she's a prisoner waiting for a sentence.

I reSist a smile.

It was me.

But I can't tell her that, or she'll be thrown for a loop if she realizes she can't recall most of her life when trapped in her episodes.

For some reason, however, I also don't want her to keep believing she cheated either, especially since she loathes that.

"It could've been nothing and a mere conjuring of your imagination," I say in my usual detached tone.

"Right? I knew it must've been. I'm not the cheating type." Her face lights up like a Christmas tree.

But then she hesitates, opens her mouth, then closes it again.

"What now?" I ask.

"If it is true...will you forgive me?"

"There's nothing to forgive, because it isn't true."

"But if it is...?"

"It is not. Full stop."

"I'd understand if you wouldn't, because I wouldn't either, you know." She places a hand on my chest. "If you dare betray me, I'll ruin your life."

"More than what you're doing already?"

"This is mere foreplay. I'll make you regret being born if you stab me in the back." She drops her hand. "Can we leave now?"

"I'll have Henderson drop you at home."

"No, we are leaving, and you're the one who will take me. We should have an early dinner and catch a West End show. Maybe *Moulin Rouge!*"

"No, thanks."

"I wasn't asking."

"And I wasn't stuttering."

"You'll spend time with me, or I'll find a man who can spare me his precious time."

A muscle clenches in my jaw as I grab her arm. "Don't you fucking dare say that again."

"Glad you agree to come." She smiles with glee. "Oh, also, you should sack Tyler from reception at King Enterprises and make Hailey senior."

"Let me guess, she praised your looks and he didn't?"

"Yeah, she's nice and professional." Her lips push out in a pout. "Besides, he was ogling my tits."

"Consider him sacked."

She laughs and shakes her head, probably thinking that she walked me straight into that decision.

Little does she know that I'm the one walking her around and around in the custom cage I've carefully constructed for her.

CHAPTER 24

AVA

I'VE COME TO THE DEPRESSING REALIZATION that my husband possesses not one single atom of fun in his gorgeous body.

He's moody and broody, and the concept of chilling completely evades him.

Really, it should be no surprise that he's an uptight arsehole with control freak tendencies, not when I've been in his orbit for...my entire life.

And yet it is. In a sense, at least.

I thought maybe he knew how to laugh, just not with me.

He's able to have a blast, but only when I'm not close.

But I don't think either is possible. At least not genuinely. He's only ever been happy when Creigh or when his parents are around, and even that isn't often guaranteed to shake his broody core.

One more reason why my idea for a night out is a fantastic way to defrost the sociopathic layer wrapped around his heart.

Though it's probably wishful thinking. But, hey, I won't know until I try.

Besides, he did accept my invitation—only after I

threatened his possessive tendencies. Anyway, a win is a win.

Naturally, we went back to the house because he refused to let me walk one more step outside in the clothes I flaunted all over not one but *both* of his workplaces.

The dress I opted for couldn't be described being modest, but it does reach my knees. Also, naturally, Eli demanded another change because half my back was on display.

A demand that was denied.

"You should've let me wear my cute skirt and top from this morning." I feign a pout after we sit at a tall platform table in a grand Lebanese restaurant in Belgravia.

Eli looks up from the menu, and the dispassion and obnoxious disregard in his gaze could trigger a few wars. "'Cute'? Is that what we're calling them?"

"What else?"

"'Audition clothes for a stripper' is more fitting."

"Hmm. I'll consider it. You know any owners of good clubs?"

He narrows his eyes to slits. "Is that sarcasm?"

"I'm dead serious. Those girlies have the best stories to tell. I'd build the most interesting girl squad ever."

"You're not stepping one foot in a strip club, Ava."

"Not even as a spectator?"

"No."

"But girls are hot."

"More reason that you will *not* go."

"I could go behind your back." I wink and play with the straw of my very virgin mojito.

"You're welcome to try." He pauses, throws an

uninterested glance at the menu, then focuses on my face again. "Do I need to put girls on my shit list as well?"

"And fire everyone in the house this time?"

"It's doable."

"Sam would hate you if she had to do all the chores."

"Not if I triple her salary."

"Not everything can be bought with money."

"Yes, it can if it's paired with both information and power. And you're not evading my question. What's the fascination with girls?"

"What do you mean 'fascination'?"

"During a nonsensical truth or dare at uni, Nikolai Sokolov, aka Bran's pet, as Lan calls him, said, 'Never have I ever fucked nor experimented with someone of the same sex.' You asked if a kiss counts, and when he agreed, you took a shot. I'm curious about the identity of said girl."

My lips drop open around the straw.

I've always known Eli to be ridiculously good with details, the devil being there and all that, but I didn't think he'd be able to recite a mundane conversation that happened over three years ago word for word.

"You weren't there during the game. How come you know so much?"

"I have my methods."

"Do your methods include quizzing Remi? Or Bran? No, it was definitely Remi. He has no concept of keeping a secret if disclosing it can serve him. What did you threaten him with?"

"Nothing much. Just that I'd decrease Ariella's access to him."

"Let me guess. Now you'd be willing to increase it if it fits your agenda?"

"Could be. But that's for neither here nor now. Who was the girl?"

"It was an accidental kiss with Cecy when we were in secondary school. We were running, I fell on top of her, and our lips touched. It was nothing."

"Cecily didn't drink."

"Because, as I said, it was nothing."

"You obviously didn't categorize it as *nothing*, or you wouldn't have taken that shot."

"You underestimate my ability to get as much alcohol in me as possible any chance I get. In the past, I mean. I'm clean now except for that drink I stole from Gemma and the others."

He traces the rim of his glass with a nonchalance that doesn't deceive me. "Do you miss the alcohol?"

"Hmm." I slurp my mojito and stare at the mint leaves. "I do sometimes, but I guess I rather miss the escapism it gave me more than the taste itself. The hangover usually came with emptiness, and I dreaded it so much that I fell back into the addiction headfirst. In reality, I don't believe I miss it, no."

I pause. It's true. I don't miss it. Not the alcohol, the mundane shallow clubbing circles, nor the dancing and fooling around and attempting to attract attention. Everyone noticed me except for the one I craved.

My gaze flits to his, and something mysterious shines bright behind those dark grays.

He feels different today, and I can't put my finger on why. Is it because we finally fucked? Is it the possibility of more?

Or is it something entirely different?

The waiter comes to take our order. After we place it, I lean my cheek on my hand and watch Eli. Like, really watch him. The light flecks of gray and blue in his stormy eyes, the sharp line of his jaw, the dispassionate look on his face. He appears a bit tired, though nothing is particularly out of place. Everything about him is controlled to the most minuscule detail.

Now that I think about it, the only time he loses control, momentarily, is when his body touches mine.

I wish I knew what he thinks about. I'd be a fly on the wall of his brain if he'd just permit me a front-row seat. Or maybe not a fly since that could be bad. A neuron. A memory, perhaps.

Except for the one when I made a fool out of myself.

"So, who knows about your unorthodox method to get me off alcohol?" I ask with no actual bitterness. Probably because I feel none. At least not anymore.

"No one does for sure. They think I helped like a very devout husband."

I snort. "If there were an award for the least devout husband, you'd win it with flying colors."

"Hardly."

"I really want to remember so I can know what on earth I was thinking when I agreed to marry you."

"It was the best decision you've ever made."

"*Hardly*," I shoot back with a smile. "You're, like, at the very end of my possible prospects."

"Possible prospects being who, exactly?"

"Nice try. If I give you names, you'll sabotage them for laughs, and I can't turn a blind eye to your toxic habits anymore." After all, I already have his attention now. I'm just not sure if it's the right type.

Or if this sort of fickle attention will ever develop into something more.

His fingers tighten around his glass the slightest bit, a change of body language I wouldn't have noticed if I weren't observing him like a hawk. "Did you wake up today and decide to transform my life into hell?"

"Don't be silly." I play with my straw. "I wake up every day with those thoughts."

He shakes his head with bitter concession, and I smile as the waiter brings me my falafel salad and hummus dip.

I spy Eli's dish—some kebab. As I eat, I watch him cutting it into minuscule pieces, but he never brings anything to his mouth. And when he does, as if for show, he puts it back down and takes a sip of his drink.

Sam's words about asking him directly pushes me to blurt out, "Why do you never eat?"

"I always eat. Otherwise, I would've expired."

"You're human, not a product. What do you mean by 'expired'? Gross." I scrunch my nose. "Also, I know you eat Sam's food, but I never see you eating outside."

"That's because I don't."

"Why do you order, then?"

"To keep up the image."

"Is there a reason why you can't have food in restaurants?"

His lips purse before they set in their usual disapproving form. "I don't trust them."

"Is this about your OCD? I mean, I think that's what it

is? I don't want to throw the term around, but you clearly
have very distinct symptoms."

"It's mild. Self-diagnosed. And yes, it plays a part."

"And the other part?"

He raises a brow. "What's with the sudden curiosity?"

"We're married, Eli. I think we should know some
things about each other. Don't you think?"

"Being married doesn't come with a free card to demol-
ish each other's privacy, so no, I don't think we should
know personal things about each other."

"Well, I do. I refuse to live with a stranger; therefore, I
will keep trying to figure you out. You can tell me yourself,
or I'll find out on my own. So can you tell me and save us
both some trouble?"

He continues cutting his food, the movements mechanical at best, and I think he's shut me outside his high walls,
but then his deep voice carries in the air. "I was poisoned
when I was maybe six. It was some maid who was sent by
one of Dad's rivals to eliminate his only heir. Mum figured
out something was wrong in time and drove me to the
hospital. I had a gastric lavage that cleared me out of harm's
way, but after that, I couldn't eat. My parents tried everything to coax me with my favorite dishes and even junk
food, but it didn't work. After I refused to put anything
in my mouth for a few days, the doctors had to pump me
with fluids and my parents consulted a child psychiatrist.
It didn't help much, and any external force only made me
withdraw further into my shell."

My lips part.

So that's the reason I've never seen him eat. He was
traumatized by an event in the past. My heart clenches at

the thought of the child version of him being so suspicious of food, he went on self-starvation.

"I'm sorry you went through that."

"Don't pity me."

"I'm not. I'm sympathizing. A concept that's foreign to you but common to most humans." I pause. "How did you come out of it?"

"Mum and Sam agreed to make all my meals. Mum tried, but she has zero cooking skills."

"Aw, bless her."

He smiles at my smile, and it takes all my self-control not to snap a picture and keep it for future reference.

"We should've eaten at home," I say with a note of guilt.

"Why? You wanted to try out this restaurant since you're a huge fan of Middle Eastern food."

"Yeah, but not if I'm the only one eating."

"My situation has nothing to do with your preferences."

"We're married, Eli. Your situation affects me whether I like it or not."

A muscle moves in his jaw as he takes a sip of his drink and then sets it down. For some reason, what I said seems to dampen the mood of this dinner. A dinner I wasn't vibing with in the first place due to his lack of participation.

So we go to the theater and watch *Moulin Rouge!* While I clap and dance and sing at the end, Eli is entirely unimpressed by the whole debacle.

"That was so much fun!" I shout and wave at the girl who was vibing with me during the show as Eli and I exit in the red glow of Piccadilly Theatre. The music continues blaring, and I sway, even when his grip stops me.

"Only if a hindrance is called fun." He places a large palm at the small of my back and expertly leads me through the crowd in a way that no one touches me.

"You're such a grinch." I place my index and middle fingers at the corners of his mouth and pull up. "Smile a little. You'd look so much hotter."

As I drop my hand, he raises a brow. "You find me hot?"

"Everyone does. At least seven girls were flirting with you earlier at the bar."

"You were counting?"

"Unintentionally."

His lips twitch in a small smile as he strokes my hip. A shiver rushes through me, and I grow pliant in his hold. It isn't fair that he's the best embrace I've ever had.

How come a monster feels so safe?

"Will you ever tell me why you married me?" I whisper.

"I told you. I need the camouflage of a stable family."

"You could've gotten that with any other girl. Why me?"

"Because it's you," he says in a cryptic tone that leaves a knot at the bottom of my stomach.

I try to ask for more clarification, but we've already reached the car.

Eli spends the whole trip looking through his phone and talking about finances with Henderson. I swear Eli breathes for money, and he's ridiculously talented at making it.

Though it's probably not money he's after; it's power.

By the time we reach the house, I feel a crushing sense of depression. Maybe because a nice night out with no quarrels is over and we'll probably not have anything similar again.

I stop at the top of the stairs, where we'll part ways for our respective rooms, and glance at him. He's standing there, his jacket in hand, and the first two buttons of his shirt are undone, revealing chiseled muscles.

Clearing my throat, I attempt a small smile. "Thanks for tonight, I had a lovely time."

He nods once, his fingers tight around the banister as if he's stopping himself from doing something.

"I...um, night," I mumble like an idiot, then try to walk with dignity and not run to my room. Or, worse, steal a glimpse at my husband, whose emotional temperament rivals the Alps.

Once I'm inside, I throw my bag on the chair and stop by the bed, feeling a chill covering my skin.

Why does it feel big and empty in here?

Maybe I should make sure Sam left some food for Eli? It's late, so I can heat it up. She won't come at me for that, and I doubt I'll burn a microwave.

At least I hope I won't.

It's just charity. Mum taught me to be a giver for those less fortunate than me. Eli's been fasting the whole day, so I'm doing him a favor.

I've just taken a step when the door bangs open and Eli is standing there, sans jacket, his nostrils flaring and his eyes a vortex of desire.

The temperature shoots up instantly, and I swallow. "I...I was going to heat you up some dinner."

He walks toward me, eating up the distance in two strides, and wraps his hand around my throat. "Be my dinner."

Then his sinful mouth captures mine.

I'm lightheaded, absolutely ensnared, and completely taken with my monster of a husband.

His tongue thrusts between my lips, claiming mine, and my heart feels so light, my body floats on the clouds as I wrap my arms around his neck.

My curves mold to his hard muscles, and I hang on to him for dear life.

When he pulls away, I breathe. "Whew. What a good night kiss."

"If you believe I'll stop after a kiss, you're in for a massive surprise, Mrs. King."

"Yeah? What do you intend to do?"

"Kiss every inch of your body, then fuck you for all the times I couldn't."

I want to ask why he couldn't before if we were married for over two years, but he pushes me against the bed and claims my mouth again, and I'm a goner.

Tomorrow is for questions.

Today I want to fully feel the best day of my life.

CHAPTER 25
ELI

SOMEWHERE IN THE BACK OF MY CONSCIOUS-ness, I'm fully aware that I shouldn't be doing this.

I flip her onto her stomach, stroking and rubbing everywhere I can touch.

The last thing my wife needs is my cock nudging against her arse, demanding access inside her, or growing rock-fucking-hard at the thought of claiming her. Owning her. Engraving myself beneath her skin.

And yet, apparently, I couldn't care less about any possible side effects of my inability to stay away.

The scents of roses and depressingly familiar candy floss saturate my nose until I'm full of her. Her smell, the feel of her soft skin beneath the roughness of mine, the visual of her creamy flesh compared to my tan complexion. The gentle, absolutely ravenous moans she releases as I rip her zipper open.

"Can you stop ruining my dresses?" she mumbles against the pillow, staying completely still as I shove away the blasphemous thing keeping me from her.

"I lack the capacity to be gentle when it comes to you, Mrs. King." I roll her hair around my fist and lower my lips to her ear. "But you knew that already when you teased me all night long."

"I...did no such thing." Her voice drips with forbidden desire and flickering lucidity. She's so fucking beautiful, I can't look her in the eye without feeling the burn in my bones.

"Is that so? Did I imagine your hand and legs not-so-accidentally brushing against my thigh?"

"Hmm. Maybe. Did it work?"

"Do you want it to work?" I run my hand down to her arse, stroking the thong that slips between the crack and then slap the inviting flesh, and she groans, her lips parting. "Judging by how wet and ready you are, I'd say you definitely do. Don't you know you're advised to steer clear of murky waters?"

"I was never good with following advice." She wiggles a little, her breathing growing shallow. "I'm *so* bad at that. Ask my doctor. Or maybe don't."

"Silly, silly fucking girl." I slap her arse again, and her head slumps forward. "You shouldn't want me."

"I could say the same about you. But we're here now, so do something. I'm a little sore, but I can take it."

"You can take my cock plowing inside you, huh?"

"Mmm."

I lick the shell of her ear, something I discovered she loves. A shaky breath rushes out of her as she whimpers, her flesh turning hot to the touch.

And I'm done for.

Fucking *finished*.

I lose my goddamn mind.

A groan leaves me as I slide a pillow beneath her stomach so she's settled in an erotic position. With another slap to her arse, I lift the thong's elastic band, then let it snap on her flesh. Her throaty moan echoes in the air, and my dick hardens and strains against my briefs as if her lips are wrapped around it.

I swiftly chase away that impossible image as I unbuckle my belt. "This is going to be fast and rough, beautiful. I can't slow down nor take it easy."

"Yes, please."

"Jesus fucking Christ." Why do I love the sound of her begging? If she so much as said *please* outside of sex, I'd let her have anything—my goddamn sanity included.

I shove down my trousers and briefs in one swift go. My engorged cock bobs against my half-exposed abs, precum shining at the tip.

My fingers find her clit, and I rub her in methodical circles. She's so wet, my fingers drip with her arousal, and an obscene sound fills the bedroom.

My wife grows pliant, her legs opening farther and her moans turning throatier and deeper.

"Call me beautiful again." She lifts herself, her fingers clenching into the mattress.

When I say nothing, she cranes her head to the side, probably to get a look at me. However, I wrap my belt around her throat and hold it and her hair as I shove her face down.

Parting her arse cheeks, I slide my cock against her soaking slit, up and down, in a torturous rhythm that tightens my abs.

Her muffled moans fill the air, and she tries to wiggle, to invite me inside her glistening cunt, but I reSist.

Barely.

My grip on the belt turns deadly, until I'm sure it'll snap under the pressure.

There's nothing I'd love more than to claim her like a fucking animal and watch her blood mix with my cum again, but that sick thought would only make me lose her for good.

So I continue rubbing our juices together, the sound echoing in the air as the smell of her sweet cunt flares my nostrils.

"Eli...oh my God..." she mumbles. "Please..."

I feel her thighs shaking as she rides and humps my cock. I remain still for a moment, watching her pink cunt sliding up and down my length in jerky, desperate movements that still look sophisticated and innocent.

Christ.

I never knew a pussy could look so fucking erotic, so beautiful that I want to break it.

Which is a goddamn problem, considering my attempts to put her back together.

Though, deep down, very deep in my demented soul, I do want to break her to fucking pieces.

Maybe I'll do that after I glue her back together so that she never finds her way out of my orbit.

My cage.

My fucking grip.

I thrust all the way inside her in one go. The sudden motion renders her frozen as a whimper falls from her lips.

Her cunt tightens around my cock, strangling me for dear life. I allow her a second to adjust, my harsh breathing matching her strained pants.

Once I feel her relaxing, I drive into her with collected deep thrusts until she's entirely slumped over the pillow.

"You look so fucking beautiful when you're being torn apart by my cock, Mrs. King."

She clenches around me, her throaty soft moans filling the air like a chant—witchcraft whose sole purpose is to dismantle me to fucking pieces.

"You're the most beautiful when your tight little cunt is being railed by me. You're dripping for me and taking my cock so well. That's it, mmm, show me how much you're mine, wife."

Her little body rocks back and forth, her arse rubbing against my groin, and I slap it a few times. She releases long stuffy moans, and I fuck her harder, deeper.

This is why I shouldn't touch my wife. Why I abstained for fucking years from claiming her. Not only is it a sure recipe for her mental decline, but she messes up my control, brings down my walls, and turns me into this sporadic entity of unhinged impulsiveness.

I don't stop when she screams into the pillow nor when her body shakes and she milks my cock.

I don't stop when she shivers and releases small moans.

I certainly don't stop when she lies there completely spent.

If anything, I go harder and faster. My balls tighten, but I don't let myself come.

Not yet.

Not now when this could be the last time I fuck her.

I blame my lack of sleep for my unleashed sickness.

"Oh God, Eli." She tries and fails to look back due to my grip on the belt. "I'm so sensitive…"

"You shouldn't have provoked me, then, shouldn't have flaunted yourself in barely there clothes and offered what's mine to the public. Now you'll take my cock as punishment and thank me for it like a good wife." I slap her arse.

She groans. "Let me...let me look at you."

"No."

"Please...I want to see you." The desperate lust in her voice almost demolishes the very last of my resolve.

I'd give anything to thrust my tongue in her mouth as hard as I'm thrusting my cock, to own her in irrevocable ways that can't be undone.

I pull out to the tip and almost flip her onto her back. *Almost.*

The image of her frigid eyes and the unattainable void in her expression flash before me, and I slam back in her again, tightening the belt so she stops talking.

Then I fuck her like a madman.

I fuck her so raw, she slides back and forth and the headboard hits the wall with loud bangs.

My fingers find her clit, and she squirms, fighting the unavoidable, but I tease and circle and press her pleasure button until she trembles around me. Her muffled moans fill the air as my abs tighten, my balls grow heavy, and I come inside her inviting cunt in waves.

The release is even stronger than last night. This is why I've kept my distance. I knew whetting my appetite once wouldn't be enough and that I'd need to do it again and again before I'd ever be satisfied.

Even now, as I watch a streak of my cum sliding down her thigh, I want to restart the ownership process all over again.

As she slumps forward, I release the belt, letting her head rest on the pillow.

I pull out mid-orgasm and decorate her red arse with my cum. She hisses at the contact against her sensitive skin, and I part her cheeks, massaging it into the crack and pressing it into her virgin hole.

"We need to prep you so you can take my cock in this tight little hole, Mrs. King."

"So you can keep fucking me from behind?" Her head is turned sideways, but she's not looking at me, her lips set in a line. Her face is flushed and dripping with both desire and defiance.

I can smell one of her tantrums from a mile away, which is a good sign, all things considered, but I still shouldn't feed her drama-prone existence.

With one last slap, I release her. "Precisely."

I walk to her bathroom and wet a towel with warm water, quickly wipe my cock clean, and tuck myself back in before I grab another towel and go back.

My wife is still in the same position, but her legs are in the air, crossed at the ankles as she stares at the bathroom door.

Her expression is softer now, and some mascara is running down from her eyes, because she cries during sex, apparently.

And she couldn't look any more beautiful.

"Why do you only touch me from behind?" she asks in a soft voice.

I ignore her and gently wipe my cum from her pussy and then her arse. I do it slowly, reluctant to erase the sign of my ownership from her skin.

"Do you not want to see my face?" Her words crack at the end.

"It's not that." I run my fingers over my angry red handprint on her porcelain skin.

"Then what is it?" she inSists. "Why can't we do any positions that involve looking at each other?"

"We're not lovers. This is only fucking, so I don't see why we should engage in any form of intimacy."

She swallows, her face reddens, and I can feel her anger radiating and growing to exponential heights.

But then she flashes me her fakest smile. One that seems only designed for me. She has no problem being like absolute sunshine to everyone else, but God forbid she smile at me.

Though she did tonight, countless times, before I smothered it.

Again.

"You're right. I'll take this as an apprenticeship to learn how to please my future lovers."

My jaw clenches. "You'll have no future lovers."

"Says who?"

"The fact you're my wife."

"This marriage is only temporary until I find the love of my life." She stands in her full naked glory and hikes her hand on her hip. "Now run me a bath."

I have to remind myself that I can't snap her fucking neck.

And that she's provoking me on purpose. Her fake-sweet smile and honeyed tone give her away.

She's just fishing for a reaction she won't get.

I head to the bathroom again and then turn on the faucet to tepid. I add her salts, bath milk, and a dozen other products. I'm checking the temperature when she steps in, leans her head against the pillow, and closes her eyes.

"Anything else, Your Highness?" I ask in a mocking tone.

"A bit hotter would be nice." She wiggles her toes in the water and releases a long sigh. "More bath milk. The whole bottle, actually."

I contemplate pouring the thing over her head, but I get distracted by the ethereal view of her pebbled pink nipples peeking through the white surface, slowly being submerged by the water.

"Is that all?" I ask once I'm done.

"Yup, all good. You can join me now."

"I will not join you."

She peels her eyes open. "Why not?"

"I don't like baths."

"You liked it just fine yesterday when you gave me one."

"I only did so because I thought you were asleep."

"And you can't do it now?" The pain in her voice would move any other man.

She has the ability to turn anyone into a puppy at her feet.

Lucky for her, I have the capacity to reSist her charms when need be.

"No," I say point-blank.

Her lips tremble, and moisture turns her eyes a glittering blue. "You're such a bastard. I really hate you."

"Good. It's dangerous to love me. But you already know that."

I turn around and leave. As I close the door, a bottle of shower gel crashes against it.

———

The next morning, I wake up refreshed after finally getting some rest.

Hungry, too, after fasting for about twenty-four hours.

I don't remember my life before I swore off food, so, in a sense, my stomach is used to surviving on my stash of protein bars or just waiting until I get home. Whenever I'm on a business trip, Sam cans her food so I won't have to go on an extended fasting journey.

I stroll into the kitchen and pause when I take a quick inventory of the table. Strawberry cake, freshly baked croissants, scones, jam, and clotted cream. The menu is definitely different from my usual granola or scrambled eggs.

Needless to say, I'm a creature of habit. It comes as a form of control. I don't appreciate any changes in my life, no matter how minute.

This is why marrying Ava was no different than inviting a disaster under my roof.

"What's the meaning of this?" I ask Sam, who's busy wiping clean some utensils.

"I thought you could use a change."

"Do you even know me? I don't like change."

"Very British of you." She pauses. "Why don't you try it? You might like it."

"Are you serious? You're well aware of my disregard for sweet things."

"Very contradictive, considering you married the sweetest girl."

I pause. Sam continues wiping away as if she didn't just drop a bomb.

"Did you just call Ava 'sweet'?"

"She is. Not my fault you're too blind to see it."

"Who are you, and what have you done to the emotionless Sam I've known my entire life?"

"I'm not emotionless. I'm selective. Like you. Now sit down and eat. And before you ask, I made nothing else and will not be making anything else."

I narrow my eyes, but since I'm hungry, I do sit down and prepare a scone with clotted cream and strawberry jam.

It tastes different, and I think it's a bit burned, but I chase away that thought. Sam would never burn anything.

"Did she take her medication last night?" I ask after I finish two scones and a croissant in record time.

"For the second time, yes. Is there a reason why you didn't check on her yourself?"

"She was mad at me."

"A pattern, apparently."

"Apparently."

The real reason is that I needed to put some distance between us. Ava has always spun around my orbit, even when she thought she'd quit me. I'm the addiction that streams in her blood whether she likes it or not, so I can't give her any fucking ideas.

She's my responsibility, my wife, and my property. I meant it when I said I could give her anything but love.

And if she keeps demanding that, she'll be the only one who gets hurt.

Her mind *can't* afford to be hurt.

"How do you like the food?" Sam asks as I swallow a portion of the cake.

"Aside from being sickeningly sweet, it's acceptable."

"Then you better show proper gratitude."

"I pay you as gratitude, Sam."

She shakes her head. "Follow me."

Repressing my perplexity, I go with the short woman to the adjoining sitting area.

My confusion slowly clears when I find my wife lying on the sofa, snoring softly while wearing a dirty pink apron. Flour smudges her cheek, and three of her fingers are wrapped in bandages.

Sam's voice carries in the air. "She woke up at the crack of dawn with me and inSisted on making you break-fast as long as I'd say I was the one who did it. She burned the first two attempts, but she kept trying to perfect her creations. She begged me not tell you who made the food, because, and I quote, 'I hate him right now.' End of quote."

My lips curve in a smile as I sit on my haunches before her and stroke the bandages on her delicate hands. Hands that weren't made for cooking nor any chores. Ava is her papa's spoiled princess and the apple of her mother's eye. Not only that, but she's adored by her grandparents and was tended to since a young age; therefore, she didn't even consider learning how to cook.

And yet she chose to make me breakfast.

"If she asked you not to tell me, why did you?" I speak to Sam, but my entire attention is on my wife.

"I find it unfair to take the credit for her effort. Especially since she woke up early despite being the opposite of a morning person. Which is why I believe you should thank her properly."

"That will only give her ideas." I reluctantly release her and rise to my full height. "She can't afford ideas."

"You're underestimating her strength."

"I'm willing to gamble on underestimating instead of overestimating her. We did it before, and she ended up in the fucking hospital."

"It's different now. Both of you are."

"Still no."

Sam sighs. "She's a good kid, Eli. She cares, and she has no qualms about showing it. I know you think she's only sensitive, but I believe you're overlooking her hidden strength and stunning self-awareness. She might not break if you tell her the truth."

"No," I let out in a clipped tone.

"She'll hate you if she finds out in a different manner. Time is *not* in your favor."

"She already hates me, so I don't see the problem with that."

"How come you're smart about everything but excruciatingly obtuse when it comes to her?"

"I'm not obtuse. I'm realistic. She'll never know and that's final."

I take one last glance at my wife's form that rivals Sleeping Beauty's.

Sam is right. Time is not in my favor.

Every day is a tick drawing Ava closer to her next episode that, according to Dr. Blaine, will be worse than the last.

The last being that she'll forget everything again.

But even if she erases me again, there's no escaping me.

I'll claim her again.

And again.

I'll carve my name beneath her skin so deeply, she'll find me in her dreams.

And her nightmares.

CHAPTER 26

AVA

"YOU SEEM DIFFERENT."

I look up from my phone after checking it for maybe the millionth time. And no, I'm totally not obsessing or anything obnoxiously similar.

My eyes meet Mama's, and she smiles softly as she passes me the popcorn bowl. Salted caramel flavor—my favorite.

We've always had girls' night—just me, her, and Ari. Oftentimes, Nan will join when she's not busy touring the world with Grandpapa in their various humanitarian endeavors.

During these nights, we watch the cheesiest chick flicks, or my comfort film, *Bridget Jones's Diary*, while we gossip about everything and nothing.

This often happens when Papa is caught up in late meetings or events for the company. Such as he is tonight. Otherwise, he wouldn't tolerate being separated from his girls, as he likes to call us.

On this occasion, we put on a Japanese drama per Ari's request. And by *request*, I mean she forced her opinion as always, and now we have to read subtitles because she refuses to watch it dubbed in English.

"Or you can, like, learn the language. It's a disgrace that most Brits only speak their mother tongue when there are so many beautiful languages out there," she said when I tried to persuade her to change the show.

"I speak Latin and French, thank you very much," I informed her.

"One is useless, and the other is practically useless as well. I, on the other hand, speak Spanish, Japanese, Mandarin, and am currently learning Arabic. Talk to the hand, peasant." She waved said hand in my face.

Mum sat between us before I could kick her, and now we're stuck with this Japanese thriller drama that's pretty interesting, actually.

But Ari will never know that, or I won't hear the end of it. She loves gloating and lacks any sportsmanship concerning anything.

She tries to steal my bowl of popcorn, although there's another one on the coffee table. I manage to shove her away but not before she snatches a handful and the rest spills all over Mama and the leather sofa.

Eli would look at me with a snobbish expression if I so much as left a crumb on his precious furniture. Now, however, the three of us just laugh as Ari and I proceed to fight over the bucket of sticky candy floss.

The mere thought of my husband has obviously clouded my senses, because Ari tugs the bucket from my grip and waggles her eyebrows at me.

I make a face and stuff my mouth full of popcorn. It's been three weeks since Eli shattered my world to pieces, ran me a bath, then made it clear he wants nothing emotional with me.

The process of hurt and comfort has been ongoing since then. He'll fuck me into oblivion but will not allow me to look at him.

He'll bring me to the edge in every position possible as long as I'm not facing him. Against his desk, on all fours, sideways from behind, slumped against the edge of the tub. Once, he walked in on me picking up a book and fucked me standing against the shelves.

It was hotter than my books, just saying.

He runs me baths afterward. Always. Without my having to ask. But he doesn't join me.

He takes me to shows and dinners—mostly because I make him. He joins me when I'm in the theater room, though he couldn't care less for my taste in films. He parades me around at events. He brings me flowers for all my performances, which have become so common lately.

But he never lets his walls down.

It doesn't matter how deep and raw his touch is, Eli's mind is still way out of reach like a faraway galaxy that's physically unattainable.

The only time I feel he loses some control is when his cock is pounding into me and driving me crazy. And yet, even then, he's powerful and in absolute possession of his resolve. Sometimes, when I beg to see his face, I feel like he'll flip me over, but he never does.

I hate myself for not being the same brand of cold he is.

But most of all, I hate that I crave his touch, that he knows all the right buttons to push to keep me coming back for more.

Yet every time he shoves me to my stomach so he can't see my face, and every time he doesn't share my bed, I feel a part of me ripping at the seams and falling away with the depressing finality of an autumn leaf.

We've been having sex regularly for the past few weeks, and by *regularly*, I mean every day. Sometimes, two or three times a day.

But I've never seen him naked. Not once.

The only time he got naked was after that first time we had sex and I couldn't open my eyes to see it.

It's been three weeks of constant mind-numbing orgasms that he makes sure I get before his, yet I don't feel closer to him than before. At least not on a deeper level like I'd like to.

Yes, our relationship is better than when I first woke up in the hospital. He's more accommodating if I'm "reasonable," and he does make time when I ask.

But it's still not...enough.

And I guess I'm coming to the awful, hideous realization that this is the closest he'll ever allow me to get.

Close enough to own, but not to like.

Close enough to eat what I cook, but not enough to let me within his walls.

Close enough to be in a marriage with benefits, but not enough to be in a real marriage.

"Ava?"

I lift my head at Mama's voice. "Yeah?"

"You just looked a bit lost in thought. Is everything okay?"

Japanese dialogue fills the room for a beat before Ari shoves the candy floss tub in my lap. "You can have it. I don't want it anymore."

I smile softly at my sister. She's always given up her things for me—like her favorite anime figurines, toy racing car, and fluffy key chain—in the hope that it'll get me out of my moody phases.

It's a habit she's had since we were little, and even though she's old enough to realize that tactic doesn't really work, she still employs it religiously.

"Is it because I said you look different?" Mama asks. "It's just about the vibe, and not anything physical."

"Definitely physical. You're glowing, Sis. Bet you're getting enough dick to use it as a facial."

"Ari!" Mum scolds. "Don't be so crude."

I grow hot.

"OMG, Mama, look, she's blushing!" My sister bounces while sitting. "Called it! Totally called it! Now, tell me, does he have the dick energy that matches his earth-shaped arrogance?"

"I will not dignify that question with an answer," I say with a clearing of my throat.

"So he does! I *knew* it. Men like him and Remi are the personification of superior sexual energy. My theory is it's in the genes."

I narrow my eyes. "I still haven't forgotten about your episode with that bastard Remi."

"What episode with Remi?" Mama asks with a raised brow.

"Hey, don't go bad-mouthing my lord and savior." She smacks me teasingly behind our mother's back. "And, dear Mama, you know I'll marry Remi. I told you so when I was, like, eleven, so don't play oblivious."

Mum's brow furrows. "I thought we talked about this already? He has no interest in you, and we don't do desperate."

"He so does." She winks at me, and I roll my eyes as she interlinks her arm with Mama's. "Please help me butter up Papa."

"You know he still hasn't come to terms with Eli. If you get with Remi, he'll surely have a stroke."

"I've been researching ways to lessen the blow. But more on that later." Ari fixates on me. "You're not avoiding the question, missy. If it's not because of Eli's dick energy, what did he do? Should I whack him for you?"

I laugh. I can't help it when she sounds so serious. "You're a gangster now?"

"I'm many dangerous things under the right circumstances."

"And you can take him out?"

"With the help of Papa, Remi, Lan, Cecy's man, and Bran's scary fiancé, who'll do anything he says, absolutely. Eli King who? He won't see us coming as I blast 'Don't Fear the Reaper.'"

I shake my head, feeling a bit lighthearted. "It's nothing like that."

"You sure? Because I can totally start a group chat."

"You'd start any group chat just to include Remi."

"True, but, like, this is also for a noble cause."

"You're such a menace." Mama hugs her and kisses the top of her head.

"I'm your and Daddy's little girl. Thank you very much."

Mama laughs with visible pride.

Once again, I wonder if she and Papa would've been happier if they'd only had Ari. She's a dangerous little hellion, but she's mentally normal.

She doesn't suffer from sleep paralysis, nightmares, and an untold Pandora's box of psychoSis madness.

I doubt she'd feel apprehensive about sharing a bed with someone else because they might see her as a monster who should be avoided.

Mama faces me with an expression that's special for me. Soft, loving, and careful. She always seems hesitant and extremely careful whenever she talks to me.

I understand. She's searching for telltale signs. Ever since they found me walking on the roof before I fell and broke my arm, my parents have been extra wary of the tiniest change.

Cecy did that at uni, too. My parents agreed to let me separate from them only if I shared a flat with her. And while she's a less scrutinizing version of them, she's still equally concerned.

It's why I prefer living with Eli. He might be distant, but at least he doesn't make me feel on edge when I'm around him.

He certainly doesn't look at me as if I'm a ticking bomb that's nearing the explosion point.

Sometimes, the atmosphere is so comfortable, I forget I have this chronic psychoSis that could manifest itself in the worst scenarios possible.

Short of our usual visits to Dr. Blaine, he doesn't ask about the pills and never brings up any of the conversations we have in her office. It's become so habitual that I almost believe I'm normal.

Almost.

Mama slides her hand around my shoulder and squeezes me closer to her. "If there's anything you want to tell me, I'm all ears, hon."

"It's nothing I can't take care of. Don't worry."

"Is Eli giving you a hard time?"

"I'm the one doing that. I mess with him as if it's an Olympic sport."

"And how does he react to that?"

"Silence mostly. Sometimes he'll glower or pinch the bridge of his nose." I stop before I say he punishes me with my arse in the air.

I didn't think I liked spanking with sex until my enigma of a husband trained me to be wet just by hearing, *Behave.* Or, *Make no mistake, if I see you smiling at others, I'll take it out on your arse, beautiful.* Or, *You're just begging to be punished, Mrs. King.*

"Bitch, please," Ari says. "He can't have the goddess without some drama. He should be thankful, if you ask me. And if he's not, we can go with my glorious assassination plot."

"Stop threatening your brother-in-law with murder," Mama says, even as she smiles.

"Only if he treats my sister right. I take no prisoners."

"Oh, really?" I cross my arms. "Heard he's providing you with constant intel on Remi."

"*Aside* from that." She mirrors my stance with a sneaky smile. "He's still my brother-in-law and family. Compromises, Ava. Have you heard of them? Word on the street is they're good for marriage. Right, Mama?"

She laughs but nods at me. "They are for sure. There's no such thing as a harmonious marriage without compromise."

"What if I'm compromising on things I don't want to compromise on?" I ask in a low voice.

"Have you tried communicating that?"

"Eli isn't the communicative type. He's worse than an army general who expects all his orders to be met."

"Are they always met?"

"Hell no. I defy him for fun, like, eighty percent of the time."

"Does he retaliate?"

I pause, thinking of all the times he just narrows his eyes, shakes his head, then walks away. "Not really."

"Then there's compromise from his side. Just because you fail to see it, doesn't mean it's not there."

"But he's infuriating, Mama."

"You still went to hell and back to marry him."

I roll my bottom lip between my teeth as I meet Ari's gaze, and she shakes her head. She doesn't want me to bring up the fact my inSistence on marrying Eli brought trouble for our parents. I apologized after I heard about that, but Mama said there was nothing to be sorry for, while Papa remained silent.

"Honestly, I didn't understand why you were so inSistent on it back then."

"Then why did you help me, Mama?"

She strokes my cheek softly. "The look in your eyes told me everything your words couldn't. Besides, with time, I came to see how this thing between you two works."

It does? How?

I want to ask since I certainly don't see it, but the last thing I want is to worry my parents any further. I'm already the worst thing that's happened in their lives, so there's no need to make it any uglier.

"It doesn't work." A familiar deep voice reaches us first

before Papa stands in front of us, his jacket in hand. "Stop indoctrinating her into believing in that useless marriage."

"Papa!" Ari wraps herself around him in a koala embrace.

I shove her away to hug him longer than needed, and then my sister and I fight over who hugs him more, just like when we were young. So Papa pulls us both to either side of him and kisses the tops of our heads.

"Are you here to announce your overdue divorce, princess?" he asks with unmasked hope.

"Cole!" Mama scolds.

"What? We all know she should ditch the loose screw and come back to live with us for life. Isn't that right?"

I smile. "I'm an adult, Papa. I can't live with you my entire life."

"Sure can. It's completely acceptable in other cultures, and we should normalize it here as well. We can start with our household. Look at Ari—she's already sworn allegiance to me for life."

"Is that so?" I tilt my head to look at her.

"Shut it," she mouths at me, then grins at our father. "Daddy's little girl for life. You'll never get rid of me."

"That's what I like to hear."

"You're so full of shit," I say.

"Ava is jealous, boo-hoo." She clings to Papa before Mama pulls her away, probably to stop her from grimacing at me.

"Have you lost weight?" Papa examines me closely, rotating my face from side to side. "I knew the prick wasn't feeding you properly. Let's sue him for neglect and get those divorce papers while we're at it."

"Cole..." Mama warns.

"Maybe he can serve some time in prison as well?" He smiles mischievously. "It'd be perfect revenge for taking away my princess. The horrified look on Aiden's face would be worth it as well."

"I'm eating just fine, Papa. He actually takes me out to dinner regularly and makes an effort to pick restaurants that serve my favorite cuisines."

"Hear that?" Mama asks with a warm smile. "Will you stop being insufferable to our son-in-law?"

"I have no son-in-law and never will." He narrows his eyes. "Did he tell you to say that? You don't need to lie, princess. I'll make him pay."

"I'm not lying, Papa." I kiss his cheek. "In fact, I promised to join him for dinner tonight, so I have to go."

"What about me? You won't have dinner with me?"

"You have Mama and Ari."

He opens his mouth to say something, but Mama stands and interlinks her arm with his.

"Go on, hon. I'll take care of your dad."

"Love you." I hug them together, then smooch Ari on the cheek before I head to the door.

Behind me, I hear Papa saying, "What's the restaurant? Maybe we'll join."

"And start a world war?" Mama asks.

"I will behave."

"You said that the last time before you locked Eli out of the house."

"It wasn't on purpose, butterfly. I genuinely mistook him for a cockroach. Not my fault he has more resemblance to vermin than humans."

I smile as I turn around and wave.

"Princess, tell me. I promise not to punch him." He pauses. "More than three times."

My face hurts from all the smiling.

Well, then, time to face my nemeSis.

CHAPTER 27
AVA

INSTEAD OF ALAN, THE USUAL DRIVER, LEO IS behind the wheel today.

I slide in the seat beside him, and he stares at me as if I've blasphemed.

"You should ride in the back, Mrs. King."

"I like to think we're friends, and therefore, I can sit here."

"Please, no."

I frown as I secure my seat belt. "I'm wounded, Leo. I thought we'd formed a bond."

"If you believe that, call me by my full name, or I'll be found buried at the North Pole."

I laugh. "You're unintentionally funny."

"I'm intentionally self-preserving." He drives off my parents' property, keeping his eyes on the road.

He wears white gloves. The entire time. I have actually never seen his hands. The other day he mentioned that he's also diagnosed with OCD and has found the most understanding boss in Eli. Probably because they share some symptoms.

All members of my husband's staff know not to touch his things with bare hands nor alter the position of his belongings without prior notice. Naturally, I'm the exception to all rules. He's fully aware that if he asks me not to do something, I'd do it out of spite.

But even I know not to provoke him when it comes to a condition he has no control over. And while I love messing with him, I also respect limits and try not to aggravate him on that side anymore.

Look at me being all mature and shit.

"Where's Alan?" I ask.

"Day off. His wedding anniversary."

"Aw, that's so cute. I'll prepare his wife a belated gift tomorrow."

He nods but says nothing. I swear Leo and Sam were personally trained by Eli to keep conversations to a bare minimum.

I powder my face and redo my lipstick. "So, what's this dinner about?"

"Have you tried asking him?"

"Yeah, and he said it's a business dinner with some important investor who's bringing his wife, and therefore, it's only tactical for me to join. He told me to keep my mouth shut, talk fashion with the woman, and behave. To which I said I can't keep my mouth shut and talk fashion at the same time. He needed to provide more comprehensible instructions."

I swear the corner of Leo's mouth pulls in a smile before he schools it.

"You also think it's funny, right?"

"I think nothing."

"Come on, you must believe him to be absurd at times."

He shakes his head once.

"You're no fun." I sigh as I slide the lipstick into my bag. "So, any further information I should know about this Mr. and Mrs.…"

"Meyers. Robert and Janet Meyers."

"Right. Them."

"Can you try not to say the wrong names, for starters?"

"Don't be silly. Rory and Jennifer Maybech. I definitely remember them."

He glances at me with confusion and probably thoughts on how to subdue me without killing me.

"I was kidding."

He narrows his eyes.

"Robert and Janet Meyers. I'm not that thick."

He seems to question that internally as he focuses back on the road. "Robert is in his midthirties and the sole heir of his family's long-standing business. They have cash to spare, and the boss needs to make sure it goes to King Enterprises' recent project. It's the only way for his father to bring him back to said project."

"Why did Uncle Aiden remove him in the first place?"

"Lack of seriousness."

I snort. "Eli kind of worships money and is a certified workaholic, so I find that hard to believe."

"He walked out of an important meeting with no reason."

"I'm sure he had one."

"Yeah. Your impromptu visit to Remi."

My lips part. "He…he left just for that?"

He nods once.

"Why didn't you stop him?"

"You believe he can be stopped when it comes to you?"

I'm starting to think the answer is a resounding no.

Worse, I have no idea what to feel about the fact I'm the reason he's in a tough situation with his father and lost a project I've often heard him discuss with Leo.

I'd like to think it's not my fault that he walked out due to a stupid reason like my attempt to provoke him, but it still nags at me.

Leo pulls up at the Ritz, and my door opens as soon as the car halts.

I should be used to the view that greets me by now, but despite the time I've spent in this man's company, the sight of him never fails to steal my breath.

He looks tall and elegant in a tailored black suit and is mouthwateringly alluring just standing there.

He narrows his eyes as I step out of the car, careful not to trip and accidentally end up in his arms.

I blame my addiction to his touch and how viciously familiar I am with those big veiny hands that he slips behind my back and then presses against my hip.

It's suicidal to feel safe in his arms, completely illogical to recognize his warmth and scent as my home, and yet I can't chase away those emotions.

If anything, the signs of withdrawal I felt for the entire day slowly disappear as his godlike presence fills my surroundings, blinding me to everything else.

"Is there a reason you're riding in the front seat?" His nonchalant voice carries in the air like a sinful promise.

It's unfair that he makes everything seem sexual in nature. I blame his voice. Superior genes and all that.

"Leo and I are friends." I wave at him. "See you later, Leo!"

The man briefly closes his eyes before he nods and drives away.

"Stop calling him that." Eli's tone turns clipped as he guides me through the entrance.

"I'm confused. His name is Leo. You know, it's short for 'Leonardo.'"

"I know who Leo is, and you will not call him that again. He's Henderson."

"Meh. I told you that's too impersonal. I prefer treating people like actual humans instead of disposables."

"His paycheck is definitely not disposable."

"Again, money doesn't buy interpersonal relationships. We need to work on that."

"You need to work on behaving during this dinner, Ava."

"Okay," I say, mostly because I feel unintentionally guilty about the whole "he blew up a business opportunity and got kicked out of the project because of me" fact.

"I mean it." He glances at me. "There have to be zero fucking mistakes tonight."

"What will I get in return?"

He drops his lips to my ear. "My tongue and cock shoved deep in your cunt and a few handprints on that arse. Whether those actions end in a mind-numbing orgasm or edging with no release is completely dependent on your behavior tonight."

His warm breaths disappear, but a shock wave of shivers breaks out down my spine.

Damn him and his crude mouth.

And why does he look completely cool and collected

while I'm on the verge of combustion? Another pair of underwear is ruined.

Fantastic.

The waiter leads us to the table, where a bald man with intense brown eyes is sitting beside a meek woman with chestnut hair, slim figure, and a stunning Vera Wang gown.

"Love the dress!" I say as I hug her in greeting. "Spring/summer Vera Wang. My favorite."

"Oh my. Thank you," she says with a shy smile. "Love your handbag. Moynat Réjane?"

"This is my precious baby." I stroke the bag as if it's an actual pet.

"At the expense of interrupting the gibberish going on, I'd love to introduce myself." The bald guy, Robert, takes my hand and places an open-mouthed kiss on the top.

I pull it away subtly and mask my disgust with my charming smile. "It's lovely to meet you both."

"The pleasure is all mine. I must say, she looks much more beautiful than the pictures, King."

"I don't believe you should be concerned with my wife's beauty. Don't you think, Mrs. Meyers?"

Janet turns into a statue and stares at her husband, who releases a loud cringeworthy laugh.

I glare at Eli as we sit down. He's been warning me to behave for two days now, but he's the one who's ruffling feathers from the get-go.

After we order food and it arrives, I'm content talking tips about the newest niche brands with Janet as the men discuss business.

I try not to be bothered by Robert's stolen glances at

my hint of cleavage and the way he suggestively licks his lips when Eli isn't looking.

He doesn't seem to care whether Janet sees him, though, and I feel a crushing pity toward her. She's a sweet woman, and although she's several years older than me, I feel the need to protect her from the slimy bastard.

I don't like him at all, but I don't show that, because Eli needs him to get back into his dad's good graces.

So I focus on Janet instead, trying to compliment her on her effortlessly chic taste.

"It's tough times for a project of that grandiosity," Robert says as he cuts through his rare-cooked steak and then glides the piece of meat through the blood like a creepy cannibal. "I applaud your confidence to make it work."

"I don't sell confidence, Robert. I sell facts. So when I tell you I'll deliver a certain ROI, that's exactly the amount you'll get. Not a dime less, though more is negotiable."

"You want my investment, King?"

"I want cooperation. A partnership, if you will. You get access to King Enterprises' resources, and I get temporary use of your cash flow."

"I can give you that. Better yet, it'll be an unconditional investment in your ongoing endeavors."

I smile. Honestly, he looks like the worst type of husband, but at least he's smart enough to trust Eli on money matters.

My husband is an expert at doubling and tripling investments, so this is in his favor.

He doesn't look pleased with Robert's words, though. His face remains neutral as he takes a sip of his drink. "What do you want in return?"

Robert drops his fork and knife to the dish but doesn't release them as his lips curl in a lopsided smirk and then points his knife at me. "Your wife for a night. You can have my wife in return."

My jaw nearly hits the floor. What the—

I stare at Janet's downward expression, her fingers curled in her lap, and the shocking realization that this is probably not the first time her husband has suggested this hits me in my bones.

My eyes fly to Eli, who sets his glass on the table, an unhinged smile curling his lips.

Oh God.

He's not thinking about it, is he? I'd cut off his dick while he sleeps if he so much as—

In a flash, Eli snatches the knife and jams it through the back of Robert's hand. The blinding strength breaks the dish, and Robert's blood mixes with the meat's as his hollow scream fills the restaurant.

All eyes are on us, and a few waiters rush over to the scene. Janet shrieks as she jumps up, then falls back to her seat.

Eli stands with eerie collectedness and buttons his jacket. "You're lucky we're in public, or that knife would've been deep in your throat. Look at my wife again, and I'll gouge your eyes out."

He grabs my elbow and pulls me up as I wobble on unsteady legs.

The waiters are fawning over Robert as he curses and acts like a spoiled brat toward the people trying to help him.

"Bin him, Sis." I pat Janet's hand as she stares up at me with lost eyes. "You deserve so much better."

Then Eli is walking me out of the restaurant amid gaping faces without batting an eye, as if he didn't just stab a man.

The night air slaps my face as we stop in front of the hotel, waiting for the car.

My tongue is still in knots, but I manage to ask in a strangled voice, "Why...why did you do that?"

"Why not?" His grip slides from my arm to my waist, tightening on my hip. "You want to spend the fucking night with Robert, Ava?"

I shake my head frantically. He sounds and looks more terrifying than when he actually stabbed the man's hand.

"Good, because there's no option for you with other men."

"Because you'd stab them?"

"Stab them, sabotage them, smash their goddamn lives to smithereens, force them to vanish without a trace. Take your pick. There's no peaceful future for any other man in your life, *wife*."

I swallow, the sound ringing in my ears. I knew Eli was behind the disappearance of my exes and any possible love interest, but I thought it was along the lines of my petty attempts to ward off the girls around him. I never thought it'd be exponentially frightening until now.

"What...what have you done, Eli?"

"The question is, what haven't I done?"

"You're sick."

"You made me sick. Next time you parade yourself around, begging for attention, I want you to think about Robert's blood and multiply it tenfold, because they'll be swimming in theirs once I'm done with them. You're my wife, and those who don't respect that fact will be dealt with accordingly."

"Including me?"

"Including you." And then his lips devour mine. It's a violent kiss I can't pull away from, and a part of me doesn't want to.

My reality flashes before me in bright red as he nips on my lip and I taste metal.

I bite his back, drawing his blood, cementing our marriage with an irreversible vow.

My husband is a full-blown sociopath, and I'm his insane, completely illogical obsession.

CHAPTER 28
AVA

IT SHOULD BE A MIRACLE THAT ELI MANAGED TO come out relatively unscathed after stabbing a man. Publicly. In an extremely affluent place.

Yet that's exactly what happened.

No charges were filed against him, and the whole thing faded away in the span of a week.

I don't think he's even taken a trip to the police station.

Unfortunately, however, the incident reached the press's grubby hands, and he couldn't exactly escape the scandalous headlines, which, in retrospect, put him in more trouble with his father—according to Leo.

Leo and I gossip now. All the time. While Sam crochets and shakes her head at us. But she loves the gossip, too. She just doesn't like to admit it.

And she's totally in our group chat of three that I named *Chamber of Gossip*. I'm no longer worried they'll out me or sell my secrets to Eli since we're a team against him.

I even overheard Sam tell him the other day to stop ordering me around. Not in those words, but it was something similar. You can bet that I hugged and kissed her chubby cheeks afterward, and she was horrified for hours.

Anyway, Leo said Eli's been dealing with the fallout

of that incident. The incident being stabbing a man and then finger fucking me in the car while I prayed Leo didn't hear us. And then as soon as we got home, Eli kept his promise and brought me to orgasm with his tongue and cock.

It still feels sick that I got off on the same hands that mutilated another person, and that I even found it hot, but I've come to the realization that I'm far from normal.

Both mentally and emotionally. Otherwise, I wouldn't be so drawn to a man who drips toxicity and charm.

But that's not for here or now.

The reason I practically invited myself over for dinner with his parents was to have a chat with my father-in-law.

Naturally, Aunt Elsa was over the moon when I called. We went shopping first, and she spoiled me rotten, bought me enough things to last me a year and inSisted I get every dress I tried on.

After dinner, however, Uncle Aiden immediately retreats to his study for some pending business calls. Before I can follow him, Aunt Elsa drags me to the sitting area.

The King mansion stands tall and proud, easily rivaling the majesty of Buckingham Palace. Its baroque architecture and intricately designed decor exude an imposing quality that perfectly reflects its owner, Uncle Aiden.

But amid the opulence and grandeur, tiny details reveal a softer side to the mansion. Cat figurines dotting shelves, niche paintings adorning walls, and the absence of pretentious statues all embody Aunt Elsa's influence in adding warmth to the house. Her efforts to make the place feel more like a home rather than just a lavish estate speaks volumes about this family. These subtle touches make the mansion feel lived in, loved in, and not just another lifeless symbol of wealth and power.

Growing up, I often wondered how Eli saw his parents' place. I know he cares for them, but he also moved out as soon as he started uni and never came back to live under their roof.

Maybe, like me, he needs a breather and his own space that's out of his parents' orbit.

"Do you want tea? Digestives?" Aunt Elsa asks as we sit on the high sofa across from the turned-off fireplace.

"I'm good."

"You didn't eat much."

"I literally have no place in my tummy anymore."

She laughs, the sound soft in the silence. "I'm glad to hear it. I wish Eli could've joined us tonight."

"He has a late meeting. You know, with everything that's going on." Which is why I chose this day to visit his parents. I don't want him around.

"Yes, that." Her brows knit together in a gentle frown before she sighs. "I'm just glad both of you are okay. I had a fright when I first heard about the incident. It brought back bad memories."

"What type of memories?"

She lifts her head, a shifty look springing in her light-blue eyes before she forces a smile. "Nothing of importance. I just wish he'd take it easy sometimes."

"Me, too," I whisper.

"Oh, I'm so sorry, Ava. It must've been scary."

"Not really. It was...*something*, but not exactly scary." I grimace. "Not sure what that says about me, though."

Especially since I fucked the guy right after and screamed his name as I came on his cock.

"It says you're his match." Aunt Elsa pats my hand. "I told you this before, but you don't remember it, so I'll say it again. I'm so happy you're with him, Ava. I always believed he needed someone like you by his side, and I'm glad he finally sees the vision."

"I'm not doing much."

"You're doing more than you think. He seems happier and more relaxed."

"Where? He's always stone-faced."

"I'm his mother. I know it when I see him. He's changed, and I like to think it's for the better." She squeezes my hand. "Thank you for helping him live a little, go out, breathe properly now and then."

"I kind of blackmail him into it."

She laughs. "And I'm grateful for that."

"God. I hope he's more like you."

"He is." She stares at an invisible spot on the wall. "Everyone thinks he's exactly like his dad, but I also brought him up and made sure to ingrain morals in him. If he ever disrespects you, I need to hear about it."

"He doesn't do that." And I mean it, he's never disrespected me. He's just a fan of breaking my heart whenever it mends itself back together.

"Good. And, Ava?"

"Yeah?"

"He's lucky to have you. I know he's hotheaded sometimes."

"Sometimes?"

"*Most* of the time, but you're hotheaded, too, young lady."

"Guilty." I raise both hands.

"Which is better than if you were meek. At least this way, you know how to handle him."

"I do?"

"Yes. The other day he was asking his father what to do if he feels like things are going so far out of control that he finds himself on the verge of snapping."

I inch closer. "And what did Uncle Aiden say?"

"If you can't afford to snap and come out of the situation unscathed or with the results you hope for, the intelligent thing to do is to walk away. Even temporarily."

My lips part. That must be why he often locks himself away from me in his study. Of course, I don't give him space and often stroll in, a book and a bucket of candy floss in hand, and proceed to read across from him, lying on the sofa with my legs up or on my stomach on the floor.

No wonder that earns me a fuck so ferocious that I can barely walk afterward and he has to carry me.

I was toying with his control when I thought I was just being a brat. Oops.

"Leo mentioned there's tension between Eli and Uncle Aiden. Do you know about that?"

"Leo?"

"Leonardo...oh, Henderson?"

"Ah. His first name is never mentioned."

"Yeah, Eli hates that I call him 'Leo.'"

"Why am I not surprised?"

"Because he can be dramatic?"

"Because he's a copy of his father in that regard. For Eli and Aiden, it's not tension. It's a rivalry of sorts, from my son's side."

"Why would he want to rival his own father?"

"Because he has this constant urge to always come out on top, and he feels like Aiden is his most worthy rival. Or Landon at times. Due to the absence of the latter, he's channeling all that energy toward his dad."

"That's not healthy."

"Tell me about it. Neither of them will back down."

"But Uncle Aiden must know how hard Eli worked on the project he got kicked out of."

"Not hard enough, as he walked out of the most important meeting for the project and then stabbed the only prospective investor. In public," Uncle Aiden says as he sits beside his wife and wraps an arm around her shoulders, slowly stroking her arm.

I've noticed that he always has to touch her in some sense, as if she's the only person who can root him in this world.

Honestly, I don't ever want to imagine him without her. Even Creighton once said neither he nor Eli can picture their dad without their mum.

He's a frightening man, not toward me since he accepted me with open arms, but he was frightening when Anni first got together with Creigh. Probably because of some unfortunate events in their story.

"It was because of me," I say slowly. "He ditched the meeting because he thought I was in danger." I lie because I don't think he'd appreciate it if I said it was due to his son's possessiveness. "And he stabbed Robert because he said his condition to invest was to sleep with me."

Aunt Elsa gasps. "That piece of shit."

The only reaction from her husband, however, is a

temporary pause of his stroking motion. "In that case, why didn't he mention it?"

"I don't know. But I can't in good conscience keep this information to myself. I wish you'd cut him some slack. He's a ridiculous workaholic, and we both know he has an obnoxious talent for making money, so the company is in good hands with him."

"That doesn't excuse his impulsive actions."

"But I just told you he did that because of me."

"And I appreciate that. I also understand his need to protect you above everything else, but that shouldn't have the power to cloud his judgment. Due to his foolish criminal actions, my father and I had to pull an absurd number of strings to keep him out of prison and are enduring being slapped with nepotism accusations. But despite that, the Meyers family is fighting back with their own connections. Robert is neither a small fish nor an insignificant fly Eli can stab and then walk away from as if nothing happened. He did not think through the consequences of his actions, and that is not a quality for a leader in this organization."

I lift my chin. "If someone suggested something similar about Aunt Elsa, would you not have done the same thing?"

"She has a point." She smiles up at him and strokes his cheek. "The apple doesn't fall far from the tree."

"I would've done worse," he admits. "But *not* in public. He should know better than to leave trails of evidence behind."

My shoulders droop with defeat because even in Eli's psychotic cases, he's never done anything in public. Even Lan thinks he's a masterful private shit stirrer with a pristine public image.

The fact he deviated from his usual pattern isn't something anyone can defend. Not even me.

Sensing my predicament, Aunt Elsa changes the subject and talks about a funny video of Creigh that Anni sent her.

I'm thinking of a way to excuse myself without disappointing her, mostly to avoid getting on Uncle Aiden's shit list. He might've heard me out and even appreciated it, but he certainly doesn't care for others stealing his wife's time. Not even his sons. He's worse than Papa in that regard.

Before I can say good night, none other than Landon walks through the sitting room's double doors, dressed in a leather jacket, black jeans, and a white tee. He runs his fingers through his hair as if he's striding through a photo shoot.

"Surprise!"

Uncle Aiden stands, and Lan goes straight to hug him.

"Miss me, Uncle?"

"Let me think on that," Uncle Aiden says as they break away.

"Wrong answer."

"The right one being?"

"*Yes*, or *absolutely*, or *I couldn't sleep thinking about you and contemplated flying over just to see you.*"

"No to all," Uncle Aiden says with a small smile.

"You know you love me. You don't have to say it." Lan drops a kiss on Aunt Elsa's cheek. "Is it just me, or do you look more beautiful than the last time I saw you?"

"Did you also tell that to your mum?" She pinches his cheek.

"Word for word. I also added that she's lost some weight—she hasn't, but she loves hearing that." He finally turns toward me and hugs me. "Barbie! How have you been without me?"

"Living just fine."

"Questionable. No one lives just fine without my godly presence. I know because I wouldn't want to live without me. You lot should pay me for having me in your lives."

I bring out my phone and put it to my ear. "Hello, MI5, Lan brought his nonsensical arrogance to Britain again. Please come pick him up for national-security purposes."

"Very funny. Getting married to Eli obviously eroded your sense of humor, aside from your common sense. Speaking of Eli, heard he's facing criminal charges?"

"No, he's not," I say. "And did you seriously just visit because of that?"

"It's a perfectly good reason to take a long-haul flight. I don't often get to laugh in his face for making a clusterfuck of a mistake."

"There will be no laughing in his face," Uncle Aiden says in a firm tone. "He knows his mistake, got punished for not considering the consequences, and is currently in the midst of finding solutions. No one needs your unnecessary gloating, Lan."

"*Thank you*," I say, inexplicably happy that Uncle Aiden is defending Eli. He might appear strict, but he and Eli share the most unique father-and-son relationship. It's not a coincidence that my husband goes only to his dad for advice, even while he tries to score points for the sake of his stupid one-sided rivalry.

"But he's never this clumsy, Uncle. Let me have my fun."

"No."

"Rest assured, I can annoy him in other ways."

"Where's Mia?" I ask.

"In the States. I only came for a few days."

"Oh God. So we get you without a leash?"

"In my full glory, Barbie. Full glory."

"Pass." I stand and smile at my parents-in-law. "I'm leaving. Night and good luck with the nutcase."

Aunt Elsa walks me to the door and inSists I take some food containers because she still believes I didn't eat much.

I walk to the car she lent me for the ride home. Their driver doesn't show up, so instead of going back and telling them that, I choose to drive it on my own. It's been a long time since I drove anyway—since the day I ruined Eli's car. Oops.

Lan slides in front of me with a devil-may-care smirk. He looks no different than a demon spawn under the drive-way's faint light.

"Now what?" I hike a hand on my hip, staring him down.

"If my ears didn't betray me, I think I heard you defend-ing Eli to Uncle Aiden."

"How long were you there?"

"Long enough to doubt my own ears. You taking Eli's side? I was honestly looking for clues of a parallel universe."

"I was...only telling the truth."

"Since when does the truth matter when it comes to your position about my cousin?"

"Since now."

"Hmm." He watches me peculiarly as he leans against the car and crosses his arms and ankles.

"What?"

"I'm contemplating whether to share a thought-provoking tidbit."

"Is it about me?"

"Certainly. But seeing things in a new light, I'm not sure if it'll do you harm or good."

"If it's about me, I'd like to know."

"Are you strong enough to take it?"

"Since when do you care about that, Landon?"

"I very much do. While I want to provoke Eli, I don't wish to end up on the top of his mile-long hit list, but since I'm here anyway, might as well make it worth my while. Let me ask you something. Are you aware your psychiatrist changed?"

"Yeah."

"Do you know why?"

"My previous psychiatrist left the UK."

"By choice?"

"What is that supposed to mean?"

"Just a question. Next one: Have you had any strange episodes lately?"

"No. I've been rather stable since I woke up in the hospital." Aside from that panic attack outside the restaurant, I haven't had any of my usual episodes. I used to be on edge anticipating the next one, but I've been so content lately that I've started to get used to this anxiety-free life.

Even if a part of me still shivers at the thought of going to sleep and constantly thinks of my next epic meltdown.

"Ever wondered why?" Lan asks.

"New meds. They're really good and have little side effects, mostly lethargy, but not too often."

"Cool."

"'Cool'? What's the meaning of this questionnaire, Lan?"

"Just bringing things into perspective. That's all."

"That's never all with you. What are you trying to tell me?"

"I don't know. Truly. It would've been different if I'd found you in your usual spot as the founder of Eli's anti–fan club, but to my dismay, you've changed."

"I...have not."

"Barbie, please. You just talked to Uncle Aiden like Eli's devout wife, who's trying to take the burn off her husband. You haven't only changed—you're diving headfirst into your old feelings for him."

"I would never give him my heart again. Not after he broke it."

"Hey, there's no need to convince me. And if it's of any consolation, I do believe he's doing this for your sake. Deep down, he cares. In his own screwed-up, twisted way, but his methods will sooner or later come to bite him in the arse."

"*Cares?* Eli?"

"A man doesn't go to the lengths of eliminating each one of your prospects and then proceed to marry you if he doesn't care."

"Ownership and care aren't the same thing, Lan."

"No, but they can coexist." He pushes off the door and opens it for me. "Should you be driving?"

"Why wouldn't I?"

He merely shrugs as I slide in and place the food containers in the passenger seat.

Lan waves at me while I pull out from my

parents-in-law's house. As I listen to cello performances by a Finnish soloist, Lan's words keep playing in the back of my head.

It's true that I had many questions after I caught Eli and even Sam in a lie, but I chose to ignore said discrepancies for the sake of my peace of mind.

Lan implied that I should consider whether or not the truth is worth sacrificing my current stability.

A few months ago, I would've always gone for the truth, but right now, as I stare at my wedding band and think of everything that comes with it, I'm not sure if that's the right solution.

Why is my truth more important than the suffering of those around me? My parents, Ari, Cecy, Aunt Elsa, and even Sam and Leo, who have been nothing but kind to me.

Eli as well. I don't think it's fair to put him through my embarrassing episodes. He has no obligation to take care of me since we're not in a real marriage.

My music comes to a halt as none other than my husband's name flashes on the screen.

I pick up with "Speak of the devil. Miss me, *darling*?"

"Are you driving?" His clipped tone fills the car with a coat of tension.

"Yeah."

"Why the *fuck*—" He cuts himself off, then speaks slowly as if he's addressing a child. "Pull over this instant and call a black cab. If they take too long, I'll come to pick you up."

"Um, no? I can drive on my own just fine."

"Pull the fuck over, Ava!"

I startle, clenching my fingers around the steering wheel.

Eli never yells at me. *Ever.* Not even when I thought he would at the height of my provocations.

I indicate to the left and pull over, then put the car in Park, mostly because I'm shaking too hard to be driving.

My ears ring, and I hear my name being called as if it's coming from underground.

An image passes through my head in a flash. I'm slumped against the side of the car.

Crimson stains mar every inch of my skin, coating my hands and thighs with a slick, sticky film. I can feel blood beneath my nails and over the pads of my fingers. The bright red pools on the ground form an abstract canvas in the dim light of the street. My breaths come in ragged gasps as I try to steady myself, my heart pounding loudly in my chest. It's as if the blood has seeped into every corner of my being, smearing me inside and out.

"Ava!" Eli's booming voice echoes in my ear, but I can't look up from the blood on my hands.

Oh no.

What have I done?

What have I—

"Ava?"

I lift my head and look at the distorted, blurry version of Eli's handsome face.

"Give me your hand," he orders in a firm voice.

I shake my head frantically. "Blood...blood..."

"Look at me. Hey, look at me. Focus on me. That's it. Good girl. Breathe. Mimic me and breathe properly. In...

out...in...out... You're doing great, beautiful. Now I want you to take my hand, okay?"

My shaky fingers rise, and the scraping of my heels on the asphalt echo like a bomb in the eerie silence.

Eli pulls me into his embrace, and everything turns black.

CHAPTER 29

ELI

FUCK.

Bloody fucking hell.

Fuck!

Henderson brings the car to an abrupt halt right across from Ava's, and I fling the door open before it properly stops and jog to the vehicle.

She went completely silent on the phone after I told her to pull over, so I had Henderson follow her phone's GPS and bring us here at the speed of light.

The last thing my wife should do is drive. She's not fit to do so by any stretch of the imagination. Worse, it's a triggering factor.

Mum and Dad should've made sure she got into the car with a fucking driver, not on her own. If Landon hadn't told me, I would've probably found her in a ditch by now.

The tightness in my steps matches that of my chest the closer I approach the car. I pause by the door and inhale a large gulp of air, readying myself for the disaster Sam, Henderson, Ariella, Cecily, and even Dad told me was coming.

The disaster of my own making.

Cold air bites into my skin as the residential area's faint lighting casts an ominous halo on the black car.

I dip my head and pause when I find Ava slumped on the steering wheel, turned away from me, her blond hair spilling in silky waves that mimic a fallen angel's.

The faint sound of a cello filters through the closed window with the smoothness of a haunting lullaby.

I pull on the handle. Locked.

Fuck.

This is the worst case of déjà vu.

The last time she was slumped and unresponsive in a car was when I tethered her to me and bound her to my side forever.

I told her she had no choice, but that was far from the truth.

She's slipping between my fingers with the perSistence of sand despite my attempts to trap her sickness. Asphyxiate it. Fucking dismantle it.

I built an hourglass, but it's been cracking for months, and I refused to see the damage. Not in the late-night walks nor the mindless existence of her ghostly version.

However, this incident is prone to shove her to the point of no return and decimate any hourglass remnants.

I couldn't care less.

If everything spills over, I'll find a way to trap her in again. Even if I have to buy every fucking desert and shove the sand back inside.

My jaw clenches as I tap on the window gently to avoid startling her, even if part of me feels she's too far gone to hear anything.

I do it again, injecting more strength behind the knock.

My wife stirs and I pause, my hand suspended in midair.

Slowly, she lifts herself and turns in my direction, her stiff movement no different than a robot's.

Fuck.

Her eyes are clouded, not empty, but also not present either. It's a mysterious mix of lethargy and alertness.

She clicks a button on the dashboard without my having to say anything.

I carefully pry the door open and lower myself so my face is level with hers in an attempt to reduce the threatening factor.

The smell of seafood fills my nostrils, but a hint of sweet flowers continues to emanate from her.

My wife gapes up at me with those deep-blue eyes that are floundering between life and death.

Like a shadow of her former self.

"Hey," I say with as much softness as I can muster.

"Hey," she mutters back, a shine gathering in her eyelids as they gradually clear. "You came."

"Of course."

"I think I had a panic attack."

"Did you take your meds?"

She frantically searches in her spilled bag, and some makeup products fall out before she produces her bottle of pills and hands it over. "I took two. Swallowed them dry."

"Good girl." I stroke her cheek, sliding my fingers to her throat and pressing on that steady pulse point.

She leans into my touch, her lips dropping open before she sucks the bottom one between her teeth.

My gaze follows the motion, and my dick definitely takes notice, failing—as usual—to read the damn situation.

She releases her lip and pushes it forward in a small pout. "You yelled at me. I didn't like it."

"Won't happen again."

"Thanks. I had fun with Aunt Elsa today and the dinner with Uncle Aiden went well."

"Good."

"She sent you food."

"I see."

"It's actually for me, but I'll share."

"I'm grateful."

"Lan came back, and he was talking shit as usual."

"It'd be shocking if he weren't."

"He could use being brought down a peg or two."

"I'll arrange it."

Her lips twitch in the tiniest smile, and I release a long exhale. It's her.

My wife is back.

I release her throat, but only so I can guide her out of the car. But she inSists on picking up all the things that fell out of her bag and the food containers.

"Hey, Leo." She waves at him as she places the containers in the passenger seat. "Be careful with these, please."

He nods.

"I'll strap them in just in case."

I tilt my head, watching her movements. They're still slightly robotic, her fingers moving in a jerky manner due to the residual tremors, but she's speaking without the haunting edge.

She's also behaving normally, so that should be a promising sign.

After she makes sure the bag of containers is strapped in, she narrows her eyes on me. "You won't object?"

"About?"

"Me calling him 'Leo.'"

"Do you want me to object?"

"Nope." She smiles and kisses my cheek. "You can be so adorable when you're compliant, babe."

And then she slides into the back seat.

I remain rooted in place, reSisting the urge to touch where her lips burned my skin.

Did she just call me *adorable* and *babe* in the same sentence after kissing my cheek?

Jesus fucking Christ.

Maybe I should be the one who sees a doctor because I want her to repeat what just happened in that exact order.

Better yet, perhaps I should have her checked in case the brat behavior underwent some dangerous mutation.

I catch a glimpse of Henderson trying to hide his creepy smile. It disappears as soon as I narrow my eyes at him.

Maybe it's time to chuck him over a cliff. I don't appreciate his recent bonding with my wife nor the way she keeps buying him stuff and making sure he eats. She's not his mother, last I checked.

I'm the only one she needs to make sure eats.

And no, I'm not being dramatic. This is perfectly normal behavior, even according to my father.

Mum said I shouldn't listen to him, but she's wrong in this instance.

I join my wife in the back seat, subtly searching for any red flags. As soon as the car moves, she faces me, a cryptic look casting a sheen over her expression.

Ava has always been an open book, including her attention-seeking behavior and over-the-top hatred during the past couple of years. I recognized what she wanted to accomplish with those attributes, and I often smashed any opportunity where she could've moved on to smithereens.

Again, and again, and fucking again.

Until she fell to her knees and could only see me as her savior.

Not anyone else. *Me.*

And yet, right now, she feels foreign. Not that ghost version of herself, but something different whose fine print I can't read.

"Why can't I drive?" she asks in a low, barely audible voice.

"It's not that you can't."

"It's that I shouldn't," she finishes. "I figured that out from your uncharacteristic anger. You were worried about me because you anticipated the panic attack. Will I get one every time I drive?"

"Most likely."

"Is that why you didn't let me drive home that time when I, uh, damaged your car?"

"Correct."

"It's a trigger?"

"Yes."

"It wasn't a trigger before I lost my memory."

"It is now."

"Why?"

"It's not important."

"According to you?"

I nod.

"Okay, but do you want to know what I think?"

"Go ahead," I say, even though I don't appreciate where this conversation is heading, let alone her apathetic tone and expressionless face.

"I think you don't want me to know about an accident that could have traumatic effects that could interfere with my state."

I drum my fingers on my thigh, exhibiting nonchalance that's the exact opposite of the roar of alarm igniting in my brain. My voice is calmer, more controlled than hers. "Have you remembered something?"

"Only a few images of me slumped by a car and staring at blood. You were there." Her cloak of neutrality slips as she gapes at me with a trembling chin. "Is it true?"

"Does my judgment on what's true and false in your memories count?"

"Yes."

"Why?"

"Because you saw me at my worst and stayed."

"What makes you think that?"

"I'm not an idiot, Eli, and I also have enough self-awareness to know you must've seen the version of me that's riddled with so many issues, she shouldn't be allowed outside, and yet you neither threw me back at my parents nor locked me up in a psychiatric facility. You never treated me as abnormal, and I'm grateful. No, I'm beyond grateful. I *owe* you, and therefore, I trust you in this regard."

"Don't do that. I can't trust myself most of the time, so neither should you."

A small smile tilts her lips, and I want to sink my teeth into that cushion and suck her blood through it. I need her to stop smiling, or else she won't like the consequences of her actions.

"I still think you're more trustworthy than my head," she whispers. "Lan mentioned things about my ex- psychiatrist and abnormal behavior, but I'll ignore that and my unreliable memories if you tell me so."

My jaw tightens. That motherfucker Landon seems to be back for his funeral. A wish I'll grant him sooner rather than later.

"What else did Lan say?"

"Nonsense as usual."

"What type of nonsense?"

A red hue covers her cheeks, and I don't like it one bit. Why the fuck is she blushing when thinking about that slimy little bastard?

She clears her throat. "Nothing important."

"Tell me and I'll decide whether or not it's important."

"It's really nothing." She eyes me carefully. "What about everything else I just mentioned? Is it also nothing?"

I can see the hope in her bright blue eyes and the need to believe in this dark fairy tale that I built for her.

I can see the next crack in the hourglass, and instead of letting nature take its course, I place one more bloodstained plaster on the pending dust devil.

I let my hand curl around her smaller one as I say, "It's nothing."

A shiver rushes through her as she releases a puff of air and flips her hand, interlinking our fingers. "Thanks."

I stare at the contrast of her fairer skin against mine and the sparkling pink nails that she often drags anywhere she can touch me. I might leave marks all over her throat, tits, and arse, but my wife never fails to leave hers as well. Even if I tie her up, she somehow finds a way to claw at me.

My phone vibrates and I ignore it, probably because it means letting her go to check it.

When it vibrates again, however, I retrieve it with my free hand.

> **Dad:** I expect you in the meeting for the Ansil project tomorrow.

Despite the absolute awkwardness of typing with one hand, I do so anyway.

> **Me:** Since when are outsiders allowed in strategic meetings?
> **Dad:** You're not an outsider. You're back on the roster.
> **Me:** Why? Pressure from Mum?
> **Dad:** And your wife.

I stare at the screen, then at Ava, who's watching me expectantly. Pressure from who, now?

My wife?

Since when is she able to pressure my dad?

> **Me:** Are you sure you don't mean YOUR wife? Last I checked she's the only one able to pressure you into anything.
> **Dad:** Ava told me the reasons why you walked out of the meeting and stabbed Robert are both

related to her. Is there a reason why you haven't shared those details yourself?

Me: I don't like to offer excuses.

Dad: I'm your father, Eli. You can use excuses with me.

Me: I don't like it and I don't want to be reinstated in the project because of my wife.

Dad: Well, you are and you should learn how to be grateful.

I lift my head to find my wife still watching me, her fingers tightening around my hand as if predicting my next move.

"What did you tell my dad?" I wrench my arm away.

She doesn't let me go easily, and one of her nails slashes against my skin.

Ava doesn't hide her look of disappointment. "The truth."

"What gave you the impression you could tell him anything?"

"The fact you're being blamed and kicked out of a project without him knowing the truth."

"If I'd wanted to tell him, I would've."

"But you didn't, so I did it for you."

"You did it *for* me? Should I offer a standing ovation? I don't need my wife to offer excuses for me. Due to your unnecessary actions, he won't even take me seriously."

"Hey. He's your dad, not your keeper, and he definitely takes you seriously."

The car comes to a stop in front of the house, and I grind my teeth. "Don't be a busybody, Ava. Are we clear?"

"I'm sorry I tried to help." Her chin trembles as she shoves the door open and gets out before she jams her head back in. "And for the record, a thank-you would've sufficed."

She rushes to the entrance as Henderson opens my door, and I swear the bastard glares at me.

"What?" I bark. "She was getting her nose in my business."

"You're married. It's both your business."

"I can't believe this. You're taking her side now?"

He merely looks away as if I'm the one being unreasonable.

"For the record," Henderson says as I step out of the car, "she was stressed about the fact she's the reason you got kicked out of the project twice and has been brainstorming ways to help. Do you believe it was easy for her to go to your father and out herself as the reason? Do you believe a proud person like her wants to be seen as your weakness by your parents?"

My jaw clenches. "You're talking too much today. Is this your two weeks' notice?"

"No, it's my humanity notice," he says with a blank face before he turns around and leaves.

My steps are long and stiff as I barge through the house. The moment I go into my room, I find Ava there, her bag on the floor and a hand on her hip.

This is the first time she's come into my room. I'm the one who usually goes to hers.

"What now?" I ask in an impatient voice as I shrug off my jacket and place it neatly on the chair.

"I want to move in."

"Move in where? We live in the same house."

"I want to move into your room."

I loosen my tie. "You're the one who wanted separate rooms."

"Well, I changed my mind."

"I didn't."

"Why?"

"Because I believe in privacy." And not triggering the fuck out of her.

"Oh, I see." She steps in front of me, forcing me to look at her. "In that case, I believe in space."

"You have all the space you need. In your room."

"Will you come over to fuck me tonight?"

"I didn't think you'd be in the mood after everything."

"I am. Angry sex is my favorite."

My cock hardens against my trousers, being a literal dick and not reading the power dynamic going on here. "Is that so?"

"Yeah. You happen to be decent at fucking me."

"*Decent*? You scream the fucking house down when my cock is filling your cunt, Mrs. King. I reckon I'm more than *decent*."

"I said what I said." She studies her nails. "Well? Will you be coming? Pun intended."

"I'll consider it."

"Consider it faster." She stands on her tiptoes and strokes an invisible crease on my shirt. "And while you're at it, consider whether you'll look at my face while being inside me, because that's the only way I'll allow you to touch me."

She goes back down and flashes me a sweet smile.

"You'll have to share my bed, too. I'm not your whore, Eli. I'm your wife, and you'll treat me as such."

I let my lips pull in a smirk. "What's the reason for this sudden change? I thought you agreed that we didn't need intimacy."

"I changed my mind. So either you give me what I want, or I'll find someone who does. Think about it, okay?"

I grab her by the elbow, digging my fingers into the skin. "There will be no someone else, Ava. That ship has long since sailed for you."

She kisses the corner of my mouth. "Then you better think fast, *babe*."

Then she waltzes out of the room, swaying her hips and flipping her hair.

And I know—I just know I'll fuck up everything for this woman.

Her lifeline included.

CHAPTER 30
AVA

"SPILL, CECY. HOW DO YOU SEDUCE THAT MAN of yours?"

My friend chokes on her juice, droplets scattering all over the table and the camera and running out of her nose.

"Gee, thanks for the lemonade shower, Ava." She wipes her nose with a napkin.

"What? Everyone knows Jeremy is physically unable to look away from you. Pretty sure he'd fuck you in public if you let him. So help a girl out and give me pointers on how you keep him coming back for more."

A blush creeps up her cheeks, and she rubs her nose. "I don't really do anything. He kind of jumps me the moment he sees me."

I look up. "God, I've seen what you've done for other people, and I want some."

"Stop being dramatic. Besides, the way Jeremy looks at me is heavily rivaled by the intense way Eli looks at you."

"Bitch, please. No need to lie just to make me feel better."

"I mean it. You're my best friend, and I love you, but you can be so blind sometimes. Also, why do you need seduction pointers? You've been complaining about being sore and achy for a while now. Though you stopped complaining over the last week."

"Ten days." I sigh as I flop back on the floor of my music room and lift the phone.

Cecy leans over on the table and abandons the manga she was reading, or pretending to. We have days where we put each other on the camera while we do our things. I'll practice or read, and she'll do the same. It's comforting to know that she's always there even if a whole ocean separates us.

"What happened ten days ago?" she asks.

"I kinda, sort of made a stupid suggestion."

"What type of suggestion?"

"A condition, actually."

"And? You're leaving me in suspense here."

"I told Eli he can't touch me unless he moves into the same room with me and that he also has to look at my face while being inside me. You know, very logical things a wife can ask of her husband. The result? The bastard completely shut me out."

I try not to sound hurt. Jeez, I'd be so embarrassed if I were talking to anyone else other than Cecy.

"Was I wrong?" I ask with a wince.

She smiles softly. "Absolutely not. I'm surprised you allowed him to get away with it in the first place."

"He made it seem as if I demanded he love me or something. Besides, even if I was hungry for affection, I kept it in. There's no way in hell I would've made myself look desperate."

"And now?"

"If I'm stuck in this relationship, I don't want to compromise on my needs."

"Gosh. I'm so proud of you."

"Yeah, well. It didn't work. And I've tried everything, you know." I count on my free hand. "I walked around the house in the most erotic nightgowns ever, and he simply didn't look at me, as if I were thin air. I barged into his study in the skimpiest clothes ever, sucking on a lollipop and making my lips all glossy and shit, and read a book on the sofa across from his desk while offering him a front-row seat to my cleavage, but he proceeded to kick me out and lock the door. I spammed his inbox with teasing pictures, and he completely ignored me. He doesn't even come home at reasonable hours anymore. We used to spend some time together before, but it's like he doesn't want to see my face now."

In- or outside of sex.

And that hurts more than I'm willing to admit.

"Hey." Cecy softens her voice, effortlessly turning on her motherly instincts. "I know it sucks, but you're doing nothing wrong, Ava. It's his loss for not appreciating you."

"Text him that."

"Will do."

"Don't. He'll know I care about this enough to talk about it with you."

"We come as a set. He can deal with it."

I grin. "Hell yeah."

"Let me ask you something." She pauses as if weighing her words. "Didn't you always say you don't like sharing a room with anyone, me included, because you don't want anyone to witness your state during a nightmare? Why is Eli the exception?"

"He knows, Cecy. *Everything*. More than he's willing

to discuss with me, apparently. Maybe it's my wishful thinking in attempting to test him further and see if he's truly accepting." In reality, I think I just don't want to sleep alone anymore.

My inSistence on always having my own room isn't because I like solitude; it's because I've been terrified of anyone seeing me at my worst.

I'd be lying if I said my fear has completely disappeared, but my yearning for company outshines it.

And inexplicably, Eli is the one whose company I'm irrevocably desperate for.

Or maybe I just don't want to admit the actual reasons aloud.

"Do you want my advice?" Cecy asks in a sly tone.

"Always."

"Isn't Lan around?"

"Ugh. That shit stirrer? Yeah, and he didn't even come with Mia or Bran, who could momentarily keep him on a leash."

"I can't believe I'm saying this, but that's even better since you can use him to do what you do best."

"Which is?"

"Provoke Eli."

"Um, Cecy? Weren't you the one who always advised me not to do that? Who are you, and what have you done to my bestie?"

"That was before you guys got married. I thought you could escape his orbit if you stopped provoking him, but that ship has sailed now."

"What makes you think it'll work when he's been acting like I'm invisible?"

"If it doesn't, you might want to start thinking about whether those compromises are your hard limits. If they are, you might also want to think about the usability of this marriage and if the convenience outweighs the heartache."

My eyes burn and blur. "Why didn't you stop me from marrying him, Cecy? It was obviously a disaster waiting to happen."

"I tried. I even told you it was going to hurt, but you said it was worth it. I'm not sure that's still the case."

"I wish I could hug you right now."

"Me, too. But, Ava?"

"Yeah?"

"Don't give up. Show him what you've got."

———

What I've got are a lot of social contacts and Lan. He can count as his own social curriculum wrapped in a bow of trouble.

There's also Remi, who's in line for second in trouble.

The three of us do what we do best—party.

We throw one on the massive yacht Eli owns. I would've thrown it at the house just to smash his OCD to pieces, but it's also my house, and I'm the only one who can wreak havoc inside it.

Besides, Sam would've killed me if I ever attempted to bring chaos to her carefully curated order, so we came up with this compromise, and she provided the catering while Leo smuggled me the keys.

I'm wearing a little pink dress with a tulle skirt and a tight sheer lace corset with built-in bra cups that cover my breasts.

In the matter of an hour, the yacht is brimming with people whose names I barely remember, nor where I met them. But then again, this is about quantity, not quality. So the more, the merrier.

I needed to get out of the funk that Eli forced me into by ignoring my existence.

"Not bad for an amateur," Remi says over the trendy DJ music as we dance to the beat. He has a drink in hand while I nurse a virgin piña colada and sway from side to side.

"Bitch, please. This isn't my first rodeo."

"To be fair, she was more of a party animal than you, Rems." Lan barely moves and is more content typing away at his phone. Judging by the pleasant expression on his face, he's definitely talking to Mia.

"See?" I raise a brow.

"Blasphemy! My lordship is the hallmark of partying. Might dress like me, talk like me, and try to be the next best thing, but it's not quite me."

"Stop stealing Eminem's lines." I push him jokingly. "And while you're at it, try not to be jealous of my goddess superiority."

"Yeah, I left that to your annoying husband." He puffs out a breath. "He made my life hell after your last impromptu visit. Tripled my workload, gave Ariella full access to my schedule, and even assigned me some stupid project that's been single-handedly destroying my colorful social life."

"Sucks to be you," Lan says with a smirk, still focused on his phone. "But then again, you're not on my cousin's level, so you better cut your losses and take whatever he dishes out in your direction."

"Hey!" I stop dancing. "I didn't invite you guys to make He-Who-Shall-Not-Be-Named the topic of discussion."

"Oh my." Lan pockets his phone and smirks with a knowing edge. "And here I thought that was the entire point of this fiasco."

"You're such a wanker."

"Which is the exact reason why you invited me, Barbie. I accept gratitude in the form of mayhem. The bigger, the better."

"Dear Lord," Remi mutters. "You invited Ariella?"

"She kind of invited herself when she found out you'd be here." I'm barely finished speaking when my sister jumps him in a koala embrace.

"I'm here! Miss me?"

"Absolutely not." He pries her off with great difficulty.

"I know you did." She smiles and blows him a kiss, then hugs me. "Sick party, Sissy."

"I have a feeling it'll be even better with your presence," I mutter.

"You can bet." She kisses me several times on the cheek. "Now, where's that brother-in-law of mine, and why isn't he behaving like a caveman for once?"

"He's not invited," I say. "It's a party for my friends, and he doesn't belong on the list."

"Ooh, sassy Ava is in full swing. We love it." She giggles.

"Suicidal as well, apparently," Lan says with a wide grin. "We definitely love it."

"Recorded and kept for possible use in future tight situations." Remi stares at his phone and nods with approval.

"I can create tight situations." Ariella licks her lips.

"Right, then." He pivots on his heel. "I need another drink."

"Wait for me!" She stops and hugs me. "I'm rooting for you."

And then she's running after Remi like a loyal puppy. No, more like a seriously vicious dog.

"Not sure if I should be worried about her or him," I mutter.

"Him." Lan nods. "Definitely him. Rems is a pure soul compared to your witch of a sister."

I kick his leg. "You're in no position to call her that when you're the devil incarnate."

He shrugs, but then his usually bored face breaks into a creepily joyful expression when his phone vibrates in his hand.

Lan doesn't even say goodbye as he picks up and walks away. "I'm putting it on the record. The worst decision of the year was flying without you, muse."

Fantastic. Now I'm on my own again.

I socialize with some friends and refuse any competitions concerning chugging indescribable amounts of alcohol. Honestly, I should be rewarded for sticking to my sobriety for so long and barely being tempted.

But then again, I feel good, mostly, and I'm impulsive as fuck when drunk, so I consider this a win.

My feet halt when I approach the bar to order another drink.

"What are you doing here?" I ask in a cool tone as none other than Gemma and her friend stand up.

Said friend is Vance, who I heard was being sent back

to Australia by his family. Naturally, I suspected Eli had a hand in it after that very public punch at the charity event, but, apparently, I heard wrong, because he's standing here just fine.

"I brought her with me. I thought you guys were friends?" He smiles in that golden-boy manner that Lan wears like a mask.

Maybe it's the same for V as well, but I never noticed it before.

"Friends don't seduce their friend's husband." I tilt my head to the side. "Right, Gemma?"

"Ava." She takes my hand between hers. "I would never."

"Please." I pull my hand free with visible disdain. "Don't gaslight me when I personally saw you bat your lashes at my husband."

"But you don't even like him." Her tone changes from pleading to snotty entitlement.

"That doesn't give you carte blanche to seduce him."

"You're being selfish."

Gemma is like me. She doesn't like being denied what she wants. But she's probably worse, in a sense. I don't pretend to be a Goody Two-shoes, whereas she made up a makeshift personality where she always appears like a damsel in distress, victimized and sickeningly nice.

And she's done it so well, never breaking out of character, even in private, that I fell for it at one point.

"*Selfish?*" I let out fake laughter. "Honey, I'm wearing his ring, so that gives me every right to be selfish over my belongings. You, however, need to remove yourself from this party and subsequently my life. I cut contact and didn't invite you for a reason. Read between the lines, please. Oh, and Eli doesn't even know your first name. He only recalls the last because he does business with your family. Sorry to break it to you, but you're not that important."

Her face grows red, and a tremor shakes her slim frame. Vance tries to step in, but I hold up a hand, signaling that he should stay out of it.

Gemma lets her bright pink lips pull in a smile even as her chin trembles and her hands fist at her sides. "And you think you are? He treats you like a valuable piece of real estate, probably for business reasons, or he wouldn't have recruited your own friends to keep an eye on you as if we're human cameras."

My mouth sets in a line, but I'll be damned if I let her see the confirmation of her words and how much they hurt me. "At least you have some use, hon."

"You're just a possession, Ava. A bright, shiny thing he took a liking to but will eventually tire of."

"Unlike you, I don't believe my worth is dependent on whether I keep a man. I have higher standards." I point behind me. "Now leave before I have you thrown out and cause a scene you don't need."

She grinds her teeth and attempts to say something, but Vance pushes her forward, and she walks out with her head held high.

"I'm sorry about that," he says as she disappears into the crowd. "I didn't know you fell out."

"Well, now you do, so I'd appreciate it if you don't shove her in my face again." I lean against the bar counter and order a mocktail before I turn back to him. "I thought you were in Australia."

"I was, but I came back." He takes a sip of his whiskey. "I must admit, I was slightly wounded you allowed him to expel me."

I tilt my head. "You insinuated I cheated on him with you while knowing my memory is unreliable, so excuse me if I chose not to fight your battle."

"Whoa." He smiles, his expression shifty. "I insinuated nothing except for us spending time together again."

"Try harder to fool me, V."

"It's true, though. We were so good together, and I do want to rekindle our relationship. He's bad news wrapped in sophisticated charm, and you know it. He's lying to you about so many things."

"And you're in the loop, how?"

"I have my contacts."

I narrow my eyes. "Have you been investigating us?"

"Him. He's attempting to destroy my family business and your life, Ava. I think it's logical for me to go after him. I don't have proof yet, but I know for a fact he did several shady things."

"Since you have no proof..." I grab my cloudy-pink mocktail and start to sidestep him.

He stands in front of me, forcing me to a halt. "You're being oblivious and naive, a combination I never thought you'd ever be accused of."

"And you're being rude to me at my own party."

"Ava." He grabs my shoulders. "Please try to see reason. Surely, you're not so far under his spell that you can't think for yourself."

"How dare you?" I shake his hands free. "Do you know my life, Vance? My predicaments? The hard choices I was forced to pick from? The decisions I had to make? The pills I have to take? The signs I have to watch out for? No. You only know the teenage version of me who pretended everything was perfect, but that's far from the truth, and that mythical version of me disappeared years ago. So don't stand there and tell me I can't think for myself. I'm not a fucking invalid!"

I whisper-yell the last part, my whole body shaking, and some of the drink spills on my fingers, turning them sticky.

"Hey, I'm sorry." He softens his voice. "I didn't mean to offend you."

"Well, you did, and you definitely meant to. I'd like you to leave. Now."

"Ava, please."

"My wife asked you to leave. Either you do that with your face intact, or you do it with your teeth falling out. Whether I break those hands you touched her with is subject to whether you remove your repugnant presence in the next ten seconds."

A possessive hand drops on my back, and I hate that his smell invades my surroundings and saturates my nostrils so that he's everything I breathe.

I stare up at him and loathe that I missed his face—as cold and emotionless as it looks. I despise the safety I feel in his embrace and the nagging thought that he's never made me feel less than normal.

Even when he's hurt me.

Vance stares between us, a grimace stretched deep on his face. "You're making a big mistake, Ava."

Eli steps forward, but I grab his arm so that I'm almost

hugging him. The last thing I want is for him to cause more public chaos and fall out even further with his dad.

Thankfully, Lan shows up and snatches Vance's collar. "Your time's up!"

I puff out a breath when he drags him out of sight. As I shift in place, my breasts brush against Eli's chest, and I look up to find his fierce gaze on me.

Placing my drink on the bar, I untangle myself from his hold. "What are you doing here? You're not invited."

"This is my yacht."

"Still not invited. Go away."

"Isn't the entire purpose of this party to get my attention and piss me off? Both have been accomplished exceptionally well."

"I'd have to care about you to attempt to get your attention. It happens that I don't."

"Ava…" He grabs my elbow. "Don't fuck with me."

"Don't touch me." I jerk away. "Now excuse me so I can go dance."

I show him a sweet smile and waltz to the middle of a group of guys from uni and dance sensually, making sure to rotate my hips and touch my waist. My fingers sink into my hair, and I grow hot under his intense gaze, falling into the rhythm.

I haven't even begun to flirt when Eli marches toward me. What…?

He never stopped me before—he only watched from afar like a creep.

"What do you want—"

"My wife." And then he lifts me in his arms like I'm a doll and walks to the lower deck.

As soon as we're inside a room, he throws me on the bed. I bounce on the mattress, then attempt to sit up.

I'm slammed back down when his weight crashes on top of me, and his fingers wrap around my throat. "I've been patient, but you don't want patient, do you? You want to be punished like a very bad wife."

CHAPTER 31

AVA

THE AIR CRACKLES WITH CRUEL INTENTIONS AS my gaze clashes with his icy, cloudy one.

An unpredictable storm that will swipe me under if I so much as breathe wrong.

Pressure builds in my stomach at the mere feel of his body on top of mine, dwarfing me, dominating, intimidating.

Absolutely addicting.

I didn't realize how much I missed him until his skin touched mine again.

I'm burning as I fall back into the orbit of the sun.

My heart races, my blood roars, but all I can do is stare at my custom-made god.

Eli yanks out his belt, the sound echoing around us like a whip, and he wraps it around my hands.

I wiggle free. "No."

"No?" he repeats with deceptive calm.

"I want to see you. Properly."

"And I want to sink my fucking teeth in your throat and mess up that skin with blood."

"Deal," I breathe out, my voice a whisper in the silence.

"Jesus fucking Christ. I tell you I want to draw your

blood and you just agree to it? Have you lost your damn mind?"

"No. I trust you won't hurt me, and I know if I ask you to stop, you will. It's a reasonable price for seeing you naked." I sit up so I'm cradling his thighs and undo the second button of his shirt with trembling fingers. "I don't like it when I'm the only one stripping. I know you do it for power, but it makes me feel like a sex doll you blow off steam into."

"Fuck." He rips open his shirt, and I gasp as the buttons fly all around and roll onto the ground.

He shoves away his trousers and briefs while balancing me on top of him. I fumble with my zipper and awkwardly pull my dress and lace panties off.

We strip in record time until we're both stark naked. For the first time ever. While I'm looking at him, at least.

I love the intense way he stares at me. My skin grows warm at the dark desire, the red-hot passion, and the need to touch me that shines bright in his eyes.

Eli tugs me back on his lap, and his huge erection nudges against my arse.

But I'm distracted by something else.

I've always known my husband to be lean but ripped. But as I glide my fingers over his broad shoulders and smooth muscles, I realize just how unfair it is that I haven't seen him naked until now.

He's perfection wrapped in human skin, and I want to touch him for eternity.

I expect him to stop me, but he lets me rub my palms over his pectoral muscles, along his abs, and...

My hands halt when I find a tattoo on his side—a

phoenix trapped in the branches of the tree of life. Crisp lines, plenty of negative space, neither big nor small, just the right size to be noticed.

For some reason, I've never pictured Eli as the type to get tattoos. He's too clean-cut for that.

I'm about to ask about it when my fingers land on a red scar near his lower abs. A gasp falls from my lips as I study the large slash.

"Wh-what happened?" I look up at him, and he stares back with an edge.

As if he's enduring me touching him, exploring him, getting to know him for once.

"Not important," he says without emotion.

Grabbing both his sides, I wiggle back and lower my head to place a kiss on the angry skin, the only imperfection in his muscled superiority.

Eli's fingers slide from my nape to my skull as he grabs a handful of my hair and pulls me back up.

The belt is in his hand, and I know he'll tie me up. As much as I enjoy that play most days, that's not the case tonight.

I push it away and drop a kiss on his shaven jaw, his throat, over his Adam's apple. "You smell so good. I love how it's as intoxicating as alcohol."

His cock grows thicker against my folds, and I grind against him, lust intensifying in my core until I'm humping his length. My arousal and his precum mix and glide, lubricating us and filling the room with a vulgar sound.

My lips brush against his, biting down on the cushion before I speak against it. "Love your taste, too. It's addictive. Almost as good as your hands."

"Shut your mouth, Ava."

"Mmm. Make me."

He shoves me against him by the hair and thrusts his tongue between my inviting lips. He kisses me like a Neanderthal, a fucking beast of epic proportions.

He kisses me like it's our first and last.

The tension ripples from my lips to the tips of my fingers, which I sink in his hair, messing it up, trying to get under his skin a little. My need for his touch bursts in fireworks of magenta and red as I wrap my legs around his waist, digging my heels into his back.

If it hurts, he doesn't complain as he kisses me deeper, dirtier, slower, as if he's savoring me.

Relearning me.

Then it's hot, fast, and dirty. He can't suck on my tongue long enough nor taste me quickly enough.

I'm so wet, it's dripping between my thighs, and he must feel it. He must know how crazy he makes me.

His hand lands on my throat, squeezing, tightening as he devours me. He pulls me up, and I tense, thinking he'll flip me around. Again.

After I've been carefully building the bridge over his icy-cold peak.

But he simply positions me on top of his hard, thick, and seriously massive cock. No idea how I've been taking this monstrosity between my legs, but that apprehension barely lingers as he speaks against my lips, his hot breath drawing goose bumps.

"You want me to lose control, Mrs. King? Want me to fuck you like a madman and stretch that tight cunt of yours to fit me? Want me to own you while I punish you?"

I nod, the motion causing my swollen mouth to brush his.

He catches my lip between his teeth as he thrusts into me. His eyes trap mine as his cock nudges in.

"Oh fuck…" I breathe as he stretches me. God, it's been some time, and he's positively huge.

"You'll take every last inch of my cock, beautiful. That's it. You're doing so well. Your cunt is welcoming me home."

I pant against his mouth, my hand wrapping around his neck, and I briefly close my eyes to engrave this sensation in the back of my mind.

"You wanted to look at me as I own you, so open those eyes. Look at what you make me do."

My lids slowly flutter open, and I whimper at the sheer intensity in his dark grays. They're worse than a storm— dangerous but alluring. I'd run right into the middle if I could.

I stroke his face. He thrusts deeper.

I kiss his cheek. He bites my neck.

Hard.

The sting rushes to the base of my stomach. Pressure builds in my core, and I clench around him.

He licks the assaulted spot on my neck and sucks on it as if he's exorcising my soul through my pulse. He bites again as he thrusts deeper, harder, and dangerously animalistic.

My moans echo in the air as I bounce on his cock, kissing his lips, his face, anywhere I can reach. I'm perSistent, as demanding as he is, and he doesn't stop me.

"You're a fucking nightmare." He grunts against my throat. "You're ruining everything."

"Good." I whimper against his mouth. "You ruined everything for me, too. I wish we could do a heart switch so you could feel what I do."

"Fuck, Ava."

He goes rougher, and I cling to him harder. My husband fucks the way he behaves. Deep and controlled. But the way he sucks on my neck is nothing short of frenzied.

There's no control when his groin slaps my arse.

There's no control when he plunges his tongue into my mouth.

His legendary self-restraint shatters against my edges, and I swallow it through his lips, tugging, nibbling, and carving my presence inside him in blood.

The pressure builds and heightens as I sink my nails into his shoulders and attempt to hide in the crook of his neck.

Eli tugs my head back with a fistful of my hair until I'm slammed by his presence again. "Eyes on me when you come for me, baby."

A violent wave of ecstasy rushes through me as I break apart. He drives into me with a harrowing rhythm, and I feel his cum fill me up as I come so hard, white stars form behind my lids and I lose my grasp on reality for a second.

But it's the type I welcome, the type I'd like to dig myself a hole and crawl into.

"Jesus, fuck. Ava!"

I blink a few times.

Somehow, I'm on my back, panting, and my husband's glorious body hovers over mine, his big hand cupping my face.

Our bodies are slick with sweat, my heartbeat is

somewhere on the moon, and my body is so achy, it's delicious.

He somehow pulled out of me; his cum is dripping between my thighs, messing up the sheets.

"Can you hear me?" he asks in a careful voice.

"Um, sorry," I whisper, hating that I ruined the most beautiful moment of my life. "It happens sometimes. I lose, um, consciousness of my surroundings. It's...nothing serious."

A small puff of air leaves his lips, and he momentarily closes his eyes.

I lean into his hand, rubbing myself against him like a puppy starved for affection. "You called me 'baby.'"

He just stares at me.

"And you actually bit me. Are you in fact a vampire? Can you turn me?"

His lips twitch in a small smile. "Do you want a bath?"

"Mmm, not here." I pull him down so his lips are inches from mine. "Take me home."

I pause, trapping my lip between my teeth at the admission I just made. That his house is my home.

When did that happen?

Thankfully, he raises a brow with obvious disregard. "What about the clusterfuck of a party going on outside?"

That's when I hear the music and the general chatter. I honest-to-God forgot about that. "Oh, the party."

"Yes, the party you threw on *my* yacht without informing me."

I shrug. "What's yours is mine. What's mine is also mine."

"By God. You're such a brat."

"Want to punish me again when we get home? Leo can end the party."

"Leo is fired for letting the party happen."

"I'll just rehire him and pay him more. With your money."

"Being married to you is obnoxiously expensive."

"Not expensive enough to cover your lack of humanity. You should consider yourself lucky."

"Lucky, huh?"

"Totally. No other woman would put up with a Tin Man. You should thank me."

"For being a pain in the arse?" he says in a deadpan voice. "Let's get a move on."

"You'll come around, babe." I brush my lips against his as he places a hand behind my back and carries me to the bathroom.

My legs lock around his waist, and I continue to explore his body, kissing him everywhere I can.

He puts an end to it too soon when we step into the shower and he fucks me against the wall.

So much for waiting for later.

———

Eli changes into some spare clothes he had Leo bring him. Then he says, "You're fired, Henderson."

I peek from the bathroom, putting on my dress. "You have been rehired and promoted, Leo! Let's celebrate later."

My husband glares at me.

I lift my shoulder. "Warned you. Not my fault you don't listen."

He shakes his head and steps out. "I need a word with Lan. See you outside."

"Okay."

He takes a step toward the door, then stops. "Behave, will you?"

I wink. "Always."

"I don't even know why I try anymore," he mutters as he steps past Leo. The latter offers me a rare smile, and I mirror it, then top it off with two thumbs-up.

Leo and Sam have been nothing but supportive during the time my husband was being a wanker. They even called him unreasonable, which I screenshotted and will frame and then place on his desk.

By the time I'm done dolling up, I breeze past all the people, who seem to have doubled in number, in search of the one person whose company I want.

I spot Eli standing outside by the deck with Lan. The cousins are facing away from me as they stare at the dark water. Light reflects on the surface like a swish of deceptive color.

"Consider this my contribution after what I said." Lan wraps an arm around Eli's shoulders.

Broad shoulders with bulging muscles that I can still make out the contours of under the blue shirt.

"I'll knock your teeth out if you don't stop provoking me, Landon. I mean it."

"Hey, relax. I didn't know Barbie was…"

Eli shoves his arm away.

"You didn't know I was what?" I ask with a smile as I join them.

"Still giving this waste of space the time of day," Lan says. "You can do so much better."

"And so can Mia," Eli shoots back.

"Nonsense. I'm God's gift to humans, and she's grateful to have me."

I place a finger in my mouth and pretend to vomit. "Your presence gives me nausea."

"Must be something wrong with your stomach."

Eli shoves him away and places an arm around my back. "Ready to go?"

"And escape the cloud of narcisSism around here? Absolutely."

"Joke's on you, Barbie!" Lan calls behind us. "You took the entire cloud with you."

Eli glares at him, and I catch him mouthing, "I'll kill you."

"Not if she manages to kill you first, Cousin," Lan says.

I laugh but still make a face at the arsehole.

During the ride back, I doze off, and I think Eli pulls me against his chest and I climb onto his lap, but I'm not sure.

The next thing I know, when I open my eyes, I'm surrounded by a familiar scent.

The soft light of a lamp illuminates my surroundings in stark detail.

My heart nearly pops out from between my ribs when I find myself cocooned in Eli's embrace. My head rests on his naked chest, my arm is wrapped around his waist, and his hand covers my back.

I'm wearing a pink nightgown, and my hair is loose, and I'm, without a doubt, covered by an ugly gray duvet while snuggling against my husband.

In his bed.

My breath hitches as I stare up at his sleepy face, at the sharp jaw and the dark lashes fanning his cheek.

This is so unfair. Why does he look hot even while sleeping?

Now I don't even want to sleep anymore and would rather watch his face.

My wedding ring shines under the soft light, and I smile. He kept the side lamp on because he knows I can't sleep in the darkness, didn't he? Even though I was out by the time he brought me here.

I'm pretty sure I woke up sometime after he carried me into the house, but I remember nothing.

My heart tightens and sinks as that truth slaps me across the face. How many more moments will I lose? How much can he take before he figures out I'm not worth the hassle?

I internally shake those depressing thoughts away and hug him tighter, hoping—no, praying—I don't wake him up with my visceral nightmares on our first night together.

My solution is to stay awake.

And I manage to do that for maybe twenty minutes, but the steady, safe beat of his heart lulls me into the deepest, most dreamless sleep of my life.

CHAPTER 32

AVA

"SOMETHING'S WRONG WITH ME."

The words leave my mouth in a haunted whisper. Probably because I never wanted to speak them aloud, let alone admit them to another person.

Said person is my psychiatrist.

My *new* psychiatrist.

The one who replaced the other psychiatrist whose fate is unknown at best and sabotaged by my husband at worst.

Dr. Blaine is a middle-aged Black woman with a pixie haircut; she's wearing a smart casual pantsuit and dainty diamond-stud earrings.

She was taken aback by my appearance at her office on Great Portland Street, mainly because I used a fake name to make an appointment.

Whenever I tried in the past, I was turned away unless I mentioned I'd be accompanied by my legal guardian. Aka my husband.

So I had to get creative.

If Blaine doesn't like it, she doesn't show it in her neutral facial expression, which could belong to monks meditating in faraway mountains.

She stares at me as I lounge on the chaise across from

her. "Due to our treatment plan, I can't speak to you in the absence of your guardian unless previously authorized by him, Mrs. King. My asSistant will arrange another appointment—"

"Because I'm insane?"

"Because I'm legally required to."

I bite down on my lower lip and then release it before I draw blood. "Then can you tell me what I can do on my own? Can I even open a bank account without his presence? Book a flight? A hotel room?"

"I'm sure you can discuss this with your husband."

I shake my head but say nothing.

For the past two weeks, we've fallen into this bubble I created for both of us. Eli ordered that my stuff be moved to his room the morning after the party. He even let me redecorate it and turn it into this odd but somehow beautiful mix of pink and gray.

Though he does grumble about the fluffy slippers he trips over and the feather robe that's on his chair. And the towel on his floor.

He's a lost organized cause. Though he'd call me chaos in a pink wrapper while picking up my things and tidying them in a neurotic way.

Since that first time, he's never fucked me while clothed again. Not once. And he always picks positions where we're facing each other, even if he ties me to his headboard.

He still looks at me.

He still curses deep in his throat when looking at me.

And I like to think that I'm carving myself inside him with every touch.

With every bath that he now takes with me and every

massage he gives me, I further swear he has hands more soothing than professionals.

The past couple of weeks have been a dream. We went to Paris for three days. Fine, it was a business trip, but he didn't tell me no when I wanted to tag along nor when I took him with me for some extravagant shopping.

He also didn't say no when I split the bags between him and Leo. What? We're overusing the poor guy, and he needs a break now and then.

But that's the thing about dreams. They're an illusion that I keep waiting to be jerked out of.

Every night, I dread sleep more than anything, even when surrounded by his strong arms.

Even after I bury my face in his neck or chest.

Even when he strokes my hair until I fall under.

"I keep having this dream about falling into a puddle of water, and when I hit the surface, it turns crimson red, and then I'm drowning in blood," I say softly.

"Mrs. King. I'm sure—"

"I'm losing time." I cut her off, my chin trembling. "I wake up and don't know where I am for a while. Sometimes, he'll talk to me and I don't hear anything because I'm not there anymore. Eli, Sam, and Leo lie to me, probably not to worry me, but I recognize when my state of fugue is getting out of control. It's happened three times in the past few weeks, that I'm aware of. And we both know if I'm conscious of those three times, then the actual percentage is much higher. I know you can't do anything for me now, but I'm asking you, I'm imploring you to increase my medication so I'm right again. But don't tell him I know. It's okay if he thinks I'm in the dark."

Tears stream down my cheeks, and I wipe them with the back of my hand. This deplorable feeling of helplessness has been eating at me from the inside out the entire time I've been laughing, joking, and holding on to the illusion that everything will fix itself.

But I should know self-healing is not an option for me. If I leave it this way, my state will only get worse, and who knows what I might do when I fall into that hideous pool of loss of consciousness?

That's what the blood in my nightmares represents.

Something unavoidable.

"Mrs. King," Dr. Blaine starts in a soft voice. "I'm afraid only your guardian can approve any increase of medication or alterations to your current treatment plan."

"Then tell him I need it. He'll listen to you. I'm sure he doesn't want to see me like this."

"If we increase the medication, you'll be lethargic more often than not."

"But I'll be conscious of my surroundings. I want to be there in my life. I don't want to lose moments because my stupid brain decided to check out. You're a doctor, so why can't you heal me? Why can't anyone heal me and give me back my life, my memories, my agency? I can only function with the help of meds, and I'm finally fine with that, I've *accepted* that, but why aren't they working effectively anymore?"

The thought that this is a phase that will soon end has been eroding me.

I don't want the end.

Not when I'm just beginning.

Not when I'm the happiest I've ever been in my life.

Dr. Blaine says nothing, but I wasn't expecting her to. I just wanted to vent to a stranger so I wouldn't hurt my family and friends nor set off my parents' alarm bells about my dreaded loss of control.

I stand and pat my cheeks. "Let me ask one thing."

"Yes?"

"Will I ever be normal enough to have children?"

She remains silent, and that's all the answer I need.

If I have children, I can't raise them, or I'll most likely be a threat to them.

Better yet, I shouldn't have them for everyone's sake.

And that will leave the heir of King Enterprises heirless. Because of me.

I came to Dr. Blaine to seek answers, but I leave with a heavy heart and tears burning my eyes.

———

That afternoon, Eli invites me to watch him be a sex god.

Sorry, I mean play polo.

It's not my fault that he looks hotter than sin in his tight white polo shirt while commanding a horse with infinite ease.

I'm so happy I brought a lace fan that matches my umbrella, because I need to cool off whenever I look at him.

The downside is that his team is playing against Papa and Remi's. Worse, Eli's accompanied by Uncle Aiden, Landon, who's staying longer than needed—probably because Mia joined him—and Bran, who came to visit his parents with his fiancé, Nikolai.

Said fiancé stands out like a sore thumb amid our

heritage dresses, Ralph Lauren blazers, and Loro Piana–acquired pieces.

Doesn't help that he shouts profanities when anyone gets within a meter radius of Bran. Mia attempts to haul him down whenever he stands, with little success.

At one point, he and Ari nearly started a fight because he called Remi a motherfucker for lightly shoving Bran, and I swear she would've clawed his eyes out if I hadn't brought her down.

As volatile as the situation is, I'm glad to get my mind off things. Even temporarily.

Besides, I'll take any opportunity to dress up and look pretty.

I'm wearing a polka-dot pink dress, the tulle underskirt adding a touch of playfulness to my outfit. Delicate lace gloves adorn my hands, matching the intricate design of my round hat. I completed the look with white-rimmed shades that shield my eyes from the bright sunlight while adding a chic and fashionable flair to my ensemble.

"This is so exciting," Mama says from beside me, rocking her vintage dress.

"More like a disaster waiting to happen. If not on the field, then here." I tug on my sister's sleeve when she tries to talk shit at both Nikolai and Mia. "Just sit down, Ari!"

"You're both going down." She does a slicing-throat motion.

"Don't threaten me with that if you can't perform it in real life," Nikolai says, relaxing his feet so they're crossed at the ankles.

Ari lifts her chin. "Who says I can't? Wanna try me, big man?"

"Why is she nothing like you?" Mia whispers to me. "She's like a more vicious version of Anni."

"Tell me about it. We better stop your brother and my sister from killing each other."

"Amen to that. Besides." She smiles with triumph. "It's obvious whose team is going to win. No offense to your dad and Remi."

"I heard that!" Ari jumps up.

"And?" Mia attempts to be oblivious. "Lan and his team are better at this."

"That's right." Nikolai puffs out his chest. "My Bran is made for elegant sports."

"So is Remi! If you don't shut up, I will…"

"What? What are you going to do with your mini size?" Nikolai drawls with contained impatience.

She gasps. "Height isn't a flex, giant."

"It is if I can squash you like an ant who's getting in my way."

"Come at me!"

"You'd drop dead before I reach you."

"Stop it, Niko," Mia whisper-yells at her brother, while I wrestle Ari back to her seat.

Mama and Aunt Elsa just laugh and then both proceed to casually cheer for their husbands as if a world war isn't at the point of erupting.

I'm the only one who's torn between my dad's and my husband's teams. So I choose to cheer whenever either of the teams scores and proceed to be called a traitor by the cult surrounding me.

Talk about trying to please everyone.

Papa and Remi pull the entire weight of their team, but

they still lose by two goals, and the last one is scored by none other than Eli.

I clap even as Ari glares at me and then says in a dramatic voice, "Mama, let's prepare Papa a pick-me-up meal and some condolences for fathering a traitor."

"Stop being so dramatic." I poke her with my umbrella. "I'm neutral."

"Neutrally eye fucking your husband," she whispers so only I can hear her. "Don't think those glasses can fool me."

I pull her by the ear until she's at my face level. "Don't lecture me if you're doing the same, you little shit."

"Well, I don't pretend. I also asked Papa to let me marry Remi if they manage to win."

"And Remi's still alive?"

She disengages from me. "Yeah, so? Though pretty sure Papa lost on purpose. Does this mean he likes Eli better than my Remi?"

I laugh despite myself. She sounds so wounded and offended at the prospect.

"He's like the greenest flag. How can Dad not prefer him over that massive red flag of a husband you have?"

"Hey!" I catch her ear again, and she kicks me teasingly.

But then I spot Eli dismounting his horse, and I lose interest in bickering with my sister. I shove her away, dust off my dress, and sit like the elegant lady I am.

He bro hugs his dad and cousins before he walks in my direction while removing his helmet.

Such a simple act shouldn't look so hot, but he has the unnerving skill of making everything look mouthwatering.

His tall legs eat up the distance in no time before he stops in front of me. A sheen of sweat covers his neck and dampens his dark locks, and I want to rake my fingers through them.

Preferably while he fucks me into oblivion and makes me forget about reality.

And now, it's impossible to keep my poker face. I squirm as he stands in front of me, blocking the sun. I'm aware of Nikolai hugging Bran and Landon going to Mia, but they soon float into the background when Eli wipes the polo ball on his shirt and then offers it to me.

"Game ball. For you."

"Aw." Aunt Elsa places a hand on her chest. "My son can be so sweet."

He flashes her a wink as I accept the ball with a stupid grin and carefully tuck it into my clutch before I stand and brush my lips against his cheek. "Thanks."

"Don't you think I deserve more than a mere cheek kiss, Mrs. King?"

"Later. Our parents are here."

"And that's a problem because? You do know they have sex, too, right?"

"Eli!"

"You might need to sit down for this, beautiful. Actually, Father Christmas is not real."

I gasp. "How dare you tarnish my delusions?"

He smiles as he tugs me toward him by the elbow and kisses my forehead.

I have no choice but to melt as tears well in my eyes. Why does he have to be so dreamy all of a sudden?

It was bad when he was a cold, emotionless monster, but now it's impossible to deny how much I'm irrevocably in love with this man.

The type of love that will break me fully this time.

I intended to take revenge, but I ended up falling deeper. What a mess.

I place a hand on his chest and pull away, plastering on a smile. "You played beautifully."

He narrows his eyes as if he can see the reason for the topic change. Sometimes, he reads me so well that it terrifies me, because now he has the power to annihilate me if he chooses to.

The power to lock me up in an asylum and marry another woman who can give him children. Maybe someone from old money, like Gemma.

The thought brings bile to the back of my throat. "But you could've taken it easy on Papa."

"He wouldn't respect me if I did."

"I still don't respect you and never will, punk." Papa tugs me away from him and kisses the top of my head. "Are you divorcing him anytime soon, princess?"

"Sorry to disappoint you." Eli pulls me back to his side. "But we'll be happily married for your lifetime and beyond, Uncle."

"Don't call me that."

"My son can call you whatever he pleases." Uncle Aiden stands by Eli's side and crosses his arms, a mischievous gleam igniting in both father's and son's eyes. "Aw, don't tell me you're upset you lost to me? *Again*."

"I'll bury you and your son six feet under right here and now."

"Papa," I whisper.

"I'd like to see you try," Uncle Aiden says.

"Dad," Eli says with a note of reprimand. "Let's take

it easy on Uncle Cole. He put so much effort into driving a wedge between me and my wife for nothing. Surely, we can be magnanimous."

"Absolutely, Son. He can be taxing when acting petty."

"Word."

"Eli!" I elbow him and try to go to Papa, but he tightens his grip around my waist, forcing me to remain in place.

"I'm here to stay, Uncle. So either you accept that and the beautiful grandchildren we'll give you, or you drive yourself to an early grave by giving yourself heart issues."

"Grandchildren, Cole." Uncle Aiden grins wolfishly. "For your information, we'll be sharing those."

"Many of them, too," Eli says, caressing my waist. "My Ava wants at least three."

"This little—" Papa lunges at Eli, or I think he does, because I've checked out.

The world turns into a buzzing mess. My heart throbs, and no air reaches my lungs.

A gentle stroke of a finger against my throat brings me back to the present. Eli, Uncle Aiden, and Papa are staring at me intently.

"You okay?" my husband asks, his brow furrowed.

I let my trembling lips flatten in a smile. "Yeah. I could use sitting down, though."

He walks me to a bench and kneels in front of me, then passes me a bottle of water.

As I take a sip, his fingers rub my knee over my dress. "Do you need to take your pills?"

I nod and start to retrieve them with a shaky hand. He

strokes my hand, bringing my movements to a stop, and then brings out the bottle and hands me two pills.

I take them and remove my glasses, letting them fall onto my lap.

My heart rate slows down to normal after a while, even though my fingers are grasping the bottle of water in a death grip.

"Better?" he asks, his fingers touching my pulse and my cheek.

I nod.

"Was it something we said? What triggered you?"

I shake my head, refusing to acknowledge the dooming reality awaiting me.

"Baby," he says with a firm voice. "You need to tell me so I can remove the potential hazard."

"Everything is a potential hazard for me."

"Then I'll remove everything."

"Don't be sweet. I can't take it."

"I'm anything but sweet. I'm a menace."

"That you are." I palm his cheek. "Can we go home? I want to annoy Sam a bit."

"Should we go to a West End show later?"

"You don't even like the theater."

"But you do."

And to cheer me up, he's willing to watch things he doesn't like.

This isn't fair. I want the cold Eli back.

"We probably can't get good tickets this late."

"I can get any tickets you want. Up to and including a meet and greet with the actors backstage for hugs and pictures. Scratch that. Only pictures. No hugs."

I smile but shake my head. "I'm not in the mood."

"What's this about, Ava? Is it due to your visit to Dr. Blaine?"

"How do you know? I took a taxi... She told you? Wait...you're having me tracked."

It's not a question but a statement.

Ever since I woke up in the hospital, I've often felt that I wasn't alone, but I deluded myself into thinking it was paranoia.

"Why?" I ask in a low tone, letting my hands fall limp on either side of me.

"I have to." His closed-off coldness peeks through, and I hate that I wished it back so soon.

"Okay..."

"Ava—"

"I get it," I say with contained bitterness. "You're worried I'll go into a fugue state and walk straight into oncoming traffic or jump off a building. So you have to make sure you know my location in order to stop it."

"Jesus Christ, it's not—"

"You're right. I could do it, and the worst part is that I wouldn't be aware of it. Like the two years I completely wiped out. I'm a ticking bomb, Eli, and we both know it."

"Nonsense. You're absolutely fine." He narrows his eyes. "What did Dr. Blaine tell you?"

"Nothing. She said she couldn't talk to me without your presence."

"And you despise that. You despise that I have any form of power over you."

"No one likes to be a puppet, least of all me. But if it's not you, it has to be Papa. If not Papa, Mama. If not Mama, someone else has to make sure I don't fuck up. I realized today that I'll never be my own person, so I'd like to eat a bucket of candy floss and watch rom-coms, please."

"No."

"No?"

Eli takes my hand in his. "I have a better place in mind."

CHAPTER 33
ELI

I'M LOSING HER.

Again.

She's slipping between my fingers.

Again.

Her presence is diminishing.

Fucking *again*.

Yet I'm grabbing scraps of her consciousness, moments of her presence, and fighting the reality of her pending fall.

"This is the place?" Ava walks to the middle of the sitting room. "Your grandma's island?"

My gaze tracks her movements—the swish of her vintage dress, the clicking of her white heels. The touch of her gloved fingers on the back of the sofa before she flashes me a mischievous grin. "I've always wondered what it looks like. I didn't think it'd be this huge and beautiful. Your gran is a lucky woman."

"You like it?"

"Yup."

"It's yours."

"Wh-what?"

"The island is yours. It's in my gran's name, and

she said she'd give it to me, considering I'm her favorite grandchild."

"And you'll just hand it over?"

"If you want it."

She twirls around and faces me, her head tilting to the side. "You'd give me anything I want?"

"Within reason."

"What's unreasonable for you?"

"You can't have another man, drive a car, nor ask for a divorce."

"Yikes. And here I thought I could find a lover and drive into the sunset in a convertible."

I narrow my eyes. "Not unless you wish to have his blood on your hands."

"Relax, I was joking." She walks around, checking the furniture and the different impressionist art paintings Mum and Gran added over the years.

A few of them are Bran's and Glyn's. The hideous sculpture of a devil is Lan's. I make a mental note to smash it to pieces before we leave.

I lean against the wall, my arms and ankles crossed as I observe and calculate my wife's every movement.

Oblivious to my neurotic attention, she walks around, releasing "oohs" and "aahs" about the pieces and snapping some pictures. "Have you spent a lot of time here?"

"Yes. Mostly during my childhood with my grandparents. Sometimes, with my parents."

She grins. "I bet you have a lot of beautiful memories."

"Possibly."

Her bright blue eyes swing in my direction. "You're not sure? Did something tarnish those memories?"

"Not particularly. I just don't connect with human emotions the way everyone else does, and therefore, I fail to consider what happened here 'good memories.' For me, it was a process that was essential to shaping my personality."

"You sound so robotic when you talk like that. No wonder you're the Tin Man." Her lips jut forward in a small pout. "Do you ever think of any memories as happy memories?"

"Plenty. Though most of them aren't socially acceptable."

"Name two happy memories."

"When Dad sat me down and told me I was born different and I have no reason to feel ashamed of it. In fact, I should be as proud of it as he is of me."

A wide smile touches her lips. "I love your dad."

"He's married."

"And so am I. Get your head out of the gutter, bro."

"I'm not your bro. I'm your husband."

She rolls her eyes. "What's your second happy memory?"

"The day we got married."

She freezes, her full lips parting. All of a sudden, she looks like a forgotten goddess. No. More of a fallen angel with broken wings. The need to snap them to pieces so she'll never fly away throbs beneath my skin like a constant sick urge.

"Ha ha, very funny." She laughs awkwardly.

"I wasn't joking."

"B-but why?" She rolls her bottom lip between her teeth, then releases the swollen red skin.

"Because I got to own you. Officially."

"Oh." Her face falls with resounding disappointment. "Makes sense."

Her movements turn lethargic as she absent-mindedly touches some of the sculptures and family photos scattered all over the place.

Gran, Mum, and Aunt Astrid can be dramatic with all the pictures they force us to take.

Ava clutches a picture in which Grandpa and Gran are sitting as he holds her hand on his lap. Dad and Uncle Levi are on his side while Mum and Aunt Astrid are on Gran's side. Glyn is wrapping her arms around Grandpa's neck from behind. Lan grins as he grabs Bran by the shoulder and I'm headlocking Creigh. This was taken about five years ago on Gran's birthday, which we spent here.

"Why did you bring me to the island?" my wife asks after a stretch of silence.

"I figured you could use a break. In Paris, you mentioned wanting a proper holiday where I'm not working."

"Why here?"

"Because no one can disturb us. It's where I come when I want to think in peace."

She stares at me. "You fly eight hours to think in peace?"

"If need be."

"And you brought me? Sure that's a wise decision, Mr. King?"

"Don't make me regret it."

"No promises." She smiles as she places the picture frame on the table. "I want to go to the beach."

"Are you sure you don't want to rest first?"

"I slept on the plane. I'm fine."

More like she barely slept. The rest of the time, she was out of it. Both physically and mentally.

But if she thinks she was sleeping, that's better.

Sam and Henderson would look at me with disapproval, and in Henderson's case, he'd beg me to finally follow Dr. Blaine's recommendations before it's too late.

But I'll chase this until the very end.

I join her on the short walk to the beach. It's late afternoon, and the sun has started its descent on the horizon, painting the sky in a shock of yellow and orange.

My wife takes off her shoes and patters on the white sand, then dips her toes in the jade-colored water.

She lets her shoes drop as she gasps. "This is so breathtaking."

"Breathtaking indeed," I say, my eyes focused on the soft slopes of her face. The charm radiating from her stabs my armor and slashes a crack that's much more fatal than the previous ones.

"The water is still warm." She kicks it with her toes. Then she whips her head in my direction with a smirk before she splashes my trousers. "Oops. I just wanted you to feel the water."

"Ava…"

She crouches and grabs a handful of water, then throws it at my chest with a laugh. "We've got to include your shirt in case it gets jealous. Is the water warm or what?"

My hand shoots up in her direction, but she darts away at the last second, and a squeal rips from her throat as she runs along the beach. Her blond strands fly with the breeze as the waves softly break on the shore.

I'm hot on her heels in seconds. I'm walking fast and

with purpose in the beginning, but then I kick away my shoes and jog after her.

My wife glances behind her, and another startled squeal bubbles out.

She picks up her pace, running as fast as her legs will allow.

My natural instinct to hunt rushes to the surface, shrouded in red-hot smoke. I catch up to her in no time, but I keep my pace steady and my breathing level.

If I get too excited, I might actually hurt that porcelain skin and shatter her breakable existence.

More than you're already doing?

The voice that used to be quieter has somehow gotten louder in the past couple of weeks.

It has become bolder with each of her soft smiles and the growth of her gullible fucking trust. It's been shaking my foundation every time she's held on to me for support, every time she's looked at me with those huge eyes that hold the vain hopes of a naive woman.

Maybe she needs to learn the hard way that she shouldn't trust me.

Not when *I* don't trust me.

"Oh my God! Stop chasing me. It's scary!" She laughs and yelps but continues to run.

Like prey.

My prey.

"Eli, stop it—" Her words end in a gasp when I grab her by the waist and lift her entirely off the sand, then set her back down.

My chest slams to her back as she breathes so heavily, she's wheezing with each inhale.

I align my lips with her ear, reveling in the shudder that shakes her entire body. "Want to know why it was scary, Mrs. King? Because you acted like prey in front of a predator. If you don't wish to be devoured, don't run away."

She turns around, a flush spreading on her cheeks, her hair wind-kissed and her lips a dark shade of her favorite color.

Broken beauty has always been the most haunting.

The most enticing, too.

"It was actually exciting to be chased. I liked it a little," she whispers, then grinds against me. "Judging by your erection, you might have liked it a lot."

And then Ava, who has more pride than the monarchy, lowers herself to her knees, her fingers fumbling with my belt.

"What are you doing?"

"Lending you a hand—or, more accurately, a mouth." She winks up at me and moistens her lips. "I've been told I'm brilliant at giving blow jobs."

Hot black rage rushes to my limbs as she frees my hard cock—which obviously isn't synchronized with my brain.

Her hands wrap around the base of my dick, and she strokes me with a rotating motion. A zap of pleasure shoots down my spine, and my abs tighten.

"Mmm. You're so big. I can't believe I manage to fit this inside me."

I sink my fingers into her hair, gathering it in a ponytail, and then yank her back not so gently. "I have no interest in your particular set of skills."

She stares up at me while still absent-mindedly stroking me. "I thought you never let me reciprocate because you didn't want to look at me. But we've passed that, so what's the issue?"

"I will not be another dick who praises your blow job abilities."

"Aw, you're jealous, babe?"

I narrow my eyes and start to pull her up.

"What if I tell you that you're the best dick I've ever seen? Because you totally are." She actually fights me to stay in position. "Let me have a taste. Please."

Fuck.

Does she know she can get me to do anything if she begs?

Even with my grip on her hair, she manages to wrap her lips around my crown, then sucks hard.

Jesus fucking Christ.

My wife stares up at me as she slides more of my length into her hot, wet mouth and pumps me at the base, her grip tightening gradually.

The fact she learned to please men from some random bastards turns me into an unhinged demon.

She's wrong. The reason I didn't want her to suck my cock isn't only about the eye contact. It's because I knew I'd transform into a raging fucking lunatic when her lips wrapped around my dick.

My free hand clenches and unclenches at my side, and the veins in my forearm pop as I tighten my grip to stop the animalistic urge flaring in my head.

Her movements are slow and sensual, and she peeks up at me the entire time, looking at me, gauging my reaction, probably.

She moans around my skin, the vibrations of her

throaty voice hardening me further. And then she releases my cock and spreads my precum against her lips.

"You done?" I ask in a somber voice.

"You really hate it?" She winces.

"I don't, but we're doing it my way." I grab her nape and tilt her head back using her hair. "I prefer fucking your throat, Mrs. King. Open your mouth."

A swallow works her throat up and down, and she wets her lips before she does as she's told.

"You're such a brat outside the bedroom, but inside, you're good at following instructions, Mrs. King. Open wider—show me how much you want me to use your mouth."

As I thrust into her inviting heat with my usual control, my wife opens wider, blinking up at me with those bright, trusting eyes, trying to accommodate me to the best of her ability.

Any ounce of reason I possess scatters like sand on the beach.

Like it does every time I touch her.

I say I'll only touch her because I'll do it my way. That I'll use, then discard her. That I'll extract my pleasure the same way I get everything in life. With method and command.

But then I slam into the beautiful chaos that is my wife.

She makes me lose control. Willingly or unwillingly.

No woman has ever done this to me. They were all commodities, faceless holes willing to be used.

She's the exception to my rules. The discrepancy in my perfectly written novel. The mutation of my biology.

It started with a sense of challenge at uni, and then

it morphed into a bizarre obsession every time she pissed me off—and she did that a *lot*. Then it suddenly became a violent possession.

A need for ownership.

The moment I identified the bug, it was already too late to extract her from my life.

Ava is the most dangerous person I've ever come across.

She can break me even while she's broken herself.

She can worm herself between my armor and my skin.

Scratch that.

As she looks at me while I fuck her mouth, I realize with depressing clarity that she's already seeped beneath my skin and she's currently flowing through my blood.

She holds on to my thighs as she lets me thrust in and out of her mouth, using her tongue for friction. Tears shimmer in her eyes whenever I hit the back of her throat.

I pull out and she pants, her breaths echoing in the silence. "Wh-why did you stop? I can take it."

"Breathe properly."

She sucks in large gulps of air, panting.

"Again."

She inhales a deep breath and exhales.

"One more time."

Her chest heaves as she regulates her oxygen intake, then opens her mouth wide.

I thrust inside in one go, using her hair as a steering wheel. My rhythm is rougher this time, more unhinged as I drive in and out. My wife never stops looking up at me, and it's that eye contact that throws me over the edge.

My orgasm is intense and long as I come deep in her

throat. She swallows as much as possible, but streaks of my cum roll down the corners of her mouth.

I pull out and tug her up by the hair and then crash my lips to hers.

She gasps as I lick my cum off her mouth, then thrust it back inside. Her moans echo in the air as she climbs up my body, wraps her legs around my waist, and kisses me senseless, raking her nails down my neck and grabbing my hair.

My crazy wife reaches between us and strokes my hardening dick, then places it at her opening. "Fuck me."

"Jesus Christ. Where's your underwear, Mrs. King?"

"I must've forgotten to wear any."

"You've been forgetting that a lot lately. I almost think it's on purpose."

"Maybe it is."

"Mmm," I growl against her lips. "Is that so?"

"Shut up and fuck me, Eli."

My cock slips from her soaked pussy to her back hole, and she writhes against me, humping, inviting me to claim my property.

I grab her arse cheeks beneath the dress, sinking my fingers into the soft flesh. "Should I fuck you here, beautiful?"

"If you want. Anything you want."

"Jesus fucking Christ. How come all your attitude disappears when my cock talks to your cunt?" I slap her arse. "Maybe it should talk to this hole as well."

"Yes, yes. Just fuck me already."

"Let me get some lube."

"It's okay."

"It's not. I'm huge, and you've never taken a cock in your arse before."

"I took the toys you put in me." She grinds against me.

I laugh. "You're cute to think any of those toys compares to my cock."

"I stand corrected." She grins, dropping a featherlight kiss on the corner of my mouth.

She can be so affectionate after sex and often showers me with hugs and kisses as if she can't get enough. My wife is definitely the type who loves to cuddle after I fuck her brains out, and although I never cared for the act before, I do with her.

I love holding her when she's entirely spent and smells distinctly like me.

While she's all wrapped around me, I walk us back to the house.

She sighs contentedly as she kisses my throat, my chin, my cheeks, my lips, and even my nose.

Anywhere she can reach is hers for the taking, and she knows it.

Too well for my liking.

As soon as we're in the bedroom, I balance her against the wall and fumble with the nightstand until I find the lube.

"I'll get on all fours if it's easier," she whispers between nibbles on my ear. She's obsessed with that spot for some reason.

"No." There's no way in fuck I'm fucking her from behind again. Not after what she told me that time.

Besides, she didn't get worse as I was afraid, so it's doable.

For now.

I put her down and pull her dress off. She removes her bra, her full breasts falling free with a gentle bounce. I get rid of my trousers and briefs in one go. My shirt follows, scattering on top of her dress.

Then I lie on my back on the bed and pull her so she's sitting on top of me.

Her lips meet mine as I squirt lube on my palm and then circle her back hole and slowly thrust two fingers inside her.

She shudders and rubs her soaking cunt against my abs.

"You're going to take my cock here, aren't you, beautiful?" I ask against her lips as I add a third finger, slowly fucking her.

"Mmm, yes, please."

"It'll hurt."

"That's okay. I trust you."

God fucking damn it.

"I meant to take it easy on you, but you're making that impossible." I lather my cock with lube, then push her up, wrenching my fingers from inside her.

I grip her waist, and she holds herself up so my cock is positioned at her back entrance. I pull her down slowly until the crown is inside.

Ava slumps forward and sinks her nails into my abs, on the scar she's never stopped asking about since the first time she saw it.

"Oh God. You're really huge."

"That's it, baby. You're taking my cock like a very good girl."

"Mmm. Fuck…" She lowers herself farther, taking

another two inches, and breathes heavily, a sheen of sweat covering her skin. Some wayward blond strands frame her face in a soft glow.

"You're doing so well."

"I am?" Her pupils dilate with the praise, and she comes down a few more inches. "Oh fuck...fuck..."

"You're so fucking beautiful. You're strangling my cock like a very good girl." I reach up and twist her nipple fiercely, knowing how much she loves a touch of pain with her pleasure.

My wife moans, throwing her head back, and I shove her all the way down.

Her whimper echoes in the air as she huffs and grabs my sides, her hands trembling slightly.

I let her adjust. We both breathe harshly, hers echoing with erotic noises.

"Relax for me, baby." I stroke her waist gently.

She stares at me, and her muscles stop being so tense.

Once I feel her softening, I drive into her with slow, shallow thrusts. She mewls and rubs her clit against my groin.

I go deeper and faster as her sounds of pleasure echo in the air. She gasps, sucking in a fractured breath every time her clit slams against my groin.

"How does it feel, beautiful?"

"Good. You feel so good."

I stop and she groans.

"Ride me, Mrs. King. Let me see how much you want me."

Leaving a hand on my stomach, she reaches back and grabs my thigh as she lifts herself up, then falls back down.

A strangled noise leaves her as she captures the corner of her lip between her teeth. Soon enough, she finds her rhythm and goes up and down in slow, sensual strokes.

I'm at the point of bursting both at how fucking tight she feels and the view of her riding me, her tits bouncing, her hands caressing my skin.

"God, you really feel so good, Eli," she breathes out in a needy voice. "Fuck me. I love it when you fuck me."

"Like this?" I thrust up when she falls down, and she slumps forward.

"Yes, yes...more..."

"You look like a fucking goddess."

"Oh God, yes!" She grinds her clit against my groin as I drive into her with deep strokes.

"I'm going to fill you with cum so you know you're only mine, wife."

"Yes... Please..."

Her lips fall open, and she tightens around me, so I sit up, sink my hand in her hair, and shove her down for a hungry, violent kiss as she shatters around my cock.

She rotates her hips and continues riding me, milking me, clenching around me.

The entire time she kisses me with frantic passion. My wife is as insatiable as I am and never gets enough.

"Come with me," she whispers against my mouth as she clenches around my cock. "Please, please."

I thrust deeper, wrapping a hand around her throat, and then I'm groaning as she moans.

The rush of the orgasm hits me with blinding strength. I come in her as I kiss her senseless.

She wraps her frail arms around me, and for a moment, we're one.

For a moment, as we kiss and she snuggles against me, I choose to think we're normal.

Ordinary.

Simple.

For a moment, I choose to forget that I have two options for my wife.

Either watch her wither away or admit her to a mental institute and watch her fall apart on the road to no return.

She might look normal now or a few days from now—a few weeks, if we're lucky—but it's an illusion.

A safety net with hidden holes.

An unsteady bridge that will crack under pressure.

Already, as I carry her to the bathroom, she looks lethargic, numb, and only half-present.

Her pulse is slow, her eyes are unfocused, and her body is stiff.

After I run the tap and check the temperature, I place her in the tub, careful to balance her head so she doesn't hit it against the edge in her daze.

I've started to move away to fetch the shower gel when a hand grabs my wrist.

"Hey, Eli?"

"Yes?" I face her, and for a moment, she looks so radiant, so fucking beautiful, pain explodes in the useless organ tucked behind my rib cage.

An organ she poked, provoked, and breathed life into; now it seems to beat only in her presence.

Her words fill the bathroom thicker than the steam. "Let's have a baby."

CHAPTER 34

AVA

IT'S IRRATIONAL AND COMPLETELY ASININE, BUT I don't take back the words I said in the bathroom three days ago.

Eli simply ignored me, slapped me with a *we'll talk about it later*, then proceeded to sweep the entire topic under the rug.

We've been going to the beach, swimming, tanning, and having more sex than porn stars—mostly because I can't get enough and I want to encourage him so I can get pregnant.

Am I being too reckless? Too unfair to the child who would live with an unstable mother?

Possibly. But I'm also desperate to engrave these moments with any method available.

I don't care what anyone says. I know myself the best, and I can recognize that my time is limited. If I'm correct, the last time I woke up in the hospital and lost two years of my life happened after a breakdown, and judging by how drastically degenerative my state is, this time will be worse than mere amnesia.

This time, the tired branch might finally break under my weight.

So I spent the past few days savoring every moment I could get my hands on. Every view, every touch, and every activity.

We went hiking, we had picnics, and he ate my food without my having to use Sam as an excuse. So when I asked if he was okay with me cooking for him, he disclosed he knew all along it was me.

He was the one who ate a slice of my cake before I doomed it to the rubbish bin.

It's strange to see him more relaxed and open about himself. Eli's talked about his childhood here, his bond with his grandparents, and the pressure he put on himself early on to be the perfect heir for the King name.

The admission that these past few days are the only occasion he's ever taken time off for himself has made me feel so bad for him.

I've been absorbing everything about him, imprinting every single detail to memory and hoping, praying that the stars collide and I never forget them this time.

Today he took me to the highest tip of a mountain to witness the most stunning sunrise.

"Here you go." He passes me a bottle of water as I collapse on a rock beneath a massive willow tree.

"I'll be sore as hell tomorrow," I grumble after I nearly empty the bottle. "But it's worth it."

My husband drops his backpack on the uneven surface as his lips pull in a wolfish smirk.

The early-morning sun slips through the trees' leaves and casts a warm glow on his sharp features. His jet-black hair shines in a blue hue, and his eyes appear lighter, like a summer cloud.

He looks hot as hell in black shorts and a tight white tee that sticks to his smooth muscles like a second skin.

"Are we talking about the hike or the way I fucked you while you were half asleep this morning?"

"Both." I grin. "Your stamina is no joke. No idea how you could go several rounds and barely pant at the end of the hike."

"It's called exercise. Something you should do more of."

"The only exercise I like is opening my legs in bed and being a princess while you do all the work. So I'll leave the stamina workout to you. Please and thank you."

He chuckles, the sound echoing around us with the sweetness of morning dew as he sits beside me. "So you're not only a troublemaking brat, but also lazy?"

"Duh." I lay my head on his lap, letting my feet dangle from the rock as I stare up at him. "I put a lot of mental effort into cello, so when I'm not doing that, I'd rather indulge in activities that require no effort whatsoever and preferably provide copious amounts of endorphins."

"Hence the rom-coms, endless shopping, and pirate romance novels."

"Not pirates. Bodice rippers."

"Bodice what?"

"Rippers. You know because they rip bodices off their women? Hey! Sort of like you. They're toxic, too. You should read them sometime and consider therapy."

"No, thanks."

"You're no fun." I pout. "They often end in pregnancies, you know. Romance novels, I mean. It's not realistic since not everyone in love or who gets married in real life has kids or even wants them, but we read romance for escapism, not realism, so everyone accepts the conventional wisdom that every happy couple needs little devils in their lives."

"I see."

"'I see'? That's all you're willing to offer?"

"What else do you want me to offer?"

"That mythical *we'll talk about it later,* maybe? How far away is later? A week? A month? Preferably a few days, which is now?"

He strokes my hair, his touch slow and gentle. "Didn't we already discuss it the other time? The bit where we both recognize you're not ready for children?"

"What if I'm never ready? Does that take the possibility of children off the table?"

"If need be."

My chin trembles. "You're the sixth generation of a wealthy and influential family. The only reason King Enterprises survives and thrives is because of successful heirs such as yourself. You're telling me you don't need one?"

"Not if it endangers you, no. I don't need one."

"Would Uncle Aiden agree? Your grandpa?"

"I'll manage them. Besides, there's always Creigh, Lan, Bran, and Glyn to keep the family registry going."

"But what about you? Surely, you want a child of your own, and I want one, too, so we can do that even if I don't get to raise him or her myself—"

"No." The word leaves him in a deep, firm voice. "I will not have children at the expense of your health."

"But you told Papa you'd give him grandchildren."

"I was just messing with him. I wasn't serious." He pauses. "So that's why you were triggered. You heard me and Dad talk about children, and you started overthinking."

"Why wouldn't I? At that time, I realized you might go heirless because of me, and I don't like being your weakness. I don't like being *anyone*'s weakness."

His fingers stroke my cheek. "You're not."

"That would be so sweet if I believed you," I say with bitterness. "Just say you'll consider it, please."

"Only if it's safe for you to be pregnant."

"That's good enough." I grab his arm. "How did you know I want three children?"

"You mentioned it in your confession letter."

My lips fall open. "Wh-wh-what do you mean by confession letter?"

"The one you wrote to me about six years ago."

"No...no way. I threw that away."

"I found it."

"And you read it?"

"Quite possibly."

"Oh God...this is so embarrassing." I hide my eyes with both hands. "Please tell me you only remember the three-children part?"

"Dear Eli." He speaks in a nonchalant voice. "You're probably wondering why I'm writing you this letter, but I had to put these feelings on paper and hope they'll somehow reach you. You see, I've had a major crush on you for years, but you always treated me like a kid who's not worth your time. It kind of hurt, but I understand that you're six years older than me, and it's both weird and creepy for you to like or even notice someone way younger than you. So I bided my time and waited for this moment to tell you how much I like you.

"Actually, I think I'm a little in love with you. Whenever I see you, I get these butterflies and feel like I'm in the presence of a god, and I want nothing more than to worship and spin in your orbit for eternity. All you have to do is treat me like your goddess, and I promise I'll stand by your side forever.

"I might not be as mature and sophisticated as the women you're familiar with, but I'm growing up, and I'm way more fashionable and stylish, just saying. Your mum is also my godmother, and we love each other so much, so we'll be the coolest mother- and daughter-in-law. You're welcome for the lack of conflict in the future and the fact you'll be marrying someone of your status.

"You might need to work hard to get Papa's acceptance, but I'll help! He looks stern and all, but really, he can't reSist my puppy eyes. I'm not saying we should get married now, but maybe in three or four years after I finish uni.

"FYI, I want three children, preferably two girls and a boy. The girls' names will be Sierra and Zoey. I'll leave the boy's name to you. I also want two dogs and three cats or three dogs and two cats. I'm open to negotiation as long as it's within that ratio. You can take your time to fall in love with me from here on. I'll wait for as long as it takes.

"PS: I need to disclose something so you're not blind-sided. I'm sure you heard from Aunt Elsa or our mutual friends that I suffer from anxiety and depression, but in reality, it's a bit worse than that, and I might need a little monitoring. However, I swear I'm mostly self-sufficient, and I'm following this new therapy plan that I'm sure will work. You have nothing to worry about. The future love of your life you now know exists, Ava."

Oh. My. God.

Can the earth open up and swallow me? Now would be great, thanks.

I peek at him through my fingers to find him staring at me as if he didn't just recite my stupid letter word for word.

"Why the hell did you learn it by heart?" I ask, trying and failing not to sound strangled.

"I have a good memory."

"You only did that to torment and embarrass me."

"I wasn't the one who wrote that."

"Ugh. Let me die in shame."

He laughs as he removes my hands from my face. "There's nothing to be ashamed of. I'm fully aware I'm irreSistible."

"Get over yourself." I prod his abs. "Besides, I was totally over you after that."

"Which is why you proceeded to vie for my attention at uni?"

"Yeah, well, if I didn't already have your attention, I wouldn't have exploited it."

"Is that so?"

"It's true! You were everywhere." I narrow my eyes. "You know, I always thought you wanted to torment me for having the audacity to like you or something, but now that I think about it, you're not the type of person who wastes time on anything without a return on his investment. So why did I have your attention?"

"It started as mild interest. A mere thought about taking

advantage of your weaknesses so I could use them against you down the line. Nothing personal. I do that to everyone. And believe me, I found a galore of faults, discrepancies, and dangerous nonchalance that I could crush you with if I chose to. You were chaotically impulsive and pathologically trusting. Two traits that would've led you to an early grave."

"And what stopped you from pushing me to said grave?"

"Unlike what you liked to believe, I never hated you prior to nor after your confession. No offense, but you held no importance to me. You were merely the kid Mum liked to dote on. I had no reason to develop any feelings for you. Though I do remember being inexplicably annoyed with your presence when we were children and might've tripped or pushed you down just because I could. That was possibly because I hated sharing my parents, and Mum cared about you too much for my liking. However, things changed as soon as you got into university."

"In...what sense?" I ask, trying not to sound hurt that he never even thought about me before, but then again, it's true that he never saw me any differently than Cecy and Glyn.

"You started to antagonize me. Repeatedly. I'm sure you can tell I'm not the type of man who can be provoked. By anyone. Least of all the kid who didn't look like a kid anymore and who certainly did not dress like a kid in those nightclubs. So that mere interest grew into deeper investment the more you and Lan plotted against me. I had to retaliate. You retaliated back. Before I knew it, that interest morphed into raw obsession and mysterious possessiveness.

I didn't understand the reasons and couldn't find a logical explanation, considering I genuinely found you infuriating and not controllable. Nonetheless, I made the decision that you couldn't be with anyone else. So I married you."

"Is that all you ever felt toward me? Obsession and possessiveness?"

"Of course not. There's always been constant fucking annoyance."

"Gee, thanks. And they say romance is dead," I joke, even though a part of me shatters against the broken edges of my stupid heart.

That idiot can't seem to take a hint and keeps attempting to heal itself from scraps.

I should know by now that Eli is capable of care but not of love. He's able to provide me with whatever I need— companionship and protection included—as long as I don't ask for his nonexistent heart.

And for some reason, that hurts worse than I would have thought.

Because as much as I try to hold on to the illusion, I can see it breaking before my eyes.

And the man I love will probably shove me aside and get on with his life down the line as I rot away with the passage of time.

———

Two days later, we go home. Mainly because Eli's called in for a work-related emergency and I want to mourn the death of the hope that my husband will ever love me.

He likes me just fine, but he *can't* love me.

I'm busy playing the cello for the fourth consecutive

hour in preparation for a possible competition. I just need to take one final chance so that whether I succeed or blow it, I'll have no regrets.

My phone vibrates on the glass coffee table. I pause, the mellow sound fading as I look at the mural clock. Quarter past eight.

Leo said they'd probably be late today and that I should have dinner, but I have no appetite, no matter how many of my favorite dishes Sam cooked. Something she let me know she despised as she shook her head and left me in peace.

I grab my phone and frown at the unknown number flashing on the screen.

"Hello?" I answer.

"Ava, it's me."

"Vance? Where's your old number?"

"I suspect it was blocked from your side."

"I didn't block you."

"Then your husband did."

"Oh."

"Like he got me kicked off UK soil for criminal charges. I'm in the airport before the travel ban takes place."

"C-criminal charges? What the hell is going on?"

"I told you he's insane, Ava. Listen, I couldn't in good conscience leave without telling you what he did."

I stand, holding my phone in a death grip. "I don't want to hear about my previous psychiatrist nor whatever he did to them—"

"It's about what he did to you!"

"M-me?" My heart lunges, and sweat breaks out on my spine.

"Remember your friend Oliver from uni?"

"Yeah. He's somewhere in South America."

"No. He went MIA, but if what I gathered from Gemma and the others is correct, I'm pretty sure Eli was involved."

"What does that have to do with me?"

"Because you married Eli quickly and without explanation right after Oliver disappeared. There has to be something there. I believe he's threatening or blackmailing you."

My grip loosens on the phone, and it falls on the table as everything rushes back in.

CHAPTER 35
AVA

TWO AND A HALF YEARS AGO

MY EYES SLOWLY PEEL OPEN AT THE CONSTANT loud sound of a *beep...beep...beep...*

My head lies on the cool surface of the steering wheel as the wind howls outside the car.

I slowly straighten, my foot shaking on the brake pedal and my heart thumping loudly in my ears.

The truck I nearly collided with drives in the distance, its bright red beams casting a halo on the otherwise-quiet, dimly lit street.

I somehow clipped or hit a pole, and now I'm stopped in the middle of the road. The driver must've swerved past me. There's some damage to the car, but it's nothing serious, and when I test it, it's drivable.

However, I've obviously lost some time because I have no recollection of what exactly happened and can only speculate.

Wait.

I fumble with my arms, touch my middle, and wiggle my toes. Everything is working. My breaths echo in the car, shallow and stuttered.

Is it possible that I died and became a ghost like in those paranormal films? Am I stuck here for unfinished business?

A knock comes on the window, slashing the silence with a violent interruption. I jump, my heart nearly spilling at my feet.

When I look up, a sigh of relief pushes past my starving lungs as I open the door. "Ollie, you scared me!"

"Is everything all right?" he asks, his gaze flitting at the now-empty street, except for my car and his, which is parked by the side of the road.

"Yup. Nearly got killed by a truck, but all is good."

I stand, but my feet fail me. Ollie grabs me by the waist and steadies me against the side of my car, his hand stroking my midsection in an uncomfortable rhythm.

He smells of cigarettes, alcohol, and overpowering oud cologne. A combination that brings nausea to the back of my throat.

"You all right there, love?"

"Um...yeah." I subtly try to push him away, but his tenuous grip hardens on my midsection until pain explodes where his fingers apply pressure.

"You don't look fine, Ava. You know what? Forget about the party. Let me take you home."

"I can drive on my own. I'm fine."

This time, I apply more strength to push him away, but he towers over me and grabs my chin, a menacing smile stretching his thin lips. "I said I'll drive you."

"And I said I can do it on my own." I frown. "Let go of me, Ollie."

"You know, that's exactly your problem, Ava. You believe all men to be playthings that you flirt with a little and suck their money dry a lot, then expect them to leave when you ask them to."

"I never asked for your money. I have my own." My voice trembles at the end.

Even though I chose to go on the defensive, a nagging feeling dictates that I remove myself from this situation as soon as possible.

My mum taught me to always follow my gut, and right now it's demanding I disentangle myself from Ollie.

He barges into my space, his expression vicious. I've never found him intimidating before, more of a pushy person who always tried his luck to get into my knickers.

However, the events are drastically different now.

I'm hyperaware of his height and width, and I faintly remember that he's one of those gym bros who make growing muscles their personality type.

His thighs brush mine, and I gulp, the sound getting trapped in my closing throat before echoing in the air.

Oliver's smirk widens like a hyena that's starting to enjoy the hunt.

"You still gave me mixed signals, and you know that. You enjoy it, right? Being an attention whore is your personality after all."

"I never asked for your attention." I lift my chin. "Back the hell off, Ollie, and I'll pretend this never happened."

I'm totally cutting him from my life after this. All this time, I was blindsided and never noticed the nefarious edges tucked beneath his easygoing facade. I remember Cecy once telling me there were rumors he abused his ex-girlfriend. She said that so I'd keep my distance from him. Did I listen? No. Mostly because I thought it didn't apply to me since I never saw him as more than a friend of the night.

Clearly, I was wrong, and I honest-to-God need to listen to Cecy more.

"Pretend it never happened?" He barks out vicious laughter that tightens my stomach and disturbs the silent darkness. "Should I curtsy, Your Highness?"

"If you don't release me this instant, I'll destroy you until nothing is left. You're messing with the wrong person, but I'll allow you to back off." I glare up at him, feigning nonchalance I don't feel. "You do know I have an influential family, right?"

He lifts his hand and slaps me so hard, my head rolls back and a buzz ricochets in my ears. A metallic taste explodes in my mouth, and I realize my lip is split open and I bit my tongue.

Before I can recover, Oliver turns me around and shoves me harshly against the car. Then he pulls up my skimpy dress. "Where's your influential family now? Maybe they'll be here to clean my cum off your dirty cunt. Let's see if it's worth all this hassle."

Reality sinks in like a load of bricks, and I blindly scratch at him. "Stop! Let me go, stop!"

"Shut your trap, bitch!" He lifts my head and slams it against the car.

The world swings and sways beneath my feet as my heels scratch on the concrete. The buzzing in my ears, the howling of the wind, and the blurriness of my surroundings feel as if they're happening to someone else.

I feel him harshly grabbing my breasts, but I can't move. My breathing gets stuck in a stuttered choke, and I hear myself whisper, "Help...please...help..."

"I said"—he bangs my head against the car again—"shut the fuck up, you damn cunt!"

Stars dance in my vision, and my arms fall to either side of me. I can feel the fight being sucked out of me as the howling wind matches my barren insides.

Maybe if I stay still, it'll be over soon.

Maybe I won't remember it.

Maybe it'll be like how I entirely forgot Bach's Cello Suite no. 4 during the competition and even forgot why the hell I was there, who the people staring at me were, and my damn identity. I'll forget this, too.

Forever.

It'll be buried in the darkness like my consciousness and part of my degenerative brain.

If there's a god out there, send a lightning strike to kill the bastard before he hurts me.

Please.

"That's right, stay still and I won't have to hurt you for long, cunt—" Oliver's voice is cut off, and I think the universe has pitied me and shoved me down into a state of numbness.

His weight disappears from behind me, and I hear a loud *thwack*.

I blink the blurry moisture from my eyes and slowly turn around, my back gluing to the car. My lips ache, my head still rings, and my legs barely keep me upright. I have to grab the top of the car for balance.

But I see it.

In the middle of the dimly lit streets.

As the wind ravages the large trees.

As my hearing sharpens and my body awakens.

Oliver is sprawled out on the ground, his body pinned beneath a larger figure.

It's Eli.

The last person I expected to save me.

His fist grips Oliver's collar, and he unleashes a flurry of punches to his face. The sound of flesh meeting concrete echoes through the air as blood splatters onto his shirt, neck, and the ground below.

My ex-friend tries to speak, but only strangled gurgles escape his throat as Eli relentlessly drives his fist into his face over and over again. Each blow lands with a sickening thud, making Oliver's features unrecognizable under the onslaught of punches and gushing blood.

I stand frozen in place, sweat beading on my back despite the cold breeze as I watch in horror. Oliver no longer reSists nor attempts to defend himself, his body limp and lifeless under the brutal assault.

Eli shows no emotion as he continues to punch and punch and *punch*. He seems almost robotic, as if he is on a mission that cannot be stopped. He doesn't even seem to notice the splatter of blood on his own shirt nor the lack of response from his victim.

A chilling realization surges through me like an electric shock—Eli couldn't care less about what he's doing. The indifference in his expression sends a jolt through my stomach, leaving me shaken and disturbed to the core.

"E-Eli..." My voice comes out as haunting as the wind.

He looks up, his jaw locked and his expression so cold, I feel the lick of ice on my skin. The contact lasts for a few seconds, but it feels like long minutes.

I've never seen him like this, so methodical in his violence, so frightening in his calm.

It's as if I'm looking at a seasoned killer.

His gaze slides back to Oliver, and he drops his head on the ground with apparent distaste, then proceeds to kick him in the ribs. "My first time murdering someone, and it's disappointingly not as euphoric as promised. If anything, I feel nothing."

"He...he...he's dead?" I whisper-yell, my throat closing around the words.

Eli rises to his full height, stares at his stained shirt with disapproval, and doesn't dignify Oliver with his attention. "Looks like it."

"Oh my God...oh my God, oh my God, oh my God..." My legs finally give out, and I slide down the car and fall on the cold asphalt as the frigid hands of panic grip me. "Let's call an ambulance. Maybe he's alive."

Eli stands before me, blocking the scene, the light, and every ounce of oxygen. "Why do you want him to be alive after he attempted to rape you?"

My breath hitches as I stare up at him. He looks like a cruel, unforgiving god. The god people prayed to during wartime so they could kill and maim as many of the enemy as possible.

And he'd grant it. In a heartbeat.

"I...I don't want him dead because of that."

"You wouldn't think the same if he'd finished what he started."

My lips part at the reminder of my wish of lightning upon Oliver just before it was instantly answered.

Eli removes his jacket and crouches in front of me as he

places it around my shoulders. That's when I realize my dress's strap is torn, and I'm shaking so wildly, my teeth chatter.

"What are you going to do?" I whisper. "You'll go to prison if this is found out."

His expression remains the same—calm, icy, and terrifyingly controlled.

Why the hell am I falling apart when he's like this? And I wasn't the one who took a man's life.

Even if I did wish doom on him.

"That's where you're wrong. If this is found out, *we* will go to prison, for I will report you as an accomplice."

"But I didn't do anything."

"Let's see whose version they believe. If you say nothing, this entire incident will vanish. We stay afloat together, or we drown together. Is that understood?"

I nod once.

"Good girl. I was confident you'd keep a secret."

My tremors turn into something entirely nefarious. I can't believe I'm feeling hot and bothered at him praising me when there's a dead body just a few meters away.

My moral compass seems to be taking the weekend off. I blame the alcohol and whatever pill I took earlier tonight.

This isn't me.

"Wh-what will you do about...?" I jut my chin in Oliver's general direction.

"Don't concern yourself with that. But you need to promise me something to ensure the survival of our alliance."

"What do you want?"

He strokes his thumb over my trembling lower lip. "Marry me, and I'll bury our secret."

CHAPTER 36
ELI

PAST

IT SHOULDN'T COME AS A SURPRISE THAT AVA refused to follow instructions and go home.

Ever since she picked up pissing me off as a sport, she's been an infuriating thorn in my side who's often scheming with Landon to make my life hell.

In theory, I shouldn't care about her attempts to rile me. More so, they shouldn't even have the capacity to disturb my immaculate control. I have no clue when this change began, when I set her in my sights as a possible target.

It could've started the day she so foolishly wrote me that letter. No. I genuinely thought of her as a naive kid who didn't know what was best for her at the time.

I began to notice her vicious pink aura when she made it her mission to drive away all the women I fucked after she enrolled in uni. She acted like I was the devil incarnate and inSisted on letting me and everyone else know how much she hated me, but then she schemed with Lan to push away any possible prospects.

So I did the same. Eye for an eye and all that.

But truly, I wished to delve into her deeper, see her for the chaotic pink ball of energy she truly is.

I wanted to find her weaknesses and bring her to her knees before me.

However, the more I find, the deeper I want to go. I've seen her hide from her best friends just so they won't witness her at her worst. I've seen her smile and laugh while her eyes are screaming for help. I've seen her looking in the mirror and reciting her name, age, and her love for cello while seeming as if she were staring through herself.

Perhaps it started then—or when she danced with small-dicked fools while her fuck-me eyes were set on me. She probably thought it was a harmless provocation, but it's backfiring and will have the direst consequence on her life.

Ava Nash should've never planted herself in my path.

She should've never vied for my attention.

Because now that she's got it, the world as she knows it will be flipped upside down.

The reason I haven't acted on these cryptic feelings to own and punish and possess the living fuck out of her is because I thought they'd eventually dissipate.

Unfortunately for her, they've grown into this furnace of chaotic emotions and an urgent need for ownership. And while I still don't have a full grasp on their meaning, she's pushed me to act on them.

She can blame herself for what will befall her.

Because here's the thing: I'm done staying in the background and delivering threats she never listens to.

It's time she personally witnesses the unpleasantness I've promised.

Her friend Bonneville divulged that their silly group of emptiness will be going to an after-party and gave me the address, inviting me over without my having to ask. A privilege of being irreSistible, if you will.

Ava nearly had a wreck on her way out of the car park because she's a reckless little shit who drives under the influence. She should pay me for making sure she doesn't die in a freak accident.

Before I can follow, I spot the blond guy who was rubbing himself all over her on the dance floor kicking his car into gear and leaving right behind Ava.

I go after him, keeping a safe distance so as not to be noticed.

He keeps the same pace as Ava, trailing her like a seasoned stalker. The blasphemy.

I'm the only one who's allowed to stalk her.

The blond guy, Oliver, if I remember correctly, turns off his headlights.

Hmm. I was going to make him disappear like all the losers she fraternizes with, but I'm positively pissed off about the sleazy look I saw in his eyes when they were dancing. The way he was stripping her naked with his gaze. The audacity of him thinking he can touch what I will own.

Yes, Ava has her own sex life like I do, but that phase will soon come to an end.

And by *soon*, I mean tonight.

From now on, no one else but me will touch her.

Fuck her.

Own her.

She'll fall at my feet until I decipher the depths of this

obsession. Then I'll get bored like I usually do and discard her like all my previous conquests.

Correction: She'll be my only conquest. I've never had to pursue anyone before her.

Which will make this so much more rewarding.

I tap my fingers on the steering wheel as I fall back farther and take a different turn so Oliver doesn't suspect anything. I want him to focus on whatever the fuck he's doing so he doesn't see me coming.

I want him to enjoy whatever thoughts he's having about Ava, because they will be his last. Instead of taking the shorter route, I follow the longer one, which sets me back about five minutes, before I turn onto the road leading to the motorway.

The first sight that greets me is of that fucker Oliver pushing Ava against her car and fumbling with her dress.

The view of her shaking uncontrollably ignites a raging fire inside my veins.

It's so wild and uncharacteristic that I see red for the first time in my life.

Murderous red.

The red I know I can never come back from.

I slam the brakes and bring the car to a halt, then step out with baffling calm. Probably because I'm reveling in the thought that Oliver's last breaths are within reach. He could've disappeared quietly like all the others, but he dared to terrorize her, to touch her with his dirty hands.

He'll no longer have the luxury of spitting his rancid breaths into a world where she exists.

I've never thought about murder before, but plotting it is easier than I presumed.

I have this crushing feeling that this won't be the last time I do something uncharacteristic for Ava fucking Nash.

The red blurring my vision morphs into a hazy black as she whimpers what sounds like, "Help..."

I'm not a knight in shining armor. What I am, however, is the only man who's allowed near her.

After tonight, Ava is fucking mine.

No matter what methods I must use to achieve that.

CHAPTER 37

AVA

THE WEDDING DAY

I CAN'T DO THIS.

The opulent grand hall buzzes with muted confusion and whispered excitement, but my vision is blurry to all the attendees.

To my family and friends who think they're sharing my happiness because I told them so.

Because I inSisted on marrying Eli despite my father's opposition and everyone else's bemusement.

All these months, I've busied myself with preparing for the wedding, so I haven't thought about what the hell I've gotten myself into. I went mental for my perfect dress, the perfect venue, and the perfect shade of flowers, but it wasn't because I cared so much. Low-key, I wished to ruin it with any method available.

I nearly trip on the hem of my dress as I reach the altar. Papa holds me upright, and I stare at his stony face through the veil. My nose still tingles from how hard I cried into his chest when he said he'd be the one to walk me down the aisle.

All the frustration, fear, and anger I felt through the

previous couple of months exploded in one go, and I cried like a baby. However, that didn't change the outcome nor my mind, despite Papa's pleas for me to think about this decision.

He categorically hates this outcome and would rather I end up on the cover of gossip magazines as a runaway bride instead of tying my fate to Eli King.

I happen to think the same.

But fear has rendered me a coward.

That night my fiancé killed Oliver, I had a panic attack and kept seeing blood on my hands. It was because of Eli, but he was also the one who got me out of it.

And now I have no way out.

So I fake a smile, and Papa reluctantly releases my arm. I feel Eli looming before us like a pending hurricane, but I focus on the safety Papa represents, the sentiment that everything will be fine as long as he's in my life.

A bigger hand envelops mine, and a rush of apprehension tightens my stomach. Papa glares at Eli, and the man I'm being forced to marry grins back.

It's sinister and threatening, like everything about him.

For a moment, I consider telling Papa the whole story. He'd help me and have Eli locked up for his crimes.

But then I recall his fight with Mama. How they seem to fall out whenever I'm the topic of discussion. Eli is right. I need to get out of their lives, or else I'll be the constant cause of their misery.

He's already my guardian now, so he has power over me no matter which way I spin it.

"You hurt my daughter and no one will find your corpse, King." Dad delivers the threat in low words.

"I look forward to officially being your son-in-law, Uncle Cole."

Papa's fists ball, but before he can punch him, Eli tugs me toward him so that we're standing facing each other. Through my veil, he looks tall, taller than usual. His height takes up all the space and sends a lick of dread through me. His face is stone-cold despite the fake smile he has plastered on his features.

I can't marry him. And it's not because he killed a man in cold blood.

It's because I'm genuinely scared he might do the same to me one day.

His reason for marrying me is to keep an eye on me. He'll make my life hell.

He'll torment me.

He'll kill the remnants of my sanity.

And the most tragic part is that my feelings for him, which never truly died, could resurface and worsen the circumstances.

I've always dreamed about marrying him, but I foolishly thought that would be done out of love.

It's wrong to get married because of blackmail. This is the most ominous start to a marriage, and I can't do it.

I have to run.

Now.

Before it's too late.

Eli leans in, and I stop breathing, my heart beating so loudly, I'm sure everyone can hear it.

His hot breath skims my ear through the veil. "Don't even think about running off on me, Ava."

My fingers shake around the gorgeous bouquet of

flowers. How does he know I plan to run? Still, I whisper, "I c-can't do this."

"You seem to believe you have a choice, but you don't. Either you stay still and go through with the wedding, or you leave. If you choose the second option, I'll find you, and I'll kidnap you to a place no one can find you. I'll lock you the fuck up, and you'll never see your parents and friends ever again. And if you prove to be a hassle, I'll slice your fucking throat and end your life as effortlessly as I did Oliver's."

I tremble as he steps back, still wearing the same sinister smile.

I've never been so terrified.

Yes, Eli has always been devious, but I never thought he could kill someone. Then I saw him punch a man to death, so now I wouldn't put anything past him.

So I believe him when he says he'll kidnap, then kill me.

My legs are frozen in place as we go through fake vows with very real consequences.

No.

The part where we say "till death do us part" doesn't seem fake at all.

The priest announces us as husband and wife, and I realize with depressing finality that I'm truly trapped with Eli for life.

He lifts my veil and wraps an arm around my waist, then tugs me toward him. I gasp when his lips seal against mine in a ferocious claim. He shoves his tongue inside and then bites mine. A metallic tang explodes in my mouth as he ravages me so fiercely, pain and intense pleasure mixing into one.

I remain limp in his arms as he kisses me with fortified ruthlessness and blind possessiveness.

As if he's making a point of staking a claim in public.

The cheers, claps, and music fade into nothingness as my ears fill with a loud buzz. I was completely taken in by this man from the beginning, and now I can no longer stop it.

He releases my mouth and whispers in a rough tone, "Mine."

CHAPTER 38
ELI

PRESENT

LACK OF SLEEP IS BEGINNING TO AFFECT MY productivity and, worse, my vigilance.

It's no longer a rare occurrence nor a fleeting occasion. I'm unable to sleep lately, whether by choice or design, and it's all due to the very rational fear that Ava could sleep-walk into her fucking death.

It wouldn't be the first time. I caught her standing at the edge of the balcony on Gran's island, her arms wide open as she smiled at the ground.

That smile still haunts me. Sadness and crushing relief brightened her ghostly blue eyes like a shooting star on a moonless night. That fleeting moment had the largest impact on me as she stood there in the night breeze, her nightgown flying with the wind, and I knew, I just knew that if I didn't pull her back, she'd fall to her death.

She'd escape me forever.

As the car comes to a slow stop in front of the house, I pinch the bridge of my nose and mentally prepare myself for another torturously paranoid sleepless night.

I down my fifth coffee for the day and get out.

Henderson follows me to the entrance, and instead of opening the door, he steps in front of it.

I raise a brow.

His deep-brown eyes appear black under the dim light as he throws tentative glances to either side of him.

"Spare me the suspense." My voice sounds tired to my own ears. "If there's anything you wish to say, say it, or move out of the way."

"This is not sustainable, sir."

"And neither is keeping you in service when you don't have your priorities straight, but here we are."

"You know full well that you can't survive on continuous lack of sleep. Your body will eventually shut down, and the consequences will be unsalvageable."

"I'm sure you and Sam will manage the estate's affairs until I'm back on my feet again."

"Just so you can shove yourself into this state again?"

"If need be. I have to be hands-on the entire time."

"Then why don't you quit your job and dedicate yourself to being her full-time caregiver?"

"I'll think about it."

"Sir!" Henderson grits his teeth, visibly vying for the patience he usually has in abundance. "If you give up everything for her, you'll eventually despise her for forcing you down this path."

"That's where you're wrong. I'd never despise her."

"Even if she's the reason you ruin the ambition you've harbored your entire life?"

"Even then."

"You'll be destructive without a purpose."

"I have a purpose. It's her."

He releases a long sigh that borders on both frustration and defeat. "I've known you since you were a child, and there has never been a time where I thought you to be impulsively irrational like you are right now. If you believe keeping her from getting proper help in a specialized institution is a form of protection, then you're sorely mistaken. You're merely delaying the inevitable, and not for the best. This will have a worse impact on her than the previous time, and it'll only end in disaster."

"Do you think I don't know that?" I snap. "Because I do. I've studied all the possible outcomes, and I'm well aware of the consequences."

"You simply don't care?"

"I simply do not want her locked up in an institution she loathes and distrusts. The last time we did that, she nearly took her own life."

"She's prone to attempting suicide even without the locking-up part."

My jaw clenches, and I have this urge to punch Henderson's face and shut him up for eternity. But that would make my wife sad, considering the infuriating bond she's formed with the man.

She's often *Leo this* and *Leo that*, perfectly channeling the energy of an extrovert who's adopted a clueless introvert.

So I shove him out of the way without inflicting bodily harm—for now. I swear to fuck, if he keeps spouting nonsense, I'll expel him to the moon.

My steps are slow, and I sway and then grab the wall for balance. Apparently, I need more caffeine.

Sam and Henderson would say I need rest.

My ears prickle at the faint sound of the cello coming from the media room where Ava usually practices. It's high-pitched and lacks the usual elegance my wife is known for in the music scene.

If anything, it's intense and jolting, filling the space with a cloak of danger and urgency.

My muscles tighten as I hurry in that direction. While I don't get alarmed at the melodies of the cello lately, this sound is a horrifying reminder of a not-so-distant version of my wife.

I grab the knob and turn, holding out hope that I'm overthinking.

The door creaks open, the noise clashing with the desperate notes of music.

My wife is perched on a chair, surrounded by a dangerous sea of shattered remnants of the glass coffee table. Crimson trails slice across her bare feet and the fronts of her legs, as though she crawled through the shards before standing on them. She continues to play her symphony of death with bleeding fingers, the bow and strings serving as instruments for her psychoSis.

Each drop of blood stains the once-pristine rug and leaves deep-red splatters on the broken screen of her phone and her light-pink dress. Even her tousled hair is marred by streaks of crimson.

Blood surrounds us, a vivid and jarring reminder of the chaos I selfishly thrust us into.

I walk toward her slowly in an attempt to keep from startling her while suppressing my need to jog, to run, to remove her from the hazardous situation.

The glass crunches beneath my shoes until I stop

in front of her and call in a firm voice over the music, "Ava?"

Her bow comes to an abrupt halt, and her fingers freeze on the tuning pegs. Slowly, she lifts her head and stares up at me with eyes both vacant and enraged. They look lost, but they also brim with a hot-red edge.

Tension crackles and blisters in the air as we maintain eye contact. Me, because I'm trying to identify if she's coming off one of her episodes. Her...I have no clue. She looks at me with a depressing fear I never thought I'd see on her face again.

"Is everything all right?" I step forward and lift a hand to touch her, check her pulse, and make sure it's beating normally.

Ava jerks back, and the cello falls from her hand and crashes against the shattered glass. Her chair scrapes the pieces and tilts under her weight, but she doesn't fall.

"Don't touch me," she says with enough bitterness to send my hackles up.

To avoid alarming her, I remain in place and shove a hand in my pocket, summoning my gentlest tone. "What's the issue?"

"You lied to me. All this time, you've been *lying* to me." Moisture clings to her lids as red covers her cheek.

"Concerning what?" I ask calmly.

"*Everything!*" she yells, her voice cracking. "You lied about our marriage of convenience. The reason behind it wasn't so we'd benefit each other. You forced me to tie the knot so you could make sure I kept your murder a secret. You threatened to take me down with you as an accomplice if I didn't comply with your proposal."

Fuck.

Fucking hell.

A muscle tightens in my jaw as the wall I carefully built around my wife crumbles to the ground in one blistering go.

"What else do you remember?" I ask with a tight voice.

It's pointless to try to make her believe none of that happened or that it's a play of her imagination. I never felt comfortable exploiting her mental state in that manner anyway, not even if it was for her sake.

"I remember *everything*. The way you made me marry you. How, when I was at the altar and contemplated running away, you reminded me that you killed someone for me and would snap my neck if I posed as any form of a problem for you." She sniffles, a tear falling down her cheek. "You threatened me with murder on my wedding day! How could you do that to me?"

"Because I couldn't afford to let you run away."

"Afraid of people gossiping if I left you stranded at the altar?"

"Afraid that was my last chance to have you."

"You mean possess me? *Own* me?"

It might have started that way, yes, but it's evolved since then, especially after she lost her memory. Ava has become an integral part of my life I cannot survive without, and that makes her a weakness, a liability, a loose thread anyone could exploit and use against me.

All this time, I've been battling the notion of cutting that thread and ridding myself of the hazard she poses, but every time, I refuse to imagine my life without her sunshine, without her pink-themed existence.

So I doubled down on my efforts. Attempted to erase the past, her illness, and everything that could turn her situation murkier.

"I'm not a thing you play with, then toss away once you're bored, Eli." Tears stream down her cheeks as she taps her chest with bloody fingers. "I *feel*. I have emotions and a heart that's been broken far too many times but refuses to die already. I'm done giving you liberty with it. Done dancing to your tune, demands, and controlling behavior."

"Is that all you remember? Demands and controlling behavior?"

"I remember you made me listen to a conversation between my parents where they were discussing my deteriorating state. Mama wanted to have me admitted to the institute, but Papa disagreed and wanted to change my psychiatrist. You did that on purpose so I'd feel guilty about being the reason for their quarrel and pose no objection to the guardianship transfer to you. You demanded I stop drinking, and when I didn't comply, you tied me up and forced me to get sober. I remember you ordering me to take my meds regularly, and when I refused, you locked me up in the psych ward for months until I was begging you to take me out. You changed my psychiatrist, separated me from the friends I partied with, and blacklisted me from all the clubs in the UK. You put a tracker on my phone and forbid me from driving again. You had people following me everywhere. I wasn't allowed to drink, party, nor even go out alone, and my only companions were your people, my parents, your parents, Ari, and Cecy. You transformed my world into a gilded cage, so yes, all I remember are demands and controlling behavior."

She's crying now. The longer she spoke, the more broken her voice turned, until she could barely talk at the end.

Everything she remembers happened way before her latest episode that ended in amnesia. Does that mean she doesn't recall the trigger?

Is she blocking that out on purpose?

Dr. Blaine said that Ava, like any neurodivergent person who's prone to trauma, strongly emphasizes the negative over the positive, and in some instances, she might choose to completely erase any good moments in favor of fitting reality into her perceived narrative.

If my wife thinks I'm the big bad wolf who ruined her life and built her a pretty gilded cage, there's no way for me to change that perception with words. The more I inSist on altering her version, the more paranoid she'll turn, and her brain might shut down as a consequence.

I made that mistake before she fell down the stairs and lost her memory. I tried explaining that, yes, I forced her to marry me, but everything else happened for a different reason than what she believed.

My wife couldn't handle the truth, and the whole debacle ended in tragedy. So I will not, under any circumstances, attempt that route again.

"You're not going to say anything?" Her pained voice and tear-streaked face are no different than a shard of glass being stabbed into my chest.

"What do you want me to say?" I ask with feigned nonchalance.

"An excuse? An explanation? An attempt to make me believe I imagined things wrong and that I'm more mentally unstable than I thought. Won't you make me question myself as usual? Aren't you an expert in manipulation and gaslighting?"

"I don't see the point." I step forward. "Let me clean your wounds."

"Step away from me!" She lunges up, and the chair knocks backward as she steps on a shard of glass.

I freeze when I see it lodging itself deep in her foot. I then fall two steps back. "I'm away. Just stop moving. I'll leave and call Sam to help you, all right?"

"Don't you dare walk away when I'm talking to you!"

My feet come to a stop again as I face her. "I'm all ears."

She sniffles, pain turning her breathing shallow, her body shaking uncontrollably. "Did you have fun stringing me along all these months and making me believe I could be normal? Did you find pleasure in giving me hope, mending the cracks in my heart while knowing full well you'd shatter it to pieces again?"

"I find no pleasure in your pain, Ava."

"Liar!" she screams. "Stop lying to me! Stop tormenting me! Just stop!"

She's walking back and forth on the glass now, and I swear to fuck, I feel every shard wedging its way into my chest.

"Okay, okay..." I put both hands up in a show of surrender. "I'll say whatever you want. Just stop hurting yourself. *Please.*"

It takes everything in me not to sweep her up in my arms and remove the glass from her skin. But I know if I do that, she'll escalate. Like an unpredictable hurricane.

My gaze flits to the cabinet where I have her emergency tranquilizer shot. We planted them in every room in the house and all the cars we use.

After that time she fell down the stairs, I promised to never let it escalate that much again. All I have to do is give her the shot and everything will be okay for a while.

Until I have to make some hard decisions. Again.

Ava stops and tilts her head. "You pity me, don't you? You feel like I'm a poor girl with a lot of issues, so you married me to feel good about yourself, didn't you? Everything was a lie. Your words, your actions, your promises. Oh my God."

"It's not like that." I take one step forward, two...

On the third, she bends over and snatches a large shard of glass in her bloodied hand, and points it at me "Stay away!"

Fuck, fuck, fuck...

I've often read history books about ways the past repeats itself, oftentimes in an endless loop, but I never thought that could be literal.

And real.

Last time, my wife held a knife. This time, it's a sharp and fucking deadly shard of glass that's currently digging into her skin.

Blood streams over her palms and wrists, then drips on the wooden floor in a sickening rhythm as she trembles, sniffles, and releases small moans of pain.

She's an absolute mess of epic proportions, and I can't push away the idea that I caused this by not offering her the help I can't provide.

The help being admitting her to an institution the

moment she woke up in the hospital. It didn't matter that she had amnesia nor that she looked normal. Dr. Blaine said it was merely a phase in her cycle, and her cycle is unpredictable. She poses a danger to herself and those around her.

She's a liability.

A mentally insane person who needs proper care.

Even her parents agreed with the doctor. Ariella and Cecily, too. Hell, my own mother has been constantly begging me to change my mind. Not to mention Henderson and Sam.

Did I listen?

No.

I saw the girl who looked at me with heart eyes and pent-up emotions and decided to take a different approach this time.

Allow her to live normally. To spread her wings and feel like ordinary people do.

And I thought things were going well. She came out of her shell, she liked me again, and she looked at me as if I were the only one she needed. Due to her memory loss, she wasn't as paranoid and scared of me because of the murder. She'd forgotten that I'd coerced her into marriage, rehab, and quitting her bad habits.

She came back into my orbit like she was always meant to.

It wasn't until now that I realized I could have possibly, probably made a massive mistake.

I remain silent and so still, I stop breathing for a while so as not to alarm her.

Ava's inhales and exhales deepen like an injured animal before her eyes widen. "Oh my God...no...no...no..."

"What's wrong?"

"No...oh God..." She bends over, hugging her stomach as if she's been shot there.

"Does it hurt? What is it, Ava?"

She straightens with stiff movements and stares at my chest with wide eyes, fresh tears streaming down her face. "I...I asked you to let me go, and you...you said no, and I...I...I stabbed you! The scar in your abdomen is because of me."

"You didn't mean to. I tried to disarm you." I speak so carefully, my voice is barely audible.

"B-but I hurt you... I..." The hand grasping the shard of glass trembles as she drops it to her side. "I stabbed you and...and...the knife fell, and I stepped backward and fell down the stairs. I hurt you...you were bleeding so much."

"I'm fine." I tug my shirt out of my trousers and show her the healed wound. "See? I'm not in pain anymore."

Her watery gaze falls to my skin, and a fresh wave of tears cascades down her cheeks. "But I *am* in pain. Right here." She hits her chest. "But especially here." She bangs on her head with a fist. "I'm in so much pain. I can't take it anymore."

"Everything's going to be all right."

"No, it won't. I think it's time I accept that." She pushes the shard of glass against her neck.

"Ava, no!"

"Divorce me, or I will kill myself." She tilts her head back and holds the glass so close to the pulse point I've been obsessing over for months. A droplet of blood cascades down her porcelain skin and soaks the collar of her dress.

"You got it. I'll divorce you. Now let go." I approach her slowly, my muscles tightening and my heart hammering.

"And you'll transfer the guardianship to Papa?"

"Yes."

"And you'll let me go? For good?"

"Yes—" Once I'm within reach, I snatch the piece of glass and throw it against the opposite wall and then wrap my arms around her from behind, restraining both her hands in front of her.

I'm panting, my breaths strained as if I've run a marathon. My wife struggles and kicks and releases animal-istic sounds.

"If you don't do as promised, I'll find a way to kill myself. Whether by throwing myself off a bridge, a build-ing, or in front of a train. I will swallow a bottle of pills or slice my wrists or even hang myself. I will do everything to take myself from your vicinity if you don't give me back my freedom. I promise I will! I promise I will!"

Her words have no different effect than if she'd stabbed me again.

No.

They're much worse.

A few months ago, she wanted to kill me to leave me. Now she's willing to kill herself just to escape me.

Fucking hell.

Keeping her restrained with one hand, I reach into the drawer behind me and retrieve the first aid kit, fumble around until I find the syringe with the tranquilizer, then gently inject it in her arm.

Ava's movements slow, and her eyes droop. As she goes

heavy in my arms, a final tear leaves her eye as she stares at me. "I'd rather die than stay married to you."

Then she goes still.

I drop my forehead to hers and allow myself to mourn my wife one final time.

CHAPTER 39
ELI

NIGHT OF THE ACCIDENT

WHEN I FORCIBLY DISCHARGED AVA FROM THE mental institute, everyone was against it.

Every. Single. One.

My father included.

However, I wasn't ready to watch her try to commit suicide again. Or worse, watch them tighten security further or place her in a straitjacket. That will not be happening under my watch, no matter how much her parents argue that discharging her is not the right solution.

Nor how much Dr. Blaine says that my wife is prone to exhibit harmful behavior to both herself and those around her. Namely me.

She's wrong.

Sam, Henderson, and I have it under control. If she gets antsy due to my presence, which admittedly happens a lot lately, I simply stay out of sight and let Sam take care of her. She's a trained medical professional and therapist, which is part of the reason my parents hired her as my nanny. She knew how to deal with my destructive behavior and handles Ava well when she's having her episodes.

She's also the one who first noticed that my wife's state worsens whenever I'm present and relayed that to Dr. Blaine.

Due to Ava's frequent episodes, I've had to stay away more than I prefer. Even tonight, I buried myself in paperwork at the office and only had Alan drive me back home when Sam texted that my wife had fallen asleep.

Here's to another night of watching her through monitors.

Although I hate to admit it, Henderson was right when he said this isn't a marriage but torture for both of us.

Ava doesn't want to be with me, and even though she's been scared of me since the wedding, she often suggests that we split up while swearing that she'll never tell anyone about the murder.

I turn crueler whenever she mentions that, but that's because it's the only method I can think of to keep her beside me. If she's scared of me, she'll never leave me.

If she's scared of me, she'll realize her survival depends on me.

Yes, I recognize that if I trust Dr. Blaine and have her admitted to the hospital for five to six months and give her time to try out her therapy method, I might get a more present wife. I'll have the girl whose life became so intertwined with mine that I can't imagine myself without her.

But the images of her strangling herself with the sheets in that goddamn dark hospital room haunt me.

I'd never put her in that place again.

Never.

I run a hand down my face and release a long sigh, then smile bitterly.

There was a day when I thought I'd get this obsession out of my system and move on with my life, but I only managed to get so attached to my wife that nausea fills my throat at the thought of losing her.

My feet halt when I find Ava at the top of the stairs. She's wearing a soft off-white silk gown, and her long blond hair frames her face like a halo.

She looks like my own fucking angel.

Broken wings and all.

Her face is passive, no emotion showing as she stares at me, both hands behind her back.

Usually, I'd touch her throat to feel her pulse—it's the surest way to know whether she's in a fugue state. If it's low, she's out of it. If it's pumping hard and strong, she's all right.

For a while, at least.

But since I shouldn't be coming in contact with her, I turn to leave as I reach for my phone to text Sam.

"Why can't you look at me?" she asks in a brittle voice, her words haunting in the silence.

"It's not that." I stop but don't face her. No matter how precious it is to hear her voice lately. She's barely talked, if at all, in the past several weeks.

"What is it, then? Why is it that even now, you don't look at me? Do you find me unsightly?"

I whirl around and curse under my breath as a tear clings to her lashes and spills down her cheek. "Never."

"Then why have you been avoiding me?" She sniffles. "I haven't seen you in a month! And before that, I didn't see you for weeks on end. This has been happening since you discharged me from the hospital. If you're repulsed by my episodes and suicide attempt, tell me to my face. Don't just disappear and leave me anxious and paranoid."

"I am not repulsed. I'd never be repulsed by you."

"You never consummated our marriage." Her words end in a sniffle before she whispers, "You...never treated me like your wife."

"You told me not to touch you."

"On our wedding night! Because I was scared and confused. I didn't mean the entirety of our marriage." She steps closer.

I step back.

I *can't* touch her.

If I do, I won't stop. I'll fuck her so hard and rough, she won't be able to walk for days.

No one can accuse me of being a saint, but I think I should be awarded the position for abstaining since the night I murdered Oliver.

But I have my reasons. One, my face triggers her.

Two, the idea of taking advantage of her lethargic mental state where she's not lucid enough to consent nor *feel* every inch of me leaves a rancid taste at the back of my throat.

So I'll remain a fucking monk until she gets better.

"You don't even want to touch me." Tears cascade down her cheeks. "Why? Why can't you *see* me, Eli?"

I stare at her glittering eyes that resemble a whirling storm. "I *do* see you. More than anything or anyone."

"Liar!" she yells. "Lies! Tell me the truth! Say you don't want to touch me because you think about replacing me with a normal woman."

"Never."

"Stop lying to me!" She lets her hands fall to either side of her, and that's when I see the huge kitchen knife she's holding.

Fucking hell!

"What do you plan to do with that, Ava?" I ask with a calm I don't feel.

She points the knife in my direction. "Let me go or I'll stab you."

"I told you. The day when you're not my wife does not exist."

Her lips tremble. "You think I can't hurt you because I had a crush on you?"

"On the contrary, I think you would exactly because of that."

"Give me my freedom back, and you can do whatever you want with the women lining up to be with you."

"No."

"I will *kill* you."

"Do it." I take a step toward her. "That's the only way you'll be free of me."

"Don't come any closer!"

I reach for the knife, but she wields it sporadically, her eyes half-closed. A sickening stabbing sound fills my ears as pain explodes in my lower abdomen.

A soft gasp echoes in the air, and Ava releases the knife, leaving it wedged in my abdomen. Her wide eyes follow the stream of blood as it soaks my white shirt and drips onto the wooden floor.

"Oh my God…" She comes closer, her hand reaching out for me, then steps back again. Fresh tears fall harder as she shakes her head. "I d-didn't mean to… I o-only wanted to threaten y-you… Oh God…."

"I'm f-fine…" I strain, touching the wound.

"Oh no…what have I done…?" She stares at the blood pooling on the floor as she backs away with trembling legs.

Toward the stairs.

"Ava!" I shout as she falls backward, and haunting *thuds* fill my ears.

For a moment, my whole world goes black.

And I know, I just know, that if she's gone, I'll make sure it's the end for me as well.

CHAPTER 40
ELI

PRESENT

I HAVEN'T LEFT MY BEDROOM FOR A WEEK.

Our bedroom.

The extravagant space now smells like her and has become the personification of her pink obsession.

Days turn into nights, and I've been floundering and running empty baths just so I can saturate my nostrils with the smell of her shower gel.

At some point, I lose all logical thought and start contemplating ways to rewind the clock so she's back where she belongs. By my side. But then I recall the last day I had her in my arms—broken, beautiful, and unconscious.

I cleaned and bandaged her wounds before I called her parents to come and pick her up.

Because I realized with looming terror that I'm a danger to her life. If she sees me again, she *will* act on her threats, and that's not something I can survive.

Even if she was bluffing, which is highly unlikely, I can't afford that risk.

Not now when she's extremely volatile.

Cole nearly beat me with a baseball bat, and Ari

cried her eyes out, telling me, "You should've listened to the doctor—look what you've done," as she hugged her mummy-like sister.

Silver patted my arm, but she didn't say anything. She didn't have to when I knew full well the decisions I had to make. I realized that when my wife lost consciousness in my arms after announcing that death is a better option than me.

So I promised Cole to send him the signed divorce and guardianship agreements first thing in the morning.

Sam packed my wife's suitcases, and Henderson helped load them into the van as I stood by my study's window watching my wife—soon-to-be ex-wife—being carried, unconscious, in her father's arms before she was driven away from me for good.

She signed the divorce papers and her father's guardianship the following day. They're just waiting for the guardianship transfer before their solicitor processes the divorce.

I told mine to give them whatever they wanted. Anything I own. Even though I doubt she'd want to take anything of mine.

She sent back all the dresses, jewelry, bags, and even cellos I bought for her over the years.

They're stacked in boxes in her old room because I refused to allow even Sam to go inside and put them back in Ava's walk-in closet.

Henderson asked me to fight the divorce through my lawyer, but it's pointless. She can have everything.

Except for this house.

I lie on her side of the bed and stare at the stupid neon-pink stars dangling from the ceiling as I pull out my phone and dial the number I've called every day since she left.

"Leave me alone, Eli," Ari snaps as soon as she picks up.

"How is she?" I ask in the silence.

"Fine."

"Elaborate."

"She's been getting remarkably better since she left your toxic orbit, but especially since Cecy came by a few days ago."

"And?"

"And that's all," she says with exasperation. Then I hear a rustling sound, a door being shut, and she lowers her voice. "Listen, just leave her alone. I mean it. I think you trigger her. She was a crying mess when she signed the divorce papers, and she sometimes bursts out in tears for no reason, and I'm sure it's whenever she thinks of you."

I'm supposed to feel good that she's also suffering through this, but no joy sparks in me. If anything, a massive sense of bitterness and an all-encompassing loss seeps through the cracks of my armor.

"I am staying away. If I weren't, I'd be there instead of talking to you on the phone. What does your father plan to do with her treatment plan?"

"That's none of your business anymore."

"Ariella, don't fuck with me. I respected her wishes and disengaged from her, but that does not mean I'll be gone completely from behind the scenes. Either tell me, or I'll kidnap the fucking psychiatrist and make her talk."

"Fine, Jesus." She pauses. "Ava wants to be admitted to the mental institution."

I sit up, my jaw clenching so hard, it hurts. "As in, your parents convinced her to?"

"Not at all."

"You mean to tell me she'd willingly go to the place she nearly killed herself to leave?"

"Yeah. She said she was tired of running away. She's also considering taking this new shock therapy method Dr. Blaine suggested, but Papa is against it. He thinks the chances of success are too low and the process is painful, and therefore, we shouldn't risk it, but you know how Ava is when she sets her mind on something."

Clearly. Considering she got exactly what she wanted by threatening me with the only thing I would never sacrifice.

Her life.

"Anyway, got to go. Stay away, Eli. I mean it." Ariella hangs up.

I lie back on the bed and turn off my phone to avoid being bombarded by the outside world.

Dad probably sacked me from the project and downgraded my position as a tactic to force me back to the living world. But I couldn't care less.

Life was bright for a moment, full of rosy colors and loud chaos, but now it's back to being bleak, gray, and hauntingly silent.

And I can't muster the energy to face any of it.

I've never wanted something and failed to get it.

Not a single thing.

And now that I've lost the one person who added equilibrium to my life, my world is tilting off its axis and creaking under the weight of depressing loneliness.

I can't trust myself to live without my wife anymore.

She kept some of my darkness at bay by giving me purpose—her. Now that she's gone, I don't trust myself not to fuck everything up in a show of epic proportions.

A knock sounds on the door.

"Leave or you're fired, Sam." I fixate on the ceiling. "You, too, Henderson."

"It's me, honey." Mum's soft voice filters through. "Please open the door."

"I want to be alone," I grumble. The last thing I want is to hurt Mum, but I'm not in the mood to speak to anyone.

"How dare you turn away your mother, you insolent punk?" Dad's voice booms on the other side. "Step away, sweetheart."

Bang!

The door comes undone, literally hanging off its hinges. Dad shoves the thick curtains open, and I squint as the strong light nearly blinds me.

I've been cooped up in here for far too long.

Sitting up, I release a sigh. "I appreciate the visit, but I still prefer to be alone."

"You look like a caveman with that unshaven face." Dad stops in front of me. "And you stink."

"Thanks for the unconditional support, Dad. Really appreciate it." I release a longer sigh as I continue in a deadpan voice, "I'm just going through an annoyingly peaceful divorce. Nothing to see here."

"Oh, honey." Mum sits beside me and strokes my back in soothing circular motions. "You've always kept your emotions and thoughts to yourself, but it's okay to let go sometimes."

"I'm fine."

"You're anything but fine." Dad sits on my other side. "No need to pretend you're doing okay after Cole got his wish."

"It's her wish, too." The words are exceptionally hard to spit out. "She wanted the divorce enough to put her life on the line for it."

Mum continues caressing my back softly. "I'm so sorry. No one deserves to go through that."

"I do. I lied to her, knowing full well the consequences wouldn't be pretty once she found out. And I was proven right, yet again."

"You did what you thought was best for the both of you." Dad squeezes my knee. "There's absolutely nothing wrong with that, and you'll not blame yourself for choosing to save your marriage. Blame Cole. That motherfucker should be blamed for half the world's problems. The other half are on Ronan."

I smile despite myself.

Of all the things Dad taught me, being unapologetic was always at the top of the list.

I also know how protective he is of his family, which is why I hid the fact Ava stabbed me from my parents. I refused to muddy the relationship between Mum and Ava or, worse, have my dad put her on his shit list for daring to harm his son.

Mum would've understood that Ava wasn't in her right mind, but he probably wouldn't have.

Not that it makes any difference now.

"Her father will admit her to the mental facility, where she might spend the rest of her life." I speak in a low tone. "The one thing I fought against is happening, and I have no power to stop it, and even if I were to come up with a plan to, I could destroy her for good."

"This might not be for the worse, you know," Mum

starts. "Remember when I often asked you to follow the doctors' suggestions? Well, that's because I experienced what it was like to live with someone like Ava."

My head tilts in her direction. "You...did?"

"Yes. When I was much younger."

"Sweetheart..." Dad says in a soft voice.

"It's okay." She smiles, but a wave of sadness saturates her voice. "I think he's old enough to know. You see, my mother was also mentally unstable, and unlike Ava, who went through rare episodes, my mother's episodes were much more frequent and violent. Dad was advised to admit her to the hospital, but he felt sorry for her and got her out almost immediately. That was a huge mistake. Not only did she hurt me, your father, several other children, and your grandfather, but she also hurt herself. I loved her so much, but at some point, that love was overshadowed by fear. If I could go back in time, I'd beg Dad to lock her up. For everyone's sake. I'm not saying Ava is the same— God no, that girl is so self-aware, it's heartwarming. She called to say she wanted to do this for herself and everyone around her. You know how proud she is, how she hates it when people babysit her. Before any of this happened, she was singing your praises because you treat her like she's normal. I know you can be as rigid in your ways as your father, but this time, maybe you need to bend slightly so you don't break."

"I'm not rigid," Dad says as if he's hurt.

"You taught him bad habits," she shoots back.

"I taught him all my superior ones."

"Including arrogance and stiffness. I should applaud you."

"Are you picking a fight, sweetheart?"

She smiles mischievously. "You think you can handle a fight, Aiden?"

As I listen to my parents bicker, Mum's words keep playing over and over in my head.

I'm reminded of why I made this choice I hate more than if I were strapped to a bridge as every car in England rolled over me.

For *her*.

For her sanity.

Her well-being.

Her *future*.

I sacrificed my peace of mind for hers, and I realize now that I would do it again in a heartbeat if I ever got a redo.

Because I care about her, more than I even realized. I wouldn't have done this for her if she hadn't already carved herself a hole in the blackness of my heart.

"Dad?" I interrupt them before they end up in the guest room ripping each other's clothes off.

"Yes?"

"She wants me completely out of her life. I can't and will *not* accept that, but I also don't want to be the reason behind her worsening state, so what do I do?"

"Easy. You wait."

"For how long?"

"As long as it takes. You'll lie low and keep an eye on her until you believe she's ready."

"What if she's never ready?"

"She will be. Ava's strong and will bounce back. Besides"—Mum pats my shoulder—"she's worth waiting for."

She is.

Since she waited years for me to come around, I can do the same.

For as long as it takes.

CHAPTER 41

AVA

"YOU NEED ICE CREAM? MORE CANDY FLOSS? Hugs?" Cecy asks from beside me, her eyes a pool of jade-colored kindness.

"Hugs, please." I lean my head against her shoulder and wrap my arms around her middle as she holds me close.

I've been demanding a lot of hugs from everyone around me lately. Probably because I won't get them as much as I'd like once I'm admitted to the institution in a few days.

To say I'm completely comfortable with that would be a massive lie, but I'm finally ready to undergo this experience on my own, even if a part of me will always dread the idea of putting that *mentally unstable* label on myself.

"You want to watch another film?" Cecy asks as the credits for *Mean Girls* play on the screen.

"Sure."

"*Bridget Jones's Diary*'s second film?"

"Yup!"

"You're so predictable." She grins down at me as she scrolls through Netflix and then selects the film.

"I'm just religious about my comfort things." I rub my face against her shoulder, fighting the onslaught of tears that I seem to be plagued with lately. "Thanks for coming at such short notice. I wouldn't have been able to do this without you."

"Always. We're ride or die, remember?"

"Hell yeah. Even if Jeremy hates me for confiscating you."

She laughs. "He'll live."

"But will he live like a normal human being, or will he live by blowing some shit up and ruining people's existence?"

"He promised to behave."

"Oooh. You're taming him."

"More like we're in this together, you know? A relationship needs some compromises from both sides for it to work."

"That's only applicable if both parties are in their right state of mind. Pretty sure there's an exception for insane partners." I stare at the opening scene of the film but don't register anything.

"Ava, you're not insane," Cecy tells me in a soft but firm voice.

"I'm just getting there?"

"Ava…"

"It's okay. The first step of overcoming a hurdle is to admit it exists."

For the past ten days, I've been thinking about all my freshly returned memories. About the turmoil and the paralyzing fear I felt during my marriage. I truly believed Eli when he said he'd kill me if I didn't obey and follow his plan.

During the first two years of the marriage, I was scared

he'd make good on his promise, and he didn't make things better by forcing me into rehab, changing my doctor and treatments, admitting me to the ward, and cutting me out of my clubbing circles.

The day when I held a knife and demanded he let me go was my tipping point after a panic attack. But he doesn't know the reason behind that episode wasn't only because my discontent had reached its peak. The actual trigger was that I saw a video of him at a party that I couldn't attend— and he didn't ask me to go—because I was a mess.

At said party, Gemma touched his arm and openly flirted with him.

While he didn't look particularly interested, he also didn't attempt to push her away.

I was livid that he'd locked me up while he paraded around with other women. I was paranoid he'd soon bring a lover home and flaunt her in my face.

So even though I was frightened, I had to destroy him before he did the same to me. And most of all, I'd had enough of cowering from him. Like a bird trapped in a cage, I wanted to shatter the bars and fly out, even if my wings were broken in the process and I had to bleed all over the floor.

But I never meant to stab him. I *really* didn't. The moment I did, I dropped the knife and couldn't stop staring at the blood that gushed out of him.

Even then, I realized I'd never truly hated him. The thought of him dying because of me hurt more than anything he'd ever done to me.

I didn't realize I was walking backward until he shouted my name and I fell down the stairs.

Having amnesia was both a blessing and a curse.

A blessing because I was no longer scared of Eli and reverted to my personality at uni, and, in retrospect, my old feelings for him resurfaced. In the first two years we were married, I didn't dare admit to those feelings because the fear of accidentally provoking him and getting killed was much stronger.

A curse because now that I remember everything, the pain has doubled and tripled until my chest can no longer carry the pieces of my broken heart.

Yes, I left Eli, but my feelings for him linger on like bitter lime stuck at the back of my throat.

"Is this about the divorce?" Cecy asks slowly.

She didn't see me break down in uncontrollable chest-heaving sobs before I signed those papers, but she heard all about it from Ari.

Mama told me maybe I should wait, and even Papa, who's been begging me to divorce Eli since I married him, said maybe I should do it when I'm calmer.

But I signed them. Even if I messed up the papers with my tears.

"It's over now," I whisper.

"Do you want it to be over?"

"It *has* to be over."

"Says who?" My friend grabs my shoulders and sits facing me. "This is your choice, Ava. If you don't want the divorce, don't go through with it."

"I asked for it. I threatened him with suicide if he didn't let me go."

"Oh."

I lower my eyes. Cecy is the only person I've told about

this, mainly because I didn't want to worry my family. "Oh? Is that all you have to say?"

"I was wondering why someone like Eli would hand over the divorce papers so easily, and now I understand. He's willing to sacrifice his only redline for your safety."

"More like he didn't want blood on his hands. He's probably glad he finally got rid of the loose screw."

"Ava..." She takes my hand in hers. "First of all, you're not a loose screw. You're just someone who's struggling by no fault of their own, and you made the hard decision to be admitted into a place you loathe in an attempt to get better. You're so strong and impressive, I don't even know how you do it. So I will *not* hear any self-deprecating rubbish again, or I will smack you.

"Second of all, I don't know if you're aware of this, but Eli didn't demand to be your guardian for controlling purposes. He really thought your parents, Ari, and even I were too soft and unable to handle hard decisions that could benefit you. We all knew you had alcoholism issues, but we were scared that if we pushed you to quit, you'd break. Not Eli. In fact, he berated us for babying you and letting your state deteriorate so badly. He got punched by Uncle Cole for it, by the way, but he still said he'd do it his way and that none of us were allowed to interfere. That psychiatrist he kicked off the continent? He was caught on the verge of selling your and other patients' confidential information to some pharmaceutical conglomerate, so Eli made sure he could no longer breathe in your vicinity.

"That first admission into the psych ward was due to pressure from everyone after your constant panic attacks and fugue states. Uncle Cole was about to take him to court for negligence if he didn't agree. He reSisted it to the very end, but even after it happened, he visited you daily and spent a few hours with you no matter how busy he was. Sometimes, you recognized him, and other times, you didn't, but he was by your side every day until you used the sheets to try and strangle yourself. He discharged you the following day, despite the doctors' advice to put you on intensive watch and keep you for further observation.

"He threatened to have the entire institution shut down if anyone stood in his way as he carried you out. He vehemently refused to admit you again after that and chose to look after you himself. Sam told me he barely slept because he wanted to personally watch and keep you out of danger. He's the one who carried you back to bed from your sleepwalks. If you fell into a puddle of mud, he's the one who bathed you and changed your clothes. He banned alcohol from the house and even stopped drinking it himself.

"After you fell down the stairs and woke up in the hospital without memories, he tried to start anew. He knew you might get worse, but he held on to the small hope that you'd get better instead. He forbade anyone from telling you any of the painful memories and wanted you to live normally, even if it was temporary. When he saw that you rekindled your relationship with the cello after a long time, he became a charity's top patron and forced them to invite you for a performance. He knew that if they gave you the chance once, you'd charm them with your skills and the invitations would become organic. He kept his distance, not because you stabbed him nor because he hated you, but because the doctor thought his face triggered you."

My chin trembles as fragmented memories of Eli picking me up, carrying me, and gently putting me to bed play in my head in a loop. Several realizations hit me as well.

He didn't have missionary sex with me in the beginning because he believed looking at his face would trigger me. He only changed that after I demanded it and he saw I was okay.

He never took off his clothes because he didn't want me to see the stab scar and somehow regain my memories of that time.

Eli didn't care that I'd stabbed him. He only cared that I'd be hurt if I were to remember.

The man who killed someone in front of me in cold blood, then used the murder to tie me to him and made a toxic number of people disappear because they breathed wrong near me shouldn't be this psychotically endearing.

He just shouldn't.

"Ava...why are you crying?" Cecy wipes my cheeks with her sleeve.

"Because I'm willing to forget that he forced me to marry him. Hell, a part of me already forgot that. And another part liked that he forced me because I have stubborn pride that forbids me from admitting I wanted that. Cecy...I think I love him. No. Pretty sure I'm *in love* with him, which is why I broke down when I recalled everything and was hit by the lies. I couldn't handle the betrayal and the fact that everything could be a lie."

"Finally. It's about time you realize what we've all known for years." She smiles. "Are you going to talk to him?"

I shake my head frantically.

"Ava...you might not see him for months or years after you're admitted."

"That's okay. I can't trust myself not to splinter to pieces and become an emotional mess if I see his face. I let myself believe in an impossible fairy tale where we'd form a happy family together, but it was all an illusion."

"If anyone can make it happen, it's you."

"Not in my current state. I *stabbed* him, Cecy. Even if he's able to overlook that, I can't. I'm terrified about the thought of hurting him again—even unintentionally. It's why my brain chose amnesia. The idea that I caused him pain broke me so much that I couldn't survive with my memories intact."

"So you'll give up? Just like that?"

"Just like that. Unless I make sure I'm no longer a threat to him, and most importantly, to myself, so that he doesn't have to deal with an invalid."

"You're *not* an invalid. And you can tell him what you think. If the unholy number of calls he makes to Ari and me is any indication, I'm sure he'll wait for as long as it takes."

"I don't want him to wait. It's better if he moves on."

"That's virtually impossible."

"He's a man with a lot of responsibilities on his shoulders. He'll get over this bleak chapter in his life."

"And you'll let him?"

"Why wouldn't I?"

"Ava...you turned into a raging witch at uni whenever you saw a woman around him. You made it your mission to chase them away as if they were poisonous flies, and we both know you did that because you couldn't handle seeing him with someone else. You *still* can't, considering all the murder plans you've had about other women flirting with him over the past few months. And now you're telling me you'll *willingly* watch him move on?"

"I have to. I have to be mature enough to let go of what's never been mine." My next words come out in a strangled tone. "Even if it hurts."

"Aww, come here." Cecily hugs me as I cry softly against her.

I wish it was the last time I cried because of Eli King.

But my tears seem to believe they belong to him.

Like everything else about me.

CHAPTER 42
COLE

I RECOGNIZED MY LIFE WOULDN'T BE PEACEFUL the moment this motherfucking twat walked up to my eldest daughter the day she was born and kissed her on the mouth.

That was when he was a six-year-old twat.

At the time, my life flashed before my eyes, and I swear I saw myself slicing his throat with a blunt knife—so it'd hurt more and he'd die slowly—then breaking his legs and burying him in a ditch.

Without his organs.

Those would be sold on the black market for an average price because they'd surely be rejected by their host, considering he's a toxic parasite.

Unfortunately, I missed a few chances to execute my murder plan, mainly because the twat's twatty father had been accompanying him at all times as if he caught a whiff of what I'd do to his son if I ever found him alone.

Before I knew it, he'd grown into a man who was able to fight me off. But I have people looking into autopsy-proof poison. Sure, it's not as gory nor glamorous as my original plan, but it'd do to eradicate him from my eldest princess's life.

For good.

However, he came to his senses and granted her a divorce and even revoked guardianship rights, so I thought, *Great. Now I'm finally rid of the twat.*

Time to celebrate.

Alas, that hasn't been the end of him.

For two months, Eli "Parasite" King has been dropping by the institute during Ava's sleep time and spends the entire night watching her through the door like a fucking creep.

No kidding. I watched him once as he stood there, both hands in his pockets, for seven fucking hours.

A few weeks ago, the doctor allowed him to sit by her bedside, and he started holding her hand. He also reads her these ridiculous romance novels that he doesn't look to be enjoying one bit, but he keeps buying them because she likes them—her mother's influence. He bought an out-of-print version for over two thousand quid just because.

He times himself and always leaves half an hour before she usually wakes up. Then he comes back the next day for the same routine. He's never missed a night. Not even when he has dark circles and looks like he could use some sleep.

Or an early introduction to his grave.

Not even when I tried to kick him out. Not only did he refuse to comply, but he also tried to turn both my wife and younger daughter against me.

Silver and Ari said things like "Well, they're not officially divorced."

"You can't file a restraining order on Eli, Cole."

"He only visits when she's sleeping, Papa. Can't you be nice? He tried his best, he clearly misses her, and he's lost weight."

"Once again, you can't file for a restraining order, Cole."

Sure I can, but I'm afraid that won't be enough to stop him.

I swear his brain could be studied to gain insight into psychopaths who don't bat an eye after offing their victims.

He's too cold, too calculating, too unruffled for my liking. If I hadn't seen the footage where he let Ava stab him, then tried to save her from falling, I would've thrown him in a grave and relieved humanity of his existence a long time ago.

It doesn't help that my daughter has always looked at him with heart eyes, as if he's the only man in the world for her.

I love Ava and would give her the moon and the stars if she ever asked for them, but her taste in men is depressingly mediocre.

Why did it have to be that twat of all twats?

Granted, I probably wouldn't like any of the other twats either, since no one is worthy of my princess, but I could at least tolerate them.

Eli, though, has his father's face. Which means it's often begging to be punched.

I tighten my fist as I stride toward him and Aiden, my feet sinking into the plush carpeting of the reception area. Velvet sofas line the walls, and the air is heavy with their rotten existence.

Father and son stand near the front desk, their voices low as they discuss something.

"What are you doing here during the day?" I grit out and point at Aiden. "And why is *he* here?"

"He wanted to visit," Eli says, his gaze flitting behind

me as if he can see her in the hallway. "Today is the last day of the first phase of the new therapy. Is she more lethargic than usual?"

"That's none of your business."

"Just stop being a petty little bitch and answer the question, Nash," Aiden says. "He's being respectful, and if you don't appreciate the effort he's exercising to put up with your obnoxiousness, I'll knock your teeth out."

I stand toe to toe with him. "I'd like to see you try."

"Please stop." Eli releases a long sigh. "I'm not in the mood for your usual bickering and would rather talk about my wife."

"Ex-wife."

"The divorce isn't processed yet," he says point-blank.

"It will be soon."

"Until then, she's my wife."

"I wonder where he learned this level of delusion." I glare at Aiden. "It's your obnoxious influence again."

"Thank fuck for that."

"Uncle Cole," Eli says. "Please."

"Don't 'Uncle' me. And Dr. Blaine said she's better than she initially anticipated."

"I already spoke to Dr. Blaine. I don't care for the technical side of things and would rather know how she's doing in real life."

I can tell he hates that he lost control over her state and that he can't monitor her at all times like he did before. I can also tell it's taking all his restraint not to force himself into her life again so he won't hurt her.

I respect that about him. I also respect that he always puts her well-being before his.

Ultimately, though, I still despise the twat from the bottom of my heart. He can blame his father for it.

I release a long sigh. "She's slowly recovering. She hasn't had an episode in three weeks, and the lower dose of medicine has helped reduce the level of lethargic phases. Silver and Cecily are with her, talking about a nonsensical film. Ari will probably join them after uni. Now, you'd better leave before she sees you."

He nods. "I'll be back later."

"I'd rather you weren't."

"I will be." He casts a glance at his father. "I'll wait for you outside. Don't stay long, as it's best she doesn't see you either."

Aiden and I watch as Eli walks out with that edge of infuriating arrogance both father and son excel at.

If I didn't know Eli was suffering, I'd think he was completely normal, with the level of calm he projects onto the outside world.

"Stop thinking about ways to eliminate my son." Aiden stands in front of me, effectively blocking my view. "And no, you can't poison him."

"You should've kept him far away from my daughter like I asked twenty-three years ago. This whole mess is because of you."

"Nonsense. This whole mess happened because you refuse to admit your daughter is a grown-up who can make her own decisions, and if that means tying her life to Eli's, so be it."

"Over my dead body."

"Can be arranged for my son's happiness."

"Is that a threat?"

"Maybe."

We glare at each other for a long beat before he releases a strained breath. "Listen, wanker, I don't give a fuck about your edgy attempts to threaten him every time you see him, but it's different now. He's lost weight. He barely eats, sleeps, or functions properly. Creighton flew back from the States to stay with him, and Elsa has been worried sick about him. *I am* worried about him. Every day, he comes to work looking like a functional zombie who's susceptible to undergo cardiac arrest at any given moment. The only thing that's pushing him to survive is Ava. So if I can overlook the fact she stabbed him, you can also overlook your nonsensical bias."

I narrow my eyes. "He told you about the stabbing?"

"He went the extra mile so I wouldn't know, and I let him believe I was in the dark. You and I both recognize he did that to protect Ava from my wrath and to avoid tarnishing our relationship, so stop being a bastard and let the kids be, would you?"

That would be possible if Aiden hadn't stolen Silver's first waltz from me. Or if the fact he was her first fiancé, even if it was fake, didn't exist.

And no, I still haven't forgotten about that, and I never will.

"Don't give my son a hard time, or I'll come for you, Nash," Aiden says in a dark tone.

"Then come for me, King."

We glare at each other for a few more moments. The only reason he disengages is because his precious son is calling him.

"We'll be in-laws for life, Nash. I hope you're also

mentally prepared for Remi and Ari, because they're already happening in the background."

Aiden walks away before I can shove him against the wall and choke him to death. The prick loves antagonizing me, so the last bit is *not* true.

I'm struggling as it is with the first part.

And no, I still don't accept Eli. Even if he's a bit more tolerable than his father.

After fetching some ridiculously named coffees from the local shop, I walk back to Ava's room.

My steps halt when I hear laughter. Good God. It's been a long time since I heard my daughter laugh so freely and sound so happy.

She's been a little social butterfly since she was born, but her light has been stripped away by the abnormal neurons in her head. Neurons she has because I was selfish enough to procreate and pass down faulty genes to her.

But Silver is right. I wouldn't have it any other way. We would've loved our little miracle no matter what.

Ava, however, struggled so much, especially during her teenage years and beyond, and my sweet girl tried her best to hide and was in denial for far too long.

She's slowly healing now. Ava doesn't seem to care about the pain that comes with this loathsome therapy method. If anything, she goes in with a blinding amount of hope that puts me to shame for ever opposing the experiment in the first place.

My daughter is much stronger than me and her mother combined. She might have fallen into black holes in the past, but right now not only does she want to get better, but she's also working hard for it.

"By the way, Cecy," Ava says. "I started reading this book you brought me the other time, but it's like I've read it before. Though I don't remember."

There's a pause and I curse. That bastard Eli must've read it for her.

"Oh, who knows?" Cecily laughs awkwardly. She's as honest and as caring as her mother, Kim, and that makes her shit at lying.

"Am I losing time again?" Ava asks in a spooked voice. "Please tell me if I am."

"No, no," Silver says. "I might have read the book aloud while you were sleeping."

"Ah, that makes sense." She puffs out a small sigh. "Hey, Mum?"

"Yes?"

"Has...uh...Eli ever asked about me?"

I peek through the ajar door, and the hopeful expression on Ava's face nearly gives me a stroke.

Jesus Christ.

She really loves the twat, doesn't she? I should've believed her tears when she signed those divorce papers— they were more honest than her words or the multiple injuries slashed along her body.

"Yes, he has." Silver smiles. "Constantly."

"Still bugging me and also Ari," Cecily offers needlessly.

"But he hasn't visited once." Ava stabs the wisps of candy floss in the bucket, her lips pushing into a pout as if she were a child.

"I thought you didn't want to see him?" Silver asks.

"I don't. But that doesn't mean he shouldn't visit at all."

"You're such a contradiction, Ava." Cecily laughs. "Would you meet him if he comes by?"

"Nope."

I open the door, and she looks up with renewed hope. Her expression falls a little upon seeing me, but then she smiles. "Papa, where have you been?"

"Getting you girls coffee." I pass her a cup. "Your favorite hot chocolate with marshmallows."

"Thanks, Papa." She grabs the cup between both hands. "For everything. Mama and Cecy, too. Ari as well. I wouldn't have been able to do this without your support."

"You'll never get rid of me." Cecily hugs her.

"Pretty sure Jer will get rid of me if you keep taking these constant trips to the UK."

Cecily laughs. "He'll survive. Besides, he'd do the same for his friends, so he gets it. Truly."

As they keep talking back and forth, I sit down on the sofa beside my wife, and she interlinks her arm with mine as she leans her head on my shoulder.

"Is everything okay, handsome?" she asks in a low voice.

I love how Silver can gauge my mood without my having to say anything. How she figured out my tells and uses them to soothe me and console me.

This woman has been my everything since I was eight years old. Over four decades later, she's still my safe space just like I'm hers.

She still stirs my hot-blooded need to be with her at all times. People say marriage gets monotonous or dull with time, but that's because they never experienced marriage or parenthood the way we did. If anything, it made us stronger and closer.

Ava was our miracle. The child we had after a false start and a long relationship, so the fact she's suffering has hurt us more than anything, and we might have argued about some things, but ultimately, it's brought us together as a family.

Even Ari has matured exponentially in the past few months. Like her sister, though, she has horrible taste in men.

I stare down at Silver's bright eyes, turned deeper and wiser with age. "I'm coming to frightening realizations about our girls."

"Like?"

"Like I have to let them go."

"Aww, bless you." She strokes my arm. "I'm surprised you only just figured this out now."

"This isn't funny. I think I'm having a midlife criSis, butterfly."

"Then we'll get through it together, like we have with everything else."

"That we will. Have I told you how much I love you today?"

"Doesn't hurt to hear it again. Love you, too." She kisses me softly.

"Get a room, guys," Ava says, and then I hear her and Cecily giggling.

But I don't stop kissing my wife.

We were in the dark for so long that I refuse to ever shove us into the darkness again.

And she's right. We'll get through this.

I don't doubt that I can go to hell and back as long as Silver is by my side.

Even if that means making hard decisions such as aborting my murder plans concerning Eli.

For my daughter's happiness.

———

Cole: I might not murder Eli after all.

Aiden: Finally came to your senses?

Cole: Don't make me regret it.

Xander: Oh my. You're finally accepting Eli as your son-in-law?

Aiden: As he should have a long time ago. They've been married for years.

Cole: I wouldn't call him a son-in-law yet. This is merely a probation period. I might go back to my murder plans at a later date.

Levi: Unfortunately, you can do nothing if your daughter loves the bastard.

Xander: Tell me about it, Captain. I was hoping my Cecy would get bored by now, but she's planning to marry the lizard.

Aiden: You took said lizard on a fishing trip, just the two of you. Just admit that you like Jeremy just like Levi loves that tattooed guy.

Levi: His name is Nikolai, peasant. And he's more tolerable than his cousin.

Xander: I was forced into that bonding trip with Jeremy for my daughter's sake. I totally did NOT enjoy it.

Ronan: Sorry I'm late. I know you miss me. Hey

@Cole Nash, please roll out the red carpet and thank your lucky stars. My beautiful catch of a son, Remi, wants to marry that hellion daughter of yours, Ari. I accept dowry in the form of a few buildings.

Cole: Over my dead fucking body.

Aiden: Told you it was coming. RIP.

Xander: *brings popcorn*

Levi: What can I say? Our children take after us.

CHAPTER 43
AVA

THREE MONTHS LATER

"HAPPY BIRTHDAY!"

A playful burst of vibrant pink confetti explodes into the air, filling the space with its whimsical tendrils, which lightly tickle my cheeks and settle on my dress.

My parents' elegant reception area is adorned with cascades of white and pink balloons as if this is my sixteenth birthday.

In the middle of it all stands a towering cake decorated with fluffy candy floss toppings, serving as the centerpiece for this special occasion. It feels as if I've stepped into a dream world surrounded by my favorite people.

Today is my twenty-fourth birthday, but it's also the day I'm officially discharged from the clinic.

Not because I asked nor because Papa put pressure on the doctors, but because Dr. Blaine decided I could function properly in society without posing a threat to either myself or others.

Apparently, I exceeded her expectations with the experimental therapy. It wasn't all sunshine and roses, though. I felt like giving up on multiple occasions, and I cried myself to sleep more than I'd like to admit, mainly because it got so lonely and I was missing a certain Tin Man.

And while I'll never live medication-free, my episodes are under control and can be managed. I haven't had one in two months, and I feel reborn.

Like I can tackle the moon and hug the stars.

I can pursue cello professionally if I choose to. Sure, I'm slightly petrified at the thought of standing onstage in front of an audience and judges again, but all this progress will be for nothing if I don't take control of my life and make the best of it.

"Thanks, everyone!" I smile, accepting a massive pink dahlia bouquet from Papa and Mama.

Ari and Cecy strangle me with a hug.

Glyn pushes them away to hug me, and I think I hear her sniffling in my neck.

Then it's Anni's turn. She squeals. "I love the dress, girl!"

"Yours is stunning!" I touch the fluffy tulle material. "Why is the bow undone, though?"

She blushes.

"My bad." Creigh pulls her toward him with a hand on her hip.

"Seriously, control yourself." I roll my eyes. "It's *my* birthday."

"And?" he asks with a poker face.

"Creigh!" Anni scolds softly, her face still red. Then she blurts, "We're moving here permanently, so we'll get a lot of shopping done. I can't wait!"

"Finally, girl!"

"I'll move back, too. Eventually." Lan grabs Creigh by

the shoulders. "No need to throw roses at my feet nor be overly excited."

"Excited?" Remi breathes heavily. "More like horrified. I can only imagine the drama you'll bring and the lives you'll ruin."

"Maybe I'll start with yours, Rems. How about that?"

Remi puts his phone to his ear. "Mum, come pick me up."

"Cut it out, Lan." Ari stands beside Remi and wraps an arm around his waist. "Or I'll knock your teeth out."

"Shaking in my boots as we speak," Lan says in a dispassionate tone.

I can see Papa narrowing his eyes on Ari even as Remi attempts to disengage from her hold. Pretty sure they've become an item over the past couple of months, considering Ari's changing mood.

My sister and I not only have synchronized periods but also, apparently, synchronized heartbreaks.

Though she seems to have found her happy ending recently, while I'm still attempting to put up a brave front.

Even now, as I'm surrounded by my friends and family, feeling loved, appreciated, and so damn lucky to have them, I can't chase away the black pit growing in my chest.

I believed I'd get over him with time. Maybe not right away but eventually.

Surely there'd be a day when I'd go to sleep and not think about his warmth enveloping me. When I'd wake up and not picture myself snuggling impossibly closer to him or being served breakfast in bed.

I can't take a bath anymore, can't sleep, can't watch my films, can't even read my romance books without thinking of him. He's the hero of all my novels. I think he has been for a long time.

Hell, I've been dreaming about him reading those books to me as I lay my head on his lap. In the dream, Eli will stroke my cheeks, kiss my forehead, and tell me in a deep, soothing voice to sleep tight.

And somehow, I end up doing just that.

It shouldn't be this way.

So what if I've had a crush on him for as long as I can remember? I'm young and should have been able to move on by now.

I should be able to recognize the toxicity and choose to run away from it.

From *him*.

Yet I keep being tugged back in with an invisible string. And the last thing I wish is to cut it off.

After I put my bouquet in a porcelain vase, I go to the kitchen to grab a drink.

What I find, however, is Jeremy caging my best friend against the wall and eating her face.

"You guys are not helping at all," I grumble as I swing the fridge open, grab a can of lemonade tonic, and mix it with a Diet Coke in a glass.

"Sorry," Cecy whispers.

"She should apologize to me for stealing you all this time," Jeremy shoots back as he hugs her to his side.

"Jer!" She hits his chest. "We talked about this."

"I'm sorry," I say after a pause. "I know it was hard for you to let her go, and if you didn't love her and respect her wishes, you wouldn't have allowed this. So thank you. I promise not to steal her time too much in the future."

He raises a brow. "Apology accepted."

"Ava…" She swallows. "You'd do the same for me, so don't make it sound like it's a hassle."

"I don't take you for granted, Cecy. I know I'm lucky to have you." I sigh. "Now I have to stop before I start crying."

"Please don't," Jeremy says. "Or she won't leave with me."

"I won't, you oaf." I glare at him. "You hurt her and I slice your throat. Got it?"

Cecily laughs. Jeremy's eyebrows are nearly touching his hairline by this point.

"Instead of worrying about her very happy relationship, why don't you talk to that husband of yours and fix your own?" he says. "We'll all be a lot more relaxed."

I take a sip of my drink and add more lemonade, just to turn it as bitter as my insides. "There's no relationship to fix. And he'll be my ex-husband soon."

"How soon? Because his nightly visits to you don't imply he's considering you an ex."

"Jeremy, why would you tell her that?" Cecily scoffs. "I told you it was a secret."

"She deserves to know."

"W-wait." The glass shakes in my hand. "Eli visited?"

"Every single night," Jeremy says. "Like clockwork."

"Cecy?"

She puffs out a breath. "He didn't want us to tell you, and even the doctor thought it was a bad idea in the beginning because he might trigger you."

"W-was he there last week?"

"Yeah."

"The week before?"

"Yup."

"The month before?"

"Uh-huh."

"Did you miss the 'every night' bit?" Jeremy asks with drawn eyebrows. "Here I thought I had a bizarre best friend, but yours could compete with Nikolai's level of weirdness, Lisichka."

"Stop being mean."

"I'm not mean. I'm truly concerned." He waves a hand in front of my face. "Are you all right? Blink if you can hear my voice."

"What did he do when he visited?" I ask Cecily—or more like blurt out in a rush of words.

"In the beginning, he stood outside the entire night. Then he sat by your bedside and read books to you."

"Oh my God." I thought I was dreaming about him all this time, but he was actually there.

I was hurt and conflicted, and immeasurably heartbroken that he'd never visited, only to find out he did it religiously.

He came to see me for five whole months.

Every single day.

I thought maybe he'd moved on while I was floundering in my permanent feelings for him, but that can't be the case if he was there all this time, right?

A weight lifts off my chest, and crushing hope rushes through me as if someone has breathed new life into me. It mounts, coils, and whispers tunes of expectation into my bruised heart.

As absurd as that sounds.

For the rest of the evening, I keep thinking about him—more than usual, I mean.

My pride forbids me from going to him. Or perhaps it's fear that this is all just wishful thinking. What if this entire thing backfires and I end up being the one who's hurt?

I'm listening to Remi and Lan talk nonsense when my phone vibrates.

My heart nearly spills on the floor when I see his name. *Tin Man* surrounded by two hearts.

I'm such a hopeless case. I didn't change it after I left the house, probably because he never called nor texted.

Tin Man: Happy birthday.

My heart falls as I read and reread his words. I type *That's all?* and then delete it. *And here I thought you forgot I existed*, then delete it. *Why do you still have the ability to break my heart, you damn twat?*

Delete.

He knows it's my birthday, and instead of offering a present like everyone who's sane, he chose to send me a dry text.

Me: I'm coming to pick up the rest of my things.
Tin Man: Sam already removed everything of yours and sent it to your parents.
Me: Not everything. I'm missing a few things.
Tin Man: Noted.

Noted? *Noted?*

What the hell is wrong with this damn Tin Man? The

realization that he might be done fighting for me sends nausea down my throat.

Still, after everyone leaves, I ask Papa's driver to drop me off at what I used to call my home.

As the car rolls to a stop in front of the house, my lungs fill with melancholy, and I struggle to breathe. Memories I experienced in every nook of this house engulf me, and for some reason, they're all happy ones.

They're all about the precious feeling of being safe and protected. Treasured and adored.

As much as the first couple of years of marriage were filled with paranoia, the period after I woke up with amnesia was the happiest time of my life. Which is why the thought of losing Eli makes me tremble in dread.

My inhales turn deep and sharp when I find Sam and Leo waiting by the entrance. They both smile as I step out of the car.

I jump them both in a hug. "You guys! I missed you so much."

"We saw you last week," Sam says with her usual snobbishness, but she pats my arm affectionately.

"That's a week too long." I grin as I pull away.

They both visited me regularly but often replied to my question of *How is everyone in the house?* with vague answers that never included their precious boss.

"Happy birthday." Sam points behind her. "I made you a very pink crochet blanket for when you snuggle to watch your films."

"I saved your 'ugly plants,' as the gardener calls them, from being axed," Leo says.

"Aw, you guys are so sweet!"

"You mentioned a few things you wanted to pick up?" Sam asks with a hint of curiosity. "I don't recall missing anything important."

"Uh, you did," I say distractedly, peeking behind them as if I might catch a glimpse of their boss.

"What?" Leo asks.

"Um…you know, those potted plants. I want to take them."

"I see," Sam says with a raised brow. "We can ship them to you."

"Sounds good."

"Perhaps you'd want to take a look at them first?" Leo says.

"Fantastic idea!"

Sam stays behind because she needs to tackle some chores while Leo accompanies me. I physically stop myself from asking whether Eli is in the house.

Don't tell me he left once he heard I was coming over.

As soon as we're inside the greenhouse, my lips fall open. The crossbred plants I thought would be long dead by now have grown into exquisite beds. Not only that, but they've multiplied to occupy the entirety of the greenhouse.

Their long leaves and colorful roses make the space look like a small paradise.

"Oh my God, Leo! Did you do this?"

"No." He scratches the back of his head. "I only had to stop the gardener from axing them one time. In truth, the boss saved them and made this happen. When the gardener disagreed, he fired him and got another one who grew them into what they are right now."

My chin trembles. Why does he keep doing this if he refuses to see me?

"Is he here?" I whisper.

"In his study." Leo pauses, then hesitates. "Do you want to see him?"

"No. He didn't come to greet me, even though he knows I'm here."

He releases a heavy sigh.

"What?" I ask, playing with a petal.

"It's just ridiculous at this point."

"What's ridiculous?"

"You came all the way here for mythical missing things, but you refuse to go to him, and he's made men disappear from your surroundings since university instead of admitting he has feelings for you."

"Eli's had feelings for me since uni? Are you serious?"

"As a heart attack. He was confused about said feelings, so his solution of choice was to eliminate any competition."

"He was just being petty."

"Were you also only petty when you sabotaged all his possible relationships?"

"No," I admit aloud. I truly didn't like the sight of him with anyone else. Besides, he encouraged me by doing the same, so we fell into that toxic pattern.

"Which is why he allowed it, even knowing full well you were behind all those abnormal actions."

"H-he knew? How?"

"Landon."

"That damn traitor!"

"He said he was being Cupid."

"A grotesque one."

"If you say so." Leo shakes his head. "I'll be outside if you need anything."

After the door closes behind him, I stand there for what seems like forever, staring at the house through the glass.

For some reason, I can feel an invisible thread tugging at me with relentless ferocity.

Perhaps I should see Eli one final time just to curse him and get this load off my chest.

You know what?

I storm toward the door.

How dare he ruin my birthday and my new beginning?

How dare he act so considerate if he's going to hurt me—

My hand freezes on the handle when I open the door.

An electric buzz streams beneath my flesh, and my heart beats so loudly, I'm surprised it doesn't fall out at my feet.

Eli stands before me in his tall intimidating glory.

He's wearing black trousers and a white T-shirt that doesn't quite strain against his shoulders like before. He's lost weight, but his face has somehow become more beautiful.

Or maybe that's just because I miss him.

I want to kiss him.

To drown in the edges of his deep-gray eyes again. To start anew.

Despite everything.

But I force myself to remain still because I'm not that desperate.

Actually, I am *that* desperate. For a touch, a skim of his fingers, even.

I want him with everything in me. I love him with my incomplete sanity and my heart, which he broke once upon a time, which only mended itself because of his unconditional care and protectiveness. The past five months were an atrocious hell because I couldn't touch him.

I couldn't bury my face in his neck and fall asleep smelling him.

I couldn't see the look in his eyes when he stares at me.

All this time, I've been starving, pining, completely and utterly lost, and heartbroken, and defeated.

Yet it was the thought of him that made me work harder on myself. I wanted to be whole so I'd no longer hurt him nor be his weakness. I wanted to get better so all his sacrifices for me wouldn't go to waste. But I can't admit any of that aloud for fear of making a fool of myself.

Again.

"What are you doing here?" I ask in a low murmur.

"Henderson said you fell, but he clearly lied." His eyes taper as he runs them down the length of me with observant intensity. The moment ends too soon when he releases a worn-out sigh and turns around. "I'll be out of your hair."

His back muscles strain against his shirt as he walks across the cobbled pavement with firm steps.

Wait.

I take a step forward.

Wait! I scream in my head.

"Wait," I whisper, but he doesn't hear me and keeps drifting away.

Out of reach.

Out of my life.

"I want my things back!" I shout at the top of my lungs.

He comes to an abrupt halt, but he doesn't turn around. "Ask Sam, and she'll get it sorted for you."

"My watch. The one that you're wearing," I blurt. "I bought it, not Aunt Elsa, and now I don't want you to wear it anymore. Give it back!"

He glances back at me, his voice deep, smooth, and cryptic. "No."

"I told you I'm the one who had it made."

"I know. Mum mentioned that a couple of years ago. It's mine now, and I don't give away what's mine."

"I thought I was yours, too, at some point, but you had no issue giving up on me."

I hate the tremor in my voice, in my limbs, in my insides.

But what I hate the most is the possibility that I can never be with him again.

I don't need doctors to tell me that I would've never fixed myself if it weren't for him. He gave me purpose, something to fight for. He also fought for me so many times during the years of our marriage.

After I calmed down and recalled everything he'd done for me, and after Sam told me all the sleepless nights he spent, all the sacrifices he made for my comfort, I knew that I had to fight, too.

It's not fair that I ended things before I cleared my head.

I don't want to leave him. Not when I need him more than air. I need the unconditional comfort and safety he offers. Even if he doesn't love me, he cares. And that's enough.

For now.

He faces me fully, a muscle working in his jaw. "I never gave up on you. I only presented you with what you asked for."

"Divorce?"

"That's what you wanted, Ava." His voice darkens. "May I remind you that you held your life in the balance for it?"

"That was before I learned about what you did for me, how you took care of me all this time, and how you visited me every day. You did everything to make me happy and asked for nothing in return, and I know how uncharacteristic that is for you. How I'm an exception. I don't take your sacrifices for granted."

"And that changes something?"

"It changes *everything*."

He strides toward me, his emotions spilling from him with every step. It's a vortex of passion, adoration, desire, but mostly hope.

As crushing and grandiose as mine.

"Don't fuck with me." He stops in front of me, his chest rising and falling with his harsh breaths. "If this is your method of revenge—"

"Tell me you'll love me. You'll try to, no matter how long it takes. Tell me your care, adoration, and protection will develop into love someday, and I'll forget about the divorce."

He shakes his head.

My heart falls.

"There's no need to wait." He strokes my cheek, and my skin ignites at the contact. "You have already captured my heart, body, and soul, Ava. I have no clue when it started, but at some point, my possessiveness and obsessiveness with you turned into this inferno of emotions where I was prepared to lose you if it meant protecting you.

That's when I realized I was in love with everything about you, whether it's your obsession with pink, candy floss, or cheesy books and films. The lack of you has stripped my world of color and made me realize you're my sole light in the darkness. It's why I killed for you and would do it again in a heartbeat. I'd kill everyone if it meant I'd get to keep you. Perhaps that's not the healthiest form of love, but it's all I have. The heart you slowly awakened is entirely yours to do with as you please."

I stare at him through blurry vision as tears well up in my eyes.

Eli loves me.

All this time, he's been *in love* with me. The truth is, I've suspected it since I learned about all he did for me, but I didn't dare hope. Now, however, all my little-girl dreams are bursting at the seams.

"What if I break your heart?" I whisper in a brittle voice.

"You already did, five months ago when you said you'd rather die than be with me, but by all means, if you wish to do it again for when I broke yours all those years ago, this is the time to go for it."

I shake my head frantically. "I'm done carrying pain and heartbreak. I want a clean slate and a new start. Besides, I never meant to hurt you nor cause you pain. Yes, I did think about revenge at one point, but I never got to the point of executing it. I couldn't bear it. The reason I came undone that day was because I didn't know about your sacrifices for me and was terrified that all your actions in recent months were a lie or that you were pitying me."

He wipes a tear that falls down my cheek. "I never

pitied you. I might have hidden things from you, but that was because I refused the very notion of triggering you or pushing you toward the episodes you were experiencing before falling down the stairs. I was sincere in everything we did together."

"I know that now." I reach my hand out and palm his face. "I'm sorry I stabbed you."

"You didn't mean to."

"I still stabbed you, and it hurt me as much as it hurt you, if not more. So I couldn't see you unless I made sure I'd never cause you pain again, whether consciously or unconsciously."

"I'm proud of you, beautiful. I know these past five months were hard, but you did so well."

A rush of endorphins flows through me, but I force it and the flood of tears down. "I did it for me, but also for you. For us. Thank you for being there every night. For being so supportive even when I pushed you away. It means so...*so* much to me."

"I'll always be there." He strokes my cheek, my nose, the corner of my mouth, wiping all my tears with eyes so soft and loving, I want to drown in them.

"Even if I get worse?"

"Especially if you get worse."

"Even if I don't want you?"

"Even then. Though you've wanted me since you were a kid; I doubt that will ever change."

"That's true." I chuckle through my tears before it slowly dies out. "I'm sorry I threatened you with suicide. It'll never happen again."

He nods, a flash of pain passing behind his eyes.

And this is when I know I hurt him deeply, probably as much as he hurt me in the past.

The Tin Man feels, and it's because of me.

"I love you, Eli. I've been in love with you since I was a clueless little girl. What started as a naive crush deepened into this uncontrollable love where I'd do anything for you. Including forgetting about all the pain in the past."

"You'd do that?" he murmurs.

"In a heartbeat. We've been apart for far too long. We misunderstood each other for such a long time, too. I think it's time for us to start a new life together."

"Together," he echoes, and then his lips brush against mine.

It's a sweet kiss in the beginning, but then he deepens it, stealing my breath and my future.

The love of my life might not be conventional, but he's all mine.

CHAPTER 44

AVA

MY MOANS ECHO IN THE HALL AS ELI CARRIES me into our bedroom while his lips devour mine.

I should probably tone it down, especially since Sam and Leo were grinning and clearing their throats as we passed by the entrance hall. But honestly, I'm too happy. And turned on.

It's a travesty that I didn't get to touch my husband for a whole five months.

Still clashing his tongue against mine, Eli reaches out to slide my zipper down, his fingers skimming my heated skin and leaving a war of goose bumps.

"God, I fucking missed you." He grunts against my lips. "I missed your scent, your taste." He licks my swollen lips, then sinks his teeth into the lower one, then kisses my nose. "Your lips, your nose, your eyes, your body, your laughter, and even your goddamn bratty behavior. I missed your everything."

His lips trigger tingles wherever he kisses me, and every part of me throbs with both adoration and boundless excitement.

When he lays me down on the bed, I wrap my arms around his neck, kissing his cheek, his nose, and his eyelids, then brushing my lips against his. "I missed you, too, so, *so* much, it was driving me insane."

"You're never leaving my sight again, Mrs. King."

"Never."

He drops one final peck on the tip of my nose, then lowers his head and undresses me one piece at a time, then kisses his way down the valley of my breasts, then sucks on my hard nipples for so long, I come a little.

In my defense, it's been too long.

I grab his shirt and awkwardly undress him until we're both stark naked. God damn. I almost forgot how mouth-wateringly hot my husband is. No wonder I couldn't and will never get over him.

He's the only type I've ever had, and no one else compares.

His muscles strain and flex under my touch as I caress his tattoo.

"What does this mean?" I breathe out.

"The phoenix is you." He kisses my throat, sucking on my pulse, and I arch, giving him further access.

"M-me?"

"You're a beautiful mythical being who can be born from the ashes of your illness."

"And the tree of life?" My words end on a moan as he keeps sucking and devouring my throat.

"That's me. I believed I could contain your rebirth, every time."

"Oh, Eli." I clutch his cheeks and kiss him, wedging my tongue between his teeth and sucking on his.

I want him.

I need him.

I can't live without him.

"Fuck me." I pant against his lips. "I've been abstinent for months, and that's no different than torture."

He chuckles, the sound echoing around us like a lullaby.

I pout. "That's not funny."

He curls his index finger and bops me on the nose. "Not in the least."

"Then why were you laughing?"

"About how we agree for once. Five months without you nearly turned me into a madman."

"Does...that mean there were no other women?"

"Baby. You think I have the capacity to consider other women when you own me?"

"Good. Because I'm the jealous type and can be as possessive as you."

"Is that so? I almost didn't catch that."

It's my turn to laugh, but it ends in a moan when he captures my lips in a searing kiss as he slides inside me. I open my legs wider and wrap them around his thighs, digging my heels into his toned muscles.

Oh God.

His dick feels huge, and I whimper as his lips wrench from mine, leaving a trail of saliva between us.

"You're so tight, Mrs. King." He strains as he pulls out a bit, then thrusts in again. "Your cunt is welcoming me home, isn't it?"

"Yes..." I moan, my insides clenching around him for dear life.

"Again." He slides out, then rams back in. "That's it. Take my cock like a very good girl."

"Oh God."

"Again." He repeats the same motion over and over until I'm moaning his name so loudly, I'm surprised I don't bring the whole house down. "Tell me you're mine."

"Yours. Always, yours…oh fuck…"

"Again." He thrusts all the way in, and I see stars behind my lids.

"Eli!"

"You're so fucking beautiful when you're screaming my name. So fucking addictive. I'm never leaving this cunt again." He reaches between us and teases my clit. "*My* cunt."

A rush of pleasure mounts to frightening heights as he fluctuates between deep, controlled thrusts and a frantic, rough rhythm. I can't reSist the madness of him.

Of us.

"I'm not leaving," I whisper as I kiss his chin, his lips, his cheek. "Never *ever* again."

"Good girl."

The praise sends my body into a frenzy of emotions and lust.

I hold on to him for dear life as the orgasm washes over me with blinding intensity. I clench around him, and he curses deeply as he follows. I can feel his cum filling me, but all I can focus on are his lips seeking mine.

He kisses me like it's our first and last. At the same time.

He kisses me like he'll never stop kissing me.

There's something excruciatingly searing about this moment. He engraves himself deep inside me, as I am carving myself into him.

There's no future where we're not together. I believe it.

I see it in his eyes as he stares at me with a heartwarming intensity that's all Eli.

"I love you, Mr. King. I'm all yours."

"Love you, too, Mrs. King."

And then he's kissing me again.

I fall into him and welcome our new life together with a happy, tearful smile.

EPILOGUE 1
AVA

THREE MONTHS LATER

THE HALL ERUPTS IN LOUD APPLAUSE AS JEREMY kisses Cecily at the altar—or more like he devours her face.

I tear up as I hoot and applaud and make all the noises with Ari, Glyn, Anni, and Mia. We're all dressed in pink bridesmaid dresses—yes, it was my idea.

But then again, Cecy basically left all the strategizing side of things to me, and I might have gone overboard and given the planners a headache.

Anyway, I'm the reason she picked the stunning Vera Wang dress that makes her look like a legit fairy-tale princess with her silver hair and elegant makeup. I'm so going to have a field day with all the photography ideas I have for later.

On Jeremy's side, Nikolai, Kill, Gareth—Kill's older brother—and some other guy I've never seen before hoot and bump fists.

Nikolai and Bran got married exactly two months ago in a stunning Tuscany destination wedding because Nikolai *refused* to get married after Jeremy. My guess is that he was just too eager to have Bran as his husband. I've never seen my friend so happy as when he was professing his undying love to Nikolai.

Not only that, but Kill and Glyn will get married next month. Lan and Mia in six months. Anni and Creigh set the date for a year from now. Oh, and Ari will probably follow soon after if she has a say in it.

I have an abundance of weddings to attend, I tell you. My favorite type of party nowadays.

This New York wedding has been a smashing success. I can't wait for more.

The girls and I throw flower petals as Jeremy takes Cecy by the hand and they walk out of the hall amid cheers.

I think I catch Uncle Xan wiping a tear as Aunt Kim strokes his shoulder. He asked Cecy to change her mind and break up with the "lizard," as he calls Jeremy, ten times over the past week, only to be refused.

On the bright side, he seems to get along better with Adrian—Jeremy and Anni's dad—than Uncle Aiden does. There's going to be drama during Creigh's wedding. I can already tell.

I've been trying to ignore the security and the different stone-faced bodyguards roaming around the church. A Russian Orthodox church—as per the Mafia's rules.

Another thing that pissed Uncle Xan off. I think it has less to do with his Protestant heart and more to do with the fact this means his daughter is marrying into the organization whether he likes it or not.

But then again, Cecy doesn't seem to mind. She has the cutest relationship with her mother-in-law, and her father-in-law—who's a scarier-looking version of Jeremy—dotes on her.

She's been smiling nonstop today and glowing like a motherfucking queen.

"Gotta follow Cecy and make sure she gives me the flowers," Ari says, then winks at Remi. "See? I'm working hard for our future."

He tries to hide a smile but fails miserably. Ari grins back, kisses him on the cheek, and then rushes behind the newlyweds.

I catch a glimpse of Papa sighing like an old man with the world's weight on his shoulders while Mama laughs.

Some things just never change.

"Are you done being a social butterfly for the month?" Warm breath tickles my ear as Eli slides to my side and wraps an arm around my middle.

I stare up at him and fall in love a bit deeper. My gaze is drawn to his breathtaking presence, drinking in every detail of his handsome form. The crisp lines of his tuxedo accentuate the sharp angles of his face, making him appear even more striking. His hair is styled to perfection, each strand falling into place with effortless grace. His piercing gray eyes, normally stormy and intense, soften as they meet mine.

Over the past few months, we've been traveling, staying on the private island longer than necessary. We've been talking and getting to know each other better and on a more intimate level.

I've never felt so alive, so cherished and loved, as when I'm with him.

I used to be plagued by cancerous dread and a vicious loss of confidence whenever I saw him. I used to be injected with a shot of pain because the sight of him reminded me of my broken heart.

The pain expanded and transformed into bitterness the more I realized I couldn't have him. He was like the sun, and I thought I was meant to orbit around him but never get close or else I'd burn.

But he proved with actions more than words how much I'm an integral part of his life and how, like me, he can barely function if I'm not there.

I'm not delusional about who my husband is. I know for a fact Vance vanished the moment he landed in Melbourne and no one has a clue where he is.

It's another disappearance Eli orchestrated, but I have no interest in asking about it. Maybe I'm as morally broken as he is, because I would do the same if another woman came close to him.

I fix his bow tie, letting my nails trace along his skin. "The day is just starting. We still have the reception and photos."

"How many photos?"

"*Lots*. As many as possible."

"Don't you have enough photo albums? Both digital *and* physical?"

"There are never enough memories. You'll all look back at my achievements and thank me for freezing all these moments."

"Not if I have to sacrifice *you* for these moments." He tightens his grip on my waist. "I've been suffering marital neglect, Your Honor."

I laugh and then murmur, "You literally fucked me first thing this morning, Eli. When I was barely awake. How is *that* neglect?"

"Mmm. But you didn't let me eat your cunt for breakfast as usual. I'm starving."

"Eli!" I whisper-yell, searching our surroundings, which are thankfully empty. "We're in a church."

"And we're married. I'm positive the church approves of the holy union."

"Not if your words are unholy."

"Is that a yes on a late breakfast?" He raises a brow.

"Later, okay?"

"You know I can't function properly without my habits."

I laugh, the sound echoing around us like a symphony of joy. Honestly, he can get extremely insistent about his morning routine. It doesn't matter if I try to wake him up with my lips around his cock or if he fucks me or not. He always needs to eat me out before he starts his day.

Not that I'm complaining or anything.

"This isn't funny," he grumbles. "I can't wait for this wedding to be over to take you back home. I'll devour you everywhere, Mrs. King."

"Not the kitchen counter, or Sam will throw a fit."

"Then Sam will be sacked."

"You can't sack my friend. I won't allow it."

He scoffs. "No idea how you made the lonely, antisocial club conSisting of Henderson and Sam your friends and continue maintaining it."

"Probably the same way I made you fall in love with me—I'm irreSistible."

"That you are." He kisses the tip of my nose, and I feel like I'm melting.

God. Why does he have the ability to reduce me to a puddle of emotions with the merest touch?

"Hey, Eli?"

"Yes?"

"Have I been sleepwalking lately?"

He pauses. "Why are you asking?"

"I don't think I have, but the more I'm certain of something, the more it's not true. Give it to me straight. Don't sugarcoat it nor attempt to hide the truth for my benefit, please."

"It happened once, a month ago, but as Dr. Blaine said, it was due to the stress of your rehearsals for the competition. It was brief and normal. Nothing was alarming."

"Are you sure that's the only one?"

"Positive."

"Maybe it's the only one you're aware of."

"Impossible, considering I never let you out of my sight, beautiful."

I release a breath.

"What are you worried about?" He strokes my cheek, my hair, my pulse point, which I learned is how he can gauge my state of mind. "Do you believe the pills' effects are waning? Do you feel something's off?"

God. I love his caring, protective side and how easily it comes out at the hint of my discomfort.

"No and no, which is why I'm worried." I release another breath. "I'm so happy that, sometimes, I believe this is a simulation and I'll wake up to my harsh reality one day."

"You're real." He brushes his lips against mine and glues our foreheads together. "*We* are real, baby."

I smile and stroke his nose against my cheek. "I know, but I want more."

"Anything. If you ask for the moon, I'll lay it at your feet."

"Nothing that excessive." I hesitate. "I...want children. *Our* children."

"Then you will have them. All three of them."

"R-really?"

"You thought I'd say no?"

"Yeah, well. You weren't as open to the idea when we last talked about it."

"That was under different circumstances. You're better now. Stronger. Livelier. If you want children, I'll impregnate you with as many of them as you wish."

"B-but what about you? Is this only for me?"

"No. It's for me as well." He rubs his erection against my stomach. "See? The idea of filling you with my baby makes me hard."

"You're awful." I laugh.

He smiles. "That aside. I only want children if you're their mother."

"I'd have no other father for them." I steal a kiss. "Now let's join the others."

"Not so fast." He lifts me in his arms. "We have to start trying to get you pregnant, Mrs. King."

My laugh fills the air as he takes me to a side room and does just that.

I fought against myself for this man, but that only made me love him deeper. Now that I'm no longer fighting, it's easier to love him more every day.

This man owns my heart and soul.

And I wouldn't have it any other way.

EPILOGUE 2

ELI

"I THINK I'M GOING TO DIE."

I stroke my wife's blond locks away from her face. "Not as long as I'm here."

"When I said I wanted three children, I didn't mean at the same time."

"I know."

"It's all because of you, bastard." She closes her eyes while sitting upright as little Sierra sucks on her nipple.

I carefully remove the bottle from Seth and then carry him to the crib so that he's lying beside his naughty sister Zoey.

The triplets are almost four months old now, which is the perfect age to give us nightmares of them waking up crying.

Sleep? We've lost the definition of that.

Yes, Sam helps and we have a nanny, but my wife refuses the notion of handing out her motherhood responsibilities, as she calls them, to someone else.

And this was after she had one of the hardest births with those three and the labor lasted an entire night. I might have threatened to murder the doctor if he didn't get her through it in one piece.

By the time she finished the exponential job of birthing three whole humans, she was exhausted, her lips were chapped, and her face had lost color, but as soon as the nurse put our babies in our arms, she was smiling and crying.

It was at that moment that I realized I have a whole family to be responsible for now. Two beautiful girls and a boy. And most importantly, their mother.

Ava calls them her stroke of luck because she won the international cello competition the day she found out she was pregnant.

She was also called to perform with one of London's most affluent orchestras when she was pregnant with them. Three times.

If she hadn't given birth, she'd be performing in Paris, Vienna, and Berlin by now.

But she's choosing to focus on our family, as she likes to remind me.

She also wants to get involved in mental health charities, with her mother's help.

My wife has a lot of ambition ever since she went on her self-imposed healing journey.

Yes, there are days when depression hits or she gets lost in her head, but those are few and far between. It took me over a year, but I'm no longer worried about her episodes, no longer dread them and the possibility that she might hurt herself.

Besides, even if she feels down, she usually calls me or comes into my office and tells me that she needs my company. She no longer hides nor feels ashamed of who she is.

Ava actively seeks out Dr. Blaine and said that, if needed, she would be ready to admit herself into the institution again for our future.

Her gradual acceptance of herself has made her more beautiful and maddening. I physically can't stay away from her for more than a day or I feel signs of violent withdrawal.

She might have been the one who experienced issues with alcoholism, but my addiction to her is even more intense.

The only difference is that I don't wish to ever become sober.

I've always felt like I lacked a sense of meaning. It wasn't until this woman chaotically bulldozed her way into my heart that I realized what it means to have a purpose, a goal, and a need to protect.

With a smile, I watch her for long minutes as she snores softly while holding our daughter.

I gently remove Sierra, and Ava startles awake. "What…? I'm right here, baby…"

She blinks a few times, watching me take our girl to her crib, and then pulls up her bra and gown.

"They're asleep?" she murmurs as she walks up to my side.

"Finally."

My wife releases a contented sigh as she leans her head on my shoulder. "I still blame your sperm for three kids all at once."

"I'll make it up to you for the rest of our lives."

"You better." She wraps her arms around my waist and

tucks herself into my side. "Mum and Aunt Elsa pointed out that they'll grow up at every stage together, but hopefully, I'll stay in one piece while they do."

"They'll have me to answer to if something happens to you."

She chuckles, and even that sounds so joyful, so different from my wife two years ago. "I can't believe you'd be picking a fight with your kids."

"You come first and they're second. Something they'll have to get used to. Now I understand and I agree with Dad's behavior completely."

"About?"

"Creigh and I always knew that, while he loves us, we'd forever be secondary to his love for Mum."

"I guess Papa is the same, which is a good thing. At least they have each other now that Ari and I are gone." She grins up at me. "We'll have each other, too, when our babies are married."

"Nonsense. I'm not giving away my girls to any sorry sod."

She bursts out laughing. "Aaaand now you're in Papa's shoes. Congrats."

"Are you teasing me?"

"I'm so going to enjoy it when that day comes. And so will Papa."

"You'll be waiting a long time because that day doesn't exist in our lifetime."

"Uh-huh." She rubs her head against my chest. "Thank you, baby."

"What for?"

"Thank you for loving me, for giving me these precious

babies, the daft dog, and the diva cat. Thank you for everything you've done for me, even when I was completely unaware of my surroundings. Thank you for your patience, your unconditional support, and for seeing and treating me as normal. Just thank you for gifting me with this beautiful life."

I caress her cheek. "I wouldn't have it with anyone else."

"I love you, Mr. King."

"And I love you, Mrs. King."

Now.

Forever.

She'll always be my wife.

Mine.

THE END

WHAT'S NEXT?

Thank you so much for reading *God of War*! If you liked it, please leave a review. Your support means the world to me.

If you're thirsty for more discussions with other readers of the series, you can join the Facebook group Rina Kent's Spoiler Room.

Next up is a new, exciting series about secret societies and morally gray characters.

Head to rinakent.com for more information.

READ ON FOR A SNEAK PEEK OF

CRUEL KING,
THE FIRST BOOK
IN THE ROYAL ELITE SERIES.

CHAPTER 1
ASTRID

YOU MAY BE NOBLE,
BUT STAY AWAY FROM KING.

THIS IS THE LAST PLACE I SHOULD BE.

Alcohol, drunk teenagers, and thumping music.

A party.

Not to be dramatic, although I probably am, this place is like my worst nightmare wrapped in super-expensive watered-down alcohol.

Now, I'm not that much of a fun-ruiner, although my best friend, Dan, would say otherwise.

Spoiler alert, don't believe anything Dan says. He's into drama and all that jazz.

But I promised him I'd attend one party before the summer starts. Since Dan is part of the football team, I expected him to take me to their usual thing—not that I know what that is, but I had an idea it'd be in some posh house in London.

However, the sneaky wanker chose *the* party. AKA the mother of all freaking parties in Royal Elite.

When Dan and I walked inside, I had to double-check to see if we were somehow trespassing into the Queen's holiday mansion and if I should tell Her Majesty that I saw the drunk captain of the rugby team piss in her pool.

To say the place is huge would be like saying the

Vikings are tiny. Okay, that was lame, but I kind of insert the Vikings in any similes I make.

Golden arcs decorate the entrance and all the way to the massive lounge area. The vaulted ceilings and the sweeping stairs only add to how ridiculously grandiose this place is—even for Royal Elite's level. Jeez. To top it off, there are butlers serving drunk teenagers more drinks than they need.

I mean, I come from money. Scratch that. Dad is rich, I'm not. However, this is on a whole different level. Even for me.

When Dan said it was party night, I thought we'd crash in one of the popular 'elite' houses.

We'd drink their expensive liquor, try to pretend that we belonged to the same school that has the future prime minister and parliament members in the making, and then piss off to nurse a hangover.

But Dan forgot to mention a tiny detail about the location of the party.

It's in the middle of freaking nowhere.

I stopped following the twists and turns Dan took with his car the moment we were out of London and no road signs came into view.

For a moment, I thought Dan was taking us to some gypsy party.

Well, this sure as hell isn't a gypsy party.

The mansion is hidden behind tall pine trees on top of a hill—no kidding. The owner is either way too private or way too gothic.

Or both.

Aside from the attendees' cars, there's nothing in sight.

Now that I think about it, this would be the perfect opportunity to mass murder everyone.

I can totally see this as the opening scene of a horror film.

You need to stop watching all those gory films. I can almost hear Dad scold in my mind. Oh, right. He's not Dad. He's *Father*.

That should summarise the formal nature of my relationship with Lord Clifford. He may or may not kill me for coming to this party without his permission.

One more reason why I follow Dan's demonic plots.

I sip from my second drink. I had one shot with Dan as soon as we arrived, but then he buggered off, so now, I'm walking around with this cocktail. There's barely a burn at the end, but I have a high tolerance, so this is nothing.

I need a distraction from the scene around me. I can't believe Dan left me—probably to go shag. Worst wingman ever.

The entire school is gathered here. Some sway to the loud, offbeat music. Outside, a few of the rugby team cannonball into the kidney-shaped pool—that has piss in it. Others howl as they play a drinking competition that I wish I had the guts to participate in.

But then again, nothing is worth jeopardising my current position in the school—I'm part of the invisible folk. You know the type: those who no one actually cares if they miss a class or two—or an entire year. And I'd like to remain that way, thank you very much.

Invisibility is a cool superpower that allows me to breeze through without any bullshit or drama.

However, if I was going to remain that way, I should've

probably chosen a less noticeable best friend than Daniel. In my defence, when I discovered his popularity, he'd already super-glued himself to me as my wingman.

Even with his popularity, I'm invisible enough that his harem of girls don't notice me when they're hitting on him.

Some of the Royal Elite students present here are still wearing their pristine uniforms with red ties and navy blue jackets. On their pockets, the school's golden logo is embroidered. The lion in a shield, topped by a crown, is a sign of both the power and corruption simmering within the walls of the school.

There's a reason the uniformed people are alone in a circle, probably discussing books. I would join in, but I doubt they'd like it when I tell them they're not supposed to wear a uniform to a party.

Even I, a total 'party terrorist'—per Dan's words—have opted for jean shorts, fishnet stockings, and a simple black top. Oh, I also wore my favourite white basketball trainers that Mum painted black stars on.

My heart shrinks at the thought of her. I take a deep breath of the alcohol and the designer perfumes permeating the air.

Fun. This is supposed to be a night of fun.

My idea of fun includes either my art studio or marathoning the latest gory film.

Just saying.

A long howl at the entrance wrenches me back to the present.

The chatter weans and the crowd parts like the Red Sea did for Moses.

When the kids trip over each other to make way, I'm

not surprised to see the football team waltzing in like freaking England's champions. Only, wait. I think they did win a game that would lead them to some sort of a school championship today.

This could or could not be the celebration party for their win.

Another tiny detail that Dan forgot to mention.

I'm not going to kill my best friend.

I'm not going to kill my best friend.

Screw it.

ABOUT THE AUTHOR

Rina Kent is a *USA Today*, international, and number one Amazon bestselling author of everything enemies-to-lovers romance.

She's known to write unapologetic antiheroes and villains because she often fell in love with men no one roots for. Her books are sprinkled with a touch of darkness, a pinch of angst, and an unhealthy dose of intensity.

She spends her private days in London, laughing like an evil mastermind about adding mayhem to her expanding universe. When she's not writing, Rina travels, hikes, and spoils cats in a pure cat-lady fashion.

Find Rina below:

Website: rinakent.com
Newsletter: subscribepage.com/rinakent
Instagram: @author_rina
Facebook: rinaakent
Reader Group: facebook.com/groups/rinakent.club
TikTok: @author.rinakent
Twitter: @authorrina